# WORTH

## LORD *of* RECKONING

# GRACE BURROWES

*Worth Lord of Reckoning* is Published by Grace Burrowes Publishing
21 Summit Avenue
Hagerstown, MD 21740
*www.graceburrowes.com*

# DEDICATION

To Kathy H., who keeps my law practice together, and often does it with a smile.

# The Lonely Lords Series

# CHAPTER ONE

"I do not have a sister."

Despite extensive experience with difficult situations and unruly clients, Worth Kettering kept his voice civil only by effort. "The topic is sensitive, you see, because I *had* a sister. You will note the past tense."

Mrs. Peese heaved herself to her feet. "My condolences on your loss, but Yolanda was quite, quite clear that you are her brother. When I reviewed the correspondence in the school's files, I found that his lordship did, indeed, name you as his alternate in the event of an emergency. This constitutes an emergency."

In all of creation, was any being more difficult to enlighten than the headmistress of an exclusive boarding school for young ladies? Kettering paced to the spotless French doors, through which, he would neither plough his fist nor run bellowing for his horse.

"I do not have a sister living on this earth. How many times must I say it?"

Mrs. Peese reminded Kettering of how he pictured the housekeeper at Trysting. Jacaranda Wyeth would share with Mrs. Peese a stout physique, energetic competence, and inflexible opinions about idleness, dirt, and the divine right of kings. With women of that ilk, he'd get nowhere using reason and probably less than nowhere using threats of force.

He turned to face the old besom and focused on the practicalities.

"Why don't I simply hire the young lady a coach and have her delivered to the earl at the family seat?" The preferred option, as far as Kettering was concerned, and it would serve Hess right for creating this mess.

"His lordship has left for Scotland, Mr. Kettering, as I'm sure you're aware."

"For God's sake, I am not aware of the earl's holiday schedule!"

She folded her arms across an ample bosom. By her lights, Kettering had likely committed three mortal sins in one sentence: He'd raised his voice, taken the Lord's name in vain, *and* disrespected a peer of the realm. God—gads, rather.

*You are a gentleman,* he reminded himself. *You are always a gentleman when dealing with ladies, clients, and children.*

Most ladies.

"Brother?" A coltish blonde stood in the doorway to Mrs. Peese's office. "Do you denounce me out of ignorance or out of spite?"

"Who the dev—deuce?"

Mrs. Peese's expression became long-suffering. "Yolanda, please return to your room. Your brother and I will negotiate the terms of your departure."

"Not if he has anything to say to it." The young lady advanced into the room, and on some level no man of business ever ignored, she upset Kettering. She was in the last throes of adolescence and tallish—all the Ketterings were tall—and she had blond hair and blue eyes highly reminiscent of Moira. This Yolanda person held out her hand, thrusting a signet ring with a unicorn crest under Kettering's nose.

A ring of the same design graced the fourth finger of his left hand. He'd been wearing it when he'd marched away from Grampion all those years ago.

"Mrs. Peese, if you would excuse my…sister and me briefly?"

"The door is to remain open," Mrs. Peese said. "Yolanda, Miss Snyder is across the hall in the guest parlor if you need her."

Mrs. Peese inhaled through her nose at Kettering, a warning of some sort. He was male and, in her world, no doubt suspect on that ground alone, and then he was alone with a young female whose nose and chin bore an odd resemblance to *his*.

"What is your scheme, miss?"

In response, she began to recite the succession of the Grampion earldom right from the first baron, a wily young fellow who'd turned Good Queen Bess's head, or so the story went. Generation by generation, the girl had it right.

"So you studied the Kettering line, because our looks resemble yours." Kettering took a seat and gestured for her to do the same. "That hardly makes you my sister. I'm what? Twenty years your senior?"

"Not quite sixteen years older than I. A portrait of your mother hangs over the mantel at Grampion Hall. Our father had it painted when our brother was a toddler, but it still hangs there, unless Hess has moved it."

"Hessian, who has conveniently decamped for points north, somewhat in advance of grouse season."

She worried the signet ring with her thumb, a habit Kettering himself still exhibited when vexed.

"In the painting, your mother wears a blue turban, like the girl in the Vermeer, and she has only one earring. The earring hangs on her right ear, the left one as you face the portrait."

"Anyone who has been to Grampion could describe that painting to you." He'd forgotten about the painting, though her recitation brought the image to mind. "You'll have to do better than that."

Over years and years of dealing with the law and those who broke it, Kettering had developed a good instinct for who was telling a desperate lie and who was telling a desperate truth. Despite his impersonation of an ill-tempered prosecutor, his instincts put this girl in the latter group.

"Hess cannot be bothered," Yolanda said. "He's hunt mad and must be off tramping the grouse moors until cubbing starts in September. No one matters to him more than his hunters and his hounds, and the library will smell of dog all winter."

Kettering rose and resumed pacing, because this would have been true of the old earl as well—and Kettering had also forgotten about the odor of hounds in the colder months. "So you're my sister and we've never met, and now the school has sent for me. What do you want?"

"Do you believe we're related?"

"Not for a moment," Kettering said, not that he would admit, in any case, because with great wealth came great caution. "You've neatly boxed me into the classic riddle of having to prove something in the negative. Why summon me now, when I had no clue as to your existence?"

"Because you must take me away from here."

"*Must,* Miss Yolanda?" Most females knew instinctively not to attempt imperatives where Worth Kettering was concerned.

Yolanda's chin came up, and yet she remained seated—a lady's prerogative. "I have nowhere to go, sir. Hess is off to the wilds of Aberdeenshire, and Mrs. Peese does not run a charitable institution. My continued presence here has become untenably awkward."

Her bravado faltered as she twitched at her skirts, and that was when Kettering saw what the unseasonably long sleeves of her dress had kept hidden: bandages around her left wrist. Thick, fresh bandages.

At her age, he'd been hopelessly prone to histrionics.

"Perhaps you'd walk with me in the back gardens?" He put the question neutrally, for some stiff-rumped minion of Mrs. Peese's was listening to every word from across the hall. "The day is pleasantly warm, and I have more questions for you."

Without touching him, without even acknowledging his proffered arm,

Yolanda led him through the French doors to the walkway outside the headmistress's office.

He gestured away from the building and put her hand on his sleeve. "This way. Now, who are you really?"

"I'm your sister, Yolanda Kettering."

"Half-sister?"

"Yes. Our father became my guardian when Mama died. I was in Papa's will, and Hess has never questioned my paternity."

The back gardens were surprisingly extensive and also well tended—a testament to the exorbitant sums charged for tuition, no doubt.

"Now you're Hess's responsibility?"

"I am not legitimate," she said through gritted teeth. "I am acknowledged, though, and I am your half-sister. Papa assumed guardianship of me because it was the best way to secure my future when Mama died, and Hess has done his duty by me as well."

"So, here you are, at one of the most exclusive boarding schools in the Midlands, and you developed a sudden urge to see your long-lost brother?"

She tugged the cuff of her sleeve down. "I don't know you, sir, but my options were limited. They're watching me all the time."

Yolanda spoke quietly, though Kettering had escorted her a good thirty yards from the building, where only roses, giant topiary hounds, or the occasional bee might overhear her.

"*They* are watching you?"

"The teachers, the other girls, the staff. If I try to escape again, they'll peach on me, and then they'll tell Hess. I know what happens to people like me."

"Dear girl, young ladies who tell great bouncers are usually thrashed soundly and given a few days of bread, water, and Bible verses."

"I'm not lying."

She wasn't telling the entire truth, either.

"Prove you are my sister. Tell me something only family would know." She was drawing him in, just as his late sister—his late full sister—had drawn him in, until it was too late, until he'd been too far gone by fraternal sentiment and his heart had held sway over his common sense.

"Your full name is Worth Reverence Kettering," she said. "Your first pony was Archibald, a piebald Shetland you were given at age six. Your second was Bucephalus, whom you were given at age nine because Archie came down with colic, and you insisted on staying at his side when Papa put him down. You told Papa you didn't ever want another horse, but grew weary of walking everywhere by the end of that summer."

"My third?"

"Ambergris," she said, as they passed a bed of tall daisies. "You rode him until you turned seventeen, when you walked away from Grampion, vowing never to return."

"I didn't vow to anybody who'd recall such folly." He hadn't even made that vow out loud. "You found my journals."

She flashed him a smile, one that exposed a terrible, winsome beauty in the near offing. "You were a dramatic young fellow."

He'd been a heartbroken idiot. "I'm not sure you're my sister, but I believe you're in difficulties. Be honest with me now, and I'll try to help you. Why do you need out of here so badly?"

"They're kicking me out," she said. "Some duke is thinking of putting his daughter here, and my unfortunate origins mean I'm *de trop*. If you can't take me off Mrs. Peese's hands, she might arrange for me to go to some sort of private sanitarium—the girls have been whispering about it all week."

Whispering where they knew she could overhear, no doubt. The compassion of rich little girls hunting in a pack was a dismaying prospect, though Kettering didn't believe for a moment the duke's daughter was the sole explanation for the present situation.

"If a place like that gets hold of me," Yolanda went on, "I'll lose my reason in truth. In the alternative, if you walk out of here today without me, Mrs. Peese might put me in a coach with Miss Snyder and deliver me to your doorstep tomorrow. She isn't about to send Miss Snyder all the way to The Lakes merely to see me safely home."

Mrs. Peese appeared at the French doors thirty yards away, her demeanor that of a warden anticipating an escape from her population of felons.

Be damned if Kettering would leave any young female to Mrs. Peese's tender mercies. "Are your reasoning powers intact, miss?"

"Not quite, but I'll bear up long enough to impress your fraternal obligation upon you."

She lifted her left hand to touch a single white rosebud, saw his gaze light on the bandages, and tucked her hand out of sight immediately.

"Pack your worldly goods," Kettering said, "and be ready to leave this afternoon when my town coach arrives."

\* \* \*

"Mrs. Wyeth!" Simmons, the butler, tapped once on the open door of Jacaranda's private sitting room. He tottered in, waving a piece of paper, his old-fashioned wig already askew at not even nine of the clock. "The most extraordinary thing has happened. Most extraordinary!"

Jacaranda gestured to her little sofa. "Please have a seat, Mr. Simmons. You must not excite your heart."

"Sound as the day I was born." He thumped his bony chest with his fist, then fell more or less bottom first onto the sofa. This was his typical method of taking a seat, the referenced natal day being a good eighty years past. "Best ring for your hartshorn, dear lady. This might overset even you."

A cat peeing in the servants' hall was enough to overset Simmons, and Jacaranda had never owned a personal stock of hartshorn, not even when she'd made her come out.

"Have some tea, sir, and calm yourself."

"We're to be visited, Mrs. Wyeth." He flourished the letter again. "Visited!"

She passed him his tea. "By whom?"

The vicar occasionally rattled out this way when he was in need of fresh air and a good game of chess. A weary traveler might stop at the kitchen door for a meal or a drink. They had visitors from time to time, of a sort.

"Himself!" Mr. Simmons waved the letter again. "Mr. K! In person! He's coming to visit, here, at Trysting!"

News, indeed, for Mr. Kettering hadn't graced his country estate with a visitation in the entire five years of Jacaranda's tenure there. Good news, in fact, for Jacaranda would enjoy at least one occasion of tending to her employer before she left her post. "Does he say if we're to make ready the family rooms?"

"Bedrooms are not a butler's concern, Mrs. W. Here, if you must have details." He passed her the letter.

"He says to prepare the family quarters." Knowing the state of Simmons's sight and the more significant of Simmons's agendas, she read the entire note aloud, "'Please ready the private family rooms, for I will be in residence starting the first of the week. Alert the staff and lay in appropriate stores for an extended stay.'"

"Well, madam." Simmons set down his tea cup, having drained it in one swallow. "You'd best get busy." He reached for one of the three tea cakes Jacaranda had set out on her own plate, revealing a second and no less familiar reason for disturbing her morning break.

"Busy, Mr. Simmons?"

"Preparing the bedrooms, dusting the parlors, cleaning the windows, turning the sheets, polishing the silver, whatever it is you do."

"That's all done regularly, Mr. Simmons. You know the routine here."

He looked disgruntled, as if somebody had stolen his mug of grog.

"The andirons might need blacking," she offered. "Though that falls to the footmen, and they are strictly your province. I've no doubt you already have your fellows dusting the library and the estate office, cleaning the outside of the windows, and sanding and beating the rugs?"

He spoke around a mouthful of tea cake. "Of course, of course. Don't suppose you could make me a list? In the excitement, a detail or two might slip from their lazy minds."

She jotted him a list—in a large, printed hand—and made him finish another cup of tea before he tottered off with his list in one hand and a second tea cake in the other.

She would miss even Simmons when she left Trysting. Simmons was a dear, and no doubt a contemporary of old Mr. Kettering, whom she envisioned toiling away in the damp and chilly confines of the Inns of Court, a muffler around his neck even in high summer.

Surely Mr. Kettering had seen at least his three-score and ten years. Why else would such an otherwise modern estate sport an octogenarian butler?

* * *

"Such wretched, wretched news!" Mama set Jacaranda's latest epistle aside and dabbed at the corners of her eyes with a lacy handkerchief.

"Is Jacaranda ill?" Daisy asked, though Jacaranda was something of a geological formation in human guise. She never took ill, never flew into hysterics, never hesitated once she'd made up her mind.

While Mama never enjoyed consistent good health.

Or a pleasant mood.

"The dratted girl reports that she's quite in the pink, but she has put off her return home to spend her summer dusting a lot of chandeliers and counting drawers full of tarnished silver. Her employer is leaving Town to ruralize at Trysting, and nothing will do but she must remain in Surrey to ready the house for him. Again, she disappoints me, and for what—to sweep mouse droppings from some old man's pantry!"

Readying the house was what a housekeeper generally did. Jacaranda probably even enjoyed doing it, and no mouse would dare set a paw in any pantry of hers.

"Would you like to hold the baby, Mama?"

Her ladyship rose, tucking the handkerchief into her bodice. "Keep that infant away from me. Children harbor illness, and my nerves are delicate right now. If Jacaranda won't come home, I simply do not know what I will do."

Daisy knew: Her ladyship would lament the disloyalty of a girl whom she'd raised *like one of her own*, ignore the requirements of a household much in need of a woman's civilizing influence, and expect Daisy to sympathize by the hour.

While all Daisy wanted was a nap.

"You could mention this letter to Grey," Daisy said, though her brother would wring her neck for that suggestion. "He misses Jacaranda, too."

They all did, even Daisy. Maybe Daisy most of all.

"Perhaps I shall do that very thing," her ladyship said, pausing in her pacing to inspect her reflection in the mirror over the parlor's fireplace. She was tall, had a fine, sturdy bone-structure, and dealt ruthlessly with any dark hairs attempting to turn gray. "No one will believe I could be a grandmother, much less three times over. I bear up remarkably well amid the chaos and strife of your brother's household, don't you think?"

"You are a marvel, Mama." Daisy had married five years ago and since saying her vows had presented her husband with two sons and a daughter. Mama had borne the late earl six children in nine years, which, as far as Daisy was concerned, qualified the countess for *marvel* status, at least.

"I must be going." Mama swept up to Daisy's seat and presented a smooth cheek for Daisy to kiss. "I vow this situation with your sister requires a resolution before I'm prostrate with nerves. Five years is far too long to indulge Jacaranda, and your brother will agree with me on this."

Daisy rose, the baby feeling as if she weighed five stone in her arms, for all the child was only a few months old. "I'll see you to the door, Mama. Please give my regards to the boys."

"Hermione Swift asked after you in her last letter. She still hasn't married off her youngest."

Mama struck the perfect balance between commiseration and gloating, as the hordes of women with whom she corresponded probably did about poor, dear Francine's step-daughter.

That headstrong Jacaranda, gone for a housekeeper, of all things!

"You must have a care for your appearance," Mama said, as the butler held her ladyship's cloak for her. "You are a bit pale, my dear, and that will never do. Eric deserves to find a pretty wife waiting for him when he comes home from his labors at the end of the day, not some drudge with"—she peered at Daisy's sleeve—"preserves on her cuffs. Pray for me, dearest. My nerves are not strong. If Jacaranda must waste what remains of her youth counting silver, she should at least count ours. We are her family, after all."

Another kiss, and Mama was off, the butler closing the door silently in her wake.

Daisy nuzzled the baby's crown and started up the steps. "We'll take a nap," she whispered to the child. "We'll dream sweet dreams and say a prayer for your Auntie Jack, because I may have just unleashed the press-gangs on her."

* * *

The difficulty with having a household of elderly retainers was that one had to do many jobs without appearing to overstep the post for which one was hired. Jacaranda could point out to Cook that raspberries had a very short season and if not picked when ripe, the entire year's opportunity for jam and pies was gone.

That way lay at least a week of cold soup, runny eggs, and weak tea.

So Jacaranda suggested the maids might enjoy a day outside and intimated that she herself would delight in the outing as well. Thus, she earned hours in the heat, keeping a half-dozen giggling, romance-obsessed girls at the task of picking berries.

Come winter, the raspberry jam would be worth the effort. At present, though, harvesting raspberries was a hot, buggy, thankless job, one that would tempt a devout Methodist out of her stays.

Jacaranda was neither Methodist nor especially devout, though on Sundays she was known to be sociable in the churchyard.

"I think that's the lot of it," the oldest of the housemaids said. "We're for a swim now, Mrs. Wyeth. You promised."

"I did promise, but keep quiet. You know the fellows will try to peek."

"So tell old Simmons to give the good-looking ones a half-day."

The women flounced off, teasing and laughing, and Jacaranda let them go without a scold. The day was broiling, and they'd picked a prodigious amount of fruit in a few hours. They'd done so, of course, because they'd been given an incentive for making haste.

With the maids off to splash about in the farm pond, Jacaranda hitched the pony grazing in the shade into the traces of the cart. She'd have to walk the little beast more than a mile to the manor house, a pony trot being a sure means of bruising fruit. The raspberries would be put up that afternoon, for even half a day in the pantry would see them mold.

Thus, Jacaranda spent the afternoon pretending she enjoyed helping with the preserves, pretending her step-mother had always made a day of such things, when in truth Step-Mama ventured no closer to making jam than when she applied preserves to her perfectly toasted bread each morning.

"Step-Mama is no fool," Jacaranda muttered when the jam was made and she could finally take off her apron. Evening had fallen, the long, soft hours of gloaming when the sun had set but the earth held on to the light.

"Your back troubling ye?" Cook asked. She'd been in Surrey for decades, but the broad vowels of the north abided in her speech.

"A twinge," Jacaranda allowed. "Putting up the fruit makes for long days."

"Raspberries is the worst for spoiling," Cook replied. "Good to have it done. Apples and pears is more forgiving. Even the cherries ain't so finicky."

"Raspberries are fragile, but we'll have preserves to put in everybody's basket at Yule."

"And shortbread." The gleam in Cook's eyes was particularly satisfied, because she'd conspired with Jacaranda to have their dairyman stagger the breeding of the heifers so they didn't all freshen at once. Staggering the herd meant Mr. Morse didn't get three months off with no milking, but it also meant the estate always had fresh milk and butter without having to buy from the neighbors.

"Did I smell shortbread baking this very morning?"

Cook's wide face split into a smile. "That you did, in anticipation of the blessed event."

"He isn't supposed to arrive for another day or two. The house hardly needed much attention to be ready to receive him."

She stated a simple fact, though Simmons's footmen had been putting in long days, indeed.

"Maybe not on your end." Cook retrieved a plate of shortbread from the pantry. "I haven't cooked for the Quality for going on five years. The larder needed attention, and I've yet to work out my menus past the first meal."

Jacaranda accepted a piece of shortbread, only one, though Cook had cut pieces sized to appeal to hungry footmen, bless her. "I don't suppose you'd show me what stores are on hand?"

"Put the kettle on, Mrs. Wyeth." Cook popped a bite of shortbread into her mouth. "This might take a cup or two of tea."

By the time Jacaranda had a week's worth of summer menus planned with Cook, full darkness had fallen and bed beckoned. The moon was up, though, and rather than make the tired staff lug a tub and water up to her room, Jacaranda threw towels and soap into a wicker hamper, along with a dressing gown and summer-length chemise.

The pond nearest the house wasn't merely ornamental. With a pump, cistern and an elaborate set of pipes, it served the stables, the laundry, and several other outbuildings. The pond was, however, relatively private, being ringed by tall hardwoods and fringed with rhododendrons on three sides.

On the fourth side was a grassy embankment, and there Jacaranda settled with her hamper. She'd done this before, usually on nights when she couldn't sleep.

On nights without a moon.

On nights when dreams were something to avoid.

Tonight, even tired as she was, sleep wasn't yet close at hand. She was ready for Mr. Kettering's arrival, but others at the house were excited, as if some handsome prince had kissed the entire staff awake. Their anticipation was like that of unruly children—impossible to ignore—and resulted in an excitement foreign to Trysting's usually placid demeanor.

Jacaranda resolved to swim away the staff's vicarious nerves, get clean, and enjoy a little privacy.

Her dress came off, then her shift and stays, then sabots, leaving her naked in the moonlight and comfortable for the first time in a long, hot day. She dove in from the rock God had positioned for that purpose and made a long, slow circuit of the pond. When she'd done her lap, she put the soap to its intended use and prepared to leave the water.

Hoof beats interrupted her consideration of the next day's list of things to do.

Hoof beats, coming up the driveway at a businesslike trot.

She was in the shallows before she realized the rider would come right past her corner of the pond on his way to the stables. Probably a truant groom who'd stayed too long at the posting inn in Least Wapping.

She toweled off hastily and shrugged into her nightgown and dressing gown, hoping the man's guilty conscience and the befuddling effects of spirits might conspire to keep her from his notice.

And they might have, except the beast was apparently a Town horse. The handsome gelding looked like that type whom squawking chickens, crossing sweepers, runaway drays, and rioting mobs wouldn't deter from his appointed rounds, but a pale blanket spread on the grass in the moonlight had the creature dancing sideways.

"Everlasting Powers, horse, it won't eat you."

A splash, as some frog took cover underwater, might have suggested to the horse his master was flat-out lying. Either that, or the animal sensed the proximity of hay, water, and fellow horses.

"Damn and blast, Goliath, would you settle?"

Goliath settled, albeit restively.

"Around to the stables with you, and at the walk if you know what's good for you." The beast must have known exactly that tone of voice, for it walked daintily on down the driveway.

Jacaranda blew out a breath of relief and folded her towel into the hamper. She did not recognize the horse, or the groom's voice, but the stable master, Roberts, knew what he was about. Housekeepers might use a pond late at night, and the occasional stable lad might go courting.

A few minutes later, a lantern sparked to life in the stable yard and voices drifted across the water. Working quickly, Jacaranda began to plait her wet hair. Whoever had wakened the stables would likely quarter with the grooms at this hour, but she wasn't about to be caught in dishabille.

"You there," a masculine baritone said from the shadows of the rhododendrons. "Explain what you're about, and explain *now*."

The tone of voice—imperious, vaguely threatening, definitely intimidating—arrived at Jacaranda's brain before the content of the words did. What registered was that she was alone, barely dressed, after dark, outside, with a strange man. The shadow detached itself from the surrounding darkness and proved to be of considerable size. She opened her mouth to scream, but nothing came out.

Her legs were not as unreliable. She would have pelted barefoot for the house, except the day before had been rainy, the bank was grassy, and Jacaranda's feet were wet.

At the last instant before she toppled into the pond, her foot slipped. Instead of a graceful arc over the water, she tumbled and fell, pain exploding in her head as she went under with a great, ungainly splash.

# CHAPTER TWO

"Breathe." Kettering pushed dark, wet tendrils of hair off the woman's forehead and spoke more sharply. "Madam, I told you to breathe."

She coughed and rolled to her side, bringing up water and yet more water. Then she shivered, even as she tried to scramble away from him.

"None of that, or you'll be back in the pond, and I am not rescuing you a second time." He eased his hold, his mind insisting she was well, despite the galloping of his heart.

"*Rescuing me?*" This time she got as far as a sitting position, her mouth working like an indignant fish's. "Rescuing me, though you all but pushed me into the water when I tried to evade your unwelcome company? I've never heard the like."

Her pique was almost humorous, given that her nightclothes were sopping wet and her curves and hollows tantalizingly obvious in the moonlight.

And yet, she had dignity, too. Damp, disheveled dignity, but dignity nonetheless.

"Madam, you panicked," Kettering said, retrieving his riding jacket from the grass farther up the bank. His coat was dusty, but he knelt and draped it over her shoulders in aid of her modesty, which would no doubt soon trouble her— for it already troubled him. "If I hadn't hauled you out of the water, you'd be bathing with Saint Peter as we speak."

"I am an excellent swimmer."

"You are an excellent scold." He settled his palm on the side of her head, brushing his thumb over her temple. "You're also raising a bump the size of

Northumbria. Nobody's an excellent swimmer when they take a rap on the noggin like this."

He took her fingers and gently guided them to the site of her injury.

"Angels abide."

He rose, and she gaped up at him. He wasn't that tall. He knew of at least one belted earl who was taller, several men who were as tall, and still the gaping abraded his nerves. He extended a hand down and drew her to her feet.

And gaped.

"I must look a fright," she said, but to him...

She was tall for a woman, wonderfully, endlessly, *curvaceously* tall. When dragging her from the water, only vague impressions had registered—some size, some female parts, not enough breathing. His coat had slipped from her shoulders as she stood, and he might as well have seen the woman in her considerable naked glory.

He picked up his coat and dropped it over her shoulders again. "I'll carry your effects, you keep the jacket, and we'll find some ice for your bruise."

"The ice stores are always low this time of year."

"Then we'll put the last of it to good use," he said, gathering up her hamper and his boots. "I'm Kettering, by the way, at your service."

When courtesy demanded that she give him at least one of her names, she remained quiet as they moved along the garden paths toward the back of the house.

The names he had for her would probably get his face slapped.

She came up almost to his chin, a nice, kissable height, and she moved with confident grace, though he kept their pace slow in deference to her injury. Truth be told, he rather liked that she didn't chatter. He could only hope she lived on one of the neighboring estates and enjoyed the status of merry widow.

Worth Kettering had a particular fondness for merry widows, and they for him, over the short term in any case. He was good for an interlude, a spontaneous passion of short duration—short being sometimes less than a half hour but invariably less than a week.

He'd studied on the matter and concluded women wanted more than a little friendly, enthusiastic rogering—that was the trouble. They wanted gestures, feelings, sentimental *notes*, bouquets, and passion, and he was utterly incapable of all but the passion.

He was so lost in a mental description of the follies resulting from females embroidering on passion—the notes and waltzes and flowers and whatnot— that he nearly didn't notice when the lady at his side preceded him into the back hallway leading to the kitchens.

Sconces were lit along the corridor, so he let her lead the way and used the time to admire the retreating view of her confident stride.

"You will please sit," he instructed his companion.

Her lips thinned, but she plopped her wet self down at the long kitchen worktable, one that had been scarred and stained when Kettering had been a lad. He was pleased to note his initials had not been smoothed off the far corner in the years since his childhood.

"I suppose tea would be in order," he decided, hands on hips. Thank a merciful God, the hearth held a bed of coals and a tea kettle ready to swing over the heat. He quickly assembled the required accoutrements, aware of his guest watching him the whole while.

"Perhaps you'd better speak," he suggested, "lest I conclude a blow to the head has stolen your faculties. I'll put some sustenance on a plate, if you don't mind. The ride out from Town is damned long—pardon my language—and I didn't intend to finish my journey with an impromptu rescue at sea."

"You certainly make yourself at home in the kitchen," the lady remarked, and her tone said clearly, she did not approve of his display of domesticity.

"I'm a bachelor, and most kitchens are organized along the dictates of common sense." He demonstrated his bachelor *savoir faire* by opening drawers and cupboards rather than leering at Trysting's cranky mermaid. "One learns to manage or one starves. Even the best staff is somewhat at a loss for how to cosset a man of my robust proportions."

Her gaze drifted over him, calmly but thoroughly. He was nearly as wet as she, and he didn't mind the inspecting—inspecting was all part of the dance— but he did mind being ravenous.

"You'll pardon me while I nip out to the ice house to find something cold for your head."

"That really won't be necessary," she said, starting to rise, only to sit right back down, her hand going to her temple.

He scowled in a manner guaranteed to silence prosy barristers and conjure files gone missing in the clerks' chambers.

"Fainting on your part would be a damned nuisance all around, madam. Keep to your seat. No head wound can be considered trivial, and the welfare of guests is taken seriously at Trysting."

"I'm not a guest."

He cut her off with a wave of his hand as he made for the back door. "Guest, trespasser, vagrant, tinker, what have you. I'm off to fetch some ice, and you will await my return."

\* \* \*

Could she make it as far as her quarters unaided before Captain Imperious of the Surrey Mounted Flotilla returned?

Likely not—not yet.

This Kettering-at-your-service must be some arrogant younger relation of Jacaranda's employer, an opportunistic nephew thinking to sponge off the old gentleman for the summer's visit, or an heir eyeing his expectations. She'd set him to rights when her head stopped throbbing and the room stopped expanding and contracting every time she moved.

The fellow wasn't entirely without use, though. He came back into the kitchen bearing a bowl of chipped ice, an incongruously cheerful red-checkered towel over his shoulder.

"Plenty enough ice left for our purposes," he said. "I'll have to speak to Simmons about ordering more."

Jacaranda had printed a reminder for Simmons regarding the ice not two days past.

"Hold still, madam."

That was all the warning Mr. Kettering gave Jacaranda before he held a towel full of ice firmly to the side of her head. The resulting pain caused her meager shortbread dinner to rebel and had her ears roaring again. When the roaring subsided, she was aware of the discomfort traveling even into her shoulder and of how the ice against her wound made her head both freeze and burn at the same time.

"Woman, you will hold still. You're in no condition to be delivering set-downs or lectures or whatever it is you're planning to deliver. Soon, your head won't hurt so badly, I promise."

His voice was brusque as he held the towel against her throbbing skull with one hand. With the other, he cradled her jaw, imprisoning her cheek against a washboard-firm stomach. His shirt was damp, of course, but through the dampness the heat of him warmed her jaw. Jacaranda should have shot to her feet with the indignity of it.

Should have scolded him smartly for his presumptuousness.

Should have delivered a set-down wrapped in a lecture tied up with a sermon.

She leaned closer to his warmth.

"Better, hmm?" He took the towel away. "Bleeding has stopped, too, thank the Everlasting Powers. Hold this here." He took her hand in his and anchored the towel to her temple again. "I'll fix us a spot of tea. You're pale as a felon awaiting sentence."

He moved off—a relief, that. Jacaranda held the melting ice for as long as she could, but the cold penetrated her hand as effectively as it had her head, and her teeth threatened to chatter. She distracted herself from the chill by watching Kettering bustle around the kitchen. For a big, rather wet man, he moved silently. He was in stocking feet—he must have left his footwear in the back hall for the Boots—breeches, waistcoat and shirt, and his clothing left nothing to the imagination.

This exponent of the Kettering male line wasn't a retiring, scrawny functionary holed up at the Inns of Court with a flannel around his dear, wattled neck. This fellow looked like he split wood, shod horses, and loaded sea-going vessels in his spare time.

His height was the first thing Jacaranda had noticed. Added to his height was his darkness: dark hair—particularly when wet, of course—and a burnished cast to his neck and forearms that suggested he frequently went without his hat—and shirt.

Beyond his appearance, he bore an energy that would have had Jacaranda scooting out of his path, if dignity would allow such a thing. Coupled with that energy was a brisk competence, which, at the moment, she appreciated.

"Drink." He put a cup of tea before her, as if she were a recalcitrant denizen of the nursery.

Jacaranda did not touch the tea cup.

"Oh, now." He set the tea tray down and lowered his presuming self right beside her. "Settle your hackles, duchess. What self-respecting Englishwoman refuses a nice hot cup of tea?" He wrapped her hands around the cup, his own cradling hers on either side of the mug. "See? Feels good. Now, don't be contrary when you know you'll enjoy your tea."

He took his hands away, having made his point, and Jacaranda's inchoate chill was abruptly supplanted by a peculiar heat rising from her middle.

"You're blushing," Mr. Kettering informed her. "I'm charmed, but you're still not drinking your tea, and until you have a sip, I can't touch mine."

She drank her tea, a cautious taste at first, but he was right: The tea was hot, strong and sweet, and the first cup of tea she'd ever had prepared by a man. The taste was disconcertingly good.

"Better, right?" He set his empty cup on the table. "I should have a housekeeper around here, and she might have something dry you could borrow to wear. It's dark out, thank the Deity. No one need see you in a servant's attire if we wrap you in a dark cloak and take you home in a closed carriage."

"I beg your pardon?" *Servant's attire?*

"I'm rather fond of the old dear," he went on, "and one doesn't want to give offense to loyal retainers. Mrs. Wyeth is the closest thing to a decent female on the premises, unless you want me canvassing the neighbors for some clothes?"

"I will wear my own clothes, thank you very much." She pushed her half-finished tea away and made to rise, but he'd boxed her in on the bench, and as soon as she gained her feet, her head sounded a trumpet fanfare of pain that blared past her neck, into her chest and arm.

"Perishing damned females, excuse the language," he muttered while he gently tugged her back down beside him. "I don't suppose you're married, and that's what all this misguided dignity is about? You will tell me now if some anxious husband must be dealt with. I insist on honesty from the women I rescue, and have no patience for mornings wasted on the field of so-called honor."

She sank onto the bench, mortified to feel another flush—it was *not* a blush—accompanying the pounding in her skull. How busy her bodily responses were after such an insignificant bump on the head.

"Naughty girl," he chided, his arm around her waist. He used his free hand to sweep her wet hair back over her shoulder, the better to mortify her by studying her wound.

"Now listen to me, duchess, because I am not at all accustomed to explaining myself." He drew his hand over her hair again, as if to move it, except the entire damp, curling mass of her sopping braid was already lying back over her shoulder. Then he did it again. And again.

"A newly discovered younger relation will join me here tomorrow—a schoolgirl, but at that dangerous, almost-hatched age, you know? Then, too, my niece will be coming along, and she's a frightfully noticing little thing, much as my late sister was. I can't offend my housekeeper's sensibilities when I've all but ignored my own property for five years. We must see you returned to your proper residence, even if you're a bit bedraggled and the worse for wear."

Still that slow, beguiling caress continued over Jacaranda's damp hair as Mr. Kettering went on. "A man has the right to ignore his possessions and estates, provided he's not negligent, but housekeepers are women, and they take on about such things. They get attached to their routines, and I've every intention of ignoring the place for another five years once I get these infernal girls sorted out. So we'll not be upsetting my dear Mrs. Wyeth, hmm?"

Jacaranda lifted her head from his shoulder, having no idea how she'd assumed such a misbegotten posture.

"You are without doubt the most conceited, managing excuse for a grown man it has ever been my misfortune to share a pond with."

His hand disappeared. "Be that as it may, you will not upset my housekeeper with airs and ingratitude, regardless of your mood, station, or dented noggin."

"There's no need for me to upset her," Jacaranda shot back. "You've already done a thorough job of it."

\* \* \*

Worth's midnight mermaid was addling his tired wits.

She was pretty, which was likely the source of the problem. He had a weakness for pretty women, though he'd learned long ago that they had no weakness for him. The pretty ones fretted at the most inopportune times about whether their hair was mussed, and he, of course, liked to muss a lady's hair. Then, too, pretty women were always looking past one's shoulder to see who was watching and to whose more interesting, titled, or wealthy side they might flit.

Still, they were *pretty*, and beauty in a female could mesmerize him, despite common sense and humiliating experience in his youth to the contrary.

The lady in his kitchen bore a touch of the exotic, all of her features and colors one detail away from perfection. Her eyes were not the fashionable blue. They were gentian, almost lavender, and so luminous as to look as though they belonged to a temple cat in human form. Her hair was not quite black, but on the curling ends looked sable, and it fell down her back in a cascade of curls and twists and flyaway strands that begged a man to write sonnets and conjure naughty fantasies.

Her hair looked in want of taming, and he liked that. She probably hated her hair, being female. He knew better.

As he rose and mentally appreciated her too-generous mouth and somewhat Nordic nose, his solicitor's brain also tried to assemble facts on a different level, for she'd intimated something about his dear Mrs. Wyeth.

"You knew how much ice was on hand," he said, as if accusing a clerk of reading his private correspondence.

She accused right back. "You aren't a little old fellow hunched over his desk at the Inns of Court."

Whatever that meant. "You knew your way to my kitchen, without the least guidance."

"I assumed you'd need somebody to keep you from stumbling into the butler's pantry. I took pity on an absentee landlord."

"Absentee owner," he retorted, his brain still unhappy with the logical conclusion.

"Absentee, in any case." Her humble bench might have been a throne for all the disdain in her glare.

"What is your name?" He softened his tone, in deference to another one of God's impending nasty jokes. She might, were there a merciful Deity, be an acquaintance of his housekeeper's, one accustomed to the friendly cup of tea after services.

Which were held five miles away, if memory served.

"My name is Jacaranda Wyeth."

"I don't suppose your dear mama is in my employ?" What sort of name was Jacaranda, and why was he doomed to deal with women who were unforthcoming regarding the simplest truths?

"I am in your employ, or I was as of recently."

"You're not quitting." He used his best unruly-client voice. Settled 'em down instantly, though the effect on little Avery was less immediate with each application.

She tipped her chin up a mere but ominous quarter inch.

Damn and blast, she was magnificent. And troublesome.

The worst of his many weaknesses was for troublesome women.

"Drink your tea." This earned him another quarter inch of chin-raising. "Please, Mrs. Wyeth, lest it grow cold."

Then the thought of warming her up, warming up all that magnificent temple cat- beautiful-exotic-Celtic-woman rippled across his imagination, and he had to sit down again.

Beside her unforthcoming self.

Of course.

She drank her tea, proving even a joking God wasn't without compassion, for Kettering needed the time to think of cold eel pie, privy rats, and those unruly clients. "You are my housekeeper, then?"

"And you are my employer." She pushed her mug away.

Worth refilled it and stirred in cream and sugar. A bachelor developed such habits, or he'd start looking about for a hostess.

"How came you to be in the pond at such an hour?"

"Today was long and hot," she said, taking a sip of her tea. "A little dip spares the maids having to lug water and the footmen having to haul the tub. The staff knows to leave me the privacy of the pond after dark."

He believed her. Not a single underfootman would dare lurk among the bushes to spy on her, lest the lad find himself turned off without a character the next morning by the vision most likely to have haunted his dreams.

"The staff is all abed?"

"Carl will be on duty by the front door. He's reliable, and we knew you might show up in advance of your coaches."

"How did you know?"

"I am in correspondence with Lewis, your house steward, who suggested you might not travel in the coach with the young ladies. Horseback is faster and likely preferable in all but wet weather."

He did not have a weakness for the *managing* variety of women, no matter how tall, pretty or troublesome. Particularly not for managing, unforthcoming women—though she'd suffered a knock on the head and hadn't *quite* been deceitful.

"Can you call a maid to stay up with you? You might slip into a coma if we let you sleep through the night."

"The blow to my temple didn't render me insensate, so much as the prospect of your unwanted attentions disconcerted me."

He was silent for a moment, trying to find a different meaning for her words and failing.

"My attentions, as you call them, were in aid of preserving your life. If you seek to put period to your existence, you have my condolences. I'm still not letting you quit, though. Not until my little family sortie in the teeming jungles of Surrey is complete."

"You have a very crude grasp of the employer-employee relationship," she informed him, finishing her tea. "Even you must understand I can give notice whenever I please."

He considered her, considered she was pale and wet and cold, and probably in need of a hot bath and some cosseting, else she would not be so sour-natured in the face of his consideration and concern.

More than physical comforts, she probably wanted privacy.

"Come." He rose and held out a hand. "I will escort you to your chambers and see you safely to bed. You can refine your insults and ingratitudes in lieu of sleep."

She took his hand, but only after perusing it as if to examine him for scales, claws, or evidence of barnyard relatives. Then she weaved when she gained her feet, which necessitated Worth once more putting an arm around her waist. That she again permitted such behavior suggested she really wasn't doing very well.

Served the ungrateful baggage right.

The housekeeper at Trysting had her own private parlor and sleeping chamber. Those hadn't moved in the five years since Worth's last visit, and Mrs. Wyeth let him escort her there without further comment.

He would *not* worry over her silence.

When they reached her door, he pushed it open, seeing no candle lit.

"This won't do," he muttered, propping her against the wall and taking down the lamp from the sconce. He lit a branch of candles in her parlor, enough that the room was minimally illuminated.

"Shall I light you a fire?"

"You shall not." She stood by the door, his jacket closed about her in a two-handed grip.

"Then get you into bed. You're one breeze away from the shivers."

"You have my thanks for your efforts." But, of course, she didn't move.

"For God's sake, woman, if I were intent on taking advantage, I'd have done so outside, in the dark, far from those who'd hear you scream, and well before you regained the use of your viper's tongue."

He moved to the bedroom and lit a candle beside her bed.

Other solicitors referred to Worth Kettering as "a detail man." The compliment was grudging, usually offered by somebody who *wasn't* a detail man. Sloppiness in a solicitor was a deadly sin, as far as Kettering was concerned, but he also understood that discipline took a man only so far toward cataloging every minute aspect of a situation.

Beyond that point, an ability to perceive details was a God-given gift.

Jacaranda Wyeth's quarters revealed myriad details to him.

She was orderly, even in her privacy.

She liked pretty things, embroidered pillow cases, aromatic roses, a soft, quilted bedspread nearly the same color as her eyes, white lace curtains. Frilly, female things that belied the no-nonsense composure of her countenance.

He withdrew from the bedroom and found her still by the sitting room door, her teeth chattering.

"Get your wet things off. I'll be back with some hot water for your ablutions, and a tray."

He left her before she could insult him again, which meant he moved quickly, replacing the lamp on the sconce and heading for the kitchen. Putting together a tray of buttered bread, cheese, and raspberry jam took no time at all. Neither did filling an ewer of hot water from the well on the range.

He didn't knock on Mrs. Wyeth's door, because his hands were full. He pushed the door open with his hip to find the sitting room empty. The door to the bedroom was closed, so he put the tray on a low table—lacy runner, bouquet of roses in a crystal vase—and tapped on the bedroom door.

"Don't you dare come in here."

"I've brought you water and sustenance. I'm off to fetch a teapot. You're *quite* welcome."

He took the time to change into a dry shirt, pajama pants and dressing gown along the way, happy to find his trunks already waiting in his room. When he returned to Mrs. Wyeth's suite with the tea tray and set it beside the food, she still hadn't emerged.

"Either present yourself now or expect company in your bedroom, Mrs. Wyeth. I can't have you falling and banging your head again." He couldn't shout, either, else he'd wake the house, and it wasn't time for that maneuver in any case, because she opened the door, a wrapper having replaced his jacket.

But, still, she was cold. Her lips were blue, her teeth chattered, and her eyes had turned to chips of periwinkle ice, for her discomfort was no doubt *all his fault.*

"For God's sake, come here." He grasped her by one fine-boned wrist and pulled her into his embrace. "You will catch an ague with all this damned pride, pardon the language." He scooped her up against his chest and settled with her on the sofa, her "d-d-don't you d-d-dare" hissed right in his ear. He twitched an afghan down from the back of the sofa and draped it over her as she squirmed in his lap.

"Hush, woman. You're cold, I'm warm, and a chill can be dangerous. Tolerate my proximity for five minutes, and I'll leave you in peace."

He ran his hand over her back, feeling the tremors of her shivering.

"Cuddle up and hold your tongue," he admonished. "You know you will otherwise crawl between cold sheets and fall asleep without getting warm. That misery can be avoided if you'll simply—"

"I hate you."

Then she subsided against him and didn't even lecture him when he rested his chin on her damp hair.

"Of course you do, but might you care to enlighten a fellow as to why?"

She burrowed closer and remained silent, suggesting her body didn't hate him.

"I have it." He gathered her into a more snug embrace as another chill shuddered through her. "If I have to ask, I don't deserve to have it explained to me."

"Brilliant."

"But hardly original. One wants a little originality in a lady's vituperations."

She made a huffy noise against his chest, but at least she'd stopped shivering.

\* \* \*

Jacaranda gave up verbally fencing with the wonderful heat source in whose arms she was nearly drowsing. She'd pay a price for this folly tomorrow, and likely for the remaining weeks of her tenure in his employ, but Worth Kettering was wearing silk and velvet, he smelled like a fresh breeze through a cedar forest, and in his arms Jacaranda felt, at least for these moments, *safe*.

He was big, brusque, officious, and far too astute, but he was offering her— pushing on her, really—a comfort more seductive than wealth or chocolate.

How long had it been since she'd been held this way? Likely since infancy. In her childhood, her papa's and step-mama's energies had been taken up with the younger children, particularly with pretty little Daisy, who'd had weak lungs as a child.

Then had come the tribulations of adolescence—height, nicknames, and the odd attentions from boys much older than Jacaranda.

She shoved that thought and all the bewildered, shameful memories that went with it aside and rubbed her cheek against the silk of Mr. Kettering's dressing gown.

He would have to wear silk.

"You're falling asleep, Wyeth, my dear."

Before she could struggle off his lap, he rose, easily, without grunting or straining or remarking on her size, and walked with her into her bedroom. He'd closed the window, probably in deference to the candle he'd lit by her bed, but that small consideration meant the room was free of drafts.

He set her on the edge of the bed, went around to the other side, and turned down the covers.

"Don't suppose you'd invite me in to warm up your sheets? I excel at warming sheets." He stacked throw pillows on a chair, a man at ease in a lady's bedroom. "No witty rejoinder, Wyeth? Shall I worry about you in truth?"

"I am speechless at your crude suggestions," she managed. "Both my bedroom and sitting room doors have stout locks. Must I use them, or have you acquired minimal notions of gentlemanly conduct at some point in your misspent youth?"

A housekeeper did not speak so disrespectfully to her employer, but he hadn't been serious about joining her in bed—she hoped. He'd been offering an insult as a bracing conversational slap to one whose wits had been wandering.

Or perhaps—intriguing notion—his remark had been intended as flirtation, a sad comment on the realities of Town life.

"Many would agree with the misspent part," he murmured, lifting back her covers. "Scoot in, my dear, or you'll start shivering again, because your hair is still damp." He frowned at that realization, the candlelight making him a displeased Bacchus. He took off his dressing gown and laid it over her pillows. "Your pillows won't take the wet."

"That dressing gown is silk." She lifted her legs to get under the covers, else he'd stand there half-clothed all night waiting for her. "I'll ruin it."

"I can't have you courting a chill. I thought we'd established that. A scrap of cloth matters little compared to the smooth running of my household."

To her horror, he sat at her hip and brushed her hair back from her forehead, then turned her head gently with a thumb to her chin.

"This scrape might start bleeding again. Try to sleep on your right side."

She obligingly shifted to her side—anything to make him go away.

"Good night, Wyeth."

"Good night, Mr. Kettering."

He rose and moved around the room, cracking her window a hair, blowing out the candle. She heard him moving in the other room, then felt the lovely weight of the afghan spread over her blankets. The light from the sitting room disappeared as he closed the bedroom door, and still she heard him, tidying up all the trays he'd brought in.

For nothing. She hadn't eaten, hadn't used the warm water, hadn't had a final cup of tea.

But she did sleep.

Eventually.

# CHAPTER THREE

"They'll be forever in there." Yolanda flopped back against the squabs and knew she was setting a bad example for her niece. Young ladies did not flop, and they did not gripe.

She had a niece, whom she hadn't known about, just as her brother Worth hadn't known he had a living half-sister. Having a niece was peculiar, when Avery seemed more like a younger sister and Worth Kettering more like an uncle. A grouchy uncle.

"Wickie won't tarry," Avery said in French. "She's devoted to me, and now she'll be devoted to you, too."

"Miss Snyder has that honor," Yolanda said, happy to practice her French on a native speaker. "At least until Michaelmas term. I wonder how much Mr. Kettering paid her for the trouble of babysitting me for three months."

Mr. Kettering. Worth. *Her brother.*

"Uncle has pots of money." Avery grinned as if Uncle had chocolates in his pockets. "Spending some on Miss Snyder won't hurt him. She looks sad to me, or angry."

"She's nervous," Yolanda said, switching to English. "She's one of those mousy little women who toils away in thankless anonymity in the classroom, and dithers over which new sampler to start as if it's a significant decision."

"Uncle thanks Mrs. Hartwick, but I don't know those other words you used—anom de something and blither," Avery said, peering out the window. "They're coming now."

"With food, thank the gods."

"Uncle says that. Thank the gods."

Uncle this and Uncle that. The little magpie worshipped the ground the man strutted around on. Yolanda had heard in great, dramatic detail in at least two and a half languages why Avery had reason to appreciate him. Avery had been orphaned in Paris for almost a year after her mother, Moria, had died, but had memorized Worth's direction, and eventually, thanks to the kindly intercession of her mother's friends, had been sent to her uncle.

A tale worthy of one of Mrs. Radcliffe's novels, right down to the way Worth doted on his niece.

Had he asked darling Avery for proof she was related to him?

To *them?*

Yolanda tucked into a hot, savory cottage pie, silently admitting that her brother may not have believed her, but he'd taken her in, bribed Miss Snyder to chaperone, and now they were off to the country.

He'd apparently bribed the coaching inns along the way, too, because the food was excellent, and the relief teams in harness in mere minutes.

Miss Snyder gave Yolanda a hesitant smile from the other bench. "It's good to see you eating, my dear. Soon we'll be at your brother's estate, and you and Avery can have a nice stroll."

She patted Yolanda's knee and took a careful bite of her meat pastry. Miss Snyder slowly, thoroughly chewed her bite, patted her lips with a serviette, then took another slow, small bite.

Another hour, the coachman had said. One more hour, a mere ten miles, and they'd be free to leave the coach.

Had it been more than that, Yolanda doubted anything in the world could have stopped her from running screaming down the road. Miss Snyder, mousy, anonymous, and whatever else could be said about her, had at least *chosen* her path in life. She could have been a governess, a laundress, a paid companion, or some lusty yeoman's wife—she was by no means ugly—while Yolanda was reduced to begging a berth from a brother nigh twice her age.

An earl's daughter with a small fortune in trust—though not a lady by title—and she'd had nowhere to go.

She chewed mechanically, lest the lump in her throat rise up and humiliate her before the brat and the mouse. A young lady with nowhere else to go could not indulge in dramatics, not in the middle of the king's highway, and not in her brother's handsome traveling coach.

* * *

"Yolanda had nowhere else to go, you see," Mr. Kettering said. "May I top off your tea?"

"Was your upbringing so backward you believe an employer should wait on his staff?" Jacaranda's tone was meant to be prim, condescending even, but what came through was sheer puzzlement. She'd been given to understand a title hung not too distant on Mr. Kettering's family tree, and here he was, dragooning her into breakfast tête-à-tête and pouring her tea.

"You'll take sugar with that, to sweeten your disposition," he said, pushing the sugar bowl toward her. "My upbringing was the best that good coin and better tutors could pound into me, but my mother died when I was quite young, and her civilizing influence soon became a distant memory. Have another raspberry crepe." He portioned one off his own plate and onto hers. "You're too thin, Wyeth. Eat." He sliced off a bite from the crepes remaining on his plate and gave every appearance of enjoying it.

Well. They were very good, the crepes, the fluffy omelet, the crispy bacon and golden toast. A piping-hot teapot nestled under embroidered white linen, and the room was redolent with the scrumptious scents of a kitchen determined to make a good showing before a long-absent master.

When had anybody, anybody *ever*, accused Jacaranda Wyeth of being too thin?

"Better," Mr. Kettering said, when Jacaranda started on her crepes. "Back to Yolanda, if it won't disturb your digestion?"

Rather than speak with her mouth full, Jacaranda made a small circle with her fork, and for some reason this had her host—her employer—smiling at her over his tea cup.

Gracious saints, that smile was *sweet*. Mr. Kettering was a dark man, dark-haired, dark-complected, dark-voiced, but that smile was light itself, crinkling the corners of startlingly blue eyes, putting dimples on either side of his mouth, and conveying such warmth and affection for life that Jacaranda had to look away.

Lewis had written that even ladies liked to have Mr. Kettering handle their private business, and in that smile, Jacaranda saw part of the reason why. Mr. Kettering was, damn and blast him, tall, dark and handsome, and blessed with that smile as well.

Thank heavens her term of employment at Trysting would soon be up.

"Your sister seems a typical young lady to me," Jacaranda said. "Your family hails from the north, do they not?"

"They do, what few of us there are," Mr. Kettering replied. "My older brother has had the keeping of the girl, but he's managed it by shuffling her from one exclusive boarding school to another, and he's lately seen to it she joined schoolmates on holidays and breaks."

"I gather she will holiday with us here for the summer?"

"Just so." His first name was Worth, Jacaranda recalled, apropos of absolutely nothing. She'd never met a man named Worth before, much less Worth Reverence.

"What can I do to make her summer more pleasant?" Jacaranda asked. "Young ladies in the area would enjoy meeting her, I'm sure."

"Then you should take her to meet them."

"Mr. Kettering, it might have escaped your shockingly egalitarian notice that I am your housekeeper, but your neighbors know my station. You will take your sister calling, not I."

His tea cup was set down with a little *plink!* of…not surprise, but disgruntlement, perhaps.

"I hardly know my neighbors in these surrounds, dear lady. Between trying to keep up with my correspondence from Town and seeing to my property here, I do not intend to make time to remedy the oversight."

Jacaranda had seven brothers, and Mr. Kettering's tone had the effect of battle trumpets summoning an experienced war horse at a dead gallop.

"You've neglected this estate for years, and we've managed well enough in your absence," Jacaranda shot back. "Your sister needs you, and no one else can see to her in this regard."

He put another half a crepe on her plate. "You don't spare your heavy guns, do you, Wyeth?"

"I have not the least idea what you mean, sir, except for a general notion that siblings ought to know and care for each other. Family ought to. I can and will make an effort to befriend the girl, and I can take Avery to play with the neighbor's children, provided you visit them first and send the requisite inquiring notes."

"I have to visit before my niece can even take her *damned doll* calling on other children?"

"You must make the girls think you'll enjoy it," Jacaranda added, just for spite. "I suggest you start with Squire Mullens immediately beyond the Millers' tenant holding. He has six daughters."

His eyes narrowed, and Jacaranda found her crepe wasn't merely good, it was delicious.

"I have taken a viper to my bosom." Mr. Kettering slathered butter on a piece of toast, then jam, then sliced it in half and put a triangle on Jacaranda's plate. "Six daughters?"

"The Damuses have eight girls, but only two are marriageable age."

"We'll start with the Damuses, and you will join me for breakfast regularly, Wyeth. I'll need your familiarity with the parish to plan the girls' social calendar." He bent to take a bite of his toast, while Jacaranda was sure he was hiding another smile.

He'd cornered her neatly, making her attendance at breakfast a show of consideration for the children, not an order.

"I will join you for breakfast." She took another bite of a crepe so light it nearly levitated off of her fork. "And only breakfast."

"Oh, fair enough, for the present. Now finish your meal. I've a notion to look at that bump on your head."

As if Worth Kettering's *notions* bore the same weight as celestial commandments or royal decrees.

"No need for that. I've quite recovered." Jacaranda chewed her toast carefully, for even toast required mastication, and the effect was to pull on that area of her head still lightly throbbing.

"You've put every bite to the same side of your mouth, my dear. Your injury pains you. Did you sleep well?"

"I did." After a time. "I usually do." Particularly when her pillow was swathed in silk.

"I usually don't," he said, frowning at his tea cup.

"Perhaps the country air will agree with you." She'd meant to say it maliciously, because he was so great a fool as to think correspondence from Town more important than a newly discovered sister.

"Intriguing thought. So what would a conscientious landowner do, were he facing my day?"

Papa had been nothing if not conscientious about his acres, and Grey followed very much in Papa's footsteps.

"A conscientious landowner would ride out. He might take his land steward, particularly after an absence, or take a few of his favorite hounds." Or he'd take a few of his more boisterous sons, and the house would, for a few short hours, be blessedly peaceful. "He'd look in on his tenants, especially those with new babies or a recent loss."

"I like babies."

Oh, he *would*. Jacaranda finished her toast.

"Will my steward know of such things? Babies and departed grannies?"

"The Hendersons lost a child this spring, a bad case of flu," Jacaranda said, pushing her nearly empty plate away a few inches. "A little girl named Linda. She had always been sickly, but they'd got her through the winter and were hoping she'd turned a corner."

He took a bite from the half crepe she'd left on her plate, chewed and arranged his fork and knife across the top of his plate. "You want me to call on these people?"

"I'll pack you a hamper. They've many mouths to feed."

"I can't ride over with a hamper on Goliath's quarters." He lifted his tea cup, examined the dregs, set it down. "Come with me?"

A request, not an order. Good behavior must always be rewarded. "To call on a tenant, I can accompany you. Their wives will be glad of another woman to chat with."

"You know their wives?"

"When your tenants have illnesses or particular needs, they send to us here and we provide what aid we can. The English countryside remains a place where one's neighbors are a source of support, and of course I know their wives."

He folded his serviette in precise thirds and laid it by his plate. "Where else do I need to show the flag?"

"These calls, the first you've made in years, aren't showing the flag." She regarded him with some displeasure, for the crepes had been very good, while the company was vexing. To deal with this man, she'd need her strength. "These people labor for your enrichment. Their welfare should concern you."

"It should," he agreed easily enough, giving Jacaranda the sense he'd lost interest in her scolds. "Let's have a look at that knot on your head, hmm?" He rose to stand beside her chair, clearly prepared to hold it for her, as if she were...a lady.

He'd love nothing more than if she fussed at him for that while he stood over her, so she held her tongue.

"Over by the window." He drew her to her feet and tugged her by the wrist to the light pouring in the east-facing window. "Turn yourself, just"—he took her by the shoulders and positioned her to his liking—"like that."

When he stepped close, she got a fat whiff of delicious, clean man. He used some sort of shaving soap that made her want to lean closer and intoxicate her nose on his woodsy aroma. The fragrance had spicy little grace notes, as well—even his scent held unplumbed depths.

"You must have a busy day of your own," he suggested, carefully tilting her head in his big hands.

"Industry is its own reward." He had offered the gambit to distract Jacaranda from his fingers tunneling through her hair, and that was decent of him, so she rallied her manners. "In truth, I have done as much preparation for your visit as I possibly can, but the house is always kept in readiness, so the burden of additional work is not great."

"Then you might enjoy coming along with me on these tenant calls?" Gently, gently, Mr. Kettering moved his touch over the knot at her temple. "Hurts, doesn't it?"

"A little." While his touch was lovely.

"The bleeding did not resume," he said, slipping his fingers from her hair, but not stepping back. "I'm glad you won't mind showing me about the farms."

He was smiling down at her again, pleased with himself, the lout, and before Jacaranda could beg to differ with him, he patted her arm.

"We'll wait until after lunch, so I can fire off a few letters first, otherwise I'll never be up to dandling babies and pinching grannies."

"Please say you would never pinch a grandmother!"

Now he did step back, his eyes dancing.

"My dear Mrs. Wyeth, I would pinch a granny, but only because she pinched me first. I know a number of grannies who aren't to be trusted in this regard. A shameless lot, for the most part. Complete tarts. Makes one look forward to his own dotage. Shall we say, one of the clock?"

"I'll have luncheon moved up to noon," she said, not taking the bait no matter how succulent, no matter how close to her nose he dangled it while looking the picture of masculine innocence. "In deference to the fact that the girls traveled for much of the day yesterday, I've planned luncheon as a picnic meal on the back lawn."

"I'm dining on the ground with children, being pinched by grannies, *and* acquiring a lot of smelly, drooling hounds, and you expect the country air to agree with me? You are an admirably cruel woman, Jacaranda Wyeth. I'll meet you at the coach house at one."

* * *

"How are you ladies settling in?" Worth put the question to his sister and his niece, who both looked quite pleased to be eating outside amid bugs and breezes, not a tablecloth in sight.

Avery, as was her habit, went chattering off in French, lightened by a dash of Italian, with the occasional foray into her expanding English vocabulary. The coach ride had been interminable; the horses had been very grand, but not as grand as Goliath; the coach fare had been very good, if difficult to tidily consume in a moving vehicle; and Miss Snyder had been as quiet as a moose.

"Mouse," Yolanda corrected, smiling—the first time Worth had seen that expression on his sister's face since her arrival at Trysting.

"What is the difference? Mouse, moose, you know I refer to a little creature for the cat to eat."

"There is a difference," Yolanda said. "Worth, have you pencil and paper?"

He passed over the contents of his breast pocket, and Yolanda started scribbling.

"Where have you seen a moose, Yolanda?" he asked, selecting a cold chicken leg to gnaw on.

"In books, unless you count Harolda Bigglesworth. Poor thing had a name like that and dimensions to match, but she was very merry."

"Shall we invite her out to the country with us?" Worth had to admit the chicken was delicious, and with a serviette wrapped around one end, not so very messy.

"We shall not," Yolanda said as she sketched. "She's been engaged to some viscount since she was a child, and association with the likes of me would not do."

"Your brother is a perishing earl." Worth waved his chicken leg for emphasis.

"Why not associate with you?"

"Your moose," Yolanda said, passing the sketch over to her niece. "He's a grand fellow, nigh as big as Goliath, and he lives in the Canadian woods."

"My goodness, he looks like a cross between a cow and a deer, but what a nose he has!"

Worth peeked over Avery's shoulder.

"You are talented," he said. "Talent is worth money, you know. I have a client who will make a tidy living painting portraits, a very tidy living. You should develop your art, Yolanda."

"Drawing is one thing they let you do," she said, tucking the pencil behind her ear.

"They *let* you do?" Worth set aside the chicken bone, for he'd eaten every scrap of meat on it.

"When you're on room restriction at school, you have your school supplies to entertain you, but only those, so I drew a great deal. Avery, will you eat every bite of that potato salad?"

Avery made Yolanda earn her salad by teaching her a half-dozen German words. Yolanda made Avery try to copy the moose, with comic results. All in all, it was a pleasurable, nutritious way for Worth to pass an hour with his…family, out of doors. On that thought, he pushed back to sit on his heels.

"My dears, I must away to impersonate a country squire. While I'm chatting up the neighbors, I can ask if any ponies are going begging in the surrounds."

"Oh, Uncle!" Avery's jubilation at the prospect of a pony knew no linguistic bounds, but Yolanda merely smiled at her niece and toyed with a bite of cheese.

"Yolanda? What say you? Shall we find you a gallant steed so you can canter about the countryside and turn all the lads' heads?"

Yolanda studied her cheese. "Good heavens, no, thank you. I've heard regular riding can make a girl's figure lopsided."

"So we'll teach you to drive," Worth suggested, "or fit you out with a left-side saddle and a right-side saddle, and you can alternate."

"That's what I shall do," Avery interjected. "I shall ride with Uncle every day."

Worth drew a finger down her nose. "No, you shall not. This is England, and it rains too frequently for daily hacks. Well, think about it, Yolanda. I must call upon the neighbors, many of whom are possessed of offspring whose acquaintance you should make. We'll be here for months, and I can't have the two of you growing lonely or bored."

Particularly not when Yolanda had been both at her fancy school.

He got to his feet and made for the coach house, but the meal, surprisingly pleasant though it had been, had left him more convinced than ever that Yolanda was hiding a great deal.

* * *

Hess Kettering, more rightly, Hessian Pierpont Kettering, Earl of Grampion, perused the first correspondence he'd received from his baby brother in five years.

*Get your lordly arse down to Trysting before Michaelmas or I'll send Yolanda home on a mail coach.*

"You'll go, won't you?" Lady Evers's eyes held concern, but only the concern of a friend. They'd tried a dalliance years ago, but neither of them had put any heart into it, and the friendship remained. Now she was spending a pretty summer morning in his library, sipping tea with him at his desk, and fretting over him—to a friendly degree.

"Worth is telling me the girl is safe with him for at least another few months," Hess said, "maybe even asking me to give him those months, but he's also issuing an invitation."

"He's hurting, Grampion. You're head of the family, and that puts the business of reconciliations squarely on your handsome shoulders. If this is the invitation you get, then this is the invitation you accept."

Surely only a friend would address him with that blend of amusement and admonition?

"Worth was always prone to dramatics, and that's what got us into this situation in the first place."

Not quite true. A young woman's duplicity had done more than a little to stir the pot of familial estrangement.

"You could have gone after him," Lady Evers said, pulling on her gloves. "He wasn't even quite an adult all those years ago."

Hessian came around the desk to scoot her chair back, now that he'd endured tea, scones, and the beginnings of a scold.

"Papa decided against retrieving him—a younger son must be allowed his pride, according to the earl—though I think it broke his lordship's heart, and then I was too busy marrying to go haring south on a goose chase."

"Your only brother and heir is not a goose."

"He acted like a goose." So, apparently, had Hessian.

Her ladyship tactfully pretended to peruse a portrait of Hess's mother hanging over the fireplace, one she'd seen dozens of times. The two bore a resemblance, something Hess noticed only now.

"Were you the soul of probity at age seventeen, Grampion?"

Yes, he had been, more fool him. He slipped her arm through his, because the time had come to gently herd her toward the door.

"I was seventeen, and that's as much as I'll admit. If I'm to heed Worth's summons, a journey of two hundred miles will take some preparation. What have you heard from Lucas?"

She prattled on about her oldest son, spending a summer in the south between public school terms, and in her voice Hess heard pride, longing, and love. Not for the first time, Hess regretted the lack of children in his own household. Grampion was beautiful, the land graciously generous, the views spectacular.

But lonely. His only consolation was that Worth had no children either, no wife, no family about except a little niece who likely understood only French, and now Yolanda, a near adult and about as sunny-natured as a hurricane.

Still, Hess wouldn't remain in the north, without niece or sister, while Worth had both, though neither would Hess go galloping south and solve all the family's problems himself—again.

\* \* \*

"Tell me about these Damuses," Worth said as he settled onto the seat of the dog cart beside Mrs. Wyeth. Goliath—trained to drive as well as ride, like any proper mount of his breeding and dimensions—was in the traces, which had required loosening the harness by a few holes in all directions.

"The Damuses are not an old local family," Mrs. Wyeth said as they clattered out of the coach yard. "She was a Dacey, and he's the second son of a baronet in Dorset. Their holding was willed to him by a grandmother, and she brought a good settlement to the union, so they prosper."

"With twelve children, that's not all they do. How about the Hendersons? Have they leporine inclinations?"

"Leporine?"

"In the nature of a hare, similar to caprine, or vulpine, in the nature of a goat, or a fox, you know?"

"My Latin is rusty. The Hendersons are a young couple who moved here from Dorset when his cousin left the property for London. They've three boys yet, now that Linda has passed on. The land is good, but they haven't been farming it for long, and it takes time to learn the way of a piece of ground."

What manner of housekeeper was brought up on Latin?

Worth turned Goliath onto the lane. "Ground is just *there*. What do you mean, learn the way of it?"

"This field tends to get boggy in spring, but mostly in the one corner, so you might plant that corner later. That field is perfect for oats, but doesn't do quite such a good job with barley. A particular irrigation ditch is always the first to back up when the leaves come off in the fall. That sort of thing."

Agricultural land was like women then, full of idiosyncrasies and quirks. "How come you, a housekeeper, to know about *that sort of thing?*"

"I wasn't always a housekeeper, Mr. Kettering. My father was responsible for a great many acres, and land doesn't farm itself."

So her father was likely a steward to some lord. Worth hoarded up that information the way some of his clients hoarded their denarii and sesterces.

"What do the Hendersons do well?"

"Her people are Irish on her mother's side, which is part of the reason they left their home county."

"We're superstitious about third-generation Irish, are we?"

"I haven't asked her for the particulars, but Mrs. Henderson can tat lace so delicate it hardly catches sunlight. Mr. Henderson has a magnificent sow by the name of William."

"A sow named William, and my livelihood depends on such as these?"

"The boys named the pig, because she lets them ride her, so she's in the way of a porcine charger."

"I hope you don't expect me to ride this great pig?"

"Don't let me stop you, if that's your inclination."

He deserved that, and it was worth the insult to know Wyeth was enjoying herself. "Goliath would never bear the shame if I rode a pig. Is there a marker for the child's resting place?"

She was silent for a moment, and Worth was pleased to have surprised her. He'd surprised himself, but he knew what it was to lose a family member, and to some people, a marker would be important.

"We'll go by the church on the way over," Wyeth said. "We can look."

They found the grave but no marker, and the curate intimated none had been ordered. Worth drew the man aside, made arrangements for something befitting a girl child, and handed Wyeth back into the gig.

"How is it you know French, Wyeth?" He slapped the reins on Goliath's shiny black rump before his housekeeper could remark his discussion with the curate.

"I had a good upbringing, and French is not a difficult language."

A steward's daughter might have a good upbringing, if her father served the nobility. "Where did you have this good upbringing?"

"Dorset."

Dorset, from whence the beleaguered Hendersons hailed, though from Worth's observation, they did not know they were beleaguered. The lady of the house had a sadness in her eyes, but she was much loved by her beamish young spouse and doted on her menfolk. Worth dutifully asked to see the magnificent sow and, while the boys rode her around the yard, inquired of Mr. Henderson if Mrs. Henderson might consider parting with some of the exquisite lace gracing their spotless cottage.

"Whyever would a grand fellow like yourself be in want of lace?"

"I'm not, personally, but I'm also not such a grand fellow that I'd pass up an opportunity to make a coin or two. Lace like that is becoming scarce, and all the fine ladies in Town will pay dearly for flounces, ruffles and mantillas. I know modistes and tailors who'd die for as much of that lace as they could get their hands on."

"You'd buy Trudy's lace?" Henderson was tall, rangy, blond and ruddy. He was also besotted with his round, red-haired Trudy, and appropriately protective of her.

"If you're willing to part with your goods," Worth said. "I'd take a commission, for arranging the London end of things, but there'd be coin for you and yours as well."

William came to a halt, like any well-trained mount, then—with the two little boys bouncing happily on her back—trotted off in the direction of the chicken coop.

"Trude's proud of that lace," Henderson said. "We've shown the boys how to tat a little, too."

"You know your lady best. Discuss it with her and send word of your decision. Seems a shame to keep work that fine a secret, though, and I could use the coin."

Henderson looked him up and down, from his brilliantly white cravat to his shiny riding boots and all the Bond Street finery in between. "Takes a bit of the ready to trick yourself out like a swell."

"More than a bit. Now, you're a married fellow. What is the secret to politely prying two women apart when a man needs to be on his way?"

Henderson's expression turned sympathetic. "Can't be done. Trude gets to visiting in the churchyard, too, and the boys have walked halfway home before I get her in the cart."

"Don't suppose that pig knows how to drive?"

"The boys are working on it. They want to be famous throughout the shire for training the realm's first draft pig."

Worth complimented the boys on William's accomplishments, scratched the pig's hairy chin, and took his housekeeper by the elbow to remove her from the Hendersons' front porch.

"Mrs. Henderson's a genius with her lace, isn't she?" he observed when he'd handed Wyeth up.

"The whole family can do work like that, but it's hard on the eyes. We'd best hurry. Looks like we're in for a squall."

"Goliath is the steady sort, and he must live up to the standards set by that pig. He'll get us home safe and sound. What did you ladies talk about?"

"The usual." She pulled her shawl closer. The temperature, which had been summery warm, was dropping as the breeze picked up. "The boys are growing, the crops are coming along, she misses her Linda, but may be carrying again already."

"The fences were not in the best repair, and I suspect one corner of the cottage roof leaks." Though Henderson hadn't mentioned either problem.

"Your steward will have a list of tenant repairs for you," Wyeth said, eyeing the sky. "A short list, but he'll want to show it to you before he spends any coin on maintenance."

"I know this steward you mention. Mr. Reilly sends me reports each month almost as detailed as yours. Is the weather always so changeable here?"

"This is England, so yes."

It might have been Worth's imagination—or wishful thinking—but it seemed to him she bundled closer to his side.

"Your bonnet might get a soaking." She likely had only the one. "May we impose on a neighbor along the way to the manor?"

"The Hendersons are the closest tenants, and the church is kept locked on weekdays."

"To prevent felons from taking refuge?"

She made no reply, and from the south came a long, low rumble of thunder.

Worth gestured with his chin, because his hands were on the reins. "A covered bridge, about half a mile ahead. We'll make it."

Goliath gave them his best bound-for-home trot, and a gust of rain spattered down, but they made the covered bridge before the heavens opened up. To Worth's surprise, his housekeeper's gloved hand was manacled around his arm when he drew the horse up in the middle of the bridge.

"You are pale as a winding-sheet, Wyeth. Is your head paining you?" He set the brake and wrapped the reins, unwilling to move until she loosened her grip.

She slipped her hands to her lap. "I hate to be out in storms. When I was a girl, I saw a tree struck by lightning, a lovely old oak I'd been playing in an hour earlier. The tree went up in flames and became an ugly, charred skeleton. My brothers thought it wonderfully dramatic. I hated it. The tree had been refuge for me."

"Brothers can be the worst." He climbed down and came around to her side of the gig. She sat straight as a lamp post, clutching her shawl around her as if a winter gale rather than a summer storm threatened. "Get you down, Wyeth. The weather must have its fifteen minutes, and Henderson said the corn can use the rain. Tell me more of these disgraceful brothers."

He lifted her from the seat before she could protest, then she stood beside him, looking pale and shivery, while he untied her bonnet and set it on the seat.

"The one I'm closest to is Grey, and he's a good brother."

Worth settled his coat around her shoulders. He liked the look of her in his clothes already, and this was only the second time he'd offered her his coat.

Fast work, though, even for him.

# CHAPTER FOUR

"Tell me about your brother Grey," Worth said, offering his arm to a woman who was not, after all, without a few human failings. "I have a perfectly useless brother in the north, and we've him to thank for Yolanda's charming presence."

"She is charming," Wyeth said, sails filling, but then a loud crack of thunder sounded right overhead and she hunched into him.

"Silly woman," Worth murmured, and his arms went around her without him thinking about it, the same as they might have gone around Avery after a nightmare. Then the rain was too loud on the roof to permit further conversation—or further endearments.

Wyeth stayed bundled against him, not quite shivering with cold, but twitchy with nerves. When the rain changed to hail, she tucked her nose against his neck and held on to him with gratifying tenacity, making no move to lecture or move off when Worth's hand settled on the back of her head and stroked her hair.

He'd never quite appreciated the potential in rainy days before, nor the value of a horse who was blasé regarding the weather.

"I'm being ridiculous," she said, when the rain slowed. "I can't seem to let go of you, though."

"You have a frightening association with storms like this, and I'm at least good for keeping off the chill." He rested his chin on her hair, which smelled wonderfully of lavender and sunshine. "You were about to tell me of your brother."

"Grey is older than I. He became head of the family quite young, and that's a difficult role when a man has eight younger siblings and half-siblings."

"You're the oldest girl?"

"How did you know?"

"How else would you have learned how to command a regiment, hmm?"

"My mama died after my younger brother Will was born. When my step-mama came along, and all the little ones appeared, I enjoyed being the big sister."

Little ones didn't simply *appear*. "I've always wished I came from a large family," Worth said, keeping an ear on the rain. "I have a brother and now a sister extant, and we have Avery. That's it. While my brother and I are estranged, my sister and I are strangers."

"Has your brother met Avery?"

"No, he has not, the wretch."

"He didn't tell you about Yolanda, did he?"

"Hard to say, because we don't exactly correspond, though I've sent him an epistle over this folly with Yolanda. The storm is moving off."

"I should move, too."

No, she should not. "Soon, my dear."

When she eased her grip a few drippy, quiet moments later, he let her step back, taking her warmth and a luscious abundance of female curves with her. Everlasting Powers, if he'd known his housekeeper was such a goddess, he'd have removed to the country years ago.

To do exactly what, he would not admit even to himself, but getting caught in storms with her was a delightful place to start.

"I'm much braver if I can remain indoors," she said, moving off to pet his horse. "He's a stalwart fellow. His name is Goliath?"

"He's a big, stalwart fellow, so yes, he's Goliath."

"Some draft in his lineage?" She winced as thunder rumbled in the distance.

"On the dam side. Let's watch the water rise." He tugged her by the arm away from his horse and brought her to the upstream side of the bridge. "I have good memories of storms, of rafting down swollen streams immediately after a deluge, of seeing all my dams swept out to sea by a good downpour. As a boy, it was wonderful."

"That must be the appeal of sons for many men," she said, taking a place along the rail beside him. "Men talk of dynasty, legacies and successions, but what a son really means is more forts in the attics, toy soldiers, and dams."

"How many brothers have you?"

"Seven, and one sister."

"No doubt you and this sister are close?"

She peered down into the roiling water. "In a way. You're being very kind."

"How will I know whose pig to throw a saddle on if I let you come to harm in a storm, Wyeth? Besides, we aren't enemies merely because we're different genders."

"Gender isn't a detail, either."

*Her* gender wasn't a detail. "I like women, I'll have you know, and not in the sense you're about to accuse me of, or not exclusively in that sense." He turned, resting his elbows on the railing, while she kept to her stream-facing position.

"You like women because they cook and clean and sew?"

"I've hired men to do those things in my London household, my dear, but no. I like women because they don't fight stupid duels over inebriated insults nobody can recall the next morning. Women don't make rude noises in public or relieve themselves against any handy wall. You have seven brothers, Wyeth, I know now you cannot be shocked. I like women—honest women, that is— because they smell good, because they give us babies, because they...what?"

"You are prissy and old-fashioned."

"You think because I'm such a large fellow I can't be fastidious?" He let her have her smirk, because it confirmed the weather was no longer unnerving her. "You think because I respect women for their inherent bravery I'm old-fashioned?"

"Bravery in what regard?"

"Leave childbearing to men and the race wouldn't last a century. All children would have to be born capable of cutting their own meat, washing their own soiled nappies, and talking themselves out of nightmares—twenty times in a twenty-four-hour period, and multiply that times the number of toddlers underfoot. Don't forget they'd have to teach themselves how to do sums and read, for men hardly know themselves after three years of university."

She gave him a funny, half-smiling perusal, then pushed off the rail.

"If we keep Goliath to the walk, we can likely find our way home now."

"You don't mind the occasional shower when we pass under a tree? I can send a closed carriage back for you." He didn't want to. He wanted to settle her right beside him on the gig again, and abruptly, the prospect of visiting his tenants shifted from drudgery to something approximating a pleasant duty.

Particularly if he could manage to dodge a few more storms with Wyeth in the process.

"A little rain isn't what unnerves me, Mr. Kettering, and I don't melt."

He handed her up, having sense enough to keep to himself the thought of circumstances under which she might, indeed, be made to melt.

\* \* \*

Worth Kettering was kind.

The realization disconcerted Jacaranda, because it required her to admit she'd been hell-bent on finding fault with him. He'd handed her down from the gig, bowed over her hand as if they'd been on a social outing, then winked at her and left her in peace.

She understood what that wink meant: *The secret of your chicken-heartedness is safe with me.*

Oh, but he didn't know the half of it. Yes, she was uncomfortable out in storms, but he didn't know she'd heard him call her "silly woman," and the affection in his tone had sent her insides prancing about. Nobody referred to her as silly, though five years ago, she'd been worse than silly. Nobody held her, stroked her hair, or offered her their jacket when she took a chill.

And nobody on the entire face of the earth wore as enticing a scent as Worth Kettering.

He'd be gone soon, though. Trysting was merely a place to find his balance with Yolanda and Avery under the same roof. If Jacaranda were lucky, a few more weeks and Mr. Kettering of the warm jacket, delicious scent, and rogue's wink would be on his way.

Then she would be on her way. She'd promised, after all, and the usual pleas and threats in Step-Mama's last epistle had borne a desperate edge.

"Mrs. W!" Old Simmons's voice was raised in a quavery approximation of a shout. "Mrs. W? Ye must come quick to the children's rooms."

He wheezed down the kitchen steps, looking mortally relieved to have found her.

"The young ladies be in a taking, Miss Snyder is wringing her hands, and ye must come." "You sit, Mr. Simmons, and catch your breath. I'm on my way."

She did not run, though. Simmons had already set a questionable example for the junior staff with his haste and shouting. She also suspected Yolanda and Avery were engaged in a version of finding their balance with each other, and among young ladies who were family, that way would not always be smooth.

"Girls, please stop shouting," Miss Snyder was saying when Jacaranda arrived at Avery's room. "I meant no offense, not to anybody. We're to help each other in this life and—Mrs. Wyeth, hello. I apologize on behalf of the children for the racket."

"These two are old enough to make their own apologies for cutting up the king's peace. Now what has caused this uproar? Avery, you first." Jacaranda closed the door and stood with her arms crossed, barely resisting the urge to tap her foot.

Avery launched a righteous volley in English liberally garnished with French, explaining that dear Wickie was off in the village on her half day, but the Miss Snyder creature attempted to brush Avery's hairs in Wickie's absence, and while an aunt might brush a niece's hairs, Miss Snyder was nobody to be assuming such privileges. Not nobody *at all*, of less consequence than a moose.

Yolanda looked abruptly away, and Miss Snyder looked down at her hands.

"Yolanda, what have you to say?"

Yolanda took a moment to compose herself, for which Jacaranda respected the girl.

"Miss Snyder was only offering to help, and Avery went off on a grand scold, and that was wrong. I am not brushing my niece's hair until she apologizes."

"I shall not apologize to somebody I don't know for forbidding her to brush my hairs."

"And yet,"—Jacaranda treated Avery's tousled hair to a slow perusal—"you can hardly come to table with your hair looking like that, can you, child? The hedgehogs will ask to make the acquaintance of your hairdresser."

Avery got a look at herself in the cheval mirror and was too young to hide a grin. "Wickie will be back, and she can brush my hairs."

"If she pleases to," Jacaranda said. "Who pays Wickie's salary, Miss Avery?"

"Uncle."

"So from whom will Wickie take her orders?"

"Uncle, but she listens to me, too."

"Miss Snyder will listen to you, too, so what do you wish you'd said to her?"

Avery studied her reflection in the mirror, biting her lower lip.

"Miss Snyder, I do not know you, and you are not my Wickie. I would not have you brush my hairs. I will brush them myself, but thank you for wishing to help."

"You love your Wickie," Miss Snyder said. "Nobody should be insulted by that. Which brush would you like to use?"

Problem solved, Jacaranda repaired to her sitting room, intent on regaining her own balance, with herself, by herself. Alas, Mr. Reilly, the land steward, patrolled the door to her parlor, a relieved smile blooming on his face when he spotted her.

"Our dear Mrs. Wyeth! There you are, and how are you on this fine day?"

Subtlety was not Reilly's forte, but he was good-hearted, if timorous. The middle of the month would soon be upon them, the master was in residence, and Reilly wasn't about to forgo his monthly cup of tea.

"I am fine, sir, and you?"

"Ready to spend an hour with a gentle lady," he said, bowing slightly. "I don't suppose you have a pot of tea on hand?"

"We'll ring for a tray." Like Mr. Simmons and half the footmen, Mr. Reilly indulged a sweet tooth at every opportunity. "How is Mrs. Reilly?"

He prattled on about his wife's sister's cousin's something or other, then wandered around to discussing his various children, at least one of whom was the brightest scholar ever to go up to university, then tiptoed up to the topic of the day with all the stealth of William, the amazing draft sow.

"I suppose I'll be handing my report to his lordship this month rather than entrusting it to the king's post. Quite a change, quite a change. But a good change, a happy change, one might say."

"*Tempus fugit*, Mr. Reilly." Jacaranda was spared further polite blather by the arrival of the tea tray. She served her guest his usual: no milk, three sugars, and six tea cakes. When Mr. Reilly was enthusiastically ruining his dinner, she started the list for him.

"The Hendersons' cottage roof is starting to leak in the front room, and the Porters' oldest son is making noises about going into London to look for work."

"Is he now? The boy will need a character, and he's a hard worker."

"His mother is most anxious to think of him in London, when he's never set foot from the shire before, but he's a good man with a horse, and there are horses everywhere."

"That he is." Reilly held his cup out for another serving, for demolishing tea cakes at such a great rate was thirsty work. "Any other little details you'd like me to include?"

She went on, recounting progress made by the tenants on various projects and needs foreseeable in the upcoming month. Early summer was a lovely time of year, when the crops were ripening, the weather mild, and a thousand pesky repairs and put-off projects could be tended to if one were diligent and organized.

Reilly's pencil and paper were out before she'd finished her list, as they usually were. He always thanked her for noting *a few trivialities* he'd missed and made noises about a woman's eye being sharper about certain things. Then he showed up a month later, smiling, inhaling cakes and biscuits, and reducing ten flooded acres of barley to a triviality.

Jacaranda didn't mind, really. An estate prospered when the senior staff were congenial and cooperative, and she was out and about with the tenants more than Reilly was. Her successor would be apprised of how things went on, and Trysting would continue to prosper.

Yolanda tapped on the door not two sips after Reilly had left.

"Come in, Yolanda." Jacaranda peered into her teapot. "I can offer you a cup, if you're of a mind."

"No tea, thank you." She advanced into the room, looking about with obvious curiosity. "Your sitting room is lovely."

"My retreat, at least it feels that way." Or *had* felt that way. "What can I do for you?"

"I wanted to ask if I could move to a different room."

"Of course, but is the bed not to your liking?"

"The bed is quite acceptable, but I'm five doors down from Avery, and I noticed the room across the hall from hers isn't occupied." She wandered around the parlor, inspecting much, touching nothing. She did lean in to sniff the white roses in a crystal vase by the window.

Her brother sniffed bouquets in the same manner.

"I can have you moved before tonight." Jacaranda rose, giving up on her tea. "If your current room is lacking in some regard, I'd rather know about it."

"Avery has nightmares," Yolanda said. "Mrs. Hartwick sleeps down the hall and has poor hearing, or she's unwilling to answer when Avery taps on her door at night. If Avery knows I'm right across the hall, she might rest easier."

"She's had a trying start in life, what with losing her parents. What shall I tell your brother regarding this change of venue for you?" Jacaranda gave her roses a drink from the pitcher on the mantel, and wondered if Yolanda might enjoy wearing a touch of rose-water scent. Young ladies could be shy about such things.

She certainly had been.

Yolanda paused before a piece of framed cutwork near the door. "Do you have to tell Worth anything?"

"He strikes me as the sort of fellow who will notice." He'd notice if his sister adopted a fragrance, too, more evidence that he leaned in the direction of being a good brother. "He doesn't hole up in the estate office, or spend the day riding out with his steward and his hounds. He's restless, I think, and unpredictable."

Yolanda paced off to study a miniature of Jacaranda's mother, a cheerful, competent woman who'd stood nearly six feet tall.

"My brother Hess said Worth has always been prodigal, a vagabond. How can he say that when Worth left home at age seventeen and has been well established in London since finishing at university?"

"Siblings sometimes see each other more clearly than anybody else." Though sometimes siblings were blind. "When will you be available for a tour of the house?"

Yolanda went back to studying the cutwork, a project Jacaranda had taken on when Daisy had become engaged, and snipping something nearly to bits had appealed strongly.

"Me? Why would I tour the house?"

"You are the closest thing your brother has to a hostess here. Some girls your age are married and presiding over their own homes, children on the way. I'd be remiss in my duties if I didn't at some point show you about the place."

"Avery will want to come."

The words held such a mix of resignation and resentment, Jacaranda smiled. How many times had she felt the same way about Daisy? Dear, little, innocent, bothersome, pesky, adorable Daisy.

"Avery will play with the Hendersons' boys some fine morning later this week, and she will adore their riding pig."

"A riding pig?"

"For small children, the beast is quite impressive, and we can use that time for more mature pursuits." Though Mr. Kettering had made a lovely fuss over William, too—perhaps because the pig was female?

"Good heavens, a riding pig. Well, yes, a tour of the house sounds preferable, if more sedate. Shall we say the next sunny morning?"

"We shall, and Mrs. Hartwick and Miss Snyder will be grateful for a break, I'm sure."

"They will." Yolanda's smile was dazzling, a more innocent version of her older brother's. "I wanted to ask you something."

Jacaranda made a mental note to regard any smiling Kettering with caution. "Please do ask."

"We're to take supper *en famille*, with Wickie, Miss Snyder, Worth, Avery and myself all together. Will you join us?"

Jacaranda hadn't seen this coming and could barely stand the expectation in Yolanda's blue eyes. "Join you?"

"Avery is comfortable with her precious Uncle Worth, but I hardly want to spend the entire meal hearing about French mice or German mice, for that matter. Wickie and Miss Snyder are both in awe of Worth because he's quite... well, he's different from their usual fare. They didn't exactly put me up to asking, but they noted you seem to deal with him comfortably."

A little too comfortably, at least in the midst of rainstorms. "What about you, Yolanda? Does the prospect of dinner conversation with your brother loom uncomfortably for you?"

"I've known him less than ten days," Yolanda said, sounding both annoyed and perplexed. "And yet we have the same laugh, the same sibling, the same niece. He got me out of that awful school the first time he was asked, which is more than I can say for our benighted brother the earl. I don't know Worth well, but I have an opportunity to change that now, so yes, dinners with him will be important to me."

She had her brother's careful diction, his rational mind, and his ability to mask true emotion behind an articulate façade. On a young girl, those abilities struck Jacaranda as a little sad.

"I'll join you, provided your brother doesn't object to eating with the help," Jacaranda said. "For the first week, anyway, and then we'll see how it goes."

"Oh, thank you!" She fired off another one of those dazzling smiles, threw her arms around Jacaranda's neck in an exuberant squeeze, then whirled and disappeared, all in the same instant.

While Jacaranda wondered firstly what she'd got herself into, and secondly, how Worth Kettering was brother to an earl and not one of his staff or his tenants seemed to know it.

* * *

Grey was a dutiful boy in some regards, also stubborn. Francine resolved to be more stubborn still.

"You must put a stop to Jacaranda's latest nonsense," she said. She'd chosen her moment well, catching him in the propagation house, where few of the servants and none of the siblings would venture without his permission.

"Good day, your ladyship." He didn't so much as glance up from the plant on the table before him, didn't offer her a bow or a smile. "If you'd give me a moment."

She'd given him years, and had he so much as bothered to set a handsome foot in the London ballrooms? No, he had not. He remained bent over his plant, some sort of knife in his hand and a smock—a servant's smock—tied about his person.

"The matter is urgent, sir, or I would not endure the heat and stench you seem to think your precious roses need."

How much coin was spent keeping this glass house heated in winter? Paying for gardeners they could ill afford?

He sliced at one branch, affixed it to the stem of the plant standing in a pot on the wooden table, and held the two together.

"If you could pass me that length of twine?"

She snatched up a piece of string about a foot long and flung it at him.

"The fate of this family's good name hangs in the balance, and you're playing in the dirt. What would your father say?"

He finished tying the two plants together with a small, symmetric bow. "He'd say, 'Good luck with the grafting, because the crosses aren't amounting to anything.'"

"Your sister is courting ruin. What will your roses matter when none of you can find wives because of Jacaranda's foolishness?"

His gaze lingered on the rose bush, and for a moment, Francine missed her late husband. He'd gazed at his roses in the same besotted fashion, and occasionally at her, too.

"Jacaranda is not foolish. Of all my siblings, she's the least foolish, and we're none of us looking for wives."

The very problem. Until one of the boys married, and married well, Francine was doomed to dwell in poverty, in a house of chaos, noise, and social obscurity—but no longer. Jacaranda would come home, the boys would be married off, the finances would prosper, and all would be well.

"You should be looking for wives. If you boys would do your duty, this family's fortunes would come right. You and Will have had plenty long enough to sow wild oats, or graft roses, or whatever it is young men do. If you won't marry, then you must at least snatch your sister from the jaws of scandal."

She drew herself up, intending to punctuate her scold with a sniff, but a sneeze caught her instead. Before she could extract a handkerchief from her bodice, Grey waved his at her.

"I notice you do not commend your own sons into the arms of the waiting heiresses."

His handkerchief smelled of the humid, dirty environs of the propagation house, which meant it bore the same scent Francine's late husband had often sported. She folded the handkerchief rather than return it to its owner.

"Do you know for whom your sister keeps house?"

"I know *where* she keeps house—a great rambling country house in Surrey, one the owner has benignly neglected for years. He's a single fellow, reported to have some coin, and Jacaranda has consistently maintained that she enjoys her duties."

Jacaranda's ability to run a regiment with a feather duster in one hand and a list in the other was exactly why she must be brought home.

"He's a single fellow, all right, and not much older than you. A bachelor supposedly raising a little niece who's half-French."

Grey took up a broom sized for the hearth and began sweeping the dirt on the table into a small pile in the center.

"This is not news, Step-Mama. I made some inquiries years ago. I myself have a niece. I wasn't aware this condemned a man to a housekeeper-less existence."

"The child must be his by-blow, and now it's said he's collected an illegitimate half-sister from boarding school."

He swept the dirt off the side of the table, into a dustbin from which dead rose branches protruded. "Many a duke has provided for his by-blows. I'd think less of the man if he sent this sister into service when he has the means to provide for her."

Grey had read law, and it had addled his brain. Either that, or he was wallowing in guilt for having permitted Jacaranda's queer start five years ago.

"Jacaranda's employer is no duke, and her place is here, with her family."

"It is," Grey said, setting the rubbish aside. "I write to her every month and remind her of that, but when I cannot afford to dower her, when she has no interest in marriage, and when her own sister is raising up babies on our very doorstep, Dorset might not be the happiest place for Jacaranda. She has promised to come home, you know."

She'd always promised to come home, then left her own dear step-mama to contend with more unruly young men than any one lady's nerves could tolerate.

"Her employer has removed to Surrey with his unsavory relations, sir. Do you think Jacaranda's reputation will not suffer?" The innuendo in Herodia Bellamy's letter had been unmistakable. "Jacaranda will be lucky to return with her virtue intact."

Grey untied his smock and hung it on a nail. Next he'd stride off on some errand known only to him.

"If Jack's employer attempts so much as an untoward smile in her direction, she'll geld him. Jack deals well with men and their households."

He at least sounded wistful. Francine took heart from that.

"She should be with family, and I've let you indulge her wayward notions long enough. You have until the end of summer to make her see reason, sir, or I'll take matters into my own hands."

He looked at his hands, which were large, elegant, and dirt-stained. "I'd advise you against anything foolish, Step-Mama. We muddle on well enough here without Jack, and she's entitled to some happiness."

*Francine* was entitled to some happiness. She was entitled to spend her summers in Bath, where Captain Mortimer spent his, where Baron Hathaway spent his, and half of Francine's correspondents spent theirs.

She was entitled to a single week free of menus and feuding parlor maids and accountings—of which Jacaranda had been prodigiously fond. She was entitled to the occasional new gown, a riding mare of her own, a small equipage. So many things she was entitled to, but they all hinged on Jacaranda bringing order to the household so Francine could get her sons married off and her finances in order.

Running the empire had to be a simpler undertaking than managing a lot of overgrown boys and their muddy boots.

"I am never foolish," Francine said, though she was growing desperate. Captain Mortimer spent altogether too much time with Penelope Shorewood, and Baron Hathaway had threatened to leave early for the grouse moors.

"You are never content," Grey said, wiping his hands with a dingy towel. "Your sons love you, you have Daisy near at hand, her babies to dote on, and still, you can't leave Jacaranda in peace. Haven't you done enough to jeopardize her prospects?"

Stubborn—as stubborn as his father, his brothers, and his sisters.

"A girl with her limitations never had much in the way of prospects, but what little remains to her will vanish if her employer brings his London cronies to the country with him. You know what house parties can be like for the help."

His lifted his jacket from the nail beside the one on which he'd hung his smock. "No, I do not know what house parties can be like for the help. My step-mother cannot bestir herself to organize a house party, though we have plenty of room, and such an event would be a simple way to introduce my brothers to any number of eager young beauties without incurring London expenses."

Good God, he was serious. He expected her, *Francine*, to spend hours planning banquets and archery tournaments and picnics and gracious—

"My nerves are troubling me," she said, heading for the door before Grey could abandon her to his weeds and mud. "I ask you to take a proper interest in your sister's welfare, and you fail to act, as usual. What would your father say?"

That parting shot was low, but Francine had seen too many barons and captains and even squires resume marital bliss with her friends and correspondents. If Grey would not take action to bring Jacaranda home, then Francine would.

# CHAPTER FIVE

Jacaranda had known dinner would be informal, because Avery was joining the adults, but Mr. Kettering hadn't ventured an opinion regarding the most suitable dinner hour.

So she'd set the time herself.

He ventured opinions on other topics all throughout the meal. First, the issue was whether Yolanda should have a mount despite her refusal to ride out with her niece. Mr. Kettering allowed as how he couldn't purchase only Avery a mount, or the girl would think she was being favored. Then the discussion turned to whether one should be allowed to eat dessert if one hadn't eaten one's vegetables.

While Wickie and Miss Snyder stoutly declared sweets should be saved as incentive to finish more nourishing food, Mr. Kettering, abetted by the young ladies, decided sweets should always be served to create a pleasant association with coming to the table generally, and children well fed enough to be eating sweets were hardly in danger of starving.

Jacaranda sipped her wine—a rare treat—and listened to the conversation without saying much. The food was good and the company congenial, but her day had been long. When the fruit and cheese were removed, she realized the entire table was waiting for her to signal the end of the meal, almost as if she were—

Well.

She rose, her chair drawn back by Mr. Kettering. He thanked Wickie and Miss Snyder for the company, kissed Yolanda and Avery on the forehead, and wished them all pleasant dreams. Jacaranda had slipped in behind the children to make her escape when a large, male hand landed on her arm.

"A word with you, Wyeth, though I don't suppose I should be calling you plain Wyeth now that we're dinner companions."

"I am plain Wyeth," she said, frowning pointedly at his hand. "What did you wish to discuss?"

"I wished to *invite* you for a stroll in the garden," he replied, leaving his hand exactly where it was. "The last of the light remains, and I'd like to air a certain topic where nobody can overhear us."

That sounded sufficiently ominous that Jacaranda let him usher her from the room.

"You won't need a shawl?"

"Our stroll will be brief." Then too, her escort had a penchant for lending her his jacket.

His lips quirked up, though he said nothing, and then Jacaranda was on the back terrace, her hand wrapped around his forearm.

"You will give my compliments to the kitchen," he said as they perambulated across the flagstones. "Dinner was excellent and the menu such that both Avery and I found much to enjoy. Please tell Simmons the wines were well chosen, too."

"I will pass your praises along." Of course, *she'd* chosen the menu and the wines. Still, his appreciation lit a small flame of pleasure in the place inside her that sought notice, a pat on the back every once in a blue moon.

"Let's move away from the house. I do not want an audience."

"This sounds serious."

"Not serious, but sensitive. Or maybe I'm sensitive."

Many people assumed—wrongly—that size and sturdy physique precluded sensitivity. She'd been at risk of making the same error where Mr. Kettering was concerned.

How lowering.

He walked along beside Jacaranda in the fading light, and to her, he looked as tired as she felt. When they'd returned from their outing to the Hendersons, he'd disappeared into the library with a morocco leather satchel and not come out until they'd sat down to dinner.

A groom had been dispatched to Town with a pile of documents, with the expectation that the full moon would allow the entire journey before the man saw his bed.

"Shall we sit?" Mr. Kettering gestured to a folly several yards off the garden path. Jacaranda knew it well, because the folly was one place she could escape to on those rare, lazy afternoons when she had a few hours to read, or nap, or write a letter or two. Afternoons when the owner of the house and his family were properly ensconced in London.

Where they belonged.

"Cushions in my gazebo? What a decadent fellow I am."

She sat, and he took the place immediately beside her.

"I'm trying to guess how you'd broach this topic, Wyeth, and I think you'd plunge in, no shilly-shallying, no dithering. I have an older brother."

"A blessing, usually, to have a sibling."

"Usually," he said, resting his arm along the bench behind them. "This brother is a fellow of some consequence, or so he thinks. We are not, as the saying goes, close."

"I am sorry to hear it."

"He and I are sorry as well, or so I think in my more charitable moments. I stormed away from the family seat as a hotheaded young idiot, and we haven't had much to say to each other since."

"These things happen in the best of families." Had nearly happened in her own.

"We need to get over it. I lost one sister to the idiot French and their inability to police their own streets. Hess lost the same sister, and yet…"

"Yet?"

"He and I lost each other long before Moira died. We can't do anything about her death, but we have Avery and we have each other. He didn't even tell me about Yolanda. I learned of her from the school, when they couldn't reach Hess and needed to expel her somewhere safe."

This was news. "She was sent down?"

"Don't suppose I mentioned that, did I? I don't have all the details, but I will be damned if I'll let another sister of mine fight battles she's too young and innocent to fight alone."

Not a one of Jacaranda's seven brothers had ever adopted that fierce, determined tone where she was concerned.

"Yolanda was fighting battles at school?"

He made a gesture Jacaranda recognized as a sign that he was fatigued, rubbing his hand over his face, top to bottom.

"Have you noticed she always wears long sleeves?"

"I had not. In a girl her age, that would be unusual this time of year." Also uncomfortable, given the heat.

"Look at her left wrist. The old besom from whom I collected her intimated that Yolanda tried to take her own life. I cannot believe this, but neither have I found a way to talk to my own sister about such a demented notion."

"You don't expect me to have that talk, do you?" She was surprised her voice was steady, for these revelations were shocking—and sad.

"If I thought you could, I'd try to foist it off on you, because I hardly have the knack of being brother to an adolescent female, but no. When Yolanda and I know each other better, I hope she'll trust me with her confidences."

He wanted his sister's trust. If Jacaranda hadn't respected him previously, she'd respect him for that alone.

"You're wise not to force the matter," Jacaranda said, though complimenting him felt awkward. "She strikes me as having a full allotment of Kettering stubbornness."

He sat back, his arm still resting along the bench behind her. "Which raises the earlier topic. My brother will pay us a visit sometime in the next few weeks, and at my invitation."

"We've plenty of room, and the house is in good trim. I wish you'd let me know the dates of his visit, though. Certain of the staff have been given holidays to see family and the like."

"Isn't that Simmons's business?"

"We cooperate, with the maids and footmen, the laundresses and grooms, so we're never too short-staffed in any one regard."

"Hessian is only one person," Mr. Kettering said. "He shouldn't be too inconvenient, though he'll doubtless travel by private coach, so that means grooms, a valet, a secretary, a coachman, and an outrider or two. He'll likely bring a second coach, so the help won't violate his privacy en route."

"So I should expect his lordship and eight to twelve other mouths to feed?"

"Everlasting powers." He rose, taking his warmth from her side. "He'll expect the state chambers, because the man bears a title."

"Was that the hard part?"

He stood on the other side of the gazebo, facing out across gardens all but shrouded in darkness. "I beg your pardon, Wyeth?"

"Admitting your brother has a title. Was that difficult?"

"Must you?"

"We are having this discussion where there's no possibility of being overheard," she said. "By your design. You and this brother do not speak, and yet you want me to ensure his visit is in every way comfortable."

"Of course I do." He turned to face her, but the moon wasn't up yet, and the sun had fled. In the gathering shadows, Jacaranda couldn't see anything of his expression.

"You aren't commanding his comfort simply as conscientious host, though."

"Wyeth, you are a managing damned female if ever there was one. Hess and I are distant for very good reasons. In hindsight, he did me a favor, and himself a disservice, but it lies between us, a great gaping awkwardness that arose before I'd even reached my majority."

"Will his countess accompany him?"

He abruptly gave her his back and resumed studying the garden. "She's dead, has been for five years."

Nothing in his voice gave away any emotion, but something about the lack of emotion spoke volumes.

"You were in love with her."

"You are beyond overstepping."

"I am observing a truth." One that raised as many questions as it answered, none of them happy.

"I was seventeen years old and callow as only a young man can be, though the young lady and I had an understanding. My brother dangled his title before her, and she fell out of love with me post-haste, so I obligingly did the same regarding her. That is as much explanation as you will have from me, and we will not discuss this again."

His voice had taken on a chilly, flat quality, and Jacaranda wished she'd brought a shawl after all. What sort of young lady could have fallen out of love with Worth Kettering, even in his most callow incarnation?

"Here." His coat, redolent with his scent and his warmth, dropped over her shoulders. He snugged it around her, then resumed his place beside her. "Youthful follies have a particularly potent ability to make one feel like a flaming idiot even years later."

Idiot folly was not entirely the province of youth, though Jacaranda had indulged in her share. She ought not to enjoy the warmth and luxury of his coat, or its scent, but she was making a bad habit of it.

"You are extending an olive branch to your brother now." Or was the overture more in the direction of Mr. Kettering's youthful self?

"I don't know about an olive branch." He ranged an arm along the top of the padded bench again. Jacaranda had been hoping he'd do that. "Yolanda will have to be launched in some fashion, even though she's a by-blow. She'll need to snare a fellow, need a settlement, and her brothers must put aside their petty squabbles for her sake."

"Right."

"Wyeth... Jacaranda..."

"Hush." She kept her eyes on the part of the far horizon glowing faintly with the promise of moonrise. "I have many siblings. Do you think I am in great charity with all of them?"

"Yes. You wouldn't countenance anything less, particularly from the males."

"I was seventeen once, too." Twenty even. Twenty, plain, too tall and more lonely than she'd even known. "My oldest brother is not at all happy that I choose to remain in service. None of my brothers are. My step-mother is nearly hysterical in her demands that I return home." Though Jacaranda's continued absence didn't seem to bother Daisy.

"And you have a deal of brothers. You must have been very foolish, to need to defy them all so badly."

Perceptive man. "I was *almost* foolish, which amounts to the same thing."

"This involved a toothsome swain, I take it?"

She remained silent, and in that silence, she forged an understanding with her employer, something in the nature of a truce, but with a dash more compassion to it.

"Men are the very devil." His arm came around her shoulders in a friendly squeeze, but then it stayed there and became half an embrace.

Jacaranda should stand up, remark the lateness of the hour, or suggest it was time to get back to the house. She knew she should, but the moon was rising, and she'd never in her more than twenty-five years watched a moonrise with a man's arm around her shoulders.

Mr. Kettering seemed lonely, too. A bit lost, even.

The first sliver of incandescent moon lipped up over the horizon, and Jacaranda marshaled her resolve to leave.

"Don't." Mr. Kettering slipped his hand into hers. "Not yet."

She subsided, letting herself have more of his warmth, not at all sure what was transpiring between them save a shared moonrise. She let her head fall to his shoulder and felt his hand stroking over her hair, once, twice.

She closed her eyes, the better to savor the sensations, the soft night air with a hint of cool, the silvery moonshine spilling over the gardens, the warmth and scent of the man beside her, and the simple pleasure of sharing a few moments with someone who'd also once been young and foolish.

When the moon was well up, Mr. Kettering drew her to her feet, but kept that arm across her shoulders as they wandered to the house. When they reached the back terrace, he stopped, kissed her forehead, and opened the door for her, then bowed, turned, and walked back the way they'd come, until Jacaranda could no longer see him for the shifting moon shadows.

* * *

Mr. Kettering wasn't at breakfast the next morning, much to Jacaranda's relief.

He'd been companionable, that was all. No man in his right mind would make overtures by moonlight to an oversized spinster housekeeper.

She didn't have to inquire regarding his whereabouts, because he'd left a note by her place at the table.

*Mrs. Wyeth,*

*I've taken my pony for a gallop and will inspect the home farm with Mr. Reilly this morning. You may impress me into exactly one tenant call after luncheon. If you would please draft notes for one neighbor call per weekday thereafter, I would appreciate it. We can discuss the children's schedule when next I see you.*

*Yours respectfully,*

*Kettering*

Respectfully.

She pondered that single word while she inventoried the linens set aside for the state chambers. Each of the earl's dozen or so servants would require lodging, and the valet and secretary would expect modest guest rooms with a footman between them at least. Then came the discussion with Cook, who was equal parts pleased and dismayed at the thought of so many more mouths to feed, particularly when one of those sported a *title*.

"They are no different from you or me, Cook," Jacaranda warned her. "They eat when they're hungry, they sleep when they're tired, or they should."

Though they tended to drink a fair bit, in Jacaranda's experience, and sometimes to impose on the chambermaids.

"If you say so, Mrs. W, but I don't suppose you'd be willing to look over the menus in advance?"

"I suppose I would, because we don't know when this relation of the Ketterings' is descending. You'll want to stock up now, and I will approve the expenses."

She made her regular inspection then, finding the new chambermaid had neglected to open the drapes in the downstairs parlor, and the downstairs footmen were taking rather too long to clean the glass lamps in the corridor sconces. She informed them exactly when the new girl would take her break—the young lady seemed canny enough—and tracked Simmons down to his favorite place to nap, the butler's pantry.

He went into transports to think the master of the household was having company, and *titled* company, and when Jacaranda left him, he was for the first time in her memory counting the silver she'd counted once a month for five years.

Her stomach was rumbling as she climbed to the third floor to check on Yolanda's new room. She found Avery with her aunt, both girls holding hands in the middle of the room.

"You start slowly, so you can learn to move the same time I do," Avery was saying. "Now, with me. Step, behind, step, *kick*. Again, step, behind, step, *kick*."

Yolanda dropped her niece's hand. "Hello, Mrs. Wyeth. Avery is teaching me a dance."

"Not one you'll need in any ballroom, I take it?"

Avery grinned and executed a lovely pirouette in arabesque. "Not for the ballrooms. Uncle's opera dancers teach me their dances while we wait for him in the kitchen."

"His—!" Jacaranda shut her mouth with a snap. "Yolanda, is your room more to your liking?"

"Very much." Yolanda smiled back at her, as if Uncle entertaining opera dancers—*plural*—wasn't a scandalous situation for a small child to know of—for any child to know of. "I can see the drive and the stables and side terrace. Trysting is really a lovely house. I'm surprised Worth doesn't spend more time here."

Jacaranda's surprise was easily contained. The wilds of Surrey suffered a paucity of opera dancers, after all.

Opera dancers. Plural. In the kitchen. Teaching Avery scandalous dances. *Angels abide.*

"Luncheon should be ready, so you'll want to freshen up." Jacaranda left them, step, behind, step, *kicking* amid a flurry of giggles, and knew the need to strangle her employer.

Men had urges over which they exercised not one bit more control than they had to. Jacaranda knew this.

"No better than they should be, the sorry lot of them," she muttered as she careened around a corner and ran into the principal author of her distress.

"You!"

"Me?"

"Mr. Kettering, you will excuse me." She leveled her most righteous glare at him and tacked left to circumnavigate him, but he stepped back and cut her off with his sheer, bodily presence.

"No, Mrs. Wyeth, I will not excuse you when you're clearly in a temper." His fingers manacled her wrist, and just that touch, warm, strong, and altogether male, made her temper snap its leash.

"I detest no man more than he who takes advantage of female innocence. You destroy something that can never be replaced, never repaired. Innocence doesn't become merely wrinkled or tarnished, it's gone forever. You leave in its place betrayal and a sorry knowledge no lady should have to bear."

"*What* are you going on about?"

"Step, behind, step, *kick*." She wrenched her wrist from his and would have flounced off, except he snatched her wrist again and pulled her into an empty bedroom, kicking the door closed behind them.

"Explain yourself, Wyeth. You aren't a woman who flies into a taking easily, so I'm doing you the courtesy of hearing you out."

He stood between her and the door, fists on his hips, and in the ensuing silence, Jacaranda realized anew that her employer was one of few people on the face of the earth who might have no trouble physically subduing her.

He was large enough, strong enough, and sufficiently unconstrained by manners when it suited him.

"Your light-skirts are teaching Avery indecent dances in your kitchen."

He locked the door, then stalked over to peer down at her. "Is it the location of the dancing, the nature of it, or the nature of the instructors you object to?"

"She's a little girl! Her mother would have wanted you to protect her from such influences, not parade them and their unfortunate morals before the child."

"You think so?"

"I know so," Jacaranda shot back. "Those women cannot help their circumstances, I know that, too, but if you intend to prey on them, can't you at least do it where Avery has no knowledge of it? Gentlemen are expected to exercise discretion even when they can't exercise control."

"You have a very bad opinion of men, don't you?" His tone was curious, and he was standing entirely too close. "For example, if I kissed you right now, you'd wallop me at the least and probably ban me from my own house. I adore a ferocious woman."

"You seek to turn the subject, and crudely. Avery should not be exposed to your debaucheries." *If I kissed you?* Despite Jacaranda's considerable anger at the man before her, her gaze dropped to his mouth. Damn him to Hades, it was a beautiful mouth, even when it wasn't turned up in that faint smile.

"Come sit with me, and I will explain to you what transpires in my London household. As a courtesy, mind you, because you're concerned for the child, not because you're entitled to explanations. One must always be mindful of setting unfortunate precedents."

When she didn't move, he took her hand and led her to a window bench. The cushion could accommodate them both—barely.

"Avery likes the opera dancers, you see." He kept her hand in his and drew his fingers over her palm. He had an ink stain on his right cuff—ink was the very devil to get out—and his touch was mesmerizing, soothing and arousing at once.

*Arousing?*

"Avery likes the dancers, or you do?"

"We both do. Moira went to Paris to study art during the Peace of Amiens, and then remained, against my judgment and Hess's. Nobody wanted her there, but I suspect she was enamored of Avery's father and unwilling to come home. Then she was *unable* to come home, and I didn't become aware of Avery's existence until the False Peace."

"I know the French are not as judgmental regarding their diversions, but the child is in England."

"She is." He laced his fingers with hers, and Jacaranda bore it, because her employer was a man who liked to touch. He touched his niece and his sister, he patted Wickie on the shoulder, and he put his arm around his housekeeper in the moonlight.

He also entertained opera dancers in his very home. She tried to withdraw her hand.

"You will hear me out, Wyeth, because I will not repeat this tale. Moira's artistic aspirations came to naught, and when Avery's father died, Moira eventually supported herself at the *opera comique*, if what Avery tells me is accurate. The dancers remind Avery of happy times with her mother. I gather the child became some sort of backstage mascot. I have an opera dancer to thank for the fact Avery arrived safely to these shores."

"You justify your choice of paramour on this basis? Your lapse of discretion?"

"Do you imagine opera dancers don't age, Mrs. Wyeth? Do you imagine they don't fall sick or suffer injury? You can turn your ankle and put it up with ice and arnica for a fortnight if you need to, but if they twist their ankles, they don't eat."

"For God's sake, you don't expect me to believe you paw these women out of charitable impulses?"

"I do not paw women, not any women, ever. If you must know, I handle investments for my opera dancers, you fire-breathing little besom."

And then he kissed her.

He settled his lips on hers, gently, so gently, while his hand came up to caress her jaw, then her hair, then to rest softly on her throat, so his thumb could brush over her cheek. His touch was sunbeam-light, warm as a breeze, and left wicked, wicked pleasure drizzling over her skin and into her mind. His mouth treasured hers, parting so his tongue could tease and taste and coax at her lips. When he eased away, Jacaranda's own mouth was parted, and her wits—and her indignation—had deserted her utterly.

"The opera dancers won't come to my office in Mayfair," he said, dropping his hand. "We meet in my kitchen, instead, where I can insist they eat some decent food, and my footmen can see them safely home. I do not *paw* them, though they're a great deal more honest about their willingness to be pawed— and do some pawing of their own—than their so-called betters. I'll see you after luncheon."

He rose and left. Jacaranda stared after him, unseeing, her hand cradling her jaw while she stifled an unaccountable urge to cry.

\* \* \*

Wyeth's kiss was a puzzle, and Worth spent most of his solitary luncheon in the library trying to decipher it when he should have been reading quarterly earnings statements.

She wasn't a virgin with regard to kissing; he'd bet his honor on that. She'd been startled to find herself lip to lip with him, but then she'd been curious, and then she'd been interested, and then she'd been...*interesting*.

One kiss was obviously not enough. He must needs kiss her again, to see if that cool, cautious curiosity could be made to burn out of control. He would parse the taste of her down to something describable, not merely "lovely" or "delicious" or "womanly."

Then there was the sound of kissing her. That soft indrawn breath of surprise, the sigh of acceptance, the hungry little moans in the back of her throat, the rustle and slide of her gown against his breeches, the almost-groan when she opened her mouth for him.

This great feast of the senses that was kissing her, he'd have it again. *They* would have it again, because if ever there was a woman from whom "no" meant "Absolutely Not Ever," it was Jacaranda Wyeth, and not even her mouth had said no.

Her kiss—her very body—had said yes.

How long would it take for her mind to realize that?

* * *

The week went flying by for Jacaranda. She was dragooned into the tenant calls after lunch, and worse, into calls on neighbors. Mr. Kettering was as stealthy about his tactics as a drunken draft sow.

"Doesn't the Damus holding lie between the Tarmans' farm and Trysting?"

"Why don't we nip in and say hello to the…Stevens? No, Steppins?"

"That's Squire Brent's place, isn't it? I think Goliath could use a drink."

And there she'd be, smiling and curtsying to the Damuses, the Steppins, and the Brents—and their myriad daughters.

"You are a fraud, Mr. Worth Kettering." They were returning from a call on the Wilders, who were tenants of longstanding, and the Kerstings, local gentry whom Jacaranda knew mostly from market and churchyard pleasantries, though she could hardly keep straight the names of their four daughters—the twins were not identical, thank God.

"Fraud is a serious offense." He steered Goliath around a turn in the lane. "In what regard do I stand accused?"

"You are afraid of young ladies."

"Flat terrified. Will you take the reins for a moment?"

He handed her the ribbons before she could protest, and then she had to sidle closer to the middle of the seat in fairness to the horse.

"They can't truss you up and drag you to the altar," Jacaranda said. "This horse has a lovely mouth."

"So do you."

"I beg your pardon?"

"Your mouth is lovely, when you aren't pinching up your lips to scold a defenseless single man for his perfectly understandable fears. The young girls can't tie me up, but they can waylay me in the rose arbor, or stumble against my person in the garden, feel faint as we're dancing at the local assembly. They know how to set tongues wagging, and many a man has been ruined for less."

"You account yourself irresistible." She didn't bother keeping incredulity from her tone.

"I account a net worth of several hundred thousand and climbing irresistible."

"Boasting of such a thing is vulgar." They tooled along in silence for about a quarter mile. "Vulgar, but impressive."

In truth, he'd been complaining more than boasting. Another quarter mile went by, and Jacaranda began to relax, because Goliath was as steady as he was magnificent.

"Is that why the opera dancers trust you? You've made yourself wealthy, so they conclude you can help them?"

"I don't know why, but it's like that story of the widow's mite. Those ladies trust me with what little they have, and I will be God-damned if I'll let it come to harm. The lordlings trying to stretch their quarterly allowance so they can gamble deeper and wench away every night don't seem nearly as worthy of my attention."

"Robin Hood, then, with a dash of arrogance thrown in."

"Where have you put your mite, Wyeth?"

He might have been sliding a hand up her thigh, so silky and intimate was his tone. The topic of her hard-earned coin was in some ways more personal than, well, kissing.

Some ways.

He wasn't teasing, not about her money. So while he pretended to study the barley fields ripening around them, Jacaranda told him which investment projects had some of her coin, which funds a little more, which ones she'd discarded as poorly managed or too speculative.

"Prudent choices, though if you diversified more, you might see a faster gain with only a slight increase in risk." He went on to suggest a modest revision to her investment strategy, and before Jacaranda knew it, they were approaching the covered bridge.

"Pull him up," Mr. Kettering said. "He's been tooling around like a good lad. He'll appreciate a chance to blow in the shade."

"You're not about to kiss me again, are you?"

Because it would be like him to lull her into lowering her guard with talk of funds and interest and projects, then ambush her with another one of those lovely, devastating kisses.

"*Kiss* you? Why, Mrs. Wyeth, for shame, and me such a virtuous lad and quite timorous where the ladies are concerned."

He popped out of the gig and came around to hand her down, except when Jacaranda gained her feet, he cupped her elbows and stood entirely too close.

"Would you like me to kiss you?" His eyes were grave, not a hint of humor in them, and his scent came wafting to her on a warm summer breeze. "Don't answer me with words, Wyeth."

He dipped his head, and then he was kissing her again, but this kiss was different. The first time he'd kissed her, he'd been making a point. She still wasn't sure what exactly his point had been, something about her judgmental nature and how much he missed his sister, probably.

This kiss was about mouths, and bodies, and the unholy pleasure of being caught up against his solid, muscular length on a soft summer day. His mouth moved over hers as deftly as an artist's brush, leaving hues of longing and unnamable sensations in its wake. He worked his kissing slowly, a seductive gentleness to every touch, even as he held her more firmly to him.

Jacaranda tucked up as close to Mr. Kettering as she could get, going up on her toes despite the warnings clamoring forth from her common sense. Those warnings weren't a matter of conscience, or morals—she was indulging in a mere kiss, and in more-or-less private—what was imperiled was her very survival.

Somehow, though, survival did not weigh in on the side of storming away in high dudgeon. Survival had nothing to do with indignation, but had everything to do with clinging to the man whose tongue was probing along her lips in delicate entreaty.

"You're too good at this," she said against his teeth.

"*We're* good at this, and we're barely getting started."

His one arm went around her shoulders, while the other settled low across her back, anchoring her more snugly and angling her so he could get a hand on her derriere and his mouth back where it belonged. He didn't clutch at her, though, he secured her so she could kiss him back without having to worry about remaining on her own two feet.

He tasted good. Like spearmint and heat, and he had the knack of asking permission with his mouth, of inviting with his tongue, and assuring with his big body. She could kiss him for a long, long—

"Mr. Kettering, *what* are you doing?"

He'd scooped her up and hefted her to sit on the bridge railing, bringing the sound of rushing water closer, which was somehow appropriate.

"I'm experimenting. Such an important matter wants a bit of science."

Then his mouth was back, but Jacaranda sat a shade higher than she'd stood, so she could wrap her arms around his magnificent shoulders and sink her hands into his dark, silky hair. Then he wedged himself between her knees, and oh, it felt imperative that she bring at least one leg around his hips and show him exactly—

He broke the kiss and captured one of her hands. "We're at risk for indiscreet behavior, my dear. This is a public thoroughfare."

She dropped her forehead to his shoulder while he took that hand of hers and stroked it over his falls.

*Angels abide!*

He was a generously proportioned man in a particular state of reproductive anticipation. His hand dropped away. Hers did not.

"Getting even, Wyeth?"

"Getting acquainted." She shaped him carefully, telling herself this was the only occasion she'd be permitted to indulge her curiosity. She was tempted to linger, but he drew in a sharp breath near her ear.

"Did I hurt you, Mr. Kettering?"

He shifted his middle back a few inches. "You torment, but I don't think you understand that. Did I hurt you?"

She lifted her head to frown at him, to fathom his meaning.

"You did not injure me, if that's what you're asking, though why such an inquiry is germane, I know not. This was a stolen kiss, and they are not, by reputation, painful."

"Please don't tell me this is your first stolen kiss."

"Kisses have been stolen from me," she said, considering him. "Not with me." She lifted away from him, but had to keep a hand on his shoulder for balance.

"I'm to be your first in at least this?"

"It's your height," she said, turning her head to watch the water below.

"Let's get you down, and you can explain that remark."

She hopped off the railing, but his hands were anchored on her hips, and all over again, she endured the strange puddling of heat in her middle that his kiss—their kiss—had caused.

"Naughty woman." He still wasn't smiling, but he seemed pleased.

She turned her back to him to study the freshet below. Was she naughty?

"Shall we negotiate now?" He made himself comfortable beside her, elbows on the railing. "Or would you prefer to settle your nerves first?"

"Negotiate?" She rather enjoyed the present state of her nerves.

"Surely it hasn't escaped your notice we're suited to a certain type of liaison, Wyeth. I'd compensate you handsomely, enough that you could put off your housekeeping and go about in Town." He watched the water, not her.

"Were it to our mutual liking," he went on, "we could even move you into Town, though there's no telling how long these things will last. I'm a decent protector, though it's been quite a while since I took on the role. I'd see you got out, to the theatre, Vauxhall, the shops. Life can't be work all the time, even for me. I suppose that's rather the point, on my end."

Inside, where Mr. Worth Kettering's piercingly blue eyes would not bother to see, Jacaranda's luncheon took to heaving disagreeably.

"No, thank you, Mr. Kettering. Shall we be on our way?"

"No, thank you, *Mr. Kettering*?" His brows knit, in consternation or indignation, she cared not which. "That was not a *Mr. Kettering* kiss, Wyeth."

"And I am not a whore. Goliath is sufficiently rested, and I must see to your dinner preparations."

"Not fair, Wyeth. I did not force you."

"No, you did not, nor will you, *ever*. I rely on that remaining artifact of gentlemanly sensibility when I ask you to take me home now."

"You're not interested in at least hearing the numbers?"

"For God's sake, I know you are a man, but I did not take you for a very stupid man. I am insulted, you dolt, not by your kiss, which was lovely, dear, sweet, and generous, but by the implication I would whore for another like it. I enjoyed it, I thank you for it, but I have no interest in your *jewels* or in being your fancy piece. Think of your opera dancers, Mr. Kettering."

She climbed into the gig and sat, hands folded in her lap, forbidding herself to say more. He must have grasped the fundamental point, for he climbed in beside her.

"Shall I drive?" she asked.

He nodded, tersely, and she tried to make charitable allowances, for he was a man and one likely used to getting his way.

Several hundred thousand times over.

And yet, he sat beside her right up to the Trysting front door, silent, unreadable, and looking like he cared not one whit for the fact that a mere housekeeper was driving him around the countryside, and refusing his offer of protection.

\* \* \*

He'd blundered badly—*and with a woman.*

Worth was comfortable making the occasional shaky investment, though less and less as his instincts and information-gathering skills had been perfected.

But with a woman...

He'd made two errors, in fact. At least two. The first was offering Jacaranda Wyeth a more or less permanent position as his mistress, when Worth had learned long ago that mistresses were a tricky lot. They became bored, and even jewels and outings weren't enough to placate them. Eventually, they resorted to provoking his jealousy, or worse, trying to get with child. No matter their skill in bed, their beauty, their wit or other charms, he parted from them at that point, with stern admonitions to himself to choose more wisely.

Wisely had come to mean temporarily. He sought the short-term, and very short-term, and very, very short-term liaison, and everybody was happier all around.

So he'd blundered and undertaken a negotiation of terms for an extended liaison.

The heat of the moment accounted for that lapse, aided by Wyeth's kisses, by her boldness, by her hand on his falls, *getting acquainted.*

Then the second, worse blunder. He'd offended the lady.

*What* had happened?

His housekeeper sailed into his house ahead of him, her skirts swishing. Her magnificent body had *happened.* Her lush, naughty mouth. Her common sense and quietly relentless compassion. Her sweet, summery scent, her phenomenal derriere, those perfect breasts, her heat, her hands…

Then that prim, hurt tone. *Think of your opera dancers, Mr. Kettering.*

He was on his horse and headed for London before the dinner bell sounded.

# CHAPTER SIX

Jacaranda was nothing if not ruthlessly honest with herself, and thus she admitted she missed her employer. He'd taken a proper leave of the children, conferred briefly with Simmons, and then decamped.

She'd driven him off, perhaps with her kisses, more likely with her speeches about his jewels—angels abide!—and his money. A fine, upstanding speech at the time, but it did nothing to help her sleep at night. She took a few nocturnal swims, doubled her vigilance regarding her housekeeping duties, and prompted Simmons to new heights of fussing and clucking over his footmen.

All for naught.

She missed Worth Kettering. Missed the scent and feel of him standing too close to her, sitting too close beside her in the gig, sending her his silent "time to go" look when the neighbors' daughters took to batting their eyes. She missed him presiding over the dinner table, teasing, entertaining, and gently chiding Avery for her manners. She missed the sound of his solid boot heels thumping along the corridors and missed his voice, bellowing for her when it was time to depart for their afternoon calls.

Missed kissing him and scolding him.

This missing was a bodily ache, different from the way she missed her siblings, or her home, or her departed parents.

All the while she inspected linens, made lists, drew up menus, and supervised the staff, she was aware of a sense of Worth Kettering's eyes on her—or somebody's eyes. The sense was strongest outside, when she took cuttings from the scent garden, or the color gardens, but it followed her into the house sometimes.

She wished her employer really had been that aged, diminutive cipher dithering away in the City. That would have been much easier.

Much.

But staying busy had long been her antidote for every ill, so she headed back up to the third floor. She'd yet to make her morning rounds there, and both girls were downcast at Mr. Kettering's departure. She opened Avery's door after a brisk knock, only to find Yolanda sprawled on a chaise with a book of Wordsworth's poetry.

"Avery's off to ride that pig, or fly a kite, or give the pig lessons in French," Yolanda said.

"I'm so bored I almost joined her."

"We haven't toured the house yet. Would that alleviate your boredom?"

"Touring the house would at least get me off my backside." Yolanda closed her book and rose. "Has the post come yet?"

"The post arrives by nine of the clock, if the stages are running on time," Jacaranda said as they left the room. "He didn't write today."

How odd to have this small grief in common with a schoolgirl.

"Again."

"You could write to him, or to your older brother."

"To tell them what?" Yolanda stopped at the top of the steps. "I haven't tried to kill myself lately?"

"Did you?" Jacaranda wanted to drag the girl a few steps back, but instead began their progress down the stairs. "Try to kill yourself?"

"No." That was all, no explanation, no emphasis.

"Well, then, not much to write about there. You might tell your brother what Avery is getting up to."

"Wickie will do that," Yolanda said, moving down the stairs at Jacaranda's side.

"She will do a version of it," Jacaranda countered. "A version that leaves out pigs and probably emphasizes penmanship. Then too, you might ask your brother to retrieve fripperies or notions from London."

This was really too bad of her. No man enjoyed trolling the ladies' shops.

Though Mr. Kettering should have written to his sister.

"Retrieve fripperies such as?"

"You embroider beautifully," Jacaranda said. "Have him pick up a particular shade of thread or a hard-to-find measure of hoop. Some sketching paper or special pencils."

"So he won't feel so badly for abandoning us here?"

"So you'll have something to do." So his sister would approve of him, even if his housekeeper could not.

Yolanda paused with her hand on the crouching-lion newel post at the foot of the steps. "He'll think I'm glad to see the thread, or the hoop, or the lurid novel, not him."

No, he would not. "He might pretend he's that thick-headed. You'll know better."

"I should make a list."

Such a Kettering, this one. "I frequently find a list useful. For example, while I don't trespass in the kitchen, per se, I do keep track of the larder and the cook's pantry."

Daisy had had no interest in learning to run a household, and Jacaranda had learned not to expect her younger sister to share those tasks with her. Step-Mama had been more preoccupied with managing her offspring and her torrents of correspondence than with household details.

"There's a great deal to know. The laundry and the medicinals alone take organization," Yolanda said as they finished up in the still room some time later.

"A systematic approach is usually best." Though how did one take a systematic approach to, say, Worth Kettering and his kisses and naughty propositions? "Labeling helps, unless the staff cannot read. If somebody comes to us without their letters, we teach them."

Yolanda left off counting the jars arranged in alphabetical order on the shelves around them. "You teach them?"

"Mrs. Reilly helps, as does Vicar, but yes. How a maid or footman takes to their schooling helps me assess how they'll fit in best at Trysting. Now, we should have a peek at the library. The footmen are possessive about it, but they'll be taking their tea break the better to flirt with the new chambermaid."

"Muriel," Yolanda said, opening a jar of vervain and sniffing. "She's friendly."

"Also pretty, which is both a blessing and a curse. Have you any questions?"

Yolanda took a pinch of vervain and crushed it between her fingers. "When is Hess coming?"

Of course the girl's loneliness would weigh more heavily than the niceties of separating spearmint and peppermint, or footmen and maids.

"Mr. Kettering did not specify a date, but all is in readiness."

"Worth will be back soon then." Yolanda said, dusting the herb from her fingers. "He won't leave us here to receive Hess without him. That would look rude."

"From what I understand—"

"They don't get along," Yolanda said, peering at the gray dusting the ends of her fingers. "Except they used to. At home, we have portraits of them together. They were peas in a pod, and in Worth's diaries—"

"You read your brother's diaries?" Jacaranda had considered herself the only sister in the history of sisters to exhibit such audacity—and courage.

"If Worth had been about at Grampion, in any sense, he might have stopped me from reading them, or respect for his privacy might have at least slowed me down."

Jacaranda led the way from the still room, which had taken on a confessional air. Or maybe the scent of vervain didn't agree with her—it was believed to repel witches.

"Suffice it to say I cannot approve of such an action, Yolanda, and I have seven brothers."

Yolanda sniffed at her fingers and made a face. "You never read their diaries? Never peeked?"

Jacaranda would not lie, exactly. "Only the oldest has a literary bent, and one doesn't trifle with him." Though sometimes one defied him outright.

They pattered on as the rest of the house was duly inspected, but it hadn't occurred to Jacaranda that Mr. Kettering would have to come home—back to Trysting, rather—to host his brother's visit, assuming he hadn't waved the man off or diverted him to Town.

The realization was mortifyingly cheering.

*  *  *

Less than two weeks at his country estate, and Worth had been spoiled for all other residences. Town was noisy, reeking and hot, and his house, which he'd always found adequately maintained, fell short of the standards at Trysting.

The windows were clean, they did not sparkle.

The carpets were beaten, they remained dull.

The food was nourishing, but its presentation unimaginative.

The house was tidy, but not…inviting.

The shops regularly sent over flowers, but the bouquets lacked fragrance and seemed to sit in their vases like sedate arrangements, not spontaneous offerings from nature.

Mimette raised her gaze from the quarterly statement Worth had drafted for her.

"You're in a hurry, ducks. You usually go over the numbers with me one by one, until I'm fair to run screaming down the street."

Mimette, or Mary, was a pretty little dancer between protectors at the moment. Her savings were thus of particular interest to her, and Worth had directed that a cold collation be prepared for their session at the kitchen table.

"I'm getting ready to travel again tomorrow," Worth said, making the decision as the words came out of his mouth. "Not being at my appointed post here in Town has created challenges."

Not being at Trysting created other *challenges*.

She gave him a genuine smile. "Challenges for you, maybe. Jones says he's never seen such peace at the office save for right after Waterloo."

"When did you hear Jones discoursing so disloyally?"

"He comes to see us dance and brings his friends, and they're a jolly bunch."

Another well-trained, competent employee would soon be domesticating. "When I'm not wreaking havoc with their fun, to hear Jones tell it. Your money is working almost as hard as you do."

"I'd take you upstairs tonight without a thought for the money, Worth Kettering, and it wouldn't be work neither—though something would be hard. You could do with a tupping." Her smile was tinged with something else now. Speculation, or maybe sympathy?

"I could." He nearly rose to take her up on her offer, because tupping had certainly been on his mind for the past week. His cock wasn't surging in its usual gleeful anticipation of a romp, though, so he kept to his chair.

Mary reached under the table and experimentally groped his flaccid length.

She took her hand away. "Whoever she is, I hope she appreciates you. Should I consider maybe taking more out of the three percents?"

"Only if you're willing to shift the degree of risk as well," Worth said, grateful for something to talk about besides tupping. Her hand had felt curiously impersonal, almost unwelcome.

He was about to send her home with a footman when he noticed the tray still held plenty of food. Nobody could eat more than an opera dancer when good, free food was on hand. Nobody. He held his interrogation until the moment of her departure.

"Mary, is your digestion troubling you?"

"Of course not." She swung her cloak over her arm, an unconsciously graceful gesture more captivating than any gratuitous fondling.

"Mary Flannery, you're dissembling with your man of business. This is not done. Lie to your priest or your protector, but not to me."

She sat back down at the table, eyeing the cold, sliced meat, buttered bread, and sliced cheese with something less than appreciation.

"Mary?"

Her hair was flaming red, her skin flawlessly pale, and her figure curvy and fit enough to haunt a man's most intimate dreams. She was one of seven, the oldest daughter. The boys would get the bulk of the family resources, buying apprenticeships in various trades. She sent money home for the girls, but her papa had a fondness for the bottle and for using his fists on his womenfolk.

"You'd best tell me who the father is." He sat beside her and slung an arm around her shoulders, wanting to howl with the infernal wrongness of the situation.

"He said he'd keep me," Mary said tiredly, leaning into him. "He kept me fifteen bloody minutes, tossed me a few coppers, and since then I haven't been able to... Well, money has been tight."

"Do you know his name?"

"One of Jones's friends, but don't involve yourself. His papa's a lord, and I was foolish."

"Does he know?"

"Nobody knows, though I think Estelle suspects and maybe Fleur."

"Then everybody suspects," Worth said, thinking through the options. "Are you feeling well enough to keep dancing for now?"

"Until I show, I can dance. That's the rule, but I'm not tall, or fat like Hera, so I've only a few weeks' work left."

"Take the rest of this with you," Worth said, gesturing at the tray. "You'll be ravenous later. Promise me you won't do anything silly while I think this over."

"I'm not the dramatic kind. Mostly, all I want to do is pee and nap."

"And shock your solicitor," Worth added, though he applauded her forthrightness. "Before I leave Town tomorrow, I'm to make some purchases for my sister at the shops. Will you be at rehearsal?"

"Miss rehearsal, and you get docked," Mary reminded him. "I'll be there."

She'd made no move to leave his side, and that more than anything else left Worth feeling inadequate, and somehow ashamed. Avery was in the country, it was a pleasant night, and Mary wouldn't have hatched any ambitious or possessive notions had he taken her up on the offer of a simple tumble between friends. A month ago, he would have blithely tripped up the stairs with her—at least until he guessed about the baby.

Hell and the devil. Fifteen minutes was a simple tumble. Worth's own record was well under that, and he hadn't even parted with a few coppers for the privilege.

*Think of your opera dancers, Mr. Kettering.*

"I will give thought to your situation, but you must not worry," Worth said. "Thomas will see you safely home and carry the leftovers so they don't go to waste. But tell me, Mary, can you tat lace?"

\* \* \*

Because Jacaranda's employer had not the courtesy to send a simple note warning her of his return, she did not rouse herself to greet him when she heard his boots thumping outside the girls' rooms farther down the hallway.

"I have come to apologize," he said, pausing in her sitting room doorway, the dust of the road still on his person.

As opening lines went, that traveled some distance toward mollifying her. To proposition one's housekeeper merited at least a personal apology. It did not merit belaboring.

"Apology accepted," she said, setting aside the first decent cup of tea she'd had all day. "Shall we send a bath up to your chambers?"

Now that he'd apologized, she wanted to devour him with her gaze, also to ignore him. Staring at her tea cup was a nice compromise, but really, to think such a scandalous proposition was to be forgiven with a few meaningless words...

"I should have sent a note," he said, inviting himself into her sitting room and appropriating the middle of her sofa. "Mind if I have a cup?"

"You apologize for the lack of a note?"

"Not well done of me, I know." He poured for himself, and Jacaranda was compelled to stare at his hands. Long, elegant fingers and broad, strong palms. They were warm, those hands, and knowing.

But their owner hadn't the sense to apologize for his brazen overtures.

"Not well done of you, indeed," she managed. "Help yourself to cream and sugar."

"I don't suppose you could order us a tray?"

"It's tea time." She rose and went to the door to signal a footman. "I am the housekeeper, I can conjure a tray of victuals on occasion. Your sister and your niece will want to greet you."

While Jacaranda abruptly did not.

"I want to greet them, too, but first I wanted to inquire as to how soon we can accommodate my brother." He downed his cup of tea in one swallow, his throat working while Jacaranda tried not to stare at that, too.

He was the most aggravating man.

"I'm ready now," she said, not liking the sound of the words as they hung in the air.

"What constitutes ready?"

"You'll interfere?"

"I'll take an interest," he said, holding his cup out for a refill.

Jacaranda obliged, willing to consider he might have apologized as artfully as he knew how.

"May we tour the state rooms, say, tomorrow morning?" he went on. "The stable master ought to be notified he'll have extra teams to deal with."

"Roberts knows," Jacaranda said, adding cream and sugar to his tea. "I'm sure Simmons told him, or Reilly. The extra linens have been washed and the curtains beaten and rehung. The good silver is polished to a shine, the lace table runners aired."

"Lace table runners?"

"All of them, because we don't know how long your brother will be joining us."

"Probably only long enough to collect Yolanda and assemble his entourage again."

"What if Yolanda doesn't want to go, but would rather stay here in the south?" Jacaranda asked, giving his tea a stir.

What was wrong with older brothers? They always assumed they knew best, always marched out smartly with their plans, never asked even an opinion, much less permission of their sisters.

He scowled at the tea she offered before accepting it from her. "If Yolanda wants to stay in the south?"

"With you."

He took a turn staring at his tea cup. "I run a bachelor establishment in Town. I always have, and I'm not connected, as my brother is."

"Your bachelor establishment boasts at least one small female child and her nanny." Jacaranda stirred her tea slowly, though it needed no stirring. "You may not be titled, though I suspect you could easily be knighted if you chose, but you are most assuredly connected. Wickie says you've paid several calls at Carlton House."

"Any pair of deep pockets is welcome to call on Prinny, and I've been considering Avery's situation. She's legitimate, or I think she is, though with the French these days, one can hardly tell."

Jacaranda's ire at his disrespectful proposition, at his abrupt absence, and his lack of warning regarding his return fueled her rising irritation at his dunderheaded notions of family.

"You are not thinking of sending that dear little child north with a stranger who's never so much as patted her head?"

"He's an earl, and he's her uncle." Mr. Kettering rose but kept his tea cup. Jacaranda suspected he did so in order to have something to stare at. "If Yolanda goes, it really won't be that much of an adjustment to add Avery to the earl's household, too."

"Worth Kettering, you have gone completely 'round the bend. Yolanda cannot be seen to disappear to the north, as if she were some eccentric spinster at the age of sixteen—or a girl in disgrace. She will need a Season, you've said so yourself, and she will need her family."

"No girl comes out at sixteen. Even I know it isn't done."

Perhaps it was a measure of his upset—over not having sent a note?—that she had to point out the obvious to him.

"In less than a year, she will be seventeen, and many girls do make their bow at seventeen. They marry at seventeen, they conceive and even bear children at that age. My own sister wed at seventeen, and very properly."

He set his tea cup down on its saucer hard and turned his back to her. Something like compassion reared its inconvenient head, but Jacaranda kept her lips closed. Let him squirm. He might treat her cavalierly—she was a woman grown who could hold her own—but his younger relations deserved better.

"Hess and I will discuss it," he said, turning back to face her after a long, silent moment.

"You ought to discuss it with the young ladies. You propose to play skittles with their lives. Avery should at least visit the family seat before you force any move on her."

"She'll love it," Mr. Kettering said, crossing his arms and leaning back on Jacaranda's window sill. "Hess keeps one of the best stables in Cumberland, and he's well liked by all. The house itself is gorgeous, stately and yet still a home, and the grounds are spectacular. We never have trouble with the help. Working for the Ketterings is a plum passed down from father to son and aunt to niece. She'll settle in at Grampion and never want to leave."

*Worth Kettering was homesick.* The longing poured out in his words, in the distant memories behind his eyes, in the wistful expression softening his features.

"You want them to have what you've rejected?"

"What I cast aside, as a youth."

"Let them have what you had as a youth, what you still have." She rose, too, and stood with her arms crossed. "Give them a choice."

"Hess is the head of our family, and his decisions will be final." Reciting the words seemed to settle something for him, but not for Jacaranda.

"You are Avery's guardian. Wickie told me so, and you are the only person on this earth who loves her like family. You came to Yolanda's rescue when dear Hess was off shooting out of season in Scotland."

"Cut line, Wyeth. We can have this argument twice daily until Hess shows up, and it won't make one bit of difference."

"Then we'll have it three times a day. Or four, or twelve."

He was scowling at her one moment, and then his lips quirked up, even as he dipped his chin to hide it.

"You are a terror, Wyeth. Did you know that?"

"I am a housekeeper, one whose family begs her to return home with each monthly letter. You thwart family at your peril, sir."

When she might have disclosed that she had heeded her family's importuning and would soon be turning in her notice, she was cut off by one footman arriving with a tray of food and another with a fresh tea service. Mr. Kettering resumed his place on the sofa, and Jacaranda settled into her rocking chair, grateful for the distraction and the distance.

"I am famished," he said, helping himself to a ham and cheddar sandwich. "I will show you every courtesy at dinner, but you'll forgive me my lapses now. I stopped only long enough to water Goliath and let him blow."

Jacaranda took a nibble of sandwich as she considered that interesting tidbit and which lapses he referred to. Lapses. Plural.

"How are matters in London?" Small talk, suitable to ingesting sustenance, she hoped.

"My house is a disgrace. My steward is a conscientious fellow, but the things you could teach him, Wyeth. I've half a mind to send him out here for a tutorial."

"After your brother departs, I should have time." Assuming she didn't return immediately to her brother's house. "If your steward takes his duties seriously, he'll not quibble about a chance to discuss them with another of similar enthusiasm."

"You are a terror who doesn't speak like any housekeeper I've known." He was back to frowning at her. "Where is this family who begs you to abandon me?"

"Down closer to the coast. Another sandwich?" *Abandon him?*

"Please." He regarded her in silence while she put more food on his plate. Rather than allow him to study her at any length, Jacaranda cast another lure.

"Tell me more about your family seat. How many acres does it encompass?"

And he was off, waxing eloquent about a place that sounded like a medium-sized slice of heaven, for all it was two hundred miles north and he hadn't seen it for half a lifetime.

Leaving Jacaranda to wonder if Worth Kettering had been banished, or if he'd exiled himself all those years ago.

* * *

The blasted woman pled a headache at dinner and took a tray in her room. Worth was aggravated at first, because he and Wyeth had settled nothing with that tea and crumpets sparring match upon his arrival, then he was relieved. They were under the same roof, he was bone tired, and perhaps she was as well.

He was restless, though, so he bade his womenfolk good night and ducked out with a towel, dressing gown, and soap, and enjoyed the privacy of the pond. The moon came up as he finished his swim, casting undulating ripples of light over the dark surface of the water.

That play of dark and light reminded him of Jacaranda Wyeth's hair and of how she moved.

Shaking that thought away, he dried off, shrugged into his dressing gown, and made his way to the house. On a whim, he took himself up to the third floor, where his sister and his niece slept.

He hadn't sent them any notes either, which was truly reprehensible of him. His housekeeper deserved a note, his womenfolk *needed* one. As he stood in the doorway of Avery's room, he recollected all the times his mother had hared off in high dudgeon, threatening never to return. He'd been relieved when she'd come blithely sailing home, though that slight, low-down sickness in the gut had never left him as he'd waited for her next dramatic exit.

"Is she still snuffling?" Yolanda stood across the hallway in nightgown and wrapper. "The poor little thing was disconsolate. I thought she'd never drop off."

"Disconsolate?" Why would Avery be disconsolate when he was back with them again?

"Her manka went missing, and she was nigh hysterical. She *was* hysterical."

"Her what?"

"Manka, or mankit," Yolanda said. "It's how she refers to the nursery blanket her mother embroidered for her. We couldn't find it anywhere, and finally Wickie told her big girls don't have blankets and if Avery didn't settle down, she wouldn't have a doll either."

"I had such hopes for Mrs. Hartwick." The woman had been the most promising of a succession of nurse-governesses, but this—

"She wasn't unkind. Big girls don't have blankets."

"No," Worth countered, "they have keepsakes, and mementos, and I happened to see that your effects include a doll, who occupies pride of place on your mantel."

She raised her chin, every inch a Kettering. "Your point?"

"Avery's blanket must be found."

Yolanda crossed the hall, went up on her toes and kissed his cheek. "I have hopes for you, brother. Good night and happy hunting."

Yolanda took her leave on that cryptic remark, and Worth opened the door to Avery's room. No candle had been left burning in the darkness, no doll tucked under her covers beside her. When Worth lowered himself to her bed, he saw her smooth little-girl cheeks were tear-stained, and her mouth worked silently, as if in want of a thumb.

"Best not wake her." Wyeth was silhouetted in the door in her nightclothes, her hair down and unbound.

The sight caused an obstruction in Worth's breathing. "You heard the racket?"

"She was pathetic." Wyeth advanced into the room. "The first honest tantrum I've seen since my brothers were very young."

"Was it your idea to threaten her dolls?"

"Angels abide, of course not." She took a rocking chair a few feet from the bed. "When children are tired and aggrieved, they can't respond rationally to threats, though it isn't my place to interfere in the nursery."

"Some would say it isn't mine."

"Some would say sending the child to Cumberland to live among a whole new set of strangers is not merely convenient for you, but in her best interests."

He brushed a lock of Avery's hair off her forehead, silently ceding his housekeeper points for tenacity and courage. "Where's her blanket?"

Wyeth rocked slowly, the tempo conveying bodily fatigue, maybe even sorrow.

"I thought that's what the fuss was about. I'll unleash the whole staff tomorrow. Blankets don't just get up and walk away. Unless the blanket has flown back to France, we'll find it."

"What if the pig ate Manka?" Avery asked sleepily. "William is *always* hungry. What if we never, ever find her? She'll be all alone." Her breathing hitched, and her little face screwed up, and she was in Worth's lap before the first tear could think of falling.

"We will find her," he assured her. "Mrs. Wyeth has said it will be so, and I say it will be so. We'll turn out every maid and footman and tell all the house cats to look for her. Hmm? Maybe your dolls saw Manka going for a great lark in the laundry cart, and she'll come back from her adventure all clean and smelling of sunshine."

"She doesn't want to smell of sunshine. She wants to smell like my m-mama."

"Like your mama?"

The blanket was years old and had literally been dragged through the gutters of Paris. The hems had a few tattered vestiges of once-lovely embroidery, but the blanket couldn't possibly smell of Moira Kettering now.

Wyeth shifted to sit beside them on the bed. "Did your mama's scent resemble this?" She held a long, dark lock of her hair under Avery's nose.

"Yes! That's the Mama-flower. Manka always smells like that. I want to sit in your lap."

She hiked herself away from her uncle and appropriated her perch of choice.

"Lavender," Wyeth said, kissing the child's crown. "Both the Kettering households use it for laundry and linen scents. I use it on my person." She shifted away and resumed her rocking chair, the child in her lap.

"Tomorrow, your uncle can show you where the Mama-flower grows here. Now is when it blooms, and the scent is quite, quite lovely," Wyeth said. "Did your mama ever sing to you when you were tired?"

"Mostly in English, which wasn't my best when I was small."

The slow rocking went on, and Wyeth's hand traced an easy pattern on the child's back. Worth felt his eyes growing heavy, and a heaviness elsewhere, too.

Not desire, though that hummed along quietly in his veins whenever he thought of the woman sitting a few feet away. Something calmer and sweeter pooled in his chest, having to do with seeing Wyeth with other children, babies even.

Everlasting Powers, save him.

"Can you hum the tune your mama sang?" Wyeth asked in drowsy tones.

And soon Wyeth had lullabied the child right back to sleep, her voice a lovely, true alto that brought comfort and peace in the darkened room.

"She's out like the proverbial candle," Wyeth said after a few minutes of silent rocking. "Can you lift the bedclothes?"

He obliged, then covered the child up when Wyeth stepped back and arched her spine, hands low on her back. While she gazed down at the sleeping child,

Worth found a cloth doll to tuck in with Avery and bent to kiss the child's forehead.

He also left her door cracked, so light from the sconces in the corridor might reach her room.

"My thanks," he said as they moved down the hallway. "God help whoever misplaced that blanket."

"The child herself likely misplaced it. You love her, you know."

"Always a fine thing, when a woman tells a man what he feels."

She stopped outside her door and peered up at him in the dim light. "I simply wore a soothing scent. You needn't be jealous."

"I'm not jealous." He wasn't, exactly, but he was made hungry in some regard by what had just transpired. Rather than examine that hunger or admit the loneliness of spirit behind it, he opened the door to Wyeth's sitting room and peered inside.

Candles burned, and a modest fire danced on the andirons. The room was cozy on a night Worth would have said was almost warm to begin with.

"I'll build up your fire," he said, moving past Wyeth into her room.

"You needn't." She followed him in. "I lit the fire only to dry my hair. I'll open my windows, because it's nearly stuffy in here now."

Stuffy and thick with lavender. "I'll bank your fire then."

He made a thorough job of a simple task, because otherwise she'd shoo him out of her quarters, when he wasn't in any hurry to leave.

"Before," he said, back to her as he knelt in front of the hearth, "when we were on the bridge? I didn't mean to insult you."

"My guess is you did not mean much of anything."

"Oh, I meant something." He straightened and put the poker aside. "We've chemistry between us, and indulging that chemistry could be lucrative for you, Wyeth."

She neither took a place on her small sofa, nor hovered by the door, but simply stood her ground at the center of the room.

"What you offered might have been lucrative in terms of coin, but costly otherwise. We need not discuss this again. Ever. "

That gave him something to think about, which might have been an adequate distraction, except it was late, they were alone, and a bed was close at hand.

Her bed.

"Most choices involve costs and benefits, my dear. You consider the costs almost exclusively." He recognized in another a trait he had honed to a fine business advantage in himself.

Her smile was such as a tutor might bestow on a particularly dim pupil. "You offered me illegitimate children I can't support, loss of reputation, potential loss of health, loss of long-term income and standing, loss of my family's regard, for starters. Let's assume I don't die in childbirth, as so many women do, and for what? A few kisses, some stolen pleasure? A little coin?"

A lot of coin, half his fortune maybe, because he could always replace the money. With her, that point would merit him nothing.

"Few of those losses would accrue unless you chose to be indiscreet. I'd protect your reputation the same as I would Yolanda's. You'd gain a few assets, paltry though they might measure in your estimation."

While this discussion alone might cost Worth his dignity, for rather than negotiating, he was perilously close to…wheedling.

"What could I possibly gain from an illicit liaison with a man who can't admit he loves his niece as if she were his own?"

The finer points of her logic escaped him. Taking care of Avery was his privilege and his duty—and Avery *was* his, unless Hessian decided to snatch her away to the north.

He sauntered close to the pillar of good sense standing where his Wyeth ought to be.

"You would gain pleasure, in which your existence is decidedly deficient, madam." He spoke gently, lest she turn the argument right back around on its source. "You would gain a friend in this life, a hand to hold, a shoulder to cry on, someone to provide bodily comfort when running your empire weighs too heavily. In short, you would gain a part of me I don't lend easily, but one you might find worth having."

He was close enough to catch the part of her scent that wasn't simply lavender, but summer flowers, and her. She regarded him with some puzzlement, and he would have given a lot to know which particular rabbit trails her febrile feminine brain was coursing.

"A part of you not *lent* easily," she said, "with interest, principle subject to collection without notice. Too much risk in those terms for a prudent investor. Nothing but risk, really. Good night, Mr. Kettering. We'll find Avery's Manka in the morning, won't we?"

He bowed and withdrew, knowing that if he touched her, the argument would progress in a different and equally fruitless direction. In her convoluted-to-him, crystal-clear-to-her way, Wyeth had communicated something in what she *hadn't* said.

She viewed a part of him was worth having, but not on the terms he'd offered. She wanted a different balance of risk and reward. That was progress, and all any negotiation wanted to remain viable was a bit of progress from time to time.

# CHAPTER SEVEN

"What will it take to wake you?"

Jacaranda knew that silky baritone, but in sleep, she did not care to heed it.

"Woman, for the love of God, wake up." A warm, large hand shook her shoulder, even as both the impatience in that voice and its anxious undertone registered.

She was comfortably face down in her pillows, a fresh breeze coming in her window. She'd been so tired last night a headache had plagued her, and then she'd lain awake pondering that odd exchange with the household despot.

Lips, on her nape. Soft, sweet, tender even, and something warmer and a touch damper than.—

She whipped over to her back. "Were you thieving a *taste* of me?"

"Good morning, or at least it will soon be morning." Mr. Kettering sat up, an infernal smile playing over those very same larcenous lips. The room was barely light, and outside Jacaranda's window, one lone bird chirped a greeting to the day.

"Get off my bed, leave this room, and do not come back, ever. If you have need of me, a maid can bring a note. Good-bye."

She tried to roll away from him, but that hand was back on her shoulder, staying her. Her bare shoulder.

Her gaze met his, and he appeared to realize at the same time she did that she'd slept without her nightclothes. Beneath the thin old quilt and sheet, Jacaranda was as naked as an opera dancer's knees.

"Wyeth, you wicked little creature." His smile became diabolical, and that hand on her shoulder shifted to trace her collarbone. "You're awake now. As am I."

"I couldn't possibly be awake, because I'm in the midst of a nightmare. Will you *please* take your hand off my person?"

The hand was gone, and so was the smile, then so was the man, for he rose and paced out of touching distance, turning his back to her.

"Thank you, Mr. Kettering, and if you will do me the courtesy to remain like that, I can find my nightclothes, though what earthly use you expect me to be without a hot cup of tea and at least a scone or two I cannot fathom."

She fished her nightgown from under her pillow while she lectured him and rose to belt her dressing gown around her waist.

"I'm somewhat decent," she announced. "Except my hair's a fright, and we're alone in my boudoir, and that cannot be decent."

He peeked, then turned around and stepped behind her to lift her hair out of her dressing gown.

"This is not a fright. Your hair could never be a fright, and when I behold you, Wyeth, I thank the Creator you do not indulge in ghastly caps and severe coronets. I found the blanket."

"Have you been up this entire night searching for that thing?"

She liked the sensation of his hands in her hair, sweeping it up and out so gently. She whipped around and glared at him accordingly.

"Not all night, but I couldn't sleep, so about an hour ago, I started looking around. Down at the stables, in the playroom, the library. I found it with the soiled linens from the girls' rooms, and it doesn't smell in the least like lavender."

"So we'll wash it on Monday." She pushed her hair out of her eyes, for it was inclined to subversive behavior when loose.

"You can't be seen to wash it, or Avery will think you're taking her mother's scent away, not refurbishing it."

"Then we won't wash it."

He glared back at her, which—though she was tempted to snicker at all this blustering over a child's blanket—also made him look rather magnificent.

"Do not patronize me, Jacaranda Wyeth. We will wash it, as soon as you show me where the blighted soap is. Then we'll let it hang in the kitchen to dry before Avery is finished breaking her fast."

"You woke me at the crack of doom to find the soap?"

His glare faltered, and he apparently found it necessary to open her window one additional inch. "You're always up at the crack of doom. Simmons complains that you make him look lazy by comparison."

"He is lazy. I like it that way, and he does a fine job, despite both age and laziness. Come with me, and we'll find your lavender soap."

The relief that flickered in his eyes caught her off guard, but really, did he think she'd let the household run out of lavender soap? In summer, for pity's sake?

They washed the blanket, then Mr. Kettering wrung it out between his hands until it was nearly dry. The only scullery maid stirring in the kitchen hared off to fetch the cream from the dairy and the eggs from the henhouse.

"I suppose you'd like me to make you a pot of tea?" Jacaranda extended the offer, knowing she would have her tea, come fire, flood or famine—*or Worth Kettering in a rambunctious mood.*

"Sit," her employer ordered. "I'll make the tea while you have a scone or two. Your disposition might benefit, if the Deity is merciful." He passed her the basket of fresh scones and put both a jar of raspberry jam and a crock of butter on the table. "Save me at least a morsel, lest I get peckish and wan."

"Peckish and wan, and given to invading your housekeeper's quarters at all hours." Jacaranda let that suffice for a riposte because the jam was wonderful, the scones perfect, and she wasn't having to make her own cup of tea.

Then too, Worth Kettering had tracked down the prodigal blanket. She very nearly congratulated him for it, but eating her scone was a higher priority. He set a cup of tea before her, then slid onto the bench beside her.

"Budge over. I am owed a scone complete with butter and jam for my heroics this morning."

She passed him her half-eaten scone, intending to hush him with sustenance, but he took a bite off it as she held it.

She put the scone on the table. "Mr. Kettering, will you cease your naughtiness?"

"Mrs. Wyeth, will you cease attributing base motives to every small gesture of flattery and flirtation that comes your way? This,"—he kissed her lips soundly, a brief, warm, raspberry-flavored kiss—"is being naughty. Now eat your scone, and I'll make you up another."

Jacaranda ate her scone, and the one he'd layered with butter and jam after that, it being far too early to debate what was and was not naughty with Worth Kettering, when she was in danger of losing track of the distinction herself.

* * *

The pond had proved a good place to cogitate, so Worth took to swimming nightly. In the water, he thought about his clients and his investments, or at least he told himself that was the purpose of his exertions.

That other thoughts intruded as he circled the pond in alternating directions was plain bad luck.

Thoughts of Avery, wreathed in smiles, unable to let go of his neck when he presented her with her blanket, fresh and fragrant.

Thoughts of Yolanda, admitting she had hopes for him. *Hopes?*

And many, many thoughts of Jacaranda Wyeth. The colder water in the deep end of the pond was particularly helpful for reining in those thoughts, but she was a puzzle, and Worth could not resist a puzzle.

She desired him, of that he was certain, and he desired her, of that he was more than certain.

But she would not have him, citing fear for her reputation and her well-being.

A frog set up a repetitive croaking in reeds on the stable side of the water, probably singing the froggy version of a serenade to his lady.

Wyeth's fears were reasonable. No matter how careful a couple was, given enough lust—Worth capacity for lust was not in doubt—conception could occur. Women died in childbirth and from the complications that followed.

No matter how discreet he and Wyeth might be, intimate relations of any regularity took place under the noses of servants, neighbors, and family. Her reputation might suffer, in which case the logical countermeasure on his part would be to—

He stopped dead in the water, momentarily sinking as his limbs stilled and the frog's croaking punctuated the stillness of the night air.

*Marry her.*

To consider such a notion ought to have given Worth a fright, but he'd learned that when attempting to solve a problem, no potential solution should be dismissed out of hand. Not on first mention.

Hessian had no children, hadn't even taken a second wife. Perhaps that was Hess's convoluted way of punishing Worth, of loading down a younger brother's conscience in a battle for the moral high ground.

High ground be damned. Conceiving children with Wyeth would be an exceedingly pleasant duty.

As the frog fell silent, and an owl's hoot floated on the soft, meadowy breeze, Worth turned the idea of marriage to Wyeth over and over in his mind. No matter how often he put the idea aside and told himself to consider some client's portfolio or financial contretemps, Wyeth-as-wife had taken up residence in his mind. He slogged up the grassy bank, wondering how Hess would react, to know such a fine and beautiful woman had chosen Worth for her own.

The idea of *belonging* to her and having her belong to him settled the matter. Marriage for them was right, it would work. The opportunity for a decent match was too practical for her not to leap at it, particularly when her intended was an earl's heir.

Worth toweled off, belted his dressing gown, and turned his steps toward the dark outline that was his long-ignored country seat.

Marriage. Who'd have thought?

\* \* \*

With Worth Kettering back underfoot, Jacaranda felt more and more often as if she were being spied upon. He lurked in doorways, watching her at her ledgers; he stopped by her parlor at tea time and helped himself to most of her sandwiches and at least three cups of tea. He found matters to discuss with her, some of which were legitimately related to his brother's impending visit.

Many of which were not.

"You'll accompany me to the Hunters' this afternoon?" he asked, setting down an empty tea cup. He'd assumed his customary place in the middle of her sofa. His arms were so long that when he laid them along the top, he spanned the entire piece of furniture.

Or maybe her sofa was that short.

"You're perfectly capable of finding your way on your own, or Goliath is," she replied, pouring herself a second cup. She always needed at least two for her morning break. "They have no daughters over the age of twelve and no riding pigs. You should be safe."

"Without older daughters, Mrs. Hunter will be particularly glad to see a woman's friendly face at her gate, and the weather is perfect for a drive."

"Simmons's knees, which are infallible, predict rain later."

"So we'll put up the top. Pass over that plate of cakes. Baked goods go stale if they sit out too long."

He was at his most determined when he was like this, casually tossing back every obstacle she threw at him, assured, relaxed. He would not be deterred, and the Hunters were the last family they had to call on.

"Mrs. Hunter is deceased," she said. "Mr. Thomas Hunter lives with his three children and his mother-in-law. He's your best farmer, the most dedicated, for all he's a young man."

Mr. Kettering paused in the midst of selecting tea cakes to put on his plate. "You admire this Thomas Hunter?"

"Of course I do. You ought to admire him, too, raising three children, providing for their grandmother, and working your land so it out-produces all the neighbors. When you're through ruining your luncheon, we can make a quick trip out."

"Such a Tartar." He popped a tea cake in his mouth, then held one up an inch from Jacaranda's lips. "You can lecture me on my shortcomings for the entire journey, both directions, but don't make me listen to your grumbling stomach."

She took a bite of cake just to get his hand out of her face, but something... not innocent flavored the exchange—while raspberry icing flavored the tea cake. Yes, he'd taken a bite of scone from her hand earlier that week, but that hadn't been entirely innocent either—on his part.

"You are tiresome," she said, getting to her feet. "I'll fetch my bonnet and shawl, and then put together a basket of provisions, so we can execute this errand you are incapable of seeing to on your own."

She left him in her sitting room, munching cake, knowing it was a bad idea to allow him to remain unsupervised in her quarters, but unwilling to tarry in his presence. He hadn't touched her since his pedagogic raspberry kiss days ago—except for helping her in and out of the gig—but when he didn't touch her, the feelings his proximity stirred were even worse.

Bodily feelings of heat and vertigo and inconvenient excitement, but feelings of the heart as well.

Jacaranda liked Worth Kettering. Liked him despite his unwillingness to shoulder the responsibility for raising his niece or launching his sister, for he had a point. The earl *should* tend to both things. The head of the family took on the jobs nobody else wanted. Hadn't Grey told her that, over and over? Grey had done it, too, and continued to do it. Witness, his letters were the most regular, and she treasured every one.

Despite the fact that her brother now wanted a specific date for her return to the family seat.

Worth Kettering and Grey Dorning would understand each other in a single glance. They were both men who went after what they wanted and let little stop them. An image came to mind of stallions meeting each other in savage battle.

Jacaranda had stopped Grey, though. Stopped him from imposing one of the most daft head-of-the-family decisions he'd ever come up with.

She was still glad about that.

She was not glad about having to travel in proximity to Worth Kettering, but Mr. Hunter was the last tenant to visit, so she packed her hamper and put aside her liking for her employer.

Also her desire for him.

They tooled out, Goliath in the traces. As they crossed the covered bridge at a smart trot, Mr. Kettering made not even a flirtatious remark. He didn't need to, not when Jacaranda could recall in wicked detail the feel of her hand getting acquainted with him through his breeches.

Angels abide, what had she been thinking?

"How long ago did Hunter lose his wife?"

"Five years or so," Jacaranda replied. "She didn't last a year after the birth of the third child, and while she didn't suffer, she did linger. Take the next right."

Goliath turned onto a smaller track, and Mr. Kettering let the horse proceed at a more leisurely trot. "What was her name?"

"He called her Mary Jean, or perhaps Mary Jane. My tenure did not predate her death. Vicar would know."

"He'd know if her grave has a marker, wouldn't he?"

"It does not, nothing save a rough stone Thomas hewed himself to resemble a rose. It's very different."

"Why hasn't he remarried?"

"You'll have to ask him." She hadn't kept her tone quite disinterested enough, and Mr. Kettering peered over at her.

"Slow down, sir. This bridge is none too sturdy." They clattered over a patch of boards, one intended to handle only light traffic.

"How does Hunter get his produce to market over such a paltry excuse for a bridge?"

"He takes the hayfields and makes a slightly longer job of it, I imagine."

"Wyeth, why doesn't Reilly note these things? The need for grave markers, the bridges gone rickety?"

"His job is to steward your land," she said, though she'd had this very argument with Reilly himself. "Trysting has no position described as steward of your people."

"Yes, it does." He let Goliath's stride lengthen as the track ran through an overgrown patch of the home wood. "I hold that position. How much farther is it to Hunter's?"

"Less than a mile. As the crow flies, this tenancy is close to Trysting, but the creeks and woods and so forth make it longer when you take the lanes. Oh, dear."

"Oh, dear, indeed." Kettering drew Goliath to a halt before a substantial tree that had fallen across the lane. "Don't suppose you packed a saw in that basket?"

"Everything but."

"I'll have a look." He passed her the reins as he climbed down from the buggy.

He released Goliath's check rein so the horse could crop grass at the roadside, then he inspected the tree. Larger than a sapling, the oak had been down long enough for the foliage to have thoroughly wilted.

"Had I ridden out daily, as my housekeeper advised me to, I would have seen this and had it removed." Mr. Kettering unbuttoned his waistcoat, then passed both jacket and waistcoat to Jacaranda.

"Your steward is responsible for the land." She'd given Reilly a schedule, which would have put him on every patch of the property at least twice a month in the growing season. "Perhaps you and he might discuss a schedule."

"Not perhaps. I'll find something to use as a lever. If I can get the damned tree loose from where it's wedged in those rocks, I can probably move it far enough to let us pass."

Jacaranda aimed her best frown at him. "Rain will soon move in. Why not turn around and let Reilly deal with this?"

"This is England. It's always about to rain, and what will Thomas Hunter think, to know I've called on every tenant save my best farmer?"

She let him disappear into the woods while she visually calculated whether it was even possible to turn the buggy on the narrow lane. Trees and rocks encroached on both sides, great nasty boulders that would not admit of buggy wheels or shod hooves.

This part of the wood was unkempt, better suited for hunting than raising firewood or lumber, but she doubted Reilly had come this way in months. Thomas Hunter could be trusted to look out for his own land, after all, and Reilly no doubt saw the man at services, assemblies and over the occasional pint.

That part of being a steward, Jacaranda could not do for him.

Mr. Kettering came striding back out of the gloomy woods, toting a stout length of dead oak that had to weigh nigh as much as Jacaranda did. He heaved and hoisted and cursed and heaved some more, until the fallen tree was free of the rocks and lying at an angle, still blocking most of the road.

"That's the hard part," Mr. Kettering said, taking off his driving gloves and slapping them against his thigh before putting them back on.

That exercise had been trying for Jacaranda, too. Beneath the thin material of Mr. Kettering's shirt, his muscles bunched and rippled with his exertions, leaving her staring at Goliath's fundament in sheer defense of her sanity.

"Would you like to put your jacket back on?"

He grinned at her, swiping the back of his glove over his forehead. "I've grown a trifle warm, and we're not done here."

A fat droplet of rain landed on Jacaranda's nose.

"We'll get a soaking now, in any case," she said, for what sky she could see through the trees had grown ominous.

Mr. Kettering pointed with his elbow. "That way, there's an empty cottage with a decent porch about twenty yards down that trail. You take the hamper, I'll fetch the horse."

A peel of thunder rumbling over the last of his words had Jacaranda out of the buggy and retrieving the hamper post-haste. She didn't like storms, didn't like the idea of getting soaking wet where Worth Kettering could find humor in it, didn't like much of anything about her day so far.

She spied the cottage, recalling it from when the estate had boasted a game keeper. The place was minimally stocked as a gamekeeper's cottage, one duty Mr. Reilly was happy to conscientiously oversee. She suspected he trysted with the occasional willing woman here, or perhaps, given his timidity and Mrs. Reilly's lack of an understanding nature, with the occasional lurid novel.

No matter. The cottage was warm and dry, and Jacaranda reached its covered porch just as the random drops coalesced into a steady shower. Several minutes later, Mr. Kettering came up the trail, leading Goliath. He waved as he took the horse around to the shed in back, his shirt already soaked to an indecent degree.

A solicitor ought not to sport such muscle. The Regent should sign a decree forbidding such a display, at least before susceptible women.

And what woman wouldn't be?

"Everlasting powers." Mr. Kettering came stomping and dripping onto the porch moments later. "You warned me, Wyeth. Go ahead and say it."

"You cut yourself." She scowled at his bleeding knuckles. "And your shirt is soaked, and the weather is hardly your fault."

She crossed her arms over her chest, because the temperature had dropped, and her own clothing wasn't exactly dry.

"Let's see what we can find inside. Right now, a towel wouldn't go amiss."

He felt above the lintel, found a skeleton key where any schoolboy tall enough would know to look for it, and unlocked the door.

He gestured Jacaranda to precede him inside, then paused in the doorway. "I was about to say, Reilly needs a talking to, given the state of the bridge, the woods, and his idea of where to hide a key, but he's at least kept this place in good shape."

He had, or his lady friends had. The cottage barely needed dusting and lacked the mildewed scent common to neglected dwellings. The wood box was full, the windows were clean, and on the shelves above the sink, a few faded towels sat neatly folded.

Over in the corner, an old tester bed was made up, knitted blankets folded across its foot, canopy nowhere in evidence.

Jacaranda rubbed her arms as another rumble of thunder sounded, even louder than the last one.

"The storm is still gaining on us," Mr. Kettering noted. "Best get a fire going, and I hope you won't mind if I get out of this wet shirt." He wasn't asking permission. He was disrobing as he spoke, removing shirt, boots and stockings.

Jacaranda tried not to watch.

While the rain against the windows began a steady roar, she took longer to remove her bonnet than she ever had in her life. Her fingers shook, and her insides felt odd, and she could not get the image of Mr. Kettering's damp, naked chest out of her mind. She also could not get her dratted bonnet off, a hairpin having caught on some part of the straw or wiring.

"Wood's nice and dry," Mr. Kettering said, scratching a flint and steel over some dead pine needles. A spark obligingly leapt, and to Jacaranda, even that— the spark falling on dry tinder, the flames eagerly licking up into the air—had prurient connotations.

What on earth was wrong with her?

"That should take the chill off." He rose in one graceful flex of muscles. "We'll hang your bonnet from the rafters, and it will be dry in no time."

Her only good bonnet would be ruined if she kept fussing at it. Her gaze fell on a box on the mantel, one decorated with a carving of the belladonna flower.

"Sit." She patted the back of a ladder-back chair then retrieved the box, finding it contained the same supplies its twin did at Trysting. "I'll clean up your knuckles."

He obliged but turned the chair backward so he could straddle it and extended his hand.

"This situation is fortuitous," he said.

"Finding a box of medicinals was fortuitous." She dabbed a clean cloth on his knuckles. "You are still bleeding." She held the cloth snugly over his abused flesh. "I thought you had gloves on."

"Had to take them off to work with the wet harness and buckles, but I like holding hands with you, Wyeth. Take your time, and don't forget to kiss me better."

She peeked at his knuckles, then closed the cloth over them again. "You are tenacious."

"So are you. I like that about you."

He could not know how susceptible she was to such a compliment. "My brother says I'm unnaturally stubborn for a woman." Now, where had that come from?

"With seven brothers, you'd have to be."

She took the cloth away again. "This might sting a bit."

She applied a pungent brown astringent, and he winced, so she blew on his knuckles to ease the sting.

"Let it dry, and don't be mucking about in the ashes or Goliath's stall until it does."

"Goliath has an open shed," Mr. Kettering said. "He can amble around or crop some grass, and I dipped him a bucket from the cistern out back. Now, we're safe and warm, and he is, too. What shall we do with this boon?"

"Boon?"

"I told myself to be patient." He stood and crossed to the braided rug before the hearth. "I told myself sooner or later, I'd catch you in the pond, or reading late at night, or in some situation where we're guaranteed privacy."

"The rain should let up soon," she said, a sense of unease rising at his words.

"I can be very quick," he went on, casually unfastening his falls. "When I want to make a point."

He stepped out of his damp breeches and hung them from a nail on the rafter nearest the fire. And that gesture, that simple reaching, without a stitch on, was so blatantly, masculinely beautiful, Jacaranda wanted to tell him to hold the pose so she might memorize it. His skin was darker above his waist, but the musculature of his arms, legs, belly, and back was all of a smooth, powerful, healthy male animal piece.

Blessed angels, he was beautiful.

He took the towel he'd been sitting on and wrapped it around his waist, and Jacaranda wanted to weep.

"Like what you see, Wyeth? I like what I see, too."

"You will not come any closer," she said, holding up a hand.

He stopped in his tracks. "Suppose not. I'd like it much better were you the one to do the approaching."

"In God's name why?" She couldn't keep her eyes averted, much as common sense was screeching at her to do just that. When she looked, she wanted to touch, and if she touched, she'd want to *be* touched.

"A fellow needs to know his attentions are welcome," he said, subsiding onto the raised stone hearth. "What better sign of welcome than when a woman makes the overtures?"

"I thought you understood I am not interested in your overtures." With the last of her resolve, she turned her face so the brim of her bonnet took him from her sight, and that was…a mercy.

"You're interested in my overtures. You're not interested in earning coin by returning them. I applaud your scruples. The alternative makes a great deal of sense to me upon sober reflection."

Sober reflection eluded Jacaranda where Worth Kettering was concerned. "A great deal of sense?"

"I'm not without sense, Wyeth, but I am without clothes. Why don't you come investigate the bargain I'm offering?"

"What bargain?"

She was reduced to inane questions, in part because he'd chosen that moment to cross the room and crack a window, the better to help the fire in the hearth catch. The Italian masters hadn't sculpted a man as breathtaking as Worth Kettering. He was a mature David, he was Vulcan, he was the exponent of all that was attractive and dangerous in a healthy adult male.

And he was nigh naked in a secluded cottage *with her*.

"That should draw better," he said. "I'd suggest getting you out of your wet things, but then you'll stay in them until lung fever carries you off. I'm not sure what motivated you to keep your bonnet on indoors, though."

She resumed tugging at the infernal bonnet, but the ribbons were damp, which made working the knot difficult. "I'm not as wet as you. You were out in the rain longer."

"If you need help with your bonnet, I am happy to oblige." He bounced down onto the bed, and the creaking of the ropes had Jacaranda's insides bouncing as well. "You brought a brush in your reticule, didn't you?"

"Comb. I can see to myself." Though when she removed her bonnet, she would look a fright.

He flopped back on the mattress so his legs hung over the side of the bed, and his words were addressed to the rafters.

"I may not have moved in quite the highest circles, but I am gentleman enough that you must know I wouldn't force you. Let me get rid of that bonnet for you, Wyeth. You fancy it, and it's fetching, in a rural sort of way. At the rate you're going, you will soon be bald and the bonnet fit only for consumption by William the Famous Draft Sow."

He wouldn't force her. Jacaranda could be stark naked and the only woman left on earth, and he wouldn't ever force her. That realization settled her down enough that she gave up ruining her bonnet and her coiffure.

"Come here, closer to the fire." He sat up and patted the bed beside him, hiking a knee onto the mattress.

"How can you be so casual about being nearly…about being undressed like that?" She lowered herself to the mattress as if it were not up to her weight, as if it might start moving without notice.

He shifted, and the bed bounced. "I can strut about as God made me because I am a man in the presence of a female who likes the look of me unclothed. Then too, my clothes are wet, and wet clothes don't flatter much of anybody. Damned uncomfortable, too, and in the most inconvenient locations. How many pins do you use, for pity's sake?"

"My hair is thick and takes a lot of pins."

But not so many that his deft fingers couldn't work under the brim of the bonnet to withdraw the offending pins that snared the bonnet onto her head. He set the pins on the bedside table, lifted the bonnet away, and her hair went tumbling down her back in a single thick braid.

"You have the knack of smelling luscious, Wyeth." He buried his nose in a handful of her hair. "Diabolical of you."

"You have the same knack. Few men do. Will you sniff at me all afternoon, or surrender my bonnet?" She'd prefer the sniffing, of course. Vastly prefer it.

He rose and hung her bonnet on a nail along the same rafter that held his clothing, then returned to the bed. "You're still sporting a few pins, and when attending a lady, I am nothing if not thorough."

She didn't feel so much as a tug or a yank on her scalp as he withdrew the last pins from her braid. He was that careful with her—or that experienced at tending to a woman's hair. She was still marveling at his skill when a boom of thunder literally shook the cottage.

"I hate storms," she said, hunching in on herself. "In Dorset, we don't get the Atlantic storms they do in Devon and Cornwall, or not so many, but we get the Channel weather, and it's bad enough."

"You're safe here, Wyeth." His arm came around her shoulders, and his lips applied themselves to her temple. "Perfectly safe."

He sat back a moment later, and Jacaranda wondered what that embrace had been about. Reassurance? When he was wearing only a *towel*? His arms had been warm and strong about her, and the reassurance in his voice had been convincing.

"My mother died in a storm," she said, back to him. "She was out on the water with a boating party, and the weather came up suddenly. Some of them made it back, but she wasn't a good swimmer."

He brushed a hand over her nape. "I am sorry, love. How old were you?"

"I was nearly three, Grey was six, Will about five."

"I was eight when my mother died. There's no good age for a child to lose a mother."

"You think about Avery losing Moira, don't you?" She did not glance over her shoulder, for the conversation had taken an unlikely turn, though she preferred it to his ridiculous banter.

"Of course I do." Another caress, this one pretending to tuck a lock of hair over her ear. "I think of Yolanda, losing both parents, and I realize whatever differences I might have had with my father, he at least did me the courtesy of surviving until I was able to make my own way in the world. Parents are supposed to see to that much."

He regretted the terms on which he'd parted from his father. Jacaranda could hear his regret, could feel it in his hand tracing the curve of her shoulder.

"I had my papa until I was seventeen, and my step-mother is still at home." Though Jacaranda wondered who was running Grey's domicile, for dear Step-Mama hadn't the knack.

"She was left with a lot of children. A lot of boys." Another slow caress, this time under her damp braid, over her nape.

"She was, but Grey was down from university before Papa died, and Step-Mama hasn't had to manage all the boys herself. Grey takes his responsibilities seriously."

"As do you."

"Papa did too." She stifled a yawn, because those little touches of his and the rain on the roof were combining to send an insidious languor through her. Then too, the fire was warming the interior of the cottage nicely. "Papa told me he remarried to ensure Will and Grey wouldn't be overly burdened managing the family's holdings."

"You believed him?"

"Why wouldn't I?"

"Five extra spares, Jacaranda?" His tone held humor, and when she glanced at him over her shoulder, his eyes did as well.

"Papa was very conscientious." While Step-Mama was very delicate, if her letters were to be believed.

"Just as you are conscientious about my house?" His arms went around her again, and he pulled her back against the warmth of his chest.

"I try." Though he would have to find a successor for her soon. She ought to tell him so.

"You succeed beautifully."

When he complimented her like that, and held her this way, Jacaranda felt beautiful, too.

Trouble invariably had the ability to entice and please while promising certain disaster.

"The rain isn't letting up." She made the observation to fill the silence stretching between them, though she didn't move. He didn't either, but remained sitting behind her on the bed.

"Which means that rickety little excuse for a bridge might be washing out," he said. "If I were you, I really would get out of that wet dress, Jacaranda Wyeth. Keep your chemise on if you want, but don't take a chill for the sake of modesty. I first came upon you in sopping wet nightclothes, if you'll recall. I've seen your treasures, you've seen mine, and nobody has gone insane with thwarted lust."

He had seen her treasures, or all but, and the dress *was* damp.

"I do not want to encourage your wrongheaded notions," she said, getting off the bed. "Neither do I consider myself the stuff of insane lust."

Or even sane lust.

"I could not imagine encouraging your wrongheaded notions." He lifted the covers and scooted under. "What? My clothes are wet, and unless you want me prancing about in a towel—which I'd be happy to do, so greatly do I seek to court your notice—then the least ridiculous place for me to be is under these covers."

He tossed his loin-towel onto the hearth and made a great display of getting comfortable under the covers.

"What am I to be doing, prancing around in my shift while you stay warm and cozy?" She started to unbutton her bodice, back turned to him, when his voice came floating over her shoulder.

"You should join me in this nice, cozy bed. We've much to discuss."

"Such as?" Her impending remove to Dorset wasn't something she'd bring up unless she was fully clothed and her hair neatly pinned.

"How you like your pleasures, for one thing. How I like mine, for another."

"I *will not* be your mistress."

"No, but that leaves sensible alternatives, which I am prepared to offer you. Come to bed, love, so we might discuss them like sensible, if nearly naked, adults. It's time you had a little of what you want out of this life."

That was such a startling pronouncement, Jacaranda had no ready retort. With her back to him, she mentally reviewed his words, for a trap lurked among them somewhere—and a truth.

"I have a great deal of what I want in this life," she said, getting back to her unbuttoning.

"I'm sure you've told yourself that." A pillow suffered a solid blow. "I've kissed you, my dear, more than once. You're hungry for a man, you might as well admit it."

*Love. My dear.* "I'm hungry for a— You are beyond audacious." Though he was not wrong. She was hungry for one man in particular, drat him.

"Taking you a long while to get out of a simple walking dress, Jacaranda Wyeth."

"Just Wyeth will do. How can I share a bed with you when you're talking such rot?"

"How can you not?" She heard the bed creak and suspected he'd rolled over to inspect her progress. "You take a chill easily, and I give off a deal of heat. Come to bed, and we'll talk."

"Close your eyes."

He did, the soul of docility, as she peeled out of her damp dress, hung it on yet another handy nail, got off her damp stays—thank God for old-fashioned jumps—and gingerly lifted the covers to climb in.

"Don't make me regret this."

"I said we'd talk, Jacaranda. You know my mouth is good for at least that."

She saw no point in arguing with him when he wasn't making any sense, neither did she scold him for the use of her given name.

"So talk to me, my dear." He rolled to his side, closer to her. She ought to flop to her side, give him her back, and start discussing the Damuses' marriageable daughters. "Tell me what pleasures you enjoy the most."

What sort of question was that? "I adore a perfect cup of tea. You?"

"We're English. Of course we must have our tea. Tell me something you like that you haven't shared with another, ever."

His voice blended with the patter of the rain and the crackle of the fire to invite confidences Jacaranda might yield to him, if she could only figure out his objective. "What is this in aid of?"

"Because we're to be intimate, Jacaranda Just-Wyeth-Will-Do. I'll not talk of coin, I'll not pester and flirt, I'll simply give you the pleasure you want, on your terms. You've won, love. I'm capitulating to your very sensible view of the matter. Have your way with me."

"I've won?"

"That's right." He traced her hair-line with a single finger. "From this moment forth, my duties include your regular and profound pleasuring, so start my instruction."

Regular *and* profound pleasuring? "When did you make this decision?"

One moment he was lying at her side, sleepily perusing her, the next he was over her, crouched like a tiger guarding a juicy meal. She had only an instant to meet his gaze, to see the startling heat and purpose in his eyes, before his lips were firmly moving over hers.

He tangled a hand in her hair to prevent her from evading him, but when the first moment of surprise wore off, the worse shock set in: Jacaranda didn't *want* to evade him. She didn't want to talk, she didn't want to reason, she most assuredly didn't want to flirt.

She wanted *him*.

And he was offering himself *on her terms*.

His kiss gentled as that realization brought her arms around his shoulders and had her seeking his mouth with her own.

"Better," he muttered.

It *was* better, better without many clothes, better in a bed, better with the rain pattering steadily on the roof and all the privacy in the world. Her hands went questing all over his back, learning the smooth, warm map of muscle and bone. She curled her fingers over his biceps, holding on hard as his tongue made teasing forays into her mouth.

And legs! A revelation, to learn that a kiss could even involve her longest, strongest limbs. The ones she'd wanted to twine around him on the bridge, the ones she could clutch about his flanks so tightly now.

The kiss built, like a fire finding a nice, cool draft to feed on, spreading out through her body, taking over her reason. She sank her hands into his hair and arched her hips up, only to meet a hard column of flesh against her belly.

"Easy," he murmured against her neck.

"We have to stop," she said, even as she got a hand over his muscular backside and clutched him hard.

"We do?"

"We're not married."

He smiled against the juncture of her shoulder and her neck. "Then we'll stop soon, but because we're here for your pleasure, we'll see to a few details first."

Jacaranda had seven brothers. She'd overheard a lot, and she knew there could be pleasure for women, for some women. Wicked, lucky women. She went quiet beneath him and smoothed a hand through his hair.

Worth Kettering would give her this pleasure, on her terms.

She shouldn't.

She absolutely shouldn't.

But his discretion was utterly trustworthy, and when would Jacaranda

Wyeth, aging spinster, rural housekeeper, *ever* have the chance to learn of these pleasures, if not with him? It wasn't that men like Worth Kettering came along so seldom, it was that they never came along. *Never.* Not in Dorset, not in Surrey, not in London's most fashionable ballrooms, not anywhere Jacaranda Wyeth had been or would be in the future.

She repeated the caress, not for him, though he seemed to like it, but for her. She found pleasure in simply stroking his hair, feeling the silky clean abundance of it slipping through her fingers. He closed his eyes and moved into her hand.

"You will show me these details, Worth Kettering, but we cannot… That is, I don't see how, without…"

"Bless you. Trust me, we won't. I won't. This is for you."

His voice had changed to a husky whisper, his body above hers became somehow languid, his muscles softer and more sinuously powerful. Under the covers Jacaranda went from warm to hot.

Wonderfully hot with a slow, spreading excitement that started in her middle and had her sighing against his chest.

"I'll show you." He sipped at the spot below her ear. "You'll let me show you."

She tucked a leg around his hips. "Show me soon, please?"

"Not soon." He lifted up, and no smile lit his handsome features. "This is for you, and we'll do it right. I promise you that, and I keep my word."

She hid her face against his throat as one of his big hands cradled the back of her head.

He held her like that, sheltered by his warm, naked body and tucked snugly against his strength. In the middle of all the pleasure and wonder and curiosity, Jacaranda withstood a spike of…hurt, of loneliness for herself, for all the times she'd needed to be comforted and treasured and *known* thus, and it had been denied her.

Daisy had this precious intimacy. Had had it whenever she pleased for the past five years.

"Hold on to me." His voice was raspy, and then he rolled them so she straddled him.

She burrowed down onto his chest, for if she sat up, her breasts would be very much on display, despite her shift. "This is novel."

"You are shy. One would not have surmised this, given how you campaign around the house like Wellington on a forced march."

His hands moved on her, stroking her hair, her back, her shoulders. God help her, there was pleasure in these simple caresses. Pleasure, comfort, and something soothing.

Caring?

"I cannot help my size. Or my name."

"What has your name to do with the matter?" He gathered her closer. A hug, but more than a hug, too.

"My brothers are creative little intellects, and my name was an endless challenge to them."

"So you were Jack the Giant?"

"And Jack Boots. Jackanapes, Beanstalk, and all manner of unflattering appellations. I honestly do prefer Wyeth. Grey says my mother called me that."

"She called you by your last name? I suppose that's better than my father's appellation for me."

"Which was?"

"Spare. Hess he referred to exclusively by his title, and I was Spare. 'Spare, why aren't you at lessons?' That sort of thing."

"You have such a beautiful name." She murmured his name because that was a pleasure, too. "Worth Reverence Kettering."

He closed his eyes, and she feared she'd misstepped, but then his arms closed around her again. Perhaps the unforeseen spikes of loneliness were not unique to her.

She leaned forward and kissed him, intending it as a comfort to him, to them both, but then his palm cradled her jaw, and he shifted his body, bringing his erect flesh up against her sex. With his tongue and his hips, he started a slow, undulating rhythm, and she fell into it, moving with him, catching his sighs in her mouth, giving him her own.

"Let me touch you," he whispered, slipping that hand from her jaw to her collarbone. "Lift up one inch, Wyeth. I want to touch you."

"Close your eyes," she said, for she knew good and well where he sought to put his hand. She lifted up, letting her own hands trail over his shoulders and chest. "You are beautiful," she said. "Breathtakingly, unfairly beautiful. Why is such size handsome on a man and ungainly on a woman?"

His eyes opened, and she wanted to cross her arms over her breasts, but she also wanted, more than anything, to not be ashamed.

"Listen to me," he said, untying the bows down the front of her chemise, even as his gaze stayed locked with hers. "A man of my size can find few women who don't feel like dolls in my arms, much less in my bed. I've tried to find pleasure with the daintier females, Wyeth, but they cultivate an air of frailness that's at least partly genuine."

His words were so...so unexpected, Jacaranda didn't protest at his caresses to her bare midline.

"With a typical woman, I cannot express my passion," he went on. "I must move about carefully. And at the risk of forever losing your esteem, I have to say the fit with such women is abysmal. One can be joined at the mouth, or elsewhere, but both at the same time without contortions. For a man who takes his kissing as seriously as his swiving, the result is eternal frustration. *You are perfect.* I would not give up one iota of your height and strength, not if God Almighty promised me the earth to see it so."

He settled one hand over either breast. "You are perfect, Jacaranda Wyeth."

And then she was perfectly shocked, because he leaned up and put his mouth to one breast, while his bare hand fondled its twin. All the arousal he'd awakened previously danced inside her like cloud lightning on a hot summer night.

"Beautiful," he murmured, using his free hand to caress her ribs and stomach. "Perfect, marvelous, and lovely."

He didn't merely kiss her breasts, didn't simply take her nipples one by one into the heat of his mouth, he *made love* to her. He pumped fresh air on the internal conflagration of her arousal, then shifted his hand down, and down, and conjured white-hot sparks with just his thumb.

She flinched.

"Settle, love." He stroked his thumb over a particular knot of feminine flesh again, deliberately, letting her become accustomed to such an intimate caress, though Jacaranda feared there was no becoming accustomed to the sensations he evoked.

Somebody groaned, a soft, tormented exhalation.

"Stay with me, Wyeth." He tugged gently on her nipple with his teeth. "Let me give you this."

"Too much." She hung her head, while moving her hips minutely against his hand.

"Let yourself have this pleasure of me," he said, his words harsh and soft at the same time. A span of seconds went by, the only sounds the slight creaking of the bed ropes, the rain, the fire in the hearth, and Jacaranda's breath, coming more and more quickly.

"Worth?"

"Let it"—another delicate nip—"happen."

"Blessed, everlasting, merciful...*Worth*..."

Her body seized with pleasure, burned with it, consumed her with it. He drove his finger up into her, and the pleasure roared hotter and harder, shaking her like thunder shakes even a sturdy structure.

She might have shouted his name, she might have whispered it.

Jacaranda curled onto Worth's chest fraught moments later, panting and dazed, grateful for his arms around her and the beat of his heart beneath her ear. She could not speak, and her body still hummed with the sensations he'd caused.

While her mind was in complete eclipse.

Of all the kindnesses Worth had shown her, she accounted his silence as foremost among them. When she awoke from her doze, she was still sprawled on his chest, his hands still moving slowly on her back and shoulders.

"You're with me again?"

"I am awake," she said, hiding her face against his neck.

"And?"

"And what?"

The rain pounded down on the roof, the fire crackled cheerily, and Jacaranda blushed mightily.

"Will I do, Wyeth? A man can't be kept in suspense about these things, and most of us fellows take to direction on this one limited matter surprisingly well."

"I cannot think how to respond." Understatement, or perhaps cowardice, so she tried harder for honesty. "I cannot think at all."

"That is an acceptable reply, but don't fret. We'll have years to learn one another's pleasures." He kissed her temple, and Jacaranda knew she ought to take exception to something he'd said.

*Years.*

"Years?" She made the monumental effort to lever up and beheld a man in the grip of an ominous kind of cheer. "What do you mean, years?"

"We have chemistry." He patted her bottom. "We won't be like some couples who are lucky to make it past the honeymoon without a disgust of each other."

She swung her leg over his hips and scooted back against the headboard so they weren't touching. "What honeymoon?"

"Whatever honeymoon you want. Suppose it depends on when we tie the knot, but Portugal is lovely in the autumn. I contemplated matrimony once before, as a much younger fellow, if you'll recall. Even then, I didn't favor a long engagement."

"Tie the knot?" She drew the covers up under her arms, while he lay recumbent beside her, arms behind his head. His smile was a little too smug, and the downy fur of his armpits a little too masculine—and much too intimate.

A lot too masculine.

"You can't think we're obligated to marry now," she said. "Even I know what happened in this bed cannot start a baby."

"Wyeth, I said we'd do this your way. I said you'd have what you wanted. You won." He sat up, too, no longer smiling but just as masculine. "We'll marry."

"I don't recall you proposing," she shot back. "I don't recall you asking for my opinion on this lifelong commitment."

"You're a female." He nodded once as if to assure himself of his conclusion. "You're a decent female with whom I intend to have relations, ergo, you sought marriage. I'm offering, you'll accept, and we'll *have* relations. I'm more sure of that than ever."

"I did not seek marriage," she said, quietly, vehemently. "I am attracted to you, true, badly, badly attracted. And it won't serve, I know that as well. But if I sought anything, it was in the nature of what you just willingly shared with me, and I thank you for it."

"You sought merely to dally? *With me?*"

She nodded, not sure what all his question revealed, or what it concealed. He'd sought marriage—*with her?*

"You are rejecting my perfectly honorable offer of marriage?"

He was honorable, damn him, while she was purely, utterly flustered. He posed a simple question, while she could not think, for all the emotions, untruths, and complications whirling inside her.

"Marriage would never work, not between us." And she'd never be able to explain to Grey, much less to Step-Mama why all her promises to come home had to be broken.

Again. Worse, how would she explain to Worth that yet another woman hadn't been entirely honest with him?

"Marriage between us would work," Worth said, flipping the covers back. Naked, he came around the bed and snatched at his breeches. "It would work splendidly."

He leaned down, seized her chin in his fingers, and kissed her soundly. "It would."

The next thing Jacaranda heard was an ax biting into a solid length of wood, hard. The ax blows fell again and again, until a rumble of distant thunder obliterated the sound from her hearing.

# CHAPTER EIGHT

The storm moved off, until what came down was mostly moisture dripping from the canopy around the clearing where Worth wielded his ax.

Jacaranda Wyeth didn't want to marry him.

*Thunk!*

She'd have her pleasure of him, then cast him aside.

*Thunk!*

She'd dictate her terms, and he was supposed to meekly abide by them.

*Thunk!*

He was to content himself with bodily intimacy only.

*Thunk!*

No commitment, no future, nothing to rely on…

*God in heaven.*

He put up the ax and gathered the split logs along with the detritus of his anger, for he was whining like a rejected opera dancer.

No, he was whining like a society lady propositioned and thoroughly enjoyed by one *Honorable* Worth Kettering, then promptly set aside so he might prowl for fresh game the next night.

Or later that same evening.

God's holy nightgown.

He sat on the back steps of the cottage, abruptly tired. The overgrown forest around him was beautiful, and his, and yet what did it mean? Woods meant some warmth, the occasional harvest of lumber, some fresh game, all of which his coin would buy him easily.

His coin would not buy him Jacaranda Wyeth, though, not as a mistress and apparently not as a wife.

And still, sitting on that hard plank of oak, what he wanted was her sitting beside him, her hair tickling his nose, her soft lavender scent wafting on the damp air.

"The rain's letting up."

How long had she been standing at the door, watching him rust his brain with futile thoughts?

"I could use a spot of tea, if there's any to be had." Anything to get her from his sight. Her hair was back in its tidy coiffure. She wore her chemise, his shirt clutched around her, leaving a portion of feet and calves—beautiful feet and beautiful calves—exposed to torment him.

The sight of her brought him a curious blend of lust and shame, for she had rejected him.

Was this how his former amours felt toward him? Covetous, but angry?

He fumed and steamed and pouted for a while longer, but when Jacaranda brought him a mug of honey-sweetened tea, he thanked her cordially and even smiled a bit.

Because by then—he was nothing if not tenacious, *she* had admitted as much—his pride had reasserted itself, his brain had come back to life, and he'd begun to once again plot a means of achieving his objective.

* * *

Worth Kettering was up to something. The scowling man who'd kissed Jacaranda so passionately before he'd left the cottage had turned into a smiling, cordial, gratingly good-natured fellow.

He thanked her for the tea.

He put his shirt back on when she handed it to him.

He suggested they raid the hamper while the rain tapered off, as if they were merely having a parlor picnic, not trying to put a serious misstep behind them.

While they ate, he told her stories about his clients, nothing truly embarrassing, and never naming names.

He helped her tidy up the remains of their meal.

"Is this your way of apologizing?" she asked, putting the lid on the butter crock. "Treating me to your party manners? You needn't."

"I'm the helpful sort." He passed her the butter knife. "I misread the situation, and I can apologize for that. It doesn't happen often, but at least this time, the only negative consequences devolved to me. You got what you wanted—or did you? Be honest, Wyeth, for I cannot abide dissembling females."

She set the butter crock on the table and rose. "I am not accustomed to such frank talk. I suppose you are."

Was it dissembling to not disclose even her real name?

He kept to his seat, which was a relief. If he started purring in her ear, or touching her again, she'd likely spout whatever drivel he wanted to hear.

"Between lovers, a certain openness is usually expected." He lounged in his chair, one arm casually hooked over the back. "I assume that's what you want of me, a lover?"

The question was as casual as his pose, but Jacaranda knew if she dared to meet his gaze, she'd see a light in his eyes that wasn't casual at all.

"I am out of my depth," she said, needing to see those eyes anyway. "I do not know exactly what has transpired between us. Your attentions felt good at the time, and the experience has left me off-kilter. I'm not sure what's to be gained by discussion. This cannot happen again."

"Pity." He affected a look of bewildered regret, which she did not believe for one instant. "I thought it went rather well, though I assumed you were inspecting a prospective husband, not a prospective lover."

"Not a lover." She barely got the word out, hugging her now-dry shawl closer.

He wrinkled his nose, as if catching a rank scent. "A casual romp then? They have their place, I suppose."

"Not a romp. Not anything beyond a misbegotten moment." An indulgence.

"So the most intense pleasure you've ever experienced is to mean nothing, Wyeth? Those passionate kisses and your body so trustingly naked against mine—nothing?"

His tone danced between puzzled and wounded, but now he had on his solicitor's negotiating face, and Jacaranda resumed her seat.

"I don't know what such an encounter means. Perhaps it should mean nothing. We did not... We are not lovers." He wanted honesty from her, she'd give him honesty—up to a point. Were she to acquaint him with her circumstances in every honest detail, he'd send her off to Dorset in his traveling coach before sundown, because Worth Kettering would not dally with an earl's unmarried daughter.

"I would like to be your lover." He ran a pinkie finger around the edge of the jam jar and licked a dab of preserves from his fingertip. "On that, we have both been clear, I think. You wanted something when you climbed into that bed with me, Wyeth. The question is, what?"

The quiet around them held a quality Jacaranda hadn't experienced before, patient, warm, and even a little comfortable, and it had to do with what had passed between them in that bed—so trustingly.

And with Worth's present efforts to forge an understanding with her regarding the same experience.

More honesty, then.

"I wanted to know what it was like." Jacaranda put the lid on the jam jar lest she trace the same path around the rim he had. "The curiosity doesn't go away, the wanting, simply because nobody offers you marriage. If I'm to be a spinster, I at least want to be a spinster who knows what passion can be like."

"You're a virgin?"

She shook her head, overwhelmed all over again by regrets that had plagued her for five years.

"Your previous experiences were not memorable?"

Oh, she could recall every detail of those experiences. "The whole business was disappointing. Very, very disappointing. I was disappointing."

"That is not possible," he retorted, and when she looked up, he was smiling at such an absurdity. "You could not possibly disappoint. Put the blame on the idiot who disappointed *you*, Wyeth. That's where it belongs." He patted her hand, as a friend might, and Jacaranda suspected her ignorance had been even greater than she'd supposed.

"I want you to think about something for me," he said, withdrawing his hand. "Think about what you want, and while you consider that, I will offer you what I believe that might be."

She wanted to tell him the truth without risking that he'd be disappointed in her. She wanted to go home to Dorset that instant. She wanted to kiss him as she dragged him back to the unmade bed. "What do you think I want?"

"An intimate friend, a man you can trust to see to your pleasure without making demands. Someone with whom you can learn about passion, someone who will respect your every confidence and honor your trust, even as you honor his."

She closed her eyes, because he'd articulated more than she dared to admit, even to herself. And yet, the intimate, trusting friendship he described had abruptly become more unattainable than ever.

"My family expects—"

"Don't give me an answer." He traced a pattern over her knuckles, once, but Jacaranda had new respect for his tactile flirtations. "I have made the offer. You consider it at your leisure. Consider it indefinitely, if you like."

"Your offer is dangerous," she said, sliding her hand to her lap. "Children result from such offers."

"I gave you pleasure now without risking conception, Wyeth, and that was a mere taste of what you can have, if you want it. I would never risk your reputation, not even for your pleasure. We've already come some way toward developing that friendship, and we can't undo what's happened today. I'd rather build on it."

"You wanted marriage." So had she once upon a time—look how that had ended. "I will not remain at my post in your employ forever, you know. My family needs me, and they demand with increasing urgency that I return to

Dorset."

"I offered marriage, thinking you sought a husband. What honest man of your acquaintance actually wants marriage? Have your brothers galloped up the aisle, one after another?"

No, they had not, not a one of them, not even Grey, and a wife would spare him much. If Grey were married, his pleas for Jacaranda to come home would carry much less weight.

Though what woman would marry Grey, knowing she'd have to put up with six other men in her household? Most of those fellows were Step-Mama's *sons*, and what they knew collectively about respecting female authority could fill a thimble halfway.

"I'm only a housekeeper, and you'll be back to Town in a couple of months at the latest. You've your pick of gently bred ladies to marry and married ladies to dally with—or opera dancers. Why are my desires important to you?"

He put the butter crock into the hamper. "I've inspected that inventory, and they've inspected me. They're bored and ornamental, and most of them excessively dainty. Even the taller ladies don't want their hair mussed on any occasion, and all that dodging about, pretending a mere passing acquaintance on the dance floor, is tedious. Puts a crimp in a fellow's style to be ignored the moment a title goes waltzing by."

*I cannot express my passion.* What would Worth Kettering's passion be like? Not merely his kisses, but *all* of him?

"What you want, Wyeth, is important to me because I want *you*. Simple and unflattering to the male of the species, but the truth. Your wants and mine can overlap, though, and to our mutual satisfaction. I leave the decision in your hands."

He rose, then leaned down and kissed her forehead, bringing his scent and warmth close for a mere instant.

"The rain has stopped," he said, straightening. "Let's get you dressed, bank the fire, and see about getting home, shall we?"

And so, for the first time in her life, Jacaranda was assisted into her clothing by a man, one who knew all about tapes and hooks and the proper sequence for attiring a lady. His assistance was impersonal, but not in the same way a maid's might have been. Worth's aid was a friendlier version, with a little less detachment, but no more presumption.

She liked it.

She liked that he knotted her shawl right under her breasts, but didn't touch her breasts. She liked that he laced her boots, but didn't try to move her skirts aside when he touched her ankles. She liked that he tied her bonnet ribbons, but didn't kiss her as he was leaning down to do so.

And then matters grew even worse.

He asked her to heft the second shaft on the buggy, and between the two of them, they managed to wrestle the vehicle around before hitching Goliath back into the harness. Worth—he was Worth to her, at least for now—hadn't asked her to stand by, pretending her hems weren't ruined. He'd asked her to lend her strength to get them home.

All the way back to Trysting, Jacaranda tried to talk herself out of considering this offer made by her employer. She knew the flaw in it—the flaw in herself. She'd said she wanted to *know* how intimacies with Worth Kettering felt, but beneath that honest admission came another. She wanted to *be* known, to be recognized and desired as a woman, not as a housekeeper, or useful step-daughter or a sister, bound to return home at summer's end.

The first, the bodily pleasure, she had resisted for years. Now that she'd had a sample, she could see the temptation. The sensations were hot, lush, overwhelming, and wonderful—but soon over. The second, though, that yearning loneliness to be *known*, to be valued and cherished, it had been her downfall in the past, and she'd sworn it wouldn't be ever again.

Not ever.

* * *

The business of teasing Wyeth into his arms felt all too familiar. Worth was a master of the chase, of the quick riposte and elegant parry, the flirtatious innuendo and sly double meaning. Except this time, the whole exercise was fraught. He wasn't enjoying it, not the way he should be.

He wasn't enjoying the pursuit because he wasn't engaged in a fencing match only to the first touch. He dared not admit as much to his quarry, but he was *courting* his housekeeper, and if one activity in his life had ever ended badly, it was courting.

He announced his intention to depart for London at dinner, then tucked Avery in, complete with an extravagant fuss over the wonderful scent of her Manka.

Then he sought to take private leave of his intended, whether she admitted of the distinction or not.

Jacaranda wasn't in her chambers. He had to search for half an hour, but eventually he thought to look in the logical location on a warm summer night. He was halfway down the garden path when a form stepped out of the shadows.

"Fine night for a stroll, isn't it, sir?"

Roberts, his stable master, emerged from the gloom of a tall privet hedge, a pipe between his teeth. The man was a human mountain, more than competent with farriery, and he had the slow, relaxed movements that soothed fractious beasts of any size.

Except, perhaps, a fractious employer intent on trysting with the housekeeper.

"You're out for a smoke, Roberts?"

"Most nights." Roberts took the pipe from his mouth. "So the entire family will be gathering soon?"

"The entire…" God in heaven, the man was right. When Hess joined them, four Ketterings would dwell under one roof. A veritable gathering of the clans, by their standards. "Yes, I suppose. Well, I'll be on my way. Enjoy your smoke."

"It's good," Roberts said, not budging from the path, "when family comes together. Better that way."

"For some families. When did I hire you, Roberts?"

"You didn't." He smiled slightly and stuck his pipe back in his mouth. "She did."

Across the garden, Jacaranda's pale nightclothes revealed that her swim was over and she was marching directly for the kitchen door.

Worth was too late. He considered applying a punishing right cross to Roberts's smug smile.

"What do you suppose she was doing out here?" Worth asked. "It's late to be wandering the gardens."

Roberts shrugged massive shoulders. "Perhaps she was in want of a smoke. If you're thinking to ask her, though, you'd best be waiting until morning. Sleep tight."

He sauntered off at the deliberate pace of a plough horse, one that needed no momentum to move a substantial load forward, only sheer strength in telling abundance.

Jacaranda Wyeth, the housekeeper, had hired the man?

Jacaranda, who wasn't a virgin, but who had been disappointed?

Worth shuddered at the idea of such a brute disporting with Wyeth, though in truth Roberts had no height or reach over him, just bulk.

Brute bulk, Worth told himself as he repaired to the house. Inelegant, horse-scented brute bulk, such as would never appeal to a lady of Wyeth's refinements.

* * *

Worth—*Mr. Kettering* was leaving in the morning, and to Jacaranda, his departure would bring both relief and regret. He'd asked her to consider his offer at her leisure, but there was nothing to consider, really.

She told herself that and willed herself to believe it. The day had been long, tiring, and difficult. Tomorrow, with him gone, would be easier.

Sleep evaded her relentless pursuit, so she heard the door to her sitting room creak open.

An intruder? Then a faint, cedary scent came to her.

*Him.*

"What an accommodating little thing you are, Wyeth, curled up on one side of the bed." The mattress dipped as he lifted the covers and joined her. "Your hair is damp. Surely you could have used my assistance to brush it out for you?"

"I was sleeping, if you don't mind." She rolled to her side, giving him her back.

"I couldn't sleep, not without telling you I'll miss you when I'm away."

His hand, slow, soothing and warm, traced over her nape and shoulders.

She would have decades to catch up on her sleep, to miss him and his touch.

"You could have told me at breakfast, or tonight after dinner," she said, and despite all her intentions to the contrary, a soft sigh followed the words. He wouldn't miss her. He was just being Worth.

"I would not have others overhear such sentiments," he said, moving his hand down along her spine then back up. "Nor would I keep you from your slumbers. Go to sleep, my dear."

"With you in my bed?"

"I'm harmless, Wyeth, unless you command it otherwise. Consider me an errant house cat who seeks to warm himself on your quilt, nothing more."

"You're too good at this, and you don't belong in my bed." But a crisp, scolding tone eluded her, and her words sounded as wistful as she felt. Angels abide, that hand of his was melting her bones and weighting her eyelids, and entirely, entirely too wonderful.

"Hush." His lips grazed her shoulder. "You need your sleep, and tomorrow will come soon enough."

"Sufficient unto the day…"

She let the words trail off as she sank into a cloud of ease and relaxation. He shifted closer, close enough she could feel his warmth, not so close he couldn't maneuver his hand all over her back.

Then he slid that hand down, to knead her backside, and the sheer bliss of it—and the proximity of sleep—had her sighing again. She recalled him slipping an arm around her waist sometime later, but then all she recalled were dreams.

And he joined her in those, too.

* * *

"Wyeth." Worth couldn't help a grin, because his lady was dressed, but her hair was unbound, a fly-away dark cloud of riotous corkscrews and ringlets hanging down to her hips and secured with only a simple ribbon. "My, you are a fetching sight so early in the day."

He made no move to touch her, because they were at the mounting block before the house, and a dozen pairs of eyes were no doubt glued to the window panes. He'd given his word he'd not jeopardize her reputation, and he always kept his word.

More to the point, if he put a single toe over that line, she'd dismiss him from her notice altogether. The high stakes were exhilarating, rather like a risky negotiation with several powerful parties at once.

"You've come to see me off," he suggested. "I'm touched."

"Enough of that." She shoved a wrapped parcel at him. "Take this with you, please. Mr. Henderson delivered it as a sample of Trudy's work, though she's capable of fancier pieces. And take this." A double sack, such as would go on either side of a saddle's pommel.

He gave her a puzzled look, but accepted both consignments.

"It's food," she said, crossing her arms. "For your journey. The posting inns have only indifferent fare, and luncheon is hours away."

She blushed, while Worth felt uncharacteristically self-conscious himself. With luck, he'd be in London by midday or shortly thereafter. That wasn't the point. No one attended his leave-takings, not since he'd first gone up to university. No one packed him food, no one came to see him off.

He was…touched.

"You'll keep an eye on the girls, Wyeth?" He turned as if to watch Roberts leading Goliath to the mounting block. "They've been here long enough to become bored, and that's not good."

"I'll keep an eye on them. Yolanda has discovered the library, and Avery is making some friends." She reached out as if to pat his lapel then snatched her hand back.

"Am I not quite presentable?"

"Your cravat." She loosened a fold of cloth beneath his jaw. "It worked its way under your waistcoat."

Then they spoke at the same time.

"I'll be back…"

"When will you…?"

He recovered first.

"Walk with me, Mrs. Wyeth? Roberts, I'll take Goliath now." He snatched the reins, tossed the sacks over the pommel, checked the girth, the fit of the bridle, then offered his free arm to his housekeeper only when Roberts had slowly ambled a good distance away.

"I shouldn't ask," she said. "The house will be in readiness whenever you return, if you return."

"Now what sort of friend would I be if I merely rode down the lane without even a wave farewell? Roberts is watching me like he's your jealous beau, else I would bow over your hand in parting. If you need anything in my absence, a groom can get word to me in a few hours."

"I'll remind the girls."

"I appreciate the provisions," he added, bending closer as if to hear her, but in truth sneaking a whiff of her hair. "I should be back by Wednesday. I'll send a note if I'm delayed."

"And if your brother shows up?"

"He'd best not. He'd have to move like lightning to get here so quickly, and Hess believes in enjoying the privileges of his station."

"If he shows up, we'll make him very welcome and send word."

He frowned down at her. She was quite pretty with her hair all a fright. "I really would like to kiss you, Wyeth. At least tell me you'll miss me. I expect that much honesty from you."

Oh, she scowled at that. Her swooping dark eyebrows drew together, and her mouth worked, evidence she was composing a wonderfully puritanical lecture regarding proper conduct between employer and employee. Then she curled her arm more closely around his.

"I'll miss you."

"Beg pardon? I couldn't quite hear you."

"You heard me. Now stop bothering me, and get on your horse."

"A stirring declaration if ever one graced my ears."

She dropped his arm, but now she was smiling, a soft, private smile that made him want to toss his housekeeper over his shoulder and send Goliath back to his stall.

"Be off with you," she said, stepping back. Now she was smiling *at* him. "Safe journey."

He touched the brim of his hat, swung onto his horse and cantered off down the drive. He was still savoring that smile and intermittently grinning like an idiot, when he reached his town house hours later.

\* \* \*

Jacaranda had felt like an idiot, standing at the mounting block as if she were someone who had a right to see Mr. Worth Kettering off on his journey. She was nothing, a mere housekeeper, and then he'd called himself her friend, and the early summer morning had become altogether lovely.

Worth Kettering's body housed several different men. One was the imperious, brilliant solicitor who expected immediate and unquestioning compliance with his every directive. That man was reasonable, if impatient, but he did not suffer fools.

Then there was the flirt, a reckless, heedless, strutting louse who in all likelihood left a trail of broken hearts from one end of Mayfair to the other. Jacaranda didn't approve of that fellow one bit.

Worth Kettering was a conscientious older brother, too, a man somewhat at a loss to know what duty required of him, but ready to do it for his sister and more than ready to step up to the challenge of raising his niece.

Jacaranda liked that Worth, and she respected him.

Then there was *her* Worth. An absolute puzzle, unlike any man she'd dealt with before. He desired her, intimately, but didn't force himself on her. He touched her, with his hands, and his body, and his mouth, and the feel of him was wonderful. His scent lingered, his warmth comforted, and his hands... Angels abide, his hands.

And that Worth—her Worth—was careful with her, and not only physically. He was sensitive to her pride and considerate of her in small, subtle ways, like not taking her hand while Roberts glowered from the mounting block.

*That* Worth was an irresistible combination of every naughty, lonely, spinster housekeeper's most closely guarded dreams. She needed time to gain perspective on him and on his infernal offer. Wednesday seemed much too soon, and an eternity to wait to see him again.

The solution to this situation was the same solution she'd employed many times in the past: *Stay busy*.

The next morning, Jacaranda had a lengthy list in her reticule, and Avery's hand in hers as they left their gig at the livery in Least Wapping. Yolanda was quiet beside them, but Jacaranda had the sense the girl was every bit as bright as her brother. Yolanda would notice everything and say little.

"Do you each have your pin money?" Jacaranda asked as they approached the market square.

Avery dropped Jacaranda's hand and reached for Yolanda's. "We do!"

"Then why don't you have a look around? I'm easy to spot, and I won't leave without you."

"We won't be gone long," Yolanda said as Avery tugged her off toward a table laden with the baked goods perfuming the morning air with their yeasty scent.

"So those are the Kettering ladies?" Thomas Hunter appeared at Jacaranda's side, a rangy fellow past the first blush of youth, with serious brown eyes and wavy wheat-blond hair.

"The older one is Miss Yolanda," Jacaranda said, though as an acknowledged sister to an earl, Yolanda might make her come out with the same consequence as a Lady Yolanda. "The younger is Miss Avery, a niece. How have you been, Thomas?"

"Managing. I've wondered if himself would pay a call on us."

"You're on the list, I assure you, but on our last attempt, we were thwarted by the weather."

He offered his arm, the sort of thing his neighbors wouldn't know to do, but he did, and Jacaranda let herself be escorted to a patch of shade at the side of the churchyard.

"Mayhap, Mrs. Wyeth, you and Mr. Kettering did make an attempt to visit, but found your way blocked by a tree?" He looked not at her, but rather at their friends and neighbors laughing, talking, and making their weekly purchases on the green.

"Thomas, does that hypothetical have a point?"

Jacaranda had always liked Thomas Hunter. He wasn't a sheep, waiting to be told where to graze, in what company, and for how long. He was on his way to owning a small holding, she was sure of it, and when he had his own land in hand, he'd make it amount to something.

Ambition in another she could respect. Thomas was also a devoted and patient father, and that she had to like.

"I consider myself your friend," he said quietly. "Not a close friend, but a friend nonetheless. You came when my youngest was ill and Gran had about given up."

"I will always come," Jacaranda started in, but he stopped her with a hand on her arm.

"That cottage near the property line. I use it from time to time for a little privacy. I like to read and to sketch." His ears turned red, and Jacaranda barely kept her surprise from showing. "I'm there fairly often, when we're between planting and harvest, but somebody else has used it, Mrs. Wyeth. Somebody else has made tea, chopped wood, built a fire, and made themselves at home."

Like a fist to the solar plexus, she deduced what he'd delicately implied.

Somebody had used the bed and forgotten to tidy it up.

*How* could she have been so careless? She was a *housekeeper*, had been nothing but a housekeeper for five long years.

"I believe Mr. Reilly has sought respite there on occasion," she said, her face heating. "Perhaps he was forgetful."

Thomas nodded to the vicar, who'd waved from the edge of the green. "His missus caught wind of his mischief. He hasn't set foot in the direction of my property for at least a year."

"A *year*?" This was news—bad news. "I wish you'd said something earlier. I would have sent him around."

"Why would I want to take time out of my busy day to tell Reilly what is common knowledge in the parish? The barley is doing fine, the wheat's a little slow, the pig had eight piglets, and my mare didn't catch until May, but that's acceptable, because the foal will have spring grass next year."

"Mrs. Wyeth!" Avery came bouncing along, towing Yolanda. "We found a man who sells books!" She went off into rapid, happy French, then dipped back into English, and finished with a few phrases of gesticulating Italian.

"Ladies." Jacaranda aimed a look at the younger girl. "May I make known to you Mr. Thomas Hunter, our neighbor and my friend. Mr. Hunter, Miss Yolanda Kettering, Miss Avery."

Yolanda offered an elegant curtsy, which prompted Avery into something between a bow and a curtsy.

"My pleasure, ladies, and perhaps I might escort you to the bookseller's stall.

I was headed that way myself." He offered Yolanda his arm, Avery his hand, and Jacaranda a polite bow.

The girls tripped off with him, Avery still squealing about the book of fairy tales—in English!—she'd decided to buy. Yolanda went along quietly, and yet Jacaranda saw speculation in the young woman's eyes.

Which left Jacaranda considering the question: Had Worth *known* they'd left the bed unmade, or had his wits been so scrambled that, like Jacaranda, he'd forgotten to protect their privacy with the simplest precautions?

# CHAPTER NINE

"You're the oldest daughter, right?" Worth put the question to Mary as she sat at his kitchen table, her feet up on a chair. "You were probably your mother's right hand."

"From little up." Mary sipped her tea, her rapturous expression suggesting she was savoring the first real tea she'd had in days. "I took as much burden from Ma as I could, until my sisters started coming along, and they're good workers. What was needed was more coin, so here I am."

"How are you feeling?" He dreaded her reply. She looked tired and pale and thinner in the face. That couldn't be good, but Jones hadn't yet discovered the name of the father. He would, though. Jones had yet to let Worth down.

"I'm doing well enough," Mary said, taking another sip of tea. "This settles my nerves, it does. I can feel myself coming to rights, to have a good cup of tea."

"Tea helps the digestion, which I would hazard has been troubling you?"

"A mite."

He topped up her cup and waited while she poured cream and sugar into it in quantity.

"I've a proposition for you," he said, pouring himself a cup and taking a seat at right angles to her. "Hear me out before you laugh in my face. I want to accomplish two things, and I think you can do both. The first matter relates to this household."

His plan was the best way to keep her safe, to get her the hell off her feet so the child she carried had a chance at health and a decent start in life. Then too, he'd become irrationally critical of the job his house steward was doing.

The back stoop sported mud from the mews and worse, for pity's sake.

The window in his bedroom stuck and screeched when he pried it open.

The kitchen floor near the sink was sticky, and when he thought back, it had always been sticky.

"Wants a hands and knees scrubbing," Mary said, rubbing her toe over the offending location. "Grease gets on it, then it half works into the wood, and it takes lye soap and hot water to lift it."

He toured the house with her, pointing out dozens of small lapses Jacaranda Wyeth would have set right in a heartbeat.

"I was in service for a few months when I first came to Town," Mary said when they were again gathered around the teapot. "Most of the girls make a try for service before they start dancing, though it's hard work. At least you have a roof over your head and some victuals."

"What happened?"

"Footmen, the man of the house, his sons, the tradesmen, a pack of humping louts, the lot of them, and a girl doesn't have to so much as flirt to be given the sack for the way a man looks at her. Don't suppose you've a biscuit on hand?"

"Finish your tea." He patted her hand and scavenged up a plate of shortbread that was less than a day old and brought up his second idea. She listened, munched her shortbread, and agreed to consider his offers.

What was it with women that they were all overcome by the need to deliberate perfectly sound propositions of late? Worth's musings were disturbed when Lewis came in looking like he'd distasteful news to impart.

"What is it?"

"We've a beggar in the mews, or I think he's a beggar, and he's asking for you."

"He's not asking for food or money?"

Lewis scratched his chin. "Claims he's not. Said he knows you're here, because your great, black beast is in the mews, and he'll keep coming back until you talk with him."

"You still think he's a beggar?" Worth turned down his cuffs as he rose. Some of his clients were from the highest tiers of society—he'd been to Carlton House that very morning—and some were not.

Still, he didn't recognize the weathered old salt at his back door.

The man stuck out a hand. "Name's Noonan. I used to sail with Captain Spicer, of the Drummond, years and years ago."

"I know Spicer," Worth said. "He's a good man, but the Drummond should have made port last week, and we fear for him." This was part of what he'd had to tell his regent earlier in the day. The meeting had lacked sorely for good cheer.

Noonan slapped a dusty cap against his thigh. "Fret not. Spicer was swilling rum at the same little out-of-the-way port where I laid up on Madagascar while his ship put in for repairs. They took bad storm damage, but lost not a hand."

"This is very, very good news," Worth said, thinking quickly. "The best news."

Noonan tugged the cap back on a balding pate, his grin conspiratorial. "The best news is that your cargo is in fine shape as well. Drummond said to tell you they should be along in a couple more weeks."

"Who else have you told?"

"Cap'n swore me to secrecy. Said to tell you myself and only you, and he'd consider his account with you even."

"Even it is," Worth said. "For your discretion, I'm prepared to offer you a one percent share in the venture, if you're interested?"

"As one old sailor who's weathered too many gales, of course I'm interested."

"Give me your direction. I'll send around the paperwork, but if you breathe a word of this to anyone, your share will soon be as worthless in truth as it's rumored to be now."

"I can take a secret with me to my grave, but I would like to call on Mrs. Spicer. She's no doubt heard the rumors as well."

"Leave that to me, and no matter what you hear, keep your mouth shut, and don't sell your share to anyone."

"Righty-o, mate." He turned to leave with a jaunty wave.

"Another moment of your time, Noonan. Captain Spicer's man deserves some decent sustenance and a spot of tea, unless you've pressing matters to see to?"

"I could do with a plate and pint, but I wouldn't put you to any trouble."

"This won't be trouble." Though it would be delicate, for Worth would not lie outright. "We're off to the local tavern, where we'll lament Spicer's apparent fate for any with ears to hear."

Noonan doffed his cap again and held it over his heart. "Too bad about old Spicer. He were a good sort, just took one too many chances."

"Pity," Worth said. "A real shame."

* * *

Worth was glad his schedule allowed for a leisurely midday meal, for old Noonan had done justice to many a pint. Now the game was well and truly on, because Spicer's sad fate had been toasted vociferously, until a pair of stevedores coming in from a hard morning on the docks had joined in. By next week, shares in the Drummond would be available for a farthing apiece, and shares were held in many, many hands.

Worth wanted to tell Jacaranda what was afoot, but he didn't dare put such tidings in a letter. He told neither Lewis, nor Jones, nor Mary, nor anybody.

Some of his clients had shares in the Drummond, the ones with enough to do a little high-risk investing, and Worth himself had invested heavily. The odds weren't as long as people thought, for the Drummond was stoutly constructed and the captain both experienced and sensible. The crew was made up of men who'd sailed with him on many occasions.

But still, Worth missed his housekeeper, missed that private smile she'd sent him off with, missed her summery, lavender scent, and her tart, unvarnished rejoinders.

He even missed his niece, and his sister, and the peaceful sense of repose Trysting offered for all who bided there.

When he returned to his town house, he sat at his desk, trimmed a quill pen, and considered what he could say that wouldn't offend the woman he was missing most.

*My Dear Mrs. Wyeth,*

That much wasn't offensive, and she was dear. She wasn't his, though—not yet. He finished the note anyway, sanded it, and passed it to a groom to take directly out to Surrey. When that task was complete, he contemplated what goal he should set once the Drummond had seen his holdings surpass the million-pound mark.

Oddly enough, that pleasant contemplation did not relieve him from wondering if his note would be answered.

* * *

"Come along, girls, unless you've more money to spend?" Jacaranda posed the question brightly, but a normally pleasant day at market had turned into something else.

Thomas Hunter suspected she'd trysted with her employer at that cottage. He hadn't said anything—he wouldn't—but already, Jacaranda and the man who *wasn't* her lover had been indiscreet.

"Please, Mrs. Wyeth." Avery gave her a big-eyed, pleading look. "May we not visit the sweet stall once again? I can buy Uncle some lemon drops, and maybe you would like some candied violets?"

"I'll take her," Yolanda offered. "We can meet you at the livery."

"Very well, but don't tarry, and no violets for me. We make our own at Trysting."

"Miss Kettering is a nice addition to the scenery," Thomas Hunter said, his gaze following Yolanda's retreating skirts with a particular male appreciation.

"She's sixteen, Thomas. She's not receiving yet."

"My wife was fifteen and *not receiving* when we started walking out. Don't worry, I know my place. If you're headed to the livery, I'll walk you."

He winged his arm, and Jacaranda had no choice but to take it.

"About our earlier discussion." He didn't have to dip his head to talk to her, because they were of a height. "You must pass along something to Mr. Kettering for me."

"If I can."

He kept walking steadily, farther away from the market crowd.

"Tell him…" Thomas glanced around. "Tell him I know a man gets lonely and has needs, but he'd best not trifle with a lady who can't manage what he's after. Kettering is a Town man and probably thinks the women here are like all those tarts in London—"

Oh, this was worse, much worse, than if Thomas had been scolding her directly.

"Thomas," she interrupted him. "You've made your point, but Mr. Kettering is the soul of probity with the maids and so forth. He is a gentleman."

Tom patted her hand as they approached the livery. "Gentlemen are often the worst of the sorry lot." Jacaranda saw plain as day in Thomas's dark brown eyes that he knew exactly who'd been in that cottage with Worth Kettering. He wasn't guessing, he wasn't surmising. He knew.

"What gave me away?"

He muttered something low and profane. "The sheets bore your fragrance, lavender and mille fleurs. No other lady in this shire bears quite that scent, and himself left behind a fancy monogrammed handkerchief. I'll call him out, Jacaranda Wyeth, I swear I will if he's taking advantage."

"He's not taking advantage. How do you know mille fleurs, Thomas?"

"You aren't the only one rusticating here in Surrey, Mrs. Wyeth, but you're the one holding my landlord's estate together, and I can't have mischief befalling you. I'll be up to Trysting to meet with Mr. Kettering on Tuesday, if it suits."

The hustle and hubbub of the town on market day gave them a measure of privacy, for which Jacaranda was profoundly grateful.

"Mr. Kettering may still be in Town on Tuesday, but you mustn't castigate him, Thomas."

"Why mustn't I? You haven't anybody else to speak up for you."

"I have many people to speak for me," Jacaranda countered, though those people were mostly content to dwell in Dorset. "Mr. Kettering does not force his attentions on unwilling women."

"You tell yourself that." Thomas untangled their arms, because even walking arm in arm might cause talk now that they neared their destination. "I have little girls of my own, Jacaranda Wyeth, and yet not long ago, I was an overgrown boy full of myself. I know what men are. I am one, and you can't trust us regarding certain matters. All those people who would speak for you, they're not here, are they? You've escaped their watchful eyes, just as I've slipped my uncle's leash. Now you're lonely, and Kettering's crooking his finger."

"He's not…" Well, he was, but she could hardly admit to a neighbor she'd turned down marriage to the man. "It isn't what you think."

"I would bet my mule it isn't what you think either." He stepped back when the grooms brought her gig around. "The day after himself returns from Town, I'll be on his doorstep, the soul of cordial deference—until you tell me otherwise."

"Thank you, I think."

He tipped his hat, and she curtsied in return, but the entire exchange had been disquieting, in several regards.

First, her privacy had already been compromised, though she trusted Thomas Hunter to keep his unsmiling mouth shut.

Second, her other secret—how she operated at Trysting—was also no longer exclusively hers.

Third, she wasn't entirely displeased about that. She'd seen respect in Thomas's eyes, liking, and a certain protectiveness that startled her but didn't disconcert as it might. He was behaving like a brother, and that pattern she understood, could predict, could manage.

Avery came skipping up to the gig, Yolanda a few steps behind.

"We have the lemon drops! And we saw that nice Mr. Hunter, and he had one. He kissed Tante's hand." She made a loud smacking sound and clambered into the gig.

"He is a very nice man," Yolanda said, following more sedately into the carriage, "and he has a lovely smile. He took the lemon drop only to be friendly, though. I know how men are."

Jacaranda said nothing, for it seemed everybody but she herself knew how men were. As they tooled back to Trysting, it occurred to her that in five years in the shire, she'd never once seen Thomas Hunter truly smile.

Though he'd smiled at Yolanda.

She was still pondering that mystery after supper, when Simmons brought her a note, one he'd apparently been hoarding for a properly dramatic moment.

"From Mr. K, him*self*, and addressed to you, Mrs. W!" He passed along a folded, sealed note, though a flake of wax was missing from the seal.

She didn't blame Simmons for trying, but neither would she reward his attempt at mischief.

"I'll wait until I've had my tea to read it," she said, though this prompted a ferocious scowl from Simmons. "His London house steward is likely asking after something Mr. Kettering has forgotten here and needs us to send along to Town."

"Then hadn't you better open it?" He smiled, pleased with himself, and made impatient circles with his hand.

"We'll send a groom with whatever it is." She set the note aside, out of Simmons's reach. "We'd never entrust Mr. Kettering's request to the public stage, now would we?"

"Suppose not." He turned to go, then inspiration struck. "What if it's urgent? What if he's waiting for your reply?"

"The missive bears nothing but an address on the outside, no indications of urgency at all. I'll be sure to let you know what he says, and thank you for making sure this found me promptly."

"Yes, well…"

Whatever prevarications and warnings Simmons wanted to pass along, at whatever length, were cut off by Carl, the senior footman, who hung panting against the frame of her parlor door.

"Mr. Simmons, sir, a wagon's coming up the drive, and it's loaded with baggage."

"A wagon?" Simmons's white eyebrows climbed his forehead. "Loaded?"

"Perhaps it's the earl's baggage arriving in advance of his entourage," Jacaranda suggested. "His chambers are prepared. The footmen need only shift the goods to the proper location."

"A wagon," Simmons repeated. "Such doings, such doings."

"I'm sure Carl will round up enough strong backs to see it done right," Jacaranda said, "provided you're on hand to supervise, Mr. Simmons."

"Oh, depend upon it, Mrs. W. Depend upon it."

He bustled off at Carl's side, leaving Jacaranda some much-needed privacy to read her note. She closed her sitting room door, retreated to her bedroom and closed that door, too.

The note bore none of Worth's fragrance, but it was written on thick linen paper, a crest of some sort embossed at the top, a lion sitting and a unicorn bowing and a Greek-looking female standing between them, a hand on each.

*My Dear Mrs. Wyeth,*

*I trust this finds you well, though I know the household yet anticipates my brother's arrival. I must impose on you for a written version of that tutorial you offered my house steward. Inspired by your example, I have hired a housekeeper here in Town, a young lady who like yourself had a great deal of responsibility for younger siblings and shows a penchant for putting things to rights domestically. My candidate for this post is named Mary, and life has not always dealt kindly with her, but she will benefit from correspondence with you, and perhaps later can make the journey to Trysting to learn at your figurative knee.*

*Like other propositions I have put before you, this is not an urgent request. Nobody will steal the dust from my parlor, will they? I will soon be underfoot at Trysting again, and we might discuss this situation in more detail. Until then, I remain*

*Yours,*

*Worth Kettering*

Should she be flattered? He'd noticed his town house and his country house were not maintained to the same standards. Of course, in some ways, housekeeping was more challenging in Town—the dust was awful, the city smells, the noise.

In other ways, Town was simple. Help was easy to hire, supplies and services were close at hand, and the markets, oh Lord, the markets in Town were a housekeeper's delight. Flowers, citrus fruit, spices, soaps and all manner of exotic and wonderful goods fresh from the docks.

Jacaranda put the letter down.

She hated Town. She'd always hated Town. She'd all but screeched that to her father and Step-Mama, her brothers, anybody who'd listen, that she hated Town, but in hindsight, she saw that what she hated was the Season.

Not Town.

Interesting, but hardly of any relevance.

Jacaranda took herself up to the state chambers on the second floor, where the footmen were arranging a small mountain of baggage.

"Well done, Mr. Simmons," she said, though the butler was fingering locks and straps, as if he was about to get himself into considerable trouble.

"You don't suppose we should unpack for the great man, do you? He can't be bothered to fold his own linen."

"He'll have staff, Mr. Simmons, a valet, a secretary, and perhaps even his own footmen. They'll take umbrage if we presume to know how his lordship likes his things set up."

"Take what? Umbers?"

"They will be offended," Jacaranda clarified. "I'm sure the trunks could all use a dusting, because the road between here and Cumberland is long. Then too, you might alert the stables that the baggage has arrived, and the coaches will likely follow soon. You did put the coachy and his porter in the kitchen, didn't you?"

He flapped a hand. "Yes, of course, in the kitchen. These be brass locks and hinges. Brass and shiny as a new button, they are."

He was still fingering the locks under Carl's watchful eye when Jacaranda left to interrogate the new arrivals. The baggage might have arrived days ahead of the traveler himself, or mere hours. In either case, she was ready for the earl's arrival, while her employer was not. The coachy was no help at all, though, knowing only that he'd accepted this load at the way station just north of London and driven it out to Surrey on hire.

Jacaranda penned a swift note to Mr. Kettering and took it down to the stables.

"Roberts?" She peered around, seeing not one soul, which wasn't that unusual, it being after sunset.

"Here, Missus." He came slowly down the ladder from the hayloft.

"Good evening, Roberts. Have you a groom to spare for a quick trip to Town?"

His bushy dark eyebrows knit, and he heaved a mountainous sigh. "Another quick trip to Town? I suppose his Royal Importance needs his paperwork moved hither and thither again?"

Everywhere, either insubordinate or impertinent men awaited.

"His Royal Importance feeds you, your horses and your grooms, so I suppose we'd best saddle a horse."

Roberts's white teeth flashed. "Now, Missus, I'm only grumbling. It's a long ride for a note that could be carried by a bird, isn't it now? An even longer ride when the note could likely wait for tomorrow's post, but no, we must all dash about, will we, nill we, and keep the master pleased."

Jacaranda had never heard such talk from him. "Roberts, the last time I considered it, keeping the master pleased was part of the definition of being in service, unless I mistake the matter?"

She let the question hang, but Roberts was an ally of sorts, and she had no wish to antagonize him. The outside staff, grooms, gardeners, groundsmen and so forth all took their direction from Roberts, and Reilly depended on the stable master as well for his animal doctoring.

"You do not mistake the matter," he said, giving a shrill, two-fingered whistle. "We'll get the man his note. You're right: We take his coin, we do his bidding, up to a point."

"You've grown rebellious in the summer heat, Mr. Roberts. Have you something to say?"

His size meant nothing to her, for Jacaranda understood he wouldn't use it against her. Roberts wasn't a bully, but he was his own man.

"No." He gave directions to a skinny groom who'd also come down the ladder from the hayloft, then turned back to her. "Yes. Walk with me a minute while the horse is being readied?"

Walk with him? Perhaps it was the appointed day for odd men to take her arm, except Roberts didn't, he merely paced off with her in the direction of the pond.

"A lot of excitement brewing up at the house," Roberts said, his gaze traveling to the manor's façade. "Having Mr. Kettering in residence, the young ladies, all this coming and going."

"I'd hardly call it excitement. Activity, perhaps."

"Activity, then. Now this earl fellow is down from the north to visit."

"His baggage has arrived, and my note to W—Mr. Kettering is to that effect," Jacaranda said, keeping her eyes front lest her horror at that slip show in her expression.

"I supposed it was so. You are managing well enough at the house?"

"We're doing splendidly." What on earth was he about?

"That's all right then." He patted her shoulder, an avuncular gesture that had her even more puzzled. First, Thomas Hunter now Roberts?

She withdrew her note from a skirt pocket. "Please give this to the groom. I expect Mr. Kettering will return post-haste, because he wants to greet his brother in person."

"He should. They're family, and Cumberland is a long way off."

"You'll be able to accommodate the teams and two more wagons?"

"We've cleaned out the whole carriage house and moved the work wagons to the home farm, and yes, we'll be ready. You?"

"We're ready but for Mr. Kettering's absence. I'm sure this note will remedy that situation."

"We'll see to it." He waved, then left Jacaranda standing in the garden, the scent of lavender rising all around her.

* * *

Considering His Royal Highness was tall, quite stout, and leader of one of the most powerful nations in the world, Prinny was deucedly hard to locate. Worth wasted most of the afternoon tracking him to a lawn tennis match, where the Regent was observing casually and flirting madly in the company of his familiars.

In no etiquette book Worth had read did it describe how to part a sovereign from his toadies to discuss delicate financial matters. Worth was thus reduced to whispering in the royal ear, as if imparting a morsel of salacious gossip, at which point the royal brain demonstrated the savvy for which it was occasionally known. The prince dragged his loyal subject off to the buffet, waving the hangers-on away like so many pesky mosquitoes.

Then it took still more whispering, and explaining, and assuring, and reassuring before Worth had the direction needed from His Royal Highness, and the signed documents necessary to carry it out.

By the time Worth returned to his town house, the summer moon was well up in the sky, and Lewis looked to be approaching apoplexy.

"Messenger from Trysting, sir," Lewis said, taking the documents from Worth's hand. "Mrs. Wyeth is alerting you to the arrival of a baggage coach. She expects the earl will soon arrive."

Worth stifled a curse, because his day had been long, hot and trying, but Wyeth would not have sounded the alarm on a whim. "You fed our man and saw his horse stabled?"

"We did."

"Goliath is saddled?"

"Waiting in his stall, a flask in his saddlebags."

"You've canceled tomorrow's appointments or shuffled them to the senior clerks?"

"Shuffled. You had only three, and Jones knows all your kitchen clients."

"Good enough. Did anyone think to pack me a supper?"

Lewis ran his finger around his wilted collar. "A sup…per?"

"No matter," Worth said, heading for the kitchen. "Have Goliath brought around, and I'll be out front in a few minutes. Tell Jones to get Mary Flannery moved in here by week's end, will you?"

"Of course, sir."

Worth ate cheese and buttered bread in the kitchen standing up. He stuffed an extra sandwich in his pocket, drained a tankard of summer ale, mounted his horse and headed out of Town shortly after midnight.

His arse hurt from making the journey into Town a few days earlier. Not his arse, exactly, his hip joints, and the bones upon which he sat. He was too old to be haring about like this, though as a young man, he'd ridden from Cumberland to Oxfordshire several times a year and felt nary a twinge.

So why had he come charging back into Town, when he'd known damned good and well his brother was soon to make an appearance?

To escape the nigh constant ache caused by proximity to one Jacaranda Wyeth, goddess of his rustic hearth. To see her was to desire her, and that unflattering reality had been most of what sent Worth galloping for London. Not to give her time to ponder their dealings, not to tend to the press of business, not to receive old sailors at his back door, and not to have Jones take samples of fancy lacework around to the shops for competitive bids.

And he hated—hated—this effervescent, anxious, *hopeful* feeling in his chest, the one caused by the thought of seeing her again, of climbing into her bed, pressing his lips to her soft, fragrant skin and having her roll over to wrap herself around him in welcome.

God in heaven, he was far gone. He brought Goliath down to a spanking trot, trying to pretend he wasn't eager to get home and failing to fool even the horse, who leaned on the bit right up to the foot of Trysting's drive.

* * *

Jacaranda rolled over in her bed as hoof beats pounded up the drive. A big horse, its footfalls reverberating in the dewy night air outside her open window.

The arrival was either Worth or his brother, but the earl was supposedly traveling in state, and Jacaranda had sat behind Goliath on enough outings to have an ear for the horse's gaits.

A sensation of relief swamped Jacaranda, of thanksgiving that the man should be safely arrived to his home. Not set upon by highwaymen, not crumpled in a ditch when his horse took a misstep, not retching his life away after partaking of bad ale at the coaching inns, not racketing about London, pursuing women who cared nothing for the man and only for the pleasures he might bestow on them.

Angels abide, where did such insecurities come from?

In any case, she was glad he was home. She rose and grabbed her prettiest night robe. By the time Worth came in the back door, she had the tea steeping and a tray of cold sandwiches assembled.

"There you are." He paused at the archway to the back hall, dusty, road-weary, and smiling such a smile, Jacaranda was warmed by it across the breadth of the kitchen. He held his arms wide, and she couldn't refuse such a sincere invitation.

Didn't want to, didn't care to know why she should.

"How is it possible to smell as good as you do at all hours of the day and night?" he asked, nuzzling her hair. "I could retire next week as the wealthiest man in the realm if I could bottle your scent."

"The scent comes in bottles," she said, not stepping back. "Are you hungry?"

"I am as hungry as a great white bear of the north emerging in spring after months of deprivation, and some food would be nice, too."

He was being naughty already. She withdrew from his embrace, not wanting to deal in innuendo and prurient double meanings. Not with him, not tonight, probably not ever.

"Did I say something wrong?"

"You said you were in want of food." She checked the strength of the tea. "I've put together some sandwiches and biscuits and sliced a peach from your walled garden."

"Is the hour too ungodly for a man to have a bath? If it is, I can take a swim, though you will probably slap me when I ask you to join me, won't you?"

"Not slap you, but I wouldn't join you, and no, it isn't too late for a bath. We've doubled up footmen on the night shift in anticipation of your brother's arrival."

"Which means we have two?" He sat and waited until she'd poured his cup of tea.

"Which means we have four until ten of the clock, then two until morning," Jacaranda said, bringing him his tray.

"Join me, please?" He didn't reach for his food, and he had to be starving, but she hesitated. His eyes held no flirtation, only banked patience.

He dropped his gaze to the food as if composing a blessing. "I won't order you to take a seat, Wyeth, but I am asking. I've missed you."

"For pity's sake, you mustn't say such things." She sat quickly, scowling at him for his indiscretion rather than admit she liked hearing the words.

"I'll put food in my mouth, then, to avoid the terrible endearments that might slip out." He reached for a sandwich. "When is my brother expected?"

"We haven't the first notion." Jacaranda had missed him, too, mightily. She could say it to herself, now that he was home safely, but to say it to him seemed unwise.

In the kitchen, unwise.

In private, disastrous.

"I would have been here sooner, but a client was in need of immediate services, and he is someone I avoid offending. Have something to eat. You're making me nervous, glowering at me. I'll suffer dyspepsia, and you'll glower at me for that, too."

He offered the last with a smile, a crooked, subtle version of the earlier great, beaming invitation.

To get away from that smile, Jacaranda rose. How was it she spent three days listening for Worth's arrival and now she had no idea how to go on.

"I'll get the footmen busy with your bath."

He let her go, which was a relief and a disappointment. She also stopped by Worth's chambers, finding no candles lit, his bed not turned down, not a single window open to the night breezes, and his flowers a tad thirsty.

Someone, or maybe several someones, required closer supervision.

By the time she returned to the kitchen, her employer was finished eating, but still sitting at the table, a cup of tea cradled against his flat belly. Now he looked not only road-weary but exhausted.

"I gather you'd already put in a long day when my note found you?" She bent to take the tray, and his fingers, cradling his tea cup one moment, were circling her wrist the next. She tugged, and he let her go.

"My days were long and my evenings longer."

She did not ask him where he'd spent his long evenings. She would never ask that, no matter how badly she wanted to know.

"My dear, you are not in charity with me," Worth said, frowning. "Is it something we can discuss?"

Put like that... She dropped to the bench beside him.

"Your offer?" she began.

"We're not bringing that up now. It's the middle of the night. Anybody might come seeking a late-night snack here in the kitchen, and you're in a mood. It can wait."

She was in at least eight different moods at the same time. "But your brother will be here, and I want this resolved."

"Beg pardon, sir, Mrs. Wyeth." Carl trotted down the kitchen steps, the jacket of his livery buttoned askew. "One of the grooms came staggering home from the pub and says there's a gent what talks like Mr. Kettering and looks a bit like him had a meal in the private dining room of the Bird in Paradise."

Worth started to rise, but Jacaranda caught him with a hand to his shoulder and pushed him back to his seat.

"His lordship is five miles away, if it's even the earl," she said. "Finish your tea while your bath is filled. Let the grooms know, Carl, and take up your post at the front door."

"He's only my brother," Worth muttered, dutifully draining his tea cup.

"Who has traveled two hundred miles in the summer heat to see you," Jacaranda replied. "You are here to receive him only because you came out from Town at a punishing pace, if I guess correctly."

"You do." He smiled a little. A very little. "You usually do."

"Then go enjoy your bath. I'll tidy up here and make sure the state chambers are in final readiness."

"I bow to your common sense." He rose and captured her hand in his to kiss her wrist. "I don't plan to make a habit of it, though, so stop feeling so smug."

"I do not feel... Oh, be off with you, lest your brother catch you with your hair sticking up in all directions and your feet bare."

He looked interested in that picture, so she took the tray, carried it to the sink, and began putting the tea things away, only to feel long arms slip around her waist.

"I missed you." A soft kiss to the place where her neck and shoulder joined, a tender, private, much-taken-for-granted place with a mysterious connection to her knee joints. "Every hour I was gone." Lips again, soft, sweet, warm. "I missed you."

He swept his fingers over her jaw, and then he was gone, and Jacaranda had to brace herself on the counter to remain upright.

# CHAPTER TEN

Worth's plan had misfired spectacularly.

Instead of giving Wyeth breathing room, time to accustom herself to courtship—to having an affair, if her crack-brained perspective was to be humored—leaving her to her own devices only had her doubts in full charge.

Women, vexing creatures, were strangers to logic.

A hot bath was not vexing, but having no one to share it with…

Worth had filled the hours in the saddle with daydreams of Wyeth attending his bath; Wyeth, waiting naked in her bed for him—she couldn't very well wait in *his* bed, not at this stage of the proceedings. He'd wanted another of those secret smiles from her, but she'd blessed him with one welcoming hug and a little shyness before she'd pokered up and turned housekeeper on him.

He shed his clothes as the last of the hot water was dumped in the tub and directed the footmen to be ready to empty the bath within the hour. His footmen were moving smartly, and he didn't doubt Jacaranda Wyeth had put the fear of dismissal in them should they shirk.

Jacaranda, not his butler, the estimable Simmons of the Fussing Eyebrows. Why Worth should suspect this to be the case, he couldn't say, but he more than suspected it. Hell, she had him second-guessing himself and tearing about the realm in all directions.

He lingered at his bath, hoping some calamity, such as his brother's arrival in the dead of night, would necessitate that his housekeeper interrupt him, and then he lingered out of sheer fatigue.

Given the hour, the Regent being in charity with his princess was a surer bet than Hessian's arrival, so Worth climbed out of his tub, toweled off, brushed his wet hair down—thank you very much—and put his feet into house slippers.

Then, *of course*, a knock on his door.

Jacaranda stood in the hallway a decorous two paces away from the door. "If you're through, the footmen can take the tub away."

"I'm through." He stepped back and opened the door wide. "Perhaps you'd join me in the library, Mrs. Wyeth?" He'd used his best condescending, lord-of-the-manor tone, the better to impress the footmen.

"If you insist." She spun on her heel, and he was left admiring the view while the footmen offered him sympathetic smiles, and did a little admiring of their own.

He didn't blame them. She was too magnificent not to admire.

"Look at her again like that, and I'll fire the lot of you."

The smiles became outright grins, so he left his insubordinate staff wrestling with the tub and trying not to lose their composure entirely.

It was a near thing, no doubt, because the lord of the manor was now occupying the same position with respect to his housekeeper as every other male on the property: right beneath her sturdy heel.

She'd gone to the library, as requested, and that had to count for something. When Worth joined her, she was standing by the long windows with her back to the room.

"I had enough moonlight to travel by most of the way," Worth said. "I saw not a single highwayman on my way here."

"You don't cross any heaths, and Goliath could likely outrun most any highwayman's horse."

"Then you don't worry when I'm on the king's highway in the dead of night that harm will befall me?" He did not lock the library door, the better to inspire his own good behavior.

"I worry."

She even tossed him a fulminating over-the-shoulder glance when she said it. She worried; she didn't like that she worried, but she wouldn't lie about it either.

God bless an honest woman. "Jacaranda."

Another glance, this time for presuming to use her name, he supposed, but it was late, he'd ridden to exhaustion to see her, and they would be disturbed only if his blighted brother showed up.

"What has you in such a state, Wyeth? Matters are no different from when I left, and if you're not interested in my company, you have only to say so."

"Your company?"

"My company, as in, my person sharing the same surrounds as yours. To wit, the present situation. You might as well tell me what burr is under your saddle, or I'll stoop to interrogating the children, and children see and hear everything. You know this."

Another look, exasperation tinged with misery.

"Your company, proximate to my own, was all but observed by one of your tenants at the cottage during the storm."

God's knickers. No wonder she was in high dudgeon. He mentally rearranged his chess pieces into a defensive posture.

"Was somebody peeking in the windows, then?"

"Somebody might as well have been." She turned, finally, to face him, and her expression was more hurt than peevish, and that…that drove a lance through his middle. A hot, miserable, piercing ache, of inadequacy and protectiveness.

"Come." He held out a hand. "Tell me, and I'll deal with it."

"You can't deal with it." She spat the words and glared down her magnificent nose at his proffered hand. "Thomas Hunter is a good man. He's widowed, and he doesn't begrudge you your dalliances, but he knows my perfume, and he saw…" She gave him her back again, shoulders hunched, arms wrapped around her middle to hold in the mortification—or her temper.

"What did he see, Wyeth?" Worth approached her with a greater show of confidence than he felt. "We dallied under the covers, nothing more."

"He saw the bedclothes were rumpled, and he knows we were there."

Worth wanted to be reassuring, to be kind, to be understanding, but for God's sake, a dalliance was her brilliant idea. Not his. Not this time around anyway.

"Do I take it we're engaged now?"

Her jaw started working like a pump handle priming itself for a torrent of words. All that came out was one rusty syllable: "No."

"Right." He walked up to her, stood directly before her. "We're not, because we were not caught *in flagrante delicto*, my dear. As sins go, what we did barely qualifies, if at all. You won't have me for a husband, need I remind you, so we're both back to wondering what exactly you seek from me, Wyeth. You describe this Hunter fellow as the pick of the litter, and I'd think a minor indiscretion safe with him. I'll speak to him, and you will be assured of this."

"You can't speak to him. If you *speak* to him, it will only confirm his suspicions."

"Which you no doubt entirely allayed with some fanciful tale of having been there without my company, perhaps?"

Her mouth closed with a snap. Then, "I did not."

He could see her silently castigating herself for not having been clever enough to concoct that lie on the spot for this nosy tenant, and some of his anger drained away.

"Wyeth." He risked a finger traced up the length of her forearm, pushing the sleeve of her nightrobe two inches closer to her elbow. "Cut line. Nobody saw anything, nobody will say anything. You're making a tempest in a teapot and tormenting yourself as well. In his widowed state, your neighbor has allowed himself the same pleasures, I assure you."

Possibly in the same small dwelling.

"He said as much." As concessions went, it was minuscule, but it heartened Worth enough to keep that finger moving on her forearm. Her wrist bones were so fine, so sturdy but feminine.

"Come sit." He took that wrist and tugged her to the sofa. "We'll watch the sunrise, and you'll tell me what transpired while I was absent. Did the girls behave, and has Simmons's gout flared up, and which maid is making eyes at which footman?"

She sat, not touching him, hunched forward on the couch, as if her shoulders were weary of a burden.

"The staff is all behaving well in anticipation of our guest's arrival," she said. "Simmons's knees wait until September to start bothering him. The cold mornings make it difficult for him to get under sail."

Worth smoothed her hair back over her shoulder and used that gesture to start rubbing her back, slowly, as much to soothe himself as to comfort her.

"Does anybody know where we came by Simmons? I should think he'd be out to pasture by now."

"He came down from Cumberland with your great-uncle, he says, but that would have been more than sixty years ago."

"Why haven't I pensioned him off to some snug little cottage on the South Downs?"

"I haven't asked you to, neither has Reilly, nor will we." She let out a breath and relaxed under his hand. "Simmons does well enough, and the footmen, porters, boot boys and such all take up for him when his infirmities subdue him."

"So protective." He applied a slight pressure to her neck, until he felt her sigh and give up more of her tension. "When I'm old and doddery, will you be protective of me as well?"

"I'll be in that cottage on the South Downs." Her words held no heat, no animosity. If anything, she sounded wistful.

"Tell me about this cottage," he said, moving his hand down her spine. "What color are the roses, and how many cats?"

She didn't give him a tolerant look, which he'd expected. She closed her eyes and described a fairy-tale cottage, one that smelled of fresh flowers, sheets aired in the sun and lavender sachets. She moved her hand once on her thigh, as if she were stroking the fat black cat she envisioned sunning himself on her stoop, and she spoke longingly of having all the daylight hours to read and walk and putter in her garden.

*Homesick.*

He knew the signs, knew the particularly tender brand of melancholy it brought, knew the futility of it.

"You have your cottage picked out, don't you?" He scooted up so he could put an arm around her shoulders and bring her close to his side.

"I do, but it's in Dorset, not on the Downs. My cottage sits in a lovely valley, and it's called Complaisance Cottage. My great-grandfather named it."

"Glass windows?"

"Mullioned, to let in the light and provide a view right down the hillside of the grand manor and all the formal gardens and the park and the maze. Staying in the cottage is like being at the great house but having privacy."

"You deserve this cottage," he said, realizing he knew nothing of her dreams, nothing of her aspirations besides tidily folded sheets in the linen closet and windows that didn't stick in the damp.

There was more to Jacaranda Wyeth than ruthlessly competent housekeeping, much more—but did she know that?

"Someday I will have it, if I mind my pence and quid."

He expected her to get to her feet and bid him a brisk good night on that common-sensical line, but the pull of her cottage was such that she merely turned her face to his shoulder and tried to hide a yawn.

"Carl's on duty?" He sneaked a nuzzle of her temple.

"And Jeff. They're cousins, and they'll take turns napping, but the front door is manned."

He patted her arm. "Then let's to bed, my dear. If Hess shows up at first light, we'll at least have had some rest, and as to that, you will permit me to escort you to your room."

She didn't fuss, a measure of her fatigue, or her longing for that solitary cottage. She took his arm and let him walk with her to her room. He lit a single candle for her and paused inside her sitting room door to assess her, now that she wasn't hissing and spitting and suffering paroxysms of mortification.

"I'm sorry about the rumpled bed," he said, "but you're flagellating yourself over it because you think a housekeeper should have noticed, aren't you?"

She nodded, a little sheepish, a little defensive.

"I count it a measure of success that for a few moments, Wyeth, you weren't a housekeeper, able to take pleasure only in well-beaten rugs and sparkling windows. For a few minutes, you were able to take pleasure in *yourself.*"

He saw her try to reject his reasoning, but like that snug, peaceful little cottage, a woman's right to some pleasure had a quiet, compelling allure, and she conceded his point with a nod.

"Off to bed with you," Worth said, "and my thanks for keeping the garrison on high alert. Hess will show up, and you'll be ready to take him on."

He didn't risk kissing her, didn't risk angering her with the presumption, and didn't risk his own self-discipline failing him should she decide to put aside her reservations.

*She* kissed *him*, though, a buss on the cheek, of apology for her mood, he suspected, and simple weary friendliness.

"Good night, Worth. Rest well."

He waited until her door was closed to touch the spot on his cheek she'd pressed her lips to.

She'd called him Worth.

Good night, indeed.

* * *

"You have a caller, sir." Not Carl, but Jeff the cousin who shared porter duties, disturbed Worth's breakfast and eliminated the likelihood he could linger until Wyeth appeared.

Well, damn and blast.

"Where did you put him?"

Over at the sideboard, the footman's gaze slid away.

"He were that dusty, sir. I put him in the second parlor. Tea tray's on its way."

"Have a tray sent up to Mrs. Wyeth, too, would you? The commotion last night likely set her schedule on its head."

"Mrs. Wyeth is in the gardens, sir. She's been up since the moon set. Said the flowers needed freshening in the boo-kays."

"Then take the tray to the gardens."

Just like that, Worth's staff was smirking again, staring at the ceiling or out the window.

"Fired without a character, you lot." He glared at both Jeff and the footman minding the sideboard, and for good measure at the scullery maid bringing up a fresh tea service. "Make sure it's a substantial tray, not merely tea and scones."

"Yes, sir." In unison, but to Worth's ears, their subservience had a tell-tale singsong mocking quality. Wyeth would not have countenanced such cheek.

Except, she did. However she ruled, it wasn't with an iron hand. Nobody at Trysting was in fear for their position, and nobody slacked. Worth approved of that. He did not approve of tenants reeking of the barnyard who came calling by dawn's early light to disturb a man bent on serious domestic campaigning.

Unless that tenant was this Hunter fellow, the one who had had the gall to intimate to Jacaranda she might be an object of gossip.

"Now see here," Worth began, sailing into the unprepossessing parlor only to stop in his tracks. "*Hess?*"

"You recognize me," Worth's guest said. "I'm encouraged." He held out a deliberate hand.

With equal deliberation, Worth put his hand in his brother's and shook, civilly, all the while repressing an urge to smile from ear to ear. Such an urge was not born of sense or logic. Hess had stabbed Worth in the back as cruelly as one sibling could betray another, and all the shared boyhood years before that one gesture couldn't wipe out the circumstances of their parting.

"I'm glad you've safely arrived." Worth could say that honestly, so he did. "Will your coaches be following?"

"No coaches," Hess replied. "My bags should have arrived, but I'm traveling alone to make better time."

"You want to return to Grampion before harvest, perhaps, or simply wanted this errand completed." Worth had not made this remark a question, though he'd meant to—hadn't he?

In the space of a sentence, the chasm between them loomed wider and colder. All it had taken was a few words tossed on years of near silence and some bitter history.

"I wanted to assure myself Yolanda is well. The school sent an alarming report, full of implications and innuendo. Then too, I would like to make Avery's acquaintance. You did intend to tell me about her?"

"I sent a note." Worth was saved from truly bickering by the arrival of the ubiquitous tea tray. He served his brother, glad for the distraction, glad to have something to do while he tried to recall exactly why he'd summoned the earl south.

Hess hadn't aged since early adulthood so much as matured. His hair was the same golden blond, his eyes a piercing northern blue, and his form as elegant and rangy as ever, but with more muscle, less pointless movement. Hess was a man now, the earl, not the young heir trying to fit into his papa's boots.

Women, always drawn to those golden aristocratic good looks, would be unable to resist this version of Hess. No wonder he'd left his Cumbrian moors at Worth's invitation. If Hess was interested in acquiring another countess, that variety of game abounded in the south.

"I haven't been to Trysting since we were children," Hess said, taking an armchair as Worth did likewise. "The place looks to be blooming, and your farms are thriving as well."

A compliment, Worth allowed, as he poured his tea, but what did it mean?

"I am fortunate to have good managers and excellent staff at all my households," Worth said, groping for what Hess was aiming at. Hess had been subtle but not sly as a younger man. Maybe age was honing his nasty side, for he had one. He most certainly did.

"I called on you, you know." This was offered as Hess ventured a lordly sip of his tea. "A fine gunpowder. Did you recall I prefer it?"

Yes, he had. "My housekeeper inquired. When did you call on me?"

"Two years ago." Another slow, savoring sip. "I vote my seat occasionally, when the issue matters to me or somebody makes a specific request. I'd heard you had word of Moira's death, and it seemed appropriate to express my condolences."

"She was your sister, too."

"She was, but you two were closer to each other than I was to either of you, at least in recent years. Shall we make a start on those scones?"

Over scones, raspberry jam, and clotted cream, the talk became less fraught, the teapot was emptied, and a yawning sadness welled up where Worth's resentment of his brother should be.

He didn't hate Hess. He'd forgiven him long since, in fact, realizing his brother had likely had little choice all those years ago. Some choice, perhaps, but not much, given their father's force of character and the state of the Kettering finances.

Still, resentment and mistrust lingered, and more than tea and crumpets would be needed to restore fraternal regard.

"Shall I show you the stables?" Worth asked. "I'm sure Roberts will have your horse settled in, but you were always particular about your cattle."

"I could use some exercise, and yes, the stables will do nicely. The hours in the saddle take a toll they didn't used to. What?" He frowned, looking for a moment like their father. "You think I among all men am immune to the march of time? I am not, so don't give me that look."

"Beg pardon." Worth rose and directed his guest to the door, only to find it opening before them.

"Oh!" Jacaranda Wyeth stood in the corridor in a lovely high-waisted summer dress looking about sixteen years old and, for the first time in Worth's memory, flustered. She carried a basket of flowers over her arm and a crystal vase half-filled with water. "Mr. Kettering, I'm sorry. I was told you were in the formal parlor."

"Hess is family, so we're in the family parlor," Worth improvised, but he had a sneaking suspicion he owed his staff for this bit of good fortune. He took the vase. "Mrs. Jacaranda Wyeth, may I make known to you Hessian Kettering, Earl of Grampion, and my brother, come to enjoy a southern respite. Hess, Mrs. Wyeth is our domestic genius at Trysting. She anticipates most of our needs and has the staff poised to fulfill the rest. You'll come to treasure her as I do."

"Mrs. Wyeth." Hess offered her a slight bow, a gesture of cordiality from a man who had no cause to bow to housekeepers of any stripe. "If you can keep up with this one,"—his gaze moved over Worth—"you are indeed a pearl among women."

"My thanks for the flattery from you both. The state rooms are ready for you, my lord, and I'm sure the nursery is buzzing with news of your arrival."

"The girls will just have to wait a bit," Worth cut in, setting the vase on the gate-legged table. "We're off to the stables. Perhaps the young ladies might join us for a picnic at luncheon?"

Hess's eyebrows rose at that suggestion, but Hess knew how to picnic. He might have neglected the skill, but he'd had it once, and he could revive it with practice.

"A picnic it will be," Jacaranda replied. "If you'll excuse me, my lord, sir, I will tend to my flowers."

She ducked past them, and Worth saw the speculation in his brother's eyes.

"Keep your lordly hands off," Worth said as they moved through the house. "Perhaps I'm sensitive, because you married my last fiancée, but Mrs. Wyeth is not for you, Hess. I mean it."

"Getting to the old business directly, aren't we?"

"You're the one who votes his seat, so you know the tedium of old business." Worth positively marched for the front door. "This is new business. Stay away from my housekeeper. She isn't up to your weight."

"Worth, I am here to sort out my responsibilities to various dependent females in our family, nothing more. Even so, your housekeeper is a magnificent specimen of femininity, and my own eyes tell me she's doing a proper job of managing your house. Let's leave it at that, shall we?"

A nice speech, and really, Hess had his pick of titled women. He had no need to pursue housekeepers, tweenies and chambermaids.

"Let's take the path through the gardens," Worth suggested. "The lavenders are blooming, and we can find you a sprig for your lapel."

"Why should I sport weeds on my person?"

"Because Avery considers the scent reminiscent of her mother, and that's an association you want her to make."

Worth adorned himself first with a sprig of true lavender, then found a showier bloom for his brother. Hess held still while Worth affixed the blossom to his lapel, and the moment bore a strong odor of déjà vu. How many times had they attended each other in preparation for balls, assemblies, formal dinners, and outings with the neighbors?

"Does it still bother you?" Hess asked, fingering the sprig. "That I married her?"

"I try not to think about it." Which was the truth, not all of the truth. "I was having second thoughts, but reassured myself even those were a sign she and I were meant to be together."

"You were very young," Hess said, and it wasn't a taunt or even an excuse. "Both of you, and if it makes you feel any better, she and I took years to arrive at even cordial civility. We didn't have much of a marriage, Worth."

"Legally, it sufficed." Worth surveyed his brother's *boutonnière* and found it adequate. "But, no, it doesn't help that you and she were miserable with each other. I'm sorry if you think it would."

As quickly as it had come up, the subject was dropped. Their tour of the stables went more smoothly, with various horses and architectural features keeping them from more troubling topics.

"We're dawdling," Hess said when they'd admired every equine and half the garden. "Shall we sit? I am not ready to face Yolanda, much less to meet this Avery."

"Avery is more French than English," Worth warned. "Your objective is not to command her respect, as if she were an English girl. You want her to approve of you, to like you."

"Hence the weeds. How is Yolanda?"

"Mysterious," Worth said, relieved Hess would ask. "The school said she's given to vapors and hysterics, but I've seen none. She's read half the library in a few weeks, she's unfailingly kind to both Avery and the staff, and she will be—she already is—beautiful. It gives one pause."

Hess turned his head to sniff at the sprig gracing his lapel. "And?"

"And when I met her she sported a thick bandage on her left wrist, and once I bundled Yolanda into my traveling coach, that old besom at the school insisted the girl had tried to take her own life."

"God in heaven." Hess crossed his ankle over his knee, then hiked his leg closer by closing his hand over his shin and tugging. Worth recalled his brother assuming this posture as a child, a way of reinforcing his mental defenses even then. "You and she haven't talked about it?"

"She told Mrs. Wyeth she didn't try to kill herself, but under the bandages was a healing laceration. Wyeth confirmed that much."

"An accident?"

"Possibly, or a dramatic gesture. Yolanda was not pleased to be left here in the south for years on end."

"Have you any idea how difficult it is to transport one adolescent female the length and breadth of the kingdom in anything approaching safety and comfort?"

"Yes, and I won't criticize you for leaving her at school, particularly when I had no idea of her existence."

"I wrote you, when Papa died, because you're her guardian in the event of my demise." Hess wouldn't lie about something like that, and still, his voice held no accusation.

"I moved around a lot seven years ago. Your note didn't reach me." Worth kept his tone carefully neutral, no defensiveness, no equivocation. Facts were never recited this impartially before the highest court in the land.

"I thought not." Hess trailed a finger over his *boutonnière*. "You would have at least called on her, had you known she was in your back yard. I know that now."

He said it quietly, a casual comment, but in his willingness to give Worth the benefit of the doubt, Hess opened a door. A small, unprepossessing door, half-obscured with the ivy of mistrust, but it opened on forgiveness and on understanding. Worth cast around for a means of keeping it open.

"Yolanda's safe and happy at the moment. We can sort the rest out later."

"We can." Hess got to his feet and offered a crooked, familiar smile. "Shall we get the greetings with our womenfolk over with? This lavender is making my eyes itch."

Worth stood, for the lavender was affecting his eyes, too. "Can't have that. I hope you know what a sacrifice I made when I consented to share a picnic with my family. Sitting on roots and rocks, prey for insects and wayward breezes, left to the company of shrieking children. What utter rot."

* * *

"You listen t'me." Harold Doorman poked Roberts once in the chest for emphasis. "That do not be the lord I saw at the Bird."

"You're trying to tell me two titled gentlemen dined at the Bird of Paradise in Least Wapping, Doorman? Two titles in one night?" Roberts didn't bother to hide his incredulity, for Doorman's affection for gin was legendarily constant.

"I don't know about titles." Doorman gave his cap a righteous tug. "But I do be knowing about nobs, and there was two a' them, right e'now. I looked on the register."

"And what did you see?" Harold Doorman was Roberts's oldest groom, his second in command as it were, and a favorite with the horses. It wouldn't hurt to humor him.

"My eyesight isn't so good." Doorman fell momentarily silent as one of the lads wheeled a barrow of clean straw down the barn aisle. "Looked like Castleroll or summat. Caster-reel."

"Lord Caster-reel graced our own pub, and you were on hand to witness this moment of history. Lord Grampion is here now, and his horse would probably appreciate a tour of the east paddock. Mind you're careful with the beast. He's high-strung, no matter he's been traveling for days."

At the mention of the horse, Doorman's expression turned up incongruously sweet. "Ain't met the beast too high-strung to nibble good Surrey grass, and I seen two a' them lords. I'd bet me wage on it."

Roberts was already moving off, because Doorman's grasp of Debrett's was even shakier than his grasp of sobriety at the Beltane bonfire. "See to the gelding, and I'll ask if we're to have coaching teams to deal with, or if all that scurrying about was for naught."

* * *

"No coaching teams," Hess told his brother's housekeeper. "Just myself, one tired horse, and a few bags."

"Very good, my lord." She bobbed a curtsy and trundled out of the library, though why a housekeeper was inquiring regarding a matter for the stables was a mystery. Mrs. Wyeth was a vigorous sort of woman, though, and worth the second look he'd given her earlier. She'd stand up to northern winters and to the rigors of managing a very large household, and she was more than easy to look upon.

Stealing her for Grampion would mean poaching another female from his brother's preserves, and this Hess could not afford to do.

Not in any sense.

"Are you ready to face the girls?" Worth asked, using the mirror over the sideboard to admire the lavender affixed to his lapel. "I'm sure they've been beside themselves in anticipation of seeing you."

"Meeting me, more like," Hess said. "I haven't seen Yolanda for more than two years, and young ladies change at her age with alarming rapidity."

"Why two years?"

"Because I'm a coward?" Hess offered a small smile with that admission and was rewarded with something like sympathy from his brother.

"I can guess," Worth said, leading Hess through a house that sported much sunshine and many fresh, colorful bouquets. "Yolanda came home on a visit one summer between terms and was a perfect brat the entire time, hated everything—you, the weather, Grampion, the neighbors' spotty boys, your horse, everything. At the winter holiday break, you arranged for her to spend the time with some obliging family in the south, and lo, you saved money, time, and worry, and she was happier for it, as were you and the entire Grampion household."

Hess caught a reflection of his own floral adornment, which did have a pleasant scent, for all it made a silly addition to his wardrobe.

"That's it, more or less. Then Yolanda took it into her head I was avoiding her, so she refused to come home, and now we're at some sort of impasse, when she must make her come out next year, or the year after, and has no use for her brother the earl."

"She's young." Worth bounded up the main staircase with an energy that had been characteristic of him from earliest boyhood. "Everything is a matter of great drama when we're young. And she has no mama. I think this affects girls terribly, but she seems to like Mrs. Wyeth."

"The absence of a mother, even a poor mother, affects boys terribly, too."

Before dear Worth could get his relentless inquisitiveness going on that admission, they were at the open door to the nursery suite.

"Uncle!" Avery scampered over and wrapped her arms around Worth's waist, and Hess knew a moment of envy that any female, much less one so young and happy, should greet Worth thus. Petty, but there it was. Avery was all that remained of Moira, another pretty, happy young lady, and Avery belonged to Worth. Their mutual possession was obvious in how the child smiled at him, took his hand, and positioned herself at Worth's side, all before risking a peek at her senior uncle.

"Avery, please make your curtsy to your Uncle Hess. He's come two hundred miles for the pleasure of making your acquaintance, and if you're very nice, he might even take you up on his horse with him some morning when we ride out."

"Is he a very big horse? As big as Goliath?"

"He's a very handsome horse," Hess said, going down on his haunches. "He'll need new friends while we're visiting, so he doesn't get homesick."

"Homesick." The child wrinkled her nose. That easily, Hess was frustrated with himself, because the very word had to be painful for her.

"Goliath and I will keep your horse company, then," she said, her expression shifting to a smile. "Mr. Roberts will have only happy horses in Uncle's stables. He said this to me, and he is the stable master. What is your horse's name?"

"Alfred."

Another wrinkled nose, but the smile stayed as well. "I'm sure he's a very dignified fellow, with such an English name. When can I ride him?"

A few years in France, and the child already had the knack of ordering her world to suit her preferences.

"I'll leave you two to work out your schedules while I find Yolanda." Worth's smile was diabolical as he went whistling on his way, and so Hess rose and looked for something sturdy enough that a grown man, an uncle, *or an earl,* could sit on it without risking his dignity and the integrity of his limbs.

A rocking chair was positioned to take advantage of the light by the window, but it put Hess in mind of elderly nurses with bad knees, so he chose the next most trustworthy option and sat his lordly arse on the floor.

# CHAPTER ELEVEN

"Yolanda?"

Worth knocked once and let himself into his sister's room without pausing. He was greeted by the sight of his housekeeper, sitting on the bed next to his sibling, Jacaranda's arm around Yolanda's waist, Yolanda's head on Jacaranda's shoulder.

"Hessian is here, my girl, and he'd like to make his bow to you." Worth injected briskness into his tone, false briskness, but it might fool an adolescent who didn't know him well.

"Tell him to go back to his hounds and grouse moors." Yolanda offered that, then turned her face to Jacaranda's shoulder. "He can return to Grampion and tell everyone I'm crazy."

Worth sought Jacaranda's gaze, looking for some help or insight, but Jacaranda only stroked a hand over the girl's hair and gave a small shake of her head.

"I'm angry at him," Yolanda said, sitting up. "He left me like a lame horse, dragged about from one stranger's house to the next, embroidering until my eyes crossed, and now he wants to make his bow to me?"

"Yolanda, perhaps his lordship knows an apology is in order," Jacaranda suggested.

Yolanda pulled away from her. "He'll clear his throat like an old man and look at the ceiling, his tea cup, or the nearest piece of art, and he'll get out a lot of long words which basically say he did the best he could with a baggage like me, and then he'll pack me up and haul me to the Arctic and tell me that's the best he can do as well."

"You do know him." Worth sat on Yolanda's other side. "The business about staring at art or out the window, or anywhere but looking a person in the eye, that's Hess."

"He might be a wonderful earl. He's not a very impressive brother."

Jacaranda smoothed back a lock of Yolanda's hair. "He's taken care of you, seen you educated, and spared you his company for a bit. He isn't all bad, and he's here now."

"Listen, Lannie." Worth risked taking his sister's hand, because Jacaranda's small touches seemed to soothe the girl. "Hess and I haven't even begun to discuss your circumstances. I've just met you, and Avery and I are entitled to some time with you before he spirits you away. Then too, you'll need a come out, and last I heard, the Queen wasn't making any progresses to the north, or the Regent either."

"Are you saying I can stay here? With you?"

"No, I am not." He spoke quite firmly, because females taking notions could completely ignore all reality to the contrary. "I'm saying if you have to go, it won't be just yet, and it won't be forever."

"Do you know how long winter is in the north, brother?" She snatched her hand away with an air of adolescent long-suffering, but all Worth heard was her use of the word "brother." She had two brothers, both well situated to provide for her, and only a few weeks after meeting Worth, Yolanda was choosing him over Hess.

The south over the north, too, but that was a detail.

Then he saw Jacaranda regarding him, solemnly, and knew he was at one of those points of decision that came upon a man without any warning, and forever changed the course of his situation on earth.

Worth was a brother, but what kind of brother, and to whom?

"Come." He possessed himself once more of his sister's hand. "Give Hess a chance, and when the time comes, I'll argue strenuously for letting you stay here with us at Trysting. I'm not your guardian, so I make no guarantees, but I've been known to be persuasive when I'm motivated."

He gave Jacaranda a look over his shoulder. She was smiling, and Yolanda was looking less mulish and martyred, so perhaps mediating between his siblings would bear all manner of desirable fruit.

The introduction went fairly well, with Yolanda offering her older brother a silent curtsy and Hess's mouth all but coming unhinged.

"Good God, you're beautiful," he said, walking a circle around her. "Not merely pretty, but beautiful."

"I do believe he's serious," Worth observed.

"I am utterly in earnest," Hess said. "Nobody at Grampion will recognize you as the hoyden who left us a few short years ago."

"Assuming Yolanda graces Grampion again," Worth replied. "We can discuss that some other day, when no picnic awaits us in the back gardens, yes?"

"A picnic!" Avery crowed. Then she was off in half-French, adoring picnics, and to fly the kites, and eat lots of cakes and take off the shoes and make the feets wet.

"Come, Avery." Yolanda led her niece from the room. "We must make sure the blankets are in the best spot. Footmen can't know such things."

"Of course not. Nor the uncles, but we are here to help them."

Worth took his brother by the elbow. "Come along, your lordship. We're to be shown the best spot, which no doubt lies in full view of an ant heap."

"Yolanda will not give in, will she?"

"Regarding?"

"I neglected her, and she's wroth over that, and the last place she wants to rusticate is at Grampion with me, even though sparing her such a fate is precisely why I so-called neglected her."

"Hess, she's female and young and has some reason to be put out with you. Two years she went without glimpsing you, and you're the head of her family. Did you miss her?"

"Of course I missed her." His mouth snapped shut, and he strode along beside Worth for half the length of a long corridor. "I wrote."

"She wrote back, I'm guessing, horrid little notes about embroidery and spotty boys?"

"She wrote about the animals she'd met, Worth. The house cats and cart ponies. As if she wouldn't allow me the satisfaction of hoping she might make new friends or see new sights. She punished me with those notes, and she was only fourteen years old."

"We use any weapons at hand when we're young and powerless," Worth said, hustling down the corridor, lest he take his meal in proximity to an ant heap. "You can apologize for what you believe you did wrong, and then it's up to her whether she meets you halfway or stays on her high horse. You don't have to take her north."

"I don't?" Hess stopped as if to admire the view out an oriel window that looked over the rose gardens. "What does that mean? She's too young to marry, Worth, I don't care what the old people say about it."

"The young people are usually the ones kicking over the traces to get married, but consider that Avery is only a year into living with her English uncle, and she seems quite taken with Yolanda. Then too, Yolanda will be back south in a year or two to make her come out. Why not leave her here with me and Avery?"

"As to Avery…"

Beyond the window, Yolanda and Avery were pointing at some shade beneath a towering oak while a pair of footmen moved blankets and hampers.

Worth knew what was coming, and perhaps it was best they have it out now, before too many fences had been mended. "As to Avery?"

"As head of the family, I've looked into the legal provisions for assuming guardianship of an orphaned child of a near relation," Hess began, gaze out the window.

Worth kept a hand on his brother's arm, until Hess was at least looking at where Worth touched him.

"You've been here only a few hours. I'm Avery's legal guardian, have been since before she arrived, and you needn't trouble yourself. Looking after the child helps me atone for Moira's death, if you must know, so don't feel you have to step in."

"Atone? For her death? What rot are you spouting, Worth?"

"I gave her money to go to Paris and join our maternal cousins, I gave her funds to seek instruction, I gave her the sense she had backing in case Papa cut her off. But for my short-sighted indulgence of her dreams, she'd be alive and raising her own children with a perfectly jolly English husband."

He hadn't planned on that confession, but really, who else could he make it to?

Hess looked him up and down, frowning a truly ferocious frown. He looked not like their father in that moment, but like their paternal grandfather when thunderously displeased.

"Don't be an idiot, Worth. I gave her money, too, and so, too, did Grandmamma. Moira wanted to go to Paris more than anything. Had we denied her, she might have been miserable instead of happy for the last years of her life. Think on that when you tire of beating yourself with the club of guilt."

"You gave her—?"

"Grandmamma did, too, and some jewels." Hess's gaze swung right back to the window. "Now let's rescue our luncheon from that ant heap."

Worth let him stride off, confident the ant heap would be vanquished. He was unable to do more than stare out the same window and watch as the other members of his family assembled for their meal.

*Even Hess*, notably cautious with his coin, had abetted Moira's dreams.

Jacaranda appeared at his side, a comforting presence he'd sorely missed while dealing with his brother.

"Get out there, Worth. They won't wait for you, and you won't get even a single chicken leg between now and tea."

Nor did he want a chicken leg.

He slipped an arm around her waist and whispered, "Come join us." He needed her near, now more than usually, given what his brother had told him.

She moved away to crack open the window and allow an eddy of rose-scented air into the corridor.

"This is your first meal as a family. You should *be* a family, not a family plus a housekeeper. Don't worry about Yolanda."

"The girl is plotting to overthrow the government as she knows it," Worth countered. "If I were Hess, I wouldn't turn my back on her."

"The worst that can happen is she has to go north at Michaelmas. She'll put up with one more winter at Grampion knowing you'll make her welcome next year, and once she's eighteen, Hess will have no reason to keep her up north. The better crop of bachelors always lurks near Town, and your brother can let her come south feeling like he's done his duty."

Hess gestured to a patch of grass in the sun, and Yolanda folded her arms. The blankets remained spread in the shade.

"Duty is Hess's middle name, and if you watch him, you'll realize he isn't arrogant so much as shy. He and Lannie have more in common than they think."

"She liked that, that you gave her a nickname, but Worth, you are the shy one now. Go have a meal with your family."

*Worth.* He was becoming Worth to her.

Out on the shady blankets, Hess pulled off his boots, Avery chattered away in at least two languages, while Yolanda arranged her skirts just so.

"You'll be fine." Jacaranda looked around, then went up on her toes and kissed his cheek. "You can tell me all about your ordeal later."

"Do you promise? My ordeal is likely to be harrowing in the extreme. Arachnids are quite the menace."

"Cook made chocolate crème cakes to ameliorate your suffering, but Hess won't leave you any sweets if you continue to hide here. Bide here, I mean."

"Nattering little besom." He kissed her cheek and headed down the steps, fortified by those few hints of understanding from her. It shouldn't be so. He was a grown man, wealthy, thriving in all the ways that counted, and he wasn't even really her lover. Barely her friend, in fact.

But it was so.

* * *

"Confound it, woman, budge over."

Jacaranda tugged the covers more tightly around herself. "Go away."

"I will do no such thing." Worth's weight dipped the mattress. "What in blazes are you doing with a brick in your sheets at the height of summer? You'll take a brick to your bosom but not my handsome self?"

"What time is it?"

He bounced and tugged and wiggled his long frame around until the last vestiges of sleep fled Jacaranda's mind.

"Past midnight," Worth said, sounding infernally comfy. "Hess was of a mind to get back his own over the cards. I am traumatized and exhausted by my day, also relieved of two pounds six."

"Why not seek your own bed, and then we'll both get some rest?"

Her brick, wrapped in several layers of flannel, made a solid *thunk* when Worth set it on the floor.

"You said I could tell you all about lunch," he reminded her. "When, pray, might I do that, when you dodged the evening meal with some taradiddle about a tray in your room? You evade me at every turn, so I've tracked you to your lair."

He lined his chest up along her back, and his arm came around her waist.

"Worth, begone. I mean it."

"You're denying me my audience?" His lips held a little audience along the top of her shoulder, and his hand gently pushed the strap of her nightgown aside. Under the cozy warmth of the covers, Jacaranda felt a shiver, a *thrill* along the path his fingers traced.

She was a good ten years too old to admit to thrills of any kind.

"Now is not the time," she tried again, but her voice lacked conviction, and his bodily warmth offered luscious comfort.

"Now is the only time. Yolanda addressed not one sentence to Hess directly at the noon meal, which made for a lovely verbal game of battledore, I can tell you. Hess's French is in good repair, but I fear his Italian is in worse shape than my own. My dear, you must relax."

"How can I relax when my bed has been invaded by the realm's largest magpie?"

"I'm visiting, not invading. You let bricks visit you and probably house cats."

His tone was playfully chiding, but beneath the banter lurked a question, too. If she insisted, he'd go, and he'd likely not come back until she invited him—if she invited him.

"Do I gather the brick was in the way of a hot water bottle?" he asked. "You toasted it up and brought it here to soothe a female ache?"

"You are too big for me to physically remove from this bed, but are you also too rude to comprehend the indelicacy of the topic you raise?"

He shifted to crouch over her beneath the covers, confirming Jacaranda's suspicion—her hope?—that he was naked. "I guessed correctly. The female complaint makes you cranky and out of sorts. I suspected this was the case."

Under him, Jacaranda rolled to her back, glad they had only moonlight to illuminate this exchange.

"I have a *headache*, one that makes my eyes hurt and my neck sore. Now that you know I'm indisposed, will you take yourself off?"

"Settle your feathers, dear heart." He kissed her forehead, an odd gesture that eased aches in various parts of Jacaranda's body and heart. "I haven't come to importune you, not that I won't at some point. See here." He found one of her hands and brought it to his—his member. "Hardly a prurient thought in my body, at the moment. I truly did want to talk."

He wasn't exactly flaccid, but he wasn't rampant, either.

"What did you want to talk about?" Jacaranda removed her hand two instants after she realized he'd removed his.

Worth hung over her, so she had to smooth back his hair with her fingers lest it obscure his eyes.

"I couldn't sleep," he said, climbing off of her and rolling to his back. He grabbed her hand again and kissed her knuckles. "Having Hess underfoot is disquieting."

"Family is always a challenge, which is part of the reason I've resisted orders from my siblings to return home until recently. In what way is his lordship disquieting?"

She didn't truly want to chase her visitor away, and she had told him they would talk, so she rolled up against his side and let her head fall to his shoulder. Maybe they could even talk about her upcoming return to Dorset.

"I blush to admit it," he began, his arm encircling her, "but I've treasured a sense of injury regarding the way I left Grampion all those years ago, and while I blamed my father, Hess had the last clear chance to thwart Papa's machinations."

"How old would he have been?" She set aside the question of what the young lady had been about—the young lady who'd had an understanding with Worth Kettering but had fallen out love with him "posthaste," to use his word. Jacaranda had reason to know no gently bred Englishwoman could be married against her will, thank God.

"Hess was all of twenty. No Town bronze, no tour of the Continent. He might have gone grouse hunting up in Scotland a time or two, but he was a stripling more than a man."

"You're having trouble clinging to your anger?"

He kissed her temple and spoke against her hair. "Worse than that. I feel sorry for him."

Oh, that was much worse. Jacaranda felt sorry for Step-Mama, whose situation was far from difficult. "Sorry, how?"

She aspired to feel sorry for Daisy, some distant day.

Worth snuggled her closer, and something tense and tired inside Jacaranda eased up, gave up. To be held, to have Worth's warmth and scent all around her in the dark, was lovely. Better than lovely, wonderful in fact, to cuddle up and chat in the depth of the night.

"Hess is so alone up there," Worth said, stroking Jacaranda's hair in an absent-minded caress. "I may not have bosom bows twelve deep, but I like my clients. Some of them could be friends. I like my staff, I like the neighbors you've introduced me to here. I have Avery, I have you, I have people moving about in my life. Hess has his stables and nobody to share them with. No wonder he missed Yolanda and wants to take her home with him."

*I have you.* As flummoxed as Jacaranda was by his casual claim, she did not allow herself to tarry over it.

"You have me for now, as a housekeeper, but we need to discuss that. Will you allow Hess to retrieve Yolanda?"

Worth heaved a mighty sigh, and this time he kissed her ear. "Hess is Yolanda's guardian. I can't stop him, but in his mind, I think he regards such an arrangement as fair somehow: I have Avery; therefore, he should get Lannie."

"Why can't you all have each other?" Jacaranda posed the question rhetorically, because her mind would not let go of those earlier words... *I have you.*

"We haven't the knack, my dear. Does your neck still trouble you?"

Not as much as her heart.

"That was not a gracious change of subject, Mr. Kettering, but because you won't desist and it's too dark for my blushes to affect you, yes, my head aches. I suspect the blooming flowers affect me badly."

"Poor lady. You're reduced to Mr. Kettering-ing me. On your side, and let's see if I can't help out."

Her complicity in this scheme was irrelevant, because he gently maneuvered her into the position of his liking, while he angled himself behind her.

"Close your eyes, my dear," he instructed, "and tell me more about your cottage. You had a name for it."

"Complaisance Cottage," she said, surprised he'd recall. "What on earth are you doing?"

"Relax, love." Lips brushed her nape. "My hand is warmer than that brick. You might as well put it to use." *He* put his hand to use, massaging her neck, a firm combination of stroking and squeezing that...

She groaned with the relief of it, and he had the good grace not to gloat aloud.

"What do your back gardens look like, Jacaranda, or does this cottage nestle against a wood?"

She explained how the cottage was situated, how informal plots rioting with flowers ringed the pitch of grass, and the stately old dowager oaks stood at the edge of the home wood as a backdrop. She told him about the sea birds who nipped up any scraps or crusts that fell—or were tossed—from a tea tray taken on the terrace, and about the particular scent of the breeze, depending on whether it was a sea breeze, a land breeze, or some brewing combination of both.

"You long for it," he said, his voice low and lazy in the moonlight.

"I ache with missing it," she replied, because it was dark, and that was the honesty she could give him. "Don't you miss Grampion?"

"The sentiments ebb and flow." His hand moved slowly over her shoulders now, the same way his words threaded through the darkness. "When the first snow falls here and it's so much later and less hearty than the first snows in the north, I miss Grampion. When the crocuses march forth, no hesitance or backsliding in their arrival, as if spring is a foregone conclusion, I miss Grampion. When the summer weather gets truly hot and miserable, I miss it. Not so much at other times."

Which left…? "You don't miss it in spring?" For she missed Dorset in spring.

"Spring in London is a busy time. I receive the courtesy invitations. I'm nominally heir to an earldom, single, and worth a fortune. I accept occasionally, particularly if it's a client doing the inviting."

"When you're twirling some lady down the ballroom, you don't miss your home?"

"Hush." He twisted up and over her for a leisurely kiss to her mouth, a kiss that involved

his tongue flirting with her lips, teasing and implying and promising even as he soothed and reassured. "I miss my home. Are you satisfied to have wrung this confession from me? I miss my home almost as much as you miss yours."

"I do miss my home, and my family. I've missed them for years, and that's why after all this time—"

He must have sensed that her words would be unwelcome, because he kissed her again, thoroughly, lingeringly.

Jacaranda subsided to her back, all thoughts of disclosures and partings tossed out of the bed like so many more cold bricks.

She kissed Worth back, cuddled with him, and conversed for another few minutes, but in truth Worth's hand, or his company, or something about his visit had relaxed more than Jacaranda's body. As she drifted off, Worth spooned around her and her discomforts considerably eased, she had the traitorous thought that it was fortunate she was returning to Dorset, for she could grow accustomed to his nocturnal company.

Sheer folly, that, but what wonderful, pleasurable folly.

* * *

"Do you miss having a wife?" Worth put the question to his brother as they rode out, no grooms, no steward to hinder their privacy. Thanks to Jacaranda's carping, Worth knew how to get around on his own land, knew which bridle path led to what lane and which fields had the best footing before their stiles.

"I do not miss the wife I had," Hess said. "I'm sorry if that offends."

Worth shortened his snaffle reins. "You might offend the lady's memory, but your words can't offend me."

"Why haven't you married?"

Hess might be shy, he did not lack courage.

"I've wondered that myself lately." Worth settled his weight into the stirrups. "Shall we let them stretch their legs a bit?"

They raced the entire three miles remaining to Least Wapping. Hess was at a slight disadvantage because he didn't know the terrain, but Worth had put his brother up on a former steeplechaser and Hess was an excellent rider.

Hess thwacked his horse's neck when they trotted into the yard of the posting inn. "What a prime fellow. Don't tell me he's for sale. I've no need of another gelding and Alfred's feelings would be hurt. This one has tons of bottom, tons of it."

"You truly love it, don't you? The cross-country romp that would frighten the hair off most people?" Worth swung down and handed Goliath off to a stable boy to cool out. "I haven't let Goliath have his head like that for months, but he enjoyed it."

"They weren't put on earth to pace their stalls, looking handsome and bored." In the hint of wistfulness in Hess's voice, Worth gathered an insight into his brother.

"Autumn will soon approach. Why not linger here for some of the informal meets and then stay to attend the lords?"

Hess's features composed themselves into a bland mask. "What of the harvest at Grampion? Is the corn to bring itself in off the fields?"

*Why can't you all have each other?*

Jacaranda's words echoed in Worth's mind, and he let the subject drop, but in the part of his brain that couldn't resist a complex negotiation, he began to plot and plan and strategize.

"Let's grab a pint," Worth suggested. "The horses can catch their wind before they tackle the five-mile jaunt back to Trysting, and you haven't told me of the staff at Grampion. Is Homer Gentry still your land steward, and does his wife still make those butter biscuits that melt away all of a small boy's troubles?"

"And leave him with a bellyache into next Tuesday," Hess finished the thought.

To Worth's surprise, Hess allowed himself to be interrogated about each and every person Worth recalled from his boyhood.

Two and a half pints later, Worth mentally conceded it had more likely been a matter of Worth allowing himself to ask.

\* \* \*

"What is Francine up to?" Grey hated having to ask his brother, but her ladyship's correspondence had reached flood stage.

Will tossed a stick dutifully dropped at his feet by a brindle mastiff larger than some of the ponies used in the mines.

"I am not in Step-Mama's confidence, Grey, for which I give daily thanks to my Creator. I did see her casting spells over the teapot with Mrs. Dankle."

The dog waited at Will's feet, adoring gaze turned on its owner. When Will gave some signal visible only to the beast, it bounded off across the green between the gardens and the home wood.

"Francine is ever imposing on Dankle's good nature," Grey said. "You need Ash to invent you a machine for pitching sticks into the next county, lest you tire your arm."

The dog was back in a half-dozen happy, ear-flapping bounds, the stick deposited at Will's feet as the hound dropped to its haunches.

"Step-Mama wants to spend the rest of the summer in Bath," Will said, petting the dog's great head. "If not Bath, then Lyme Regis. The older set likes to congregate where they have fond memories and to leave the house parties to us."

Where were Will's fond memories? He was a handsome fellow in the tall, dark-haired, violet-eyed cast of his siblings and had read law with the same ease some people read the Society pages of the *London Gazette*.

"I cannot afford to send Francine to Bath, and I've told her as much on several occasions." Painful occasions, for them both.

"I know that. Good boy, George."

"You name the largest dog in the realm after our sovereign?"

"I named the largest bitch in the realm after our sovereign. Her full name is Georgette. You should ask Daisy what her dear mama is up to. If Francine burdens anybody with her schemes, it's her own daughter."

At the mention of her name, the dog's ears swiveled, for she, like most females, was apparently eager to do Will's bidding.

"I'd be nervous, were I you, Will."

"She won't eat me, will you, Georgie dearest? She eats only meddling older brothers who won't send Step-Mama away for a few weeks so we can all enjoy some peace and quiet."

"Which is why I'd be worried," Grey said, letting the dog sniff at his hand. She was surprisingly delicate about it, for all her size. "I fear Francine's scheming again to get one of us matched with an heiress. I've the title to protect me, because Francine won't presume to choose our next countess. You're the next oldest, the best looking, and too fond of the ladies to tell Step-Mama to mind her own business."

Will tossed the stick again, sending it clear into the home wood. "You're saying if you deny Mama a house on the Crescent in Bath, she'll seek revenge by flinging heiresses at me?"

The dog disappeared after the stick, her path marked by rustling bushes.

"I don't know what exactly Step-Mama's about. Francine is a woman who's been discontent with her station for some time, and I haven't the knack of divining her plots. She was after me to bodily fetch Jacaranda home, claiming that this time Mrs. Dankle truly will leave us for the charms of her son's small holding."

"Dankle has earned her rest, and four grandchildren is rather a temptation."

Three grandchildren had done nothing to improve the lure of home for Francine. With each of Daisy's babies, her ladyship seemed to grow more desperate to distance herself from her children.

"Be careful, Will. If you've a notion to attend some house parties, I won't stop you."

Will gave him an odd look. "I thought you hated house parties."

"I most assuredly do. They are the delight of the unhappily married and the downfall of many a contented bachelor. You'd best see what's keeping that puppy of yours. Mr. Springboth's hound occasionally gets loose, and as far as he's concerned, your Georgie would make a prime bit of sport."

"I'll be careful, and I'll keep an eye on Step-Mama. See that you do likewise. You're not bad looking, you have the title, and for some women, that's enough."

Will loped off, his expression promising severe consequences for any presuming hound who trifled with his Georgette.

\* \* \*

"It occurred to me," Worth said as he settled in beside Jacaranda, "a storm is brewing tonight, and you might appreciate some company. No bricks, my dear?"

"No bricks." The comment was literal and figurative, because she wasn't hurling writs of ejectment at him either. Tonight she laced her fingers through his and let his hand rest over her midriff.

His patience was paying off—finally.

"You're feeling a bit more the thing?" He stole a kiss to her shoulder, the happiest occasion of thievery.

"A bit. That tickles."

"This?" He ran his nose along the top of her shoulder again. "You're like a bouquet, you know. Your shoulders have one fragrance, your hair another, you hands yet another. I could cheerfully sniff you for hours."

He had, in fact. When last he'd called upon her under the covers, her scents had quieted his mind as much as her company had.

"You'd get no rest." Jacaranda sounded happy to contemplate his misery, and her happiness meant a great deal to Worth.

"You're either coming to trust me"—he kissed her nape—"or you've secreted a frying pan under your pillow and you're confident you can subdue me with it if I get out of line."

She rolled to her back, and in the moonlight her features were breathtakingly lovely. "Are you soon to get out of line?"

And there it was, the Jacaranda Wyeth battle flag, demanding honesty and a surrender of privacy from him. He hadn't been sure even a few days ago that the sacrifice would be worth the reward, but now... He was willing to sacrifice much to have *her* honesty and *her* surrender. Willing to wait, willing to campaign all summer.

Except summer was half over, and his dear Wyeth was increasingly restless, for reasons he could not fathom.

"I will never cross the lines you draw for us," he said. "I'll push, I'll tease, I'll negotiate, and I'll dare, but you hold the reins, Jacaranda. You will always hold the reins."

"If I didn't, what would you do, were you at liberty?"

Bold question. *Clever*, bold question.

"Honestly? I'm supposed to say I'd ravish you blind, make love to you until neither of us can walk, and those would be sincere sentiments. I desire you until... Well, I simply do."

He shut up in defense of his beleaguered dignity.

"But?"

"I desire more than a quick tumble, a tickle and a poke. I'm not sure what exactly I mean, but I conclude your timing on the matter is to be trusted more than my own."

He watched her digest that, not even sure himself what he'd said, what he'd been trying to say.

"Explain something to me," she said, rolling over to her side again. "When can we pursue this 'matter' with the least risk of conception, were I so inclined?"

He couldn't help himself, he cuddled closer, a hot spike of lust giving the lie to his earlier more philosophical words. He'd meant those words of course—one did not dissemble with Jacaranda Wyeth—but her question boded well for his objectives.

Whatever they might be.

He opened his mouth to breathe in the scent of her neck. "After a lady's indisposition has departed, it's reasonably safe for a few days, a few nights. I would love to pleasure you, Jacaranda, all night."

"Yes, I know, until we're both lamed, though how that results from pleasure escapes me." She fell silent as Worth pushed her gently to her back, settling his mouth over hers before she could offer more tart, frustrated observations.

"You want to know, Jacaranda," he murmured against her mouth. "Your curiosity is consuming you. What would we be like, together? How would I feel, inside you, over you? Under you? Behind you? Just how much pleasure could I bring you with my mouth on your privy parts? Or maybe you'd like to put your mouth on me?"

He cruised that mouth of his over her features, gathering tastes and textures with his tongue: her delicate, delicate eyelashes, the exact curve of her brows, left then right, the span of the bridge of her nose, the soft buttery substance of her earlobes, the pulse at her throat.

"You are delicious, an edible bouquet."

"Stop. Worth, you must stop, now."

# CHAPTER TWELVE

Worth paused, hoping Jacaranda had ordered him to a parade rest, not the onset of yet more sexual frustration.

"You'll overwhelm me," she said, hiking up on her elbows. "I have not decided to—"

"Join," he suggested, "to join with me intimately."

"I haven't, but you said…" She traced his eyebrows with her index finger, as he'd traced hers with his tongue. "I intended that you and I should have a certain difficult discussion, and I still do. But for now, lie on your back and behave, Worth."

He rolled to his back as obediently as one of Hess's hounds and prayed to a merciful God this *behaving* was a form of progress for them. As for the difficult discussion, he could only hope that meant she was reconsidering his proposal. Difficult for her, to admit she'd erred, though in victory he would be gracious and charming. Why, he'd even—

She took up where she'd left off, imitating him, tracing her fingers over his features, then following with her mouth.

"You bathed tonight. I can smell the flowers on you."

"You like that," he said, "that I bathed for you. I get hard when I'm bathing, thinking of you doing what you're doing now." One of many times throughout the day that arousal afflicted him.

"Oh, please hush." Not her usual dismissive admonition, more a moan, a prayer, and she settled her mouth over his, ensuring his compliance.

He stayed on his back, where she'd told him to stay, and he resisted mightily the urge to roll her under him and the need to snug her body to his so he'd have something to thrust against.

He instead put all that lust and longing and frustration into his kiss, sealing his mouth to hers, cupping her head in his palm and sending his tongue foraging into her heat. He explored, he plundered, he teased, he feinted, all in aid of encouraging her own forays. When the tip of her tongue limned his teeth, his cock leapt and his belly tightened.

He dropped away from the kiss. "Too much."

"I don't understand."

She was frowning again. Frowning wasn't good.

"Hell and the devil." He took her hand and drew it down, to the arousal rampant against his belly, rampant, straining, weeping with the need for completion. "You do this to me, Jacaranda. I'm close."

"Close." She kept her hand around him as he drew his away, leaving her to grip his shaft lightly. "I see."

"Close your fingers around me. Please."

She did, her grip still too tentative.

"Tighter, love. I'm begging."

"I don't want to hurt you." But her marvelously competent hand closed around him securely, and the pleasure of it stole his breath.

"If you move your hand, fondle me, stroke me, put your mouth on me, I'll spend. I'll leave if you ask it, Jacaranda. I don't want to, but I can manage to abandon you now if I must."

A fine lie, that, and when honesty was one of the aspects of Jacaranda Wyeth he treasured most dearly.

She held him firmly, while he willed her to find the fortitude to take this step with him.

She sleeved him and moved her hand up and down about an inch. "Like this?"

"Higher." He got both syllables out through clenched teeth. "Not like... Here."

He showed her with his own hand, a few loose strokes, enough to get most of the length of him and enough that his ballocks threatened to draw up.

"Draw my stones down," he said. "Gently, yes... God's dancing slippers." The cool, soft slide of her fingers, the surprising assurance with which she complied with his request surprised him.

"You like this?" She had her hand on his cock again, letting the circle of her fingers slip up to the crown and down the shaft.

"Love...it. Jesus at the wedding feast." He had to move his hips, had to, but he kept his undulations slow, wanting to savor the torture, wanting it to build and build. Knowing she was watching him by moonlight, though, watching the tension in his face, watching his body become a mindless, pleasure-maddened beast, made the whole experience so much more intimate.

She was learning about sexual intimacy, yes, but she was learning about *him*, too.

He grabbed the pillow on both sides of his head to keep his hand from fisting around hers. Bright, hot pleasure roared through him, out through every particle and sinew he owned and on into the dark, summer night. He groaned, he bucked, he strained to withstand the bliss and strained harder to surrender to it, on and on, until he couldn't hear, couldn't see, and couldn't move for the pleasure wringing him out.

When he was once again aware of crickets chirping and the breeze billowing the curtain, Jacaranda's cheek was pressed to his abdomen, and her hand cupped his rapidly softening cock.

*Words.* Women wanted words at such times. Worth had none. Couldn't imagine when he would find any, either.

Jacaranda rose and fetched a flannel and basin from the bureau across the room. She swabbed him off and took a few brisk swipes at her fingers.

"A man's pleasure is indelicate." The most blissful indelicacy Worth had ever endured. "I'm sorry."

She set the towel and basin aside. "It's intense. I suppose you'd like to sleep?"

"Sleep, when I've just…? I'll sleep later."

"I've never seen a man do that before." She gestured vaguely at the cool air over his genitals. "My brothers were forever being coarse when they thought I couldn't hear them, but I've never…well. I was afraid I'd hurt you."

She was so brave, and so shy about climbing back into bed with him.

"Some people enjoy an element of pain. I'm not one of them, but stop looking at me as if I grew horns. I am in want of affection." He was a little alarmed at his admission, for that was the truth coming out of his idiot mouth.

Sex scrambled the brains; this was scientific fact, he was sure of it.

She climbed on the bed and busied herself rearranging the pillows he'd cast into chaos. "We've shared affection already. You can't be in want of affection."

He wanted more than simple affection, and the vexing creature would make him admit it.

"I want to know,"—he paused, gathering his courage—"I need to know you are not repulsed, you aren't shocked. This wasn't how I intended to go on. I don't want you to have a disgust of me."

She appeared to consider this, and then subsided onto the mattress, facing him, not touching him, damn it. Because she was closer to the window, her face was obscured by night shadows, and that about drove him 'round the bend.

But from somewhere, he found the resolve, the courage, to hold his position and keep his hands to himself.

"What comes now?" she asked, a frown in her voice.

*Let me hold you,* he wanted to say, but there was that frown.

"Jacaranda, what would you like to come now?"

"Honestly?"

"Love, you've seen me *in extremis* when I hadn't planned to be that way. You'll have to tell me where this leaves us, and yes, of course I expect honesty between us. I adore your penchant for honesty."

The frown intensified. "We still need to have that discussion, but can you do that *in extremis* part again?"

\* \* \*

Jacaranda's face heated as she put the question to Worth, and she battled the urge to flee. What stopped her was the suspicion, the strong suspicion, that Worth's feelings would be hurt if she tucked tail and ran.

They would be hurt even more if she unburdened herself of the two deceptions she yet perpetrated on him.

She was leaving him at the end of the summer, and her name wasn't Jacaranda Wyeth. She hoped never to burden him with the knowledge he'd dallied with an earl's spinster daughter.

"I can manage it again," he said, studying her in the moonshadows. "I need a few minutes to recover, but I could if you assisted. Is that what you want?"

He traced her eyebrows with a single finger then let that finger trail down her nose, and chin, and across her collarbones, his expression reverent.

"Sometime, yes."

"Enough of this long-distance negotiating, Wyeth." He moved across the mattress to bundle her against his side. "Slap me if I'm being presumptuous."

"Slap—" As if lying in his arms were more presumptuous than...well. She cuddled down against his chest, though the wretch could probably feel her cheeks heat.

"On my bum would be nice should the slapping appeal," he said, gathering her closer. "I'll happily reciprocate if you'd like a little spanking."

"Oh, do hush." She put her hand against his naughty mouth, but some of the awkwardness of the situation dissipated. She could see him enjoying her hand applied smartly to his backside, too.

Which gave one reason to ponder.

"This feels better," he said, his hand stroking over her hair.

"Better than what?"

"Than you, regarding me so solemnly from halfway across the Channel. Erotic intimacy is an odd business, isn't it?"

He had a name for what they'd shared. Marvelous.

"The entire business is strange." She felt him waiting, listening for her reaction, so she mustered a greater quantity of fortitude. "It's beautiful, too, and very personal."

"Intimate."

His was the more accurate word.

"Do you want to sleep now?" Because if he did want to sleep, she wanted him to sleep in her bed, so she could feast her senses on him while he lay passive, beautiful, and mysterious in her arms.

"What I want"—he gently shook her head with his hand in her hair, a scolding sort of shake—"is to know you're not disconcerted by what happened in your bed tonight. What I did was selfish, vulgar, and presumptuous."

"I am disconcerted." She pressed her lips over his nipple and tongued him while she sorted through her reactions and ways to render them into words she could bear to speak. "You taste like spices."

"Jacaranda Wyeth."

She smiled, letting him feel her mouth curve against his skin. "I felt powerful, knowing I caused the pleasure you felt."

"Ah." Relief in that single syllable. "You'd like that, having power over a man when his defenses were in disarray."

"Not just any man, for most of them have their defenses in disarray most of the time. You. I liked sharing that moment with you." In this, she could be absolutely honest.

"You're not disgusted?"

"I wanted to taste you." She bit his chin and climbed over him, probably surprising them both with her boldness. "I wanted to taste you, and kiss you, and fondle you."

The dear man threaded his hands through her hair on either side of her head and shut her naughty mouth by kissing her soundly.

* * *

Jacaranda delighted to waken in Worth's arms, to see his dark hair against her white pillowcases when the sun's first rays came stealing in the window. To watch him rouse while the birds outside the window sang to the new day, to see him open his eyes while she drowsed beside him.

These desires were dangerous. Her longing went beyond merely wanting *him*, which any woman with red blood in her veins might do. More than that, she wanted memories with him, memories of intimacies that transcended a mere joining of bodies.

Because she sought those memories, she endured his farewell kiss without embarking on any difficult discussions about Dorset and family obligations and impoverished earldoms.

She did not want to explain to him that she, of all people, hadn't been entirely forthcoming with him, and though her secrets were not shameful, exactly, they were falsehoods. Worse, the longer she allowed those falsehoods to live, the more difficult would be the reckoning for her deception.

With Worth Kettering, further intimacies would be transcendently splendid. Jacaranda knew that now, knew the look and feel and scent of him when he expressed his passion, when he was *in extremis*, as he'd put it, and she wanted more. With him, she wanted to share that passion, to know if it could ignite her own.

Which would, of course, do nothing to ensure the maids were at their tasks, the footmen weren't bothering the maids too awfully much, Simmons's knees were still working, and Cook wasn't overwhelmed.

Dawn came wonderfully early in summer, though when Jacaranda reached the breakfast parlor, she was surprised to find only the Earl of Grampion at the table.

No Worth?

"He's packing," Grampion said, rising. "I expect he'd be down here at a dead gallop did he know you were breaking your fast."

Jacaranda retreated into manners. "Good morning, my lord. I assume you're referring to Mr. Kettering?"

"I am. Did you sleep well, Mrs. Wyeth?"

He held her chair for her, so Jacaranda couldn't watch his face as he posed the question.

"I slept wonderfully," she said, the absolute, bald, unfortunate, naughty truth.

"You have that look about you." He took his seat and passed her the teapot, cream and sugar in succession. "You've roses in your cheeks."

"Thank you for the compliment." Jacaranda smiled at him, for it had been a compliment, though hardly given with a flourish. "Are you enjoying your stay here, my lord?"

He took a sip of his tea and wrinkled his handsome mouth. He wasn't a bad-looking man, though his lanky English blondness was less appealing than his brother's dark good looks.

"I am enjoying my stay, yes."

"Is there a 'but' appended to that grudging allowance?"

"Worth said you were a woman of substance." Grampion frowned at his tea now, a stout black breakfast blend Jacaranda had ordered to get the household's day off to a good start, though he might have ordered gunpowder for himself easily enough. "I should have known by Worth's lights that substance meant a tendency toward cheek as well."

"My apologies." Jacaranda appropriated a serving of eggs from the server in the middle of the table and some toast. "May I have the butter?"

This provoked a smile from the earl, which made him look younger and far more attractive—by Jacaranda's *lights*.

"Your apologies, pass the butter. I can see why Worth is so taken with you." He did pass the butter.

"Aren't you eating, my lord?" She went about buttering her toast as if the earl hadn't made a disquieting observation, hoping that Grampion simply lacked for conversation first thing in the day. *She* certainly did. "The eggs are surpassingly good."

"You needn't turn up skittish, Mrs. Wyeth. I'm out of the habit of poaching on my brother's preserves."

She put her knife and toast down, for that comment, especially from a belted earl, required a response, regardless of the household's democratic eccentricities at meal times.

"Were I, as you put it, your brother's *preserves,* then it would be up to me whether I could be poached upon, wouldn't it? And were I your brother's preserves, and he mine, I can assure you, your overtures would be soundly rebuffed."

"You don't fancy a title panting after you?" He was merely curious rather than peevish or offended.

"I don't fancy a man who would betray his brother at the same table as I am, much less with his tongue unattractively wagging in the wind," Jacaranda said. "Because you are not such a man, at least not in your present incarnation, we need hardly discuss hypotheticals over our morning tea, correct?"

"God in heaven." The words were said with exactly the same inflection Worth used. "You are a veritable Tartar." He saluted with his tea cup. "We have thoroughly hashed through my dastardly past, and I will have some of those eggs."

"You ought to talk to him about it, you know," Jacaranda said, spooning eggs onto his outstretched plate. He was a big man, almost as big as Worth, so she didn't stint.

"You expect me to eat all this?"

"You aren't a bird, my lord, and Worth has you riding all over the shire. Eat up, and be grateful. I am."

She smiled and gave a flourish with her forkful of eggs. He wasn't so bad, this earl, but he wasn't a happy man, and she felt sorry for him.

Imagine, feeling sorry for an earl. She'd thought to leave that habit behind her forever.

"I've tried talking to Worth," he said, tucking into his eggs. "He brushes the topic aside. Even as a boy, Worth was plagued by shyness."

"Bring it up again. My brothers all require persistence when one wants to parse a delicate subject, and then they want it over with as soon as may be. Cowards, the lot of them."

"Are you saying Worth is a coward?"

"Good heavens, no." Jacaranda studied her plate to hide the smile that went with the next thought: *Worth is very brave. He's pursuing me.* "You both have a capacity for shyness, and Worth is the kindest man I know. I doubt he'd want you to trouble yourself over ancient history."

"Less than fifteen years ago," the earl said, pouring himself more tea. "I am not shy."

She reached over and patted his hand. "Of course you're not."

He glared at her, just as one of her brothers might, and she wondered where this great good-humored confidence of hers was coming from. The man was an earl, for pity's sake, and she was teasing him.

She wondered if anyone was teasing her own brother like this, for Grey was a man badly in need of teasing.

"You are a baggage, Mrs. Wyeth," Grampion pronounced, but he was smiling. At last, he was smiling again. "Worth is lucky to have you."

"Worth knows this," said the man himself. He kissed Jacaranda's cheek as he swept into the room, tousled his brother's hair, and appropriated the teapot.

"Damned thing is empty," he said, taking a seat beside his brother and helping himself to the man's tea. "One has to make do. Mrs. Wyeth, my brother and I are removing to Town this morning. I've been summoned by a particularly irksome client. We should be back before too long, unless I lose my brother's company to the flesh-pots of Egypt, as it were."

The earl stole his tea back. "Worth, for pity's sake."

"You could have grown lonely up there in the north with nothing but sheep to keep you company. Natures in the south are sunnier, you'll note, because we have more opportunities to socialize convivially, and winters don't last ten and a half months. Ah, look, somebody took pity on a poor, starving lad and left me a few spoonfuls of egg."

He took the rest of the eggs, winked at Jacaranda, and stoically endured his brother's splutterings about manners and upbringings and decadent speech. A footman brought in more tea and moved the empty dishes to the sideboard before Worth waved him away.

The earl rose and bowed to Jacaranda. "I'm sorry to leave you in such company, Mrs. Wyeth, but Worth claims his client cannot wait. I'm off to finish my packing."

"Worth claims," Worth mimicked. "You'd better have your lordly arse down to the stables in thirty minutes or I'll leave you here to Mrs. Wyeth's tender mercies. She'll have you fat as a shoat and standing up with all the local beauties if you're not careful, and we have a veritable regiment of local beauties."

The earl departed, not deigning to reply, and Jacaranda was left smiling at her... Well, he was still her employer, and a little of her glee at the start of the day dimmed.

"That boy needs to visit some flesh-pots, methinks." Worth spoke loudly enough his departing brother might have heard him. "But he'll stay with me in Town, because he hasn't had time to open Grampion House. You'll manage?"

"Without you two? Of course."

This earned her a pause as Worth reached for his brother's tea again.

"I'll miss you, Jacaranda Wyeth. I can't close the door and part with you as I'd like, but I can tell you I will miss you."

"When will you return?"

"You're supposed to say you'll miss me, too." He set the tea down untasted, his morning bonhomie leaving his expression. "I wouldn't be haring back to Town now of all times if I could avoid it, but this client has a right to be concerned."

"His money is at risk?"

"He doesn't do well with high-risk investments," Worth said, clearly choosing his words, "but he needs high returns, and I've promised them to him."

"Promised, Worth?" He hadn't made *her* many promises; but then, she'd given him exactly none herself.

"Within reason. I don't like doing it, for no matter how sternly I caution him, he hears only of the potential profit, but so far, we've been lucky. Walk me to my room? I'd like to take a proper leave of you, and Hess will be down at the stables in exactly five-and-twenty minutes."

"Did you know last night that you'd be leaving this morning?"

He patted his lips with his serviette. "I did. The messenger arrived as Hess and I were putting away the cards. We saw him fed and bedded down with the grooms. He was on his way back to Town at first light. Why?"

"You should have been getting your rest," she said, unhappy with him for reasons she couldn't sort out. "Not disporting with me."

"You are not doing this." He rose and came around to hold her chair. "You are not picking a silly fight because I've been called to Town and you think I'm going happily. I'm going kicking and screaming, my love. I am well aware this timing is execrable, well aware we need to talk."

He towed her by the wrist into the hallway then dropped her hand. "Come along, please. We won't be disturbed in my room, and you should have a chance to throw things at me if it will make you feel better."

"I don't want to throw things at you." Except he was right: She did want to throw things, things that broke with a lot of noise and mess and sharp edges.

Good heavens, she was turning into her step-mama.

"Then scream at me like a virago," he suggested. "Along the lines of 'Worth, how can you run off to Town when you know I haven't made up my mind about you? This is exactly why no woman in her right mind should give you the time of day, much less fifteen minutes of her night. You dash off at the worst moment and leave a woman to wonder if she imagined all that...' Have I got it about right?"

He'd kept his voice down, which was probably why she hadn't interrupted him with a sound scolding.

"I wish you didn't have to go, though I know your business means a great deal to you."

"Less than it used to," he muttered, and this, for some reason, made Jacaranda feel better. "Less than it should."

She could not ask him if he'd consort with his opera dancers while in Town, if he'd haul his brother around to the brothels in a display of fraternal hospitality. Men were capable of living parallel lives, she knew that from being Grey Dorning's sister, and from the mistakes she'd made five years ago.

"I hardly need to pack much," he said as they reached his room. He left the door open, but disappeared into his dressing room, allowing Jacaranda to peer around chambers she'd been in often enough, but never with him.

"Do you know where my emerald cravat pin has got off to?"

"I wasn't aware you had an emerald cravat pin." She followed him into his dressing room, because a possible theft of emerald jewelry on her watch was a very serious—

He dragged her up against him and covered her mouth with his as soon as she was across the dressing room threshold.

*A morning kiss,* Jacaranda thought as pleasure bloomed. He tasted of sweetened tea and a little of desperation. She preferred the desperation.

"Damn you." He pushed her up against a wardrobe. "How can you be so composed when I want to pitch a tantrum?" His kiss became slower, less desperate, more plundering. "I want to consume you, woman, to spend hours in bed wearing you out and then hours longer while you wear me out. Or maybe I'd go first, but what an end, eh? Say you'll miss me."

He kissed her neck, holding her hands stretched above her with one of his and brushing his other down her front.

"Worth." Whispering his name was not a very impressive display of feminine authority. "*Worth Reverence Kettering.*" She got the whip-crack into it that time. "You must stop."

He hung over her, his lungs working so each inhale meant his chest brushed her breasts. "Why stop?" An incongruous, wry smile bloomed across his features, and Jacaranda was relieved to see it.

"Because in twenty minutes, you'll have to sit a horse, and I have no intention of permitting you nineteen minutes of liberties first."

A look passed across his features, arrested, then maybe chagrined. He pushed away and crossed the little room to sink down onto a daybed.

"Cruel but accurate. I really do not want to go."

"I believe you." Still, she couldn't bring herself to ask again when he'd be back. "I'll look after the girls in your absence, and for Yolanda, it might even be a relief to have some breathing space."

"That one." He stood and scrubbed a hand down his face. "I can't tell if what she wants is to stay with me, or to make Hess pay for leaving her to her own devices."

"You might talk to her about it."

"A novel idea: talk to a female about what she wants. Let's give it a try, shall we? Do you want me, Jacaranda Wyeth?"

Maybe Jacaranda was the one in need of room to breathe. "Bodily? Of course, that has never been in question."

His smile faded into puzzlement. "We should be back toward midweek. Parliament will go out of session, and I doubt Hess wants people to know he's underfoot."

Jacaranda pushed away from the wardrobe. "He's single, titled, and wealthy. They'll get word he's in Town even if he never leaves your residence." Grey had complained often enough about the London hostesses that Grampion's plight earned her sympathy.

"Hess's heir is similarly situated," Worth reminded her. "I wonder about the wealthy part of it, Jacaranda."

"In what sense?"

"Hess came down here without a single groom, for pity's sake. I take a groom when I'm going any distance, to see to the horses, for safety, in case Goliath throws a shoe, a hundred reasons. Why no groom?"

"He made it here without one, and he's a very private person, your brother."

"He is. May I tell you something?"

The subject was no longer Hess Kettering, and unease skittered up Jacaranda's spine.

"I want you to desire me," Worth said, coming to stand right before her. "I think I can *make* you desire me, in fact, but I am confounded to admit that isn't enough."

She must not let him say anything more along these lines. "We haven't even—"

He put two fingers to her lips.

"I know." The puzzlement was back. "Will you miss me, Jacaranda? Will you stop in the middle of your day and wonder what I'm up to, if I'm thinking of you? Will you smile sometimes, to recall something I said, something I did? Or am I spouting callow nonsense, thinking, maybe just a little, that you want more than bed sport of me, too?"

"That is precisely the problem," she said, trying not to be dazzled with what he'd confessed. Dazzled and heartbroken. "What I want is complicated. I'd hoped we might have time to discuss it, but now I want—"

"I want it, too. I thrive on complexity." He kissed her again, sweetly, as if her answer had been exactly what he wanted to hear.

Then he rummaged in his bureau.

"Worth, bid the girls farewell. We'll manage in your absence."

"Manage." He banged a drawer closed and held up an elegant gold and emerald cravat pin. "Bugger managing. Tell me, Jacaranda Wyeth. I will not let you out of this room until you do." They weren't touching, but his gaze bored into her with unnerving determination. "Tell me."

Jacaranda took a moment to sort through what else lurked in his gaze: encouragement, a gift of his courage, offered to her to fortify her against any fears.

All he wanted was the truth. That again.

"I'll miss you," she said, sliding her arms around his waist. "I'll say prayers for your safety, I'll listen for Goliath's hoof beats coming up the drive. When no one's about, I'll lift your pillow to my nose to bring your scent to me. I will not always be housekeeper here, Worth, but for now, I wish I had a miniature of you. I wish I had one of myself to give you."

They were courting words, also parting words. He kissed her again, each cheek, each eyelid, framing her face with his hands, suggesting he'd heard the courting part and ignored the rest.

"You'll be on horseback soon, Worth."

"Right, and I must make my bow in the nursery. Sniff my pillow all you like."

Then he was gone.

Before she left his rooms, Jacaranda stopped by the great lordly expanse of his high bed and brought his pillow to her nose.

* * *

"Good of Miss Snyder to bring Avery down to see us off," Worth said. They'd left Least Wapping in the dust, the horses had worked off their fidgets, and Hess still hadn't volunteered one word of conversation.

"I was surprised your Mrs. Wyeth didn't see you off. Shall we let the beasts blow?" He brought his horse down to the walk, the steeplechaser Worth had put him on earlier in the week. "Your housekeeper seems fond of you."

"One hopes she's fond of me. I'm more than fond of her, so don't get ideas."

"About?"

Worth smiled at his brother to ensure hostile notions remained only notions. "I overheard her at breakfast. She might as well have smacked your nose with a rolled-up newspaper."

"So that's what put you in such a fine humor? Your housekeeper—who referred to you by your *given* name, by the by—scolding me? Why didn't you call me out?"

"Same reason I didn't years ago." Worth hadn't foreseen the conversation taking this turn, but neither would he dodge the topic. "The lady makes her choice, we fellows abide by her wishes."

Hess fixed his gaze on the horse's ears. "Mrs. Wyeth is choosing you?"

"She isn't choosing *you*." Brilliant, dear, stubborn woman. "That's enough for present purposes."

"I know this will sound ridiculous, but I wouldn't want to see the woman abuse your sensibilities, Worth."

"From you, who stole my bride, that does sound ridiculous." Worth lifted his reins free of Goliath's mane. "Touching but ridiculous."

"Precisely because I did steal your bride, I'm protective of you," Hess said. "Then too, you're my only brother, my only adult sibling, my heir. Humor me and tread carefully around Mrs. Wyeth."

Hess's expression was a study in impenetrable, titled dignity, though Worth would never have taken his brother for a snob.

"You mean I'm not to offer her marriage?"

"Offer her marriage on a platter," Hess said, "but only after she's offered you her heart. I do not need to tell you women can dissemble, and we fellows, led about by something other than our common sense, don't wake up until it's too late."

"Speaking from experience, Hessian?"

"Do you recall Lady Belinda Evers?"

Worth had a vague memory of a girl who'd briefly been as tall as he'd been, before adolescence had turned him into a compilation of elbows, knees, and peculiar vocal pitches.

"She was plain Belinda Turner when I knew her—a nice girl, not given to airs."

"I have a daughter with her," Hess said. "Or I'm almost sure I do. Evers is twenty-some years Belinda's senior. She presented him his heir and spare, and then he pretty much went shooting for the duration. She told him she wanted more children, and he tried to rise to the occasion, so to speak, but frequently without adequate result. Belinda doesn't understand I know what she was about."

"This is quite a tale. How can she think to keep this secret from you?"

And how did Hess feel about not one but two women seeking taking advantage of him?

"Because she doesn't know Evers shared his woes with me over brandy, complained about having a restless younger wife who demanded children from a man old enough to be a grandpapa, and so forth."

Life in the north was supposed to be dull. "Then she batted her eyes at you over tea. You could have refused her, but you didn't."

"I almost felt as if Evers were asking for my help, truth be known. He dotes on the child. Belinda was miserable to see her boys growing up and nothing in her future but watching her husband age."

This exchange of honest confidences with Hess had veered into the "be mindful what you wish for" category of business, and yet, this *was* what Worth had wished for—his brother's trust and all that went with it.

"You use this situation with the fair Belinda and her aging spouse to punish yourself," Worth said. "I can't figure out all the details, but this was self-flagellation, wasn't it?"

"I undertook a casual affair with a willing party—or Belinda did." Hess spoke the words as if he'd rehearsed them many times. "We're friends, all of us, in some way. I don't pretend to understand it, and I'm not about to embark on such foolishness again."

Hess could tell him this, because despite all, they were still close in a way known only to brothers. The realization warmed Worth as summer morning sun could not.

"You keep to yourself because of the girl?"

"Yes, because of her. Dallying is one thing, but giving up my children to be raised by other men is quite another. Amy is nearly four and has my eyes—our eyes. I'm still waiting for Belinda to tell me she at least suspects the child is mine, but it has been years, and she's made no admission."

Amy was an artifact of grief then, for she'd been conceived soon after the death of Hess's countess. "Belinda is a loyal wife."

"Oh, right."

"Well, loyal and faithful aren't always a matched pair."

"This child might be my only progeny, Worth. You'd think Lady Evers might take that into consideration as well."

"She's trying to do you a favor, I suspect," Worth said, battling more than a twinge of consternation on his brother's behalf. "A damned strange sort of favor. I trust she loves the girl?"

"Belinda would give her right arm for her boys, but she'd give her life for that little girl. I have no doubt of that whatsoever."

The horses walked along for the better part of a mile, while Worth composed a great philosophical oratory about fate and the Almighty and one's role being mysterious. A fine speech it was, too, full of long words and poetic allusions. Also impressively boring.

London was still better than an hour away, and beside Worth, the earl remained silent.

"I'm sorry, Hess."

"For?"

"You seem doomed to lose family. Your wife, your parents, your sister, all dead. Your daughter is being raised by another, your remaining sister can't stand your household, and your brother and your niece live two hundred miles to the south. I'm sorry these hardships have befallen you."

He phrased the sentiment as a condolence, but a more accurate description for what Worth experienced would have been…pity.

Commiseration, even, for some of those losses Worth had shared, and *his* brother was also two hundred miles distant.

A damned nuisance, that.

"I've come to treasure my solitude," Hess said, "and at least my brother and I are no longer estranged."

No, they were not, though how that had happened, Worth was not sure— nor did he need to be. "Maybe your luck is changing."

"One can hope." Hess nudged his mount back up to the trot, and they exchanged not another word before reaching the town house.

# CHAPTER THIRTEEN

"Grey, you can't haul Jacaranda home by her hair."

Daisy Fromm, nee Dorning, scolded her oldest brother quietly as he paced her back terrace. Grey would be handsome if he weren't always scowling and glaring, but he was scowling now and looking determined, and that always boded ill for someone.

"It's one thing for Jacaranda to keep house when the owner is off in London, but according to Roberts, this Kettering fellow has brought a pair of children with him, likely his by-blows, and she's supposed to keep house with them *and him* underfoot. Francine says it will be the end of Jack's reputation."

As if going into service hadn't already accomplished that?

"She's been in his employ for five years," Daisy said, feeling a peculiar pang of envy. "Of course she will occasionally be under the same roof as her employer. Mrs. Dankle dwells with you, doesn't she?"

"Mrs. Dankle is sixty if she's a day. She's wiped my nose and the noses of every little Dorning foal to hit the ground. Moreover, she's given notice."

Mrs. Dankle frequently gave notice, then Francine bribed her into relenting.

"We're not horses, Grey." Daisy switched her hold on the baby in her arms, for the child was growing at a prodigious rate—just as her brothers had. "Besides, the gentry typically rusticate in summer. You're here, and you didn't even stay in Town for the closing ceremonies."

"Hang the closing ceremonies." His gaze came to rest on the infant, his glower softening to something approaching wistfulness. "This one's growing like a weed, Daze. How can Jack miss her own niece and nephews growing up?"

Perhaps because she had no children of her own?

"Jack is stubborn, Grey, and she says in her letters she's happy. If we miss her, well, that's the price we pay for loving her." The words were prevarications wrapped in platitudes, but Daisy would not burden her brother with the truth. She protected not Jacaranda's dignity with her falsehoods, but her own.

"Letters, bah." Grey ran a hand over the baby's fuzzy head, his gentle touch at variance with his scornful tone. "Little fairy tales written by women to placate men. Jack has said she'll come home at the end of the summer, but she's made similar promises and found reasons to break them. Something's amiss at Trysting. And what sort of name is that for a house? Did you know Kettering is brother to an earl?"

"I know many fine people who are siblings to an earl," Daisy said, patting the baby's back. "What is your point?"

"Jack needs to come home." Grey tossed his long frame into a wrought iron chair, its feet scraping against the terrace flagstones. "When I agreed to this scheme, I told myself she was in a pout because you'd caught your man and she hadn't. I gave it a year before she came home either towing a husband or finally ready to look for one. It has been five years, Daisy. You've three children, and she has, what? Bad knees from scrubbing floors?"

Jacaranda had her dignity, a variety of freedom, and a bit of coin to show for it—likely her figure was still comely, too—and she'd have staff to scrub those floors.

"Not all women are suited to marriage, Grey. Not all people." Though some brothers were more suited to it than they could admit.

"None of that." He'd growled the words, older-brother fashion. "I looked over this year's crop in Town. I'm off to a house party in October. I stood up with an entire bouquet of wall flowers at the local assembly."

Daisy remained silent, tucking the blanket more closely around the baby. She'd caught her man all right, but how much more of the tale Grey knew, she'd never quite fathomed. Because she did value her husband's continued existence—some days and most nights—she wasn't about to confide in her oldest brother anytime soon.

"I stopped by Least Wapping on my way south," Grey said, getting to his feet. He was restless like that, a man beset with too much energy.

"Did you see Jack?"

"I did not. I kept my distance. She seems to be coping, but I have an itchy feeling between my shoulders, Daze. I'll take some of the boys and go see what's afoot once we get the ditches cleared. Will has always been able to make her see sense, and he's confirmed that Francine is getting up to some mischief or other."

Francine was bored, fretful, and not much of a mother. Daisy could say that in part because she herself was a mother—now.

"Will thinks you should leave Jack in peace." Daisy didn't want Grey dashing off, so she did something guaranteed to keep him on that terrace: She passed her brother the baby.

"I think her eyes are changing," Grey said, peering at the little face peeking out of the blanket. Abrupt shifts of subject were symptomatic of Grey preparing to dart away on one of his queer starts. "They'll be gorgeous eyes, just like Auntie Jack has, won't they?"

"Just like Uncle Grey has," Daisy said, wondering if the ladies in London ever took a moment to admire Grey's eyes, or were too put off by his brusque demeanor.

He ran his nose over the baby's cheek, which inspired the little baggage to smiling and waving her fists. "So you don't think I should retrieve Jack?"

The smile he bestowed on the infant nearly broke Daisy's heart. Before Jack had left, Grey's smile had been much more frequently in evidence.

"If you're asking me, then no," Daisy said. "I don't think you should barge into her affairs. You're being the earl, though, not a sensible brother, and thus you'll bother Jack regardless. Please give her my love when you go storming up to Trysting."

"One appreciates honesty from one's siblings." He left off cuddling his niece, and five minutes later, Daisy let him see himself out, earl or not.

If she'd been honest, she would have told him she hoped that someday he'd turn that smile on a lady who was old enough to treasure it for the rarity it had become.

\* \* \*

The flesh-pots of London failed utterly to lure Hess from Worth's town house.

Fortunately, Mary had made significant progress bestirring the menials to spruce up the place, so it wasn't such a bad spot to abandon a guest.

Worth tracked his sovereign down at a picnic and boating party this time, discreetly offered the requisite assurances, and then stopped by Lloyds to see if the clerks had heard any pertinent gossip.

If they had, they were keeping their lips buttoned, which would be a historic first, given that Worth plied them with not only noontime ale, but also rum and decent brandy before the night was through. He spent the next morning calling upon the lady whose husband captained the Drummond and the next afternoon meeting with opera dancers and shopkeepers, then appearing to laze about in the cleaner dockside taverns.

"And where have you been all day?" Mary took his coat from his shoulders as he walked in the door. "You stink of the wharves, Mr. Kettering. This will not endear you to the laundress."

"My hard-earned coin will have to keep me in her good graces. Where's my brother?"

"Reading on the back terrace. That man reads like civilization depends upon it. Hardly touched his lunch."

"Then dinner had best be enticing, and we can serve it out back." Worth gave her an up-and-down perusal. "How are you feeling?"

"I miss the girls," Mary said, taking his hat, gloves and walking stick. "I do not miss breezing around in the altogether for a bunch of drunken louts to leer at."

"Have you talked to Jones?"

She looked away, and Worth wanted to bellow for his head office clerk then and there.

"Never mind," he said. "It isn't my business. The house is looking much improved. For that I'm grateful."

Her smile was heartbreakingly bashful as she nodded her thanks for the compliment. Worth took a surreptitious glance at her tummy and was relieved to see she wasn't showing. But then, her full apron was long and loose, and he was hardly in a position to assess changes to her figure based on personal knowledge.

Though he might have been.

He shook off that uncomfortable thought, grabbed a decanter, glasses and tray from the library, and made his way to the terrace.

Where Hess was indeed poring over a book. "Poetry, Hessian?"

"Miss Snyder claimed I'd miss a treat if I didn't make time for Byron. The man is brutally funny."

"Or simply brutal. May I offer you a drink?"

"Sit you down," Hess said. "I've been swilling lemonade all afternoon. Your terrace is peaceful, Worth. Do you ever spend time out here?"

"We'll be eating out here," Worth said, easing off his cravat.

"Did you complete your appointed rounds today?"

"Not entirely." Worth propped his boots on a low wrought iron table and cradled his drink on his belly. "His Royal Highness moves about when one wants him to hold still and can't be budged when one wants him to move. A vexing fellow."

"You're solicitor to the Regent?"

"Of course not. Prinny and I chat from time to time, about this and that." Worth took a gratifying swallow of his brandy.

"That's quite an honor, Lord Mayor of the Regent's Chit-Chat."

"It's quite a pain in the arse when I lack the requisite magic wand and secret incantations. He expects high return and low risk."

"Doesn't everybody?"

Worth thought his brother was joking at first, but Hess was completely serious. What followed was a tutorial on investment practices, with Hess asking cautious, basic questions and Worth answering as best he could without being insulting.

"It all sounds very complicated," Hess concluded. "Very modern."

"Investment strategy is as old as China in some senses. I'd be happy to invest something for you…" He let the offer hang in the air, but sensed this was perhaps the primary objective of Hess's journey south. Not Yolanda, not reconciliation, not meeting Avery, but money.

Though, quite possibly, Hess himself hadn't realized his own agenda.

Coin of the realm, blunt, cash… Money had as many names as did the male reproductive organ, and sensible people were more interested in coin than coitus.

"How much would I need to get involved with some of the more profitable ventures?"

The question was carefully, casually posed, and Worth had heard it a thousand times. Nobody looked him in the eye when they asked, and everybody hoped the answer was some insignificant amount.

Which it was not. Not by the standards of an opera dancer, not by the standards of an earl. For the dancers, Worth put together their coin and purchased a share between five or six of them, sometimes between as many as a dozen small investors. Such an undertaking was tedious and meant a flood of paperwork and a great deal of time, but he did it willingly.

"Is Grampion in financial trouble?" Worth asked gently. He and Hess had made progress with their past, and maybe this was a form of progress as well.

Hess propped his feet beside Worth's on the low table.

"I believe so, yes." He might have been commenting on the probability of rain, so bland was his tone.

"Are *you* in trouble?"

Hess's gaze remained on their boots, Hess's shiny, Worth's dusty.

"I will be. I give it less than five years. I expect I'll remarry sometime before disaster strikes."

A silence wafted by, while Worth poured them both a tot more brandy. This discussion with his brother in the lengthening shadows of day's end was like galloping a steeplechaser for three miles at top speed, then slamming into the final jump of the course.

Worth was stopped cold, stunned. Grampion had always been so gracious, so lovely.

So *expensive*, though a boy would not have realized that.

Hess had married once on impulse, or perhaps in a convoluted exercise in sibling rivalry. He shouldn't have to marry again for duty. Even Hess should have one shot at some happiness.

What a relief, after years of animosity, for Worth to experience genuine protectiveness toward his brother.

"Will you allow me to help?"

Another question gently put, and another silence, while Worth considered that single question might mean he spent the rest of his life wishing his brother would resume speaking to him.

"God, yes, Worth, I will allow you to help. I will be grateful for your help. I know I don't deserve—"

"We haven't much time," Worth interrupted, "but a particular opportunity lies in the offing now that could set you up nicely. How bad is the bleeding?"

Darkness had fallen before they went inside, moving their discussion to the library. Before Worth let Hess go up to bed, Worth had worked out the rudiments of a plan to not simply get the ancestral estate out of debt, but to turn it into a profitable venture. Putting Grampion on solid footing could take five years, but a few shares in the Drummond would shorten that estimate considerably.

Worth was content with that scenario when he considered their father had likely inherited a dismal situation fifty years ago, and done little to turn it around.

Hess refused to borrow from his brother, though, so it would be only a few shares of Drummond stock purchased, and that money was from Hess's dwindling personal wealth. Like many of his peers, he was pouring personal money into an increasingly unprofitable agricultural estate, too hidebound or ignorant to diversify his revenue sources.

"This venture with the Drummond is high risk, isn't it?" Hess asked as he rose to leave for his bed.

"That depends on how you view it, but high reward, too, and we should know in the next fifteen days which it is."

"So I'll have to stay in the south for another few weeks." Hess did not look pleased with this possibility.

"Is my hospitality so lacking?" Worth said, purposely goading his brother, because hospitality wasn't the problem.

"Your hospitality is superb, but the thought of Yolanda glaring daggers at me for weeks, then having to haul her, muttering and cursing, the length of England... One would like to have such an ordeal behind one."

"Perhaps you'll be able to turn her up sweet, or we can come to some other arrangement."

"I know my duty, Worth."

"Your duty now is to get a decent night's sleep." Worth got to his feet, fatigued to his bones, but also lighter in spirit. Setting another's financial house in order often did that for him. "Mine as well."

"About that." Hess pinned his gaze on a painting of a mare and foal, an early

Thomas Lawrence.

"Hessian?"

"You seem to have the knack of acquiring young, pretty housekeepers."

"Each of whom," Worth said, "is entirely her own woman."

Hess looked sheepish, but pleased. "That's what she said. Your Mary is quite forward."

"She's also carrying another man's child. If she told you you couldn't get her with child, it was the God's honest truth."

"Little brother, the life you live is incomprehensible to me." Hess gathered up his boots and stockings. "Though you seem comfortable in it."

He left on that observation, and Worth went in search of his housekeeper, but only to tell her he'd be leaving for Trysting in late morning.

* * *

"Hell, yes, I'll sell you my shares." James Murphy's boots thumped onto the carpet of his office. "The Drummond is accounted a complete loss, and I know what you're about, Kettering. You're trying to keep me from selling to somebody else for a farthing to the pound, so your own pile of shares won't be worth even less when you try to dump the ones you still have. It's an old trick."

"Or perhaps I believe in my captain, and the Drummond will come sailing in here one of these weeks." Worth injected a note of defensiveness under his rejoinder, though one did want to play fair—within reason.

"The captain hasn't been born of woman who can control the weather, my friend." Murphy's smile was sympathetic, but he signed over his stock certificates at face value. Worth paid him in cash, gathered a witnessed receipt, and thanked his associate very cordially.

He made six similar stops, which left him and his investors the sole shareholders in the venture, then collected his brother at the town house and once again headed back to Trysting.

* * *

"This is a sorry day, Mrs. W." Simmons shook his head like a dog with a flea in his ear. "A sorry, sorry day. The young lady snatched from our very halls, and not one witness. A right tragedy, you ask me. What will Mr. K say?"

Perhaps Mr. K would allow Jacaranda to pension Simmons off at last.

"We'll soon know Mr. Kettering's view on the matter, Mr. Simmons. I sent a note to Town, and I don't doubt he'll be here by moonrise."

"Moonrise!" The eyebrows rose to unprecedented heights, and beneath the dismay lurked a nasty element of glee to have such drama befall the house.

Jacaranda's hand formed a tight fist in her skirts.

"Mrs. Wyeth?" Carl stood a safe distance away as he addressed her. "We've searched the outbuildings and found no sign of Miss Yolanda."

"Thank you, Carl. What about the attics?"

"We're up there now, ma'am, and the cellars, too."

"Very good. Keep me and Mr. Simmons informed."

"Oh, this is dire," Simmons moaned. "What if she's not in the attics or the cellars? We've searched the grounds, her room, the outbuildings and gardens. She's not asleep in a hammock or reading by the stream. There's no note. She hasn't taken a horse or cart, and nobody has seen her since luncheon, and that was hours ago. Hours!"

"So it was, Mr. Simmons. I suggest you start praying."

He was so stunned by that pronouncement, his mouth snapped shut fast enough to have his turkey wattle shaking.

What was there to do except pray? Yolanda had been infernally quiet since the earl had come to visit, wafting around the house like a pretty ghost, holing up in the library, taking trays for lunch and breakfast.

Boot heels rang in the corridor, and Jacaranda had to hope it was a groom arriving with news, good or bad, any news at all.

"Mrs. Wyeth?" Worth Kettering stood framed in the doorway, his brother at his shoulder. "My dear, the house is in an uproar, the grooms say Yolanda is missing, and we've no footman at our front door. What on earth is going on?"

"Worth—" She took a step toward him, then realized she'd just used his *name* before his brother the earl.

And did not care. "Yolanda hasn't been seen since luncheon, and we've looked everywhere."

"This is my fault," the earl said. "She's run off because she thinks I'll dragoon her back to Grampion in chains."

"We can debate her motivations later." Worth didn't look angry, so much as focused. "Assuming Yolanda has decamped purposely, we can also take turns whacking at her backside for causing such anxiety to my staff. Let's have some tea, and Mrs. Wyeth can tell us what's been done so far to locate our sister."

"*Tea?*" Jacaranda wanted to beat the bushes herself, and Yolanda's brother was thinking of tea?

"I'll see to it," the earl said, spinning on his heel and leaving the library.

"Now come here." Worth kicked the door closed and held out his arms. "We'll find her, don't doubt it. She's a Kettering and made of fortitude, resourcefulness and determination. Hess is likely right, and this is a fit of pique, that's all."

"I am so worried," Jacaranda managed, and then she was weeping against his shoulder, so glad to see him, so relieved for once to not have to be the one who organized, and thought ahead, and encouraged everyone else.

"Young ladies loose without supervision are worth worrying about." Worth tucked his chin against her temple and held her until Jacaranda eased her grip on him. A knock at the door heralded the earl, followed by a maid bearing a tea tray. The newest maid, who would have been limited to upstairs duty under normal circumstances.

"Thank you," Worth said. "That will be all." He sat himself on the sofa and patted the place beside him. "Sit you, Mrs. Wyeth, and start from the beginning. Your lordship, butter the lady a scone and stop castigating yourself."

Jacaranda sat between them, finding the tea and sustenance helped—she hadn't eaten for hours—but so, too, did Worth's methodical approach to the entire situation and his simple, calm presence.

"When was she last seen?"

"By whom?"

"Did she receive any correspondence this morning?"

"Has she formed any particular friends in the area?"

"Has she caught the eye of any of the local swains?"

Jacaranda could answer accurately, but at the last question, she paused.

"I don't know that she exactly caught his eye, but Thomas Hunter caught hers at market. He was most gallant."

"Gallant?" The earl was on his feet. "I'll shove my gallant fist down his presuming throat if he's enticed her to folly."

"Hessian." Worth held up a cup of tea to his brother. "Yolanda would have left a note if she were eloping. She wouldn't want Avery to worry, and she wouldn't want the scandal exacerbated by a foolish alarm to the whole parish."

The earl accepted his tea, then took to staring at a portrait of some ancestor sporting lace, hose, and collar. "You're saying she was carried off against her will?"

"I'm saying I don't think she eloped with somebody she's known only a span of weeks. She has more sense than that. What does Avery say?"

"We haven't wanted to alarm her," Jacaranda replied. "She's in the nursery with Mrs. Hartwick."

"I'll fetch her." His lordship was out the door before Jacaranda could ring for a maid.

"Let him go," Worth said. "He will blame himself until she's found, and if this is a stupid stunt, Yolanda will regret it to her dying day. Eat your scone, love, and stop blaming yourself."

"If she was unhappy, I should have seen it. I was a miserable girl once, too, and I know how foolish they can be."

"You?" He held up a plate with the buttered scone on it. "Foolish? I must hear this tale, for I can't imagine such a thing." He leaned over and kissed her cheek. "For courage. We'll find her, and she had better have a good excuse for this nonsense. I don't like to see you upset, much less my brother suffering paroxysms of undeserved guilt."

That little kiss did give her courage, as did Worth being himself, flirting a bit despite the circumstances, tending to the basics—food and drink—and taking the whole matter in stride.

What would she have done if he'd still been in Town?

"I've got Avery," Grampion said as he crossed the threshold, and he did, literally, have the child. She was affixed to his back and looking around from her perch with a hesitant smile.

"Uncle Worth! I saw you come home on Goliath." She held out her arms as if she'd hug him from his lordship's back.

"My dearest niece." Worth plucked her off the earl, hugged her, and deposited her on the sofa. "Join us for a cup of tea. We've a mystery to solve."

"I've seen the footmen scurrying everywhere, and I hear them up in the attics. They never go up there. Neither do the maids." Avery looked perfectly composed as she sat beside her uncle on the sofa.

"We're hunting a treasure," Worth said, fixing her a cup of tea that was more cream and sugar than tea. "Your aunt has gone missing and you keep a close eye on her, so we're hoping you might be able to give us some clues."

"Clues?"

"Hints, ideas about where she might be."

"May I have a scone with jam?"

"You may." He tended to her request and passed her the plate. "You saw Yolanda at lunch, didn't you?"

"Of course, and she brings her book, and Miss Snyder gives her the don't-read-at-table look. A bit more jam," she said. "It's very good, the jam."

Worth dutifully took the plate back and added another dollop of jam.

"Where did Yolanda go after lunch?" he asked.

"She comes here to look at the maps," Avery said, taking the plate and managing to bite off a corner of scone without getting jam all over her fingers. "She likes the maps and said she would explore the estate. It belonged to an aunt, a long time ago, all of this."

"It did." Worth passed the child a serviette, which was wise because the jam was excessive in proportion to the scone, and disaster seemed only a lick away. "Which maps did Yolanda like to study?"

"All of them." Avery dabbed at her lips delicately. "She wants to be an intrepid explorer. What does intrepid mean?"

"Fearless. Did Yolanda like to look at the globe?"

"No, not that kind of map," Avery said, now halfway through her scone. "She liked the maps of where we are. Where we are now."

"These maps?" the earl asked from halfway across the room. "They aren't recent." He was carefully flipping the pages of a large atlas laid flat for display on a sturdy table.

"Those maps, yes," Avery said, but didn't give up her place on the sofa.

"They are maps of here, of Trysting, when the aunt owned it."

"She's right," Jacaranda said, "but the estate maps are back a few pages in that atlas. They're very detailed. I need a quizzing glass to read some of the print."

"Yolanda would study the map, then take a book with her to explore the estate while Uncle went on his calls with Mrs. Wyeth," Avery said. "May I have another scone?"

"Not yet." Worth rose and crossed to stand beside his brother. "You'll spoil your dinner, but you've been very helpful. Did Yolanda go exploring this afternoon?"

"Oh, yes." Avery gazed upon the plate of scones like a martyr contemplating heaven. "I watch from the nursery windows. Some days she goes to the paddocks to see the horses, some days she goes to the home farm to see the cows and sheep."

"Where did she go today?"

"To the home wood." Avery's fingertip made a surreptitious pass through the jam pot then disappeared into her mouth. "She likes the birds in the wood and likes to read there. She says it's cool and pretty. I think it's scary."

She pronounced the word oddly—scar-y—but her meaning was clear.

"This is not an accurate map of the home wood," Jacaranda said, peering at the atlas from the earl's other side. "The entire plot is much overgrown since former days. Something Reilly and I have remarked often."

Worth bent closer and took up the quizzing glass kept next to the atlas.

"You're right. Wouldn't Hunter's holding be right down this bridle path here?" He traced his finger along the map.

"It would be," Jacaranda said, "except those bridle paths haven't existed to speak of in my lifetime. They might be game trails now, but I think they were established more for harvesting lumber in the last century."

"So Yolanda is stumbling around in the wood looking for trails that don't exist?" His lordship's scowl was fierce. "Let's go. We don't want to lose the light."

Worth passed Avery the quizzing glass, patted her shoulder, and sent her back to the nursery. "A few minutes of organization will save us a lot of stumbling around. Mrs. Wyeth, a lane still cuts through the wood, doesn't it? Would that be this trail, here?"

Within a few minutes, Worth and the earl had a grid worked out and a system whereby one team of men would start on the lane to Hunter's holding, the other would start at the manor, and they'd meet in the middle of the wood. Footmen were being instructed to notify the grooms and gardeners and other staff when Carl tapped on the library door.

"Mr. Thomas Hunter is asking for you, Mrs. Wyeth. He wouldn't say what his business was, but his mule is in a right lather."

"Show him in," Worth said. "Mrs. Wyeth will receive him here with us."

Thomas came in, his attire too informal for this call to be social.

"Mrs. Wyeth, Mr. Kettering." He bowed to Jacaranda, he merely nodded at Worth. He shot the earl a measuring look. "I don't believe I know you, sir."

"Grampion," Worth said, "may I make known to you Mr. Thomas Hunter, one of my most industrious tenants. Hunter, I give you the Earl of Grampion, who is at this moment a very concerned brother to a certain young lady, as am I."

"She's safe," Hunter said. "She twisted her ankle, but I don't think it's broken. She's at the gamekeeper's cottage near my property, her foot up and her book within reach. She's very embarrassed, but got turned around in the wood and then took a bad step. I heard her calling on my way to Least Wapping."

Jacaranda had to sit, so great was her relief, because a young woman could come to very great harm in no time at all.

"Do we have you to thank for her comfort and care, Hunter?" Worth's tone held a pugnacious edge.

"I have shown her every courtesy," Hunter retorted, his chin lifting half an inch. "She is not at my home, but she is certainly an honored guest."

"We'd best fetch her in a cart," Jacaranda interjected, for male posturing could be interminable. "Getting from the cottage out to the track will be difficult for her."

"I'll fetch her," the earl said. "My horse can take the two of us, if Mr. Hunter would be so kind as to lead the way?"

Hunter looked the earl up and down, but held his peace.

"You might as well speak plainly," Worth said. "We are her family, and we love her, but her mind is her own, Mr. Hunter."

"She said this one"—he nodded at his lordship—"would scold her as if she were eight years old. She's not eight years old."

"Yolanda is not to blame for turning her ankle," Worth said. "I doubt his lordship will do any scolding, for he's too glad the girl's safe and reasonably sound."

The earl nodded his agreement—his capitulation—once. "Just so, but she needs her family now, though you have our thanks, Hunter. She is dear to us."

"One hoped that was the case. I'll await you in the stables." He bowed politely to Jacaranda, gave each man a nod, and withdrew.

"She's safe," Worth said, directing his comments to his brother. "She didn't intentionally alarm anyone, and she's safe."

"She's safe, but we don't know she turned her ankle. She might have concocted this whole debacle to spend time unchaperoned with your tenant. Yolanda is clever if nothing else."

"Do you have a reason to accuse her of such dramatics?" Worth asked, which was fortunate, because Jacaranda would not have put the question half so civilly.

"Wasn't it you who had to retrieve her from an exclusive boarding school for trying to do injury to herself?"

Jacaranda could keep silent no longer, for brothers would chose the most vexatious times to be difficult. "Can't you sort through that later? Right now, we need to retrieve her from that cottage, and assure her she's loved and that her absence mattered." Why could they not see this? "If you two want to continue this argument, I will happily fetch her with Mr. Hunter."

She'd carry the girl from the cottage herself if need be, though Thomas would likely appropriate that honor.

The earl's eyebrows rose, then crashed down, making him look very much like his brother. He bowed and withdrew without another word.

"You're not going with him?" Jacaranda aimed the question at Worth, who'd settled on the sofa near the tea and scones.

"I am not," he said, buttering a scone. "Hess and Lannie have matters to work out, and they'll need privacy to do it. They're both monumentally shy, and my hovering won't help."

"Eating a scone will?" Though Jacaranda was hungry, and another cup of tea wouldn't go amiss either.

"Come sit with me." He beckoned with the hand holding the scone. "And, yes, because I've been in the saddle for much of the day, I intend to eat every last scone on this plate. The jam is about gone, though."

Jacaranda sat, needing to be near him, which made no sense when the crisis was past. "I was so relieved to see you. Your brother was doubtless scandalized."

"My brother has other things on his mind just now." Worth held up the scone for her to take a bite. "A little scandalizing will be good for the fellow. He's grown Puritan in his northern wilderness."

"Puritan?"

"Lonely, but he doesn't seem to know it, or what to do about it." Worth took a bite for himself, then offered the scone to her again. "We need some tea to wash this down."

She let him ply her with tea and scones and let herself sit right next to him, absorbing his warmth and calm.

"You didn't panic," she said. "I was ready to scream, and you didn't panic."

"She isn't your little sister," Worth said. "Inside I was screaming, but you kept looking at me as if I'd know what to do, and Hess couldn't very well step in, because it isn't his property, and he was too busy blaming himself."

"You didn't blame yourself." She let her head rest against his shoulder, and he obligingly looped an arm around her.

"I most assuredly did. You simply didn't hear me. I will always bear responsibility for Moira's death, and I was fully prepared to be at fault if Yolanda had been set upon by bears, or pirates, or pixies."

Jacaranda lifted her head to glare at him. "You did not cause Moira's death. If anything, your generosity gave her a few years of happiness."

He was silent, not a brooding silent. Then, "Marry me."

"*What?*"

"I said…" He drew his finger along her arm. "Please marry me. Please."

Jacaranda watched his finger trail down her forearm, having difficulty connecting the sight with sensation, just as Worth would not be able to connect Lady Jacaranda Wyeth Dorning with his practical, plain housekeeper.

"I beg your pardon?"

"I said, please marry me. This raspberry jam is worth putting my foot in parson's mousetrap. Did you make it? I think you did. No wonder Avery was abandoning all manners for a mere taste. You could sell this, you know, retire from this life of gay abandon and buy that cottage."

She blushed hotly, probably turning nearly the color of the jam itself. "You will not bring up cottages, if you please."

"You have such a way with the imperatives, my dear." He munched away on his scone, the wretched man. "What did you mean when you said you'd once been a foolish girl?"

"Weren't you once a foolish boy?"

"Hell, yes. For years and years." He chewed more slowly, and Jacaranda hoped his teasing about marriage was done—for he had been teasing, this time.

Or he'd turned his proposal into a joke rather than endure her rejection.

The sooner she returned to Dorset, the better.

"In some ways, I'm only now getting over the tendency toward foolishness," he said, "but that doesn't answer my question, dear heart. Tell me of your foolishness."

"My past is not a fit topic." Jacaranda rose, and she could see she'd surprised him. Her past and her future were both not fit topics. "I must ensure that Cook has dinner underway, given the upheaval of the day."

"Jacaranda?" He was on his feet, too, and clearly done with his teasing.

"Sir?"

He paced across the room to join her near the door, his gait unhurried, as if he knew she wasn't about to leave until she'd heard him out.

"Thank you," he said, speaking distinctly. "I neglect to give you these words often enough, not because I don't feel grateful—I do—but because they make you uncomfortable, just as talking about your cottage does. Thank you for turning the house and staff upside down to look for my sister. Thank you for making this house a home my family can feel welcome in. Thank you for raspberry jam."

She wanted to cry. He wasn't even touching her, he wasn't teasing, and she wanted to cry.

"You're welcome." She put her fingers on the door latch and walked out from under the hand he'd settled on her shoulder—one of the more difficult departures she'd asked of herself.

"I'll see you at dinner." His words floated after her, pitched so she'd hear them, but she made good her escape and reached her room before the tears fell in quantity.

# CHAPTER FOURTEEN

"It has something to do with why you're housekeeping here in Surrey," Worth mused as he climbed into Jacaranda's bed.

Her worst nightmare and her fondest dream had come to call once again. Jacaranda buried her nose in her pillow. "You infernal man, what do you think you're doing here?"

"I've come to talk about cottages and jam pots," he said, going through the ritual of bouncing around to get the pillows and covers just so. "You would not discuss them with me earlier, and my curiosity is piqued. I would also like to know if you missed me sufficiently that you're willing to dispense certain favors in my direction."

"*My* curiosity is burning to experience a good night's sleep." Jacaranda gave him her back, putting a convincing show of sincerity in her words, almost enough to compensate for lying in bed for more than an hour, wondering if he'd join her.

He spooned himself around her. "Yolanda seemed fine at dinner."

"I think she was surprised his lordship would fetch her, and whatever he said, it seemed to clear the air between them." Worth was in Jacaranda's bed, where at least part of her wanted him, and she'd missed these late-night conversations and the simple cuddling and petting he lavished on her.

Missed them a lot, and would miss them more soon.

"Why the sigh, Jacaranda Wyeth?"

"Your hand. I am a fool for the way you rub my back."

"It relaxes me, too," he said, pausing to kiss her shoulder, "to rub your back.

May I ask you about something?"

"No, Worth. For once, you may not pose whatever question comes into the vast, busy manufactory that is your mind."

"Do you need money?"

"What sort of question is that?"

"An honest one." He sounded embarrassed. "My housekeeper in Town sends a portion of her wages home, and it occurred to me your family might be in some need."

She hadn't foreseen this, couldn't quite fathom where it was coming from or where he was headed with it, though she should have known he'd put together the pieces easily enough.

"We're not in particular need, though I haven't been home to visit for nearly two years. I have a large family, but the land is good, and we work hard." Then too, they no longer had to endure the expense of London Seasons for a young lady who did not take. "Why do you ask?"

"My manufactory specializes in producing idle curiosity. Would you trust me with your money, Jacaranda?"

Another kiss, though she had the sense her answer mattered far more than his casual tone suggested.

"If you needed it, yes, I would trust you with my money."

She'd have been better advised to give him her money than her heart—more fool her.

"I might need it," he said, and the relief in his tone was unmistakable. "Give me another week or so to sort matters through. I'd give you a note of hand, or a promissory note, if you preferred."

"I don't need any notes." She rolled over to try to see him, but the moon was either behind its clouds or not up yet. "I'll withhold your raspberry jam if you game it away."

"My word is good with you?"

"You're in my bed, after dark, without benefit of clothing, so yes, I'd say a modicum of trust lies between us." Not as much trust as he deserved, though.

"Hess is nearly rolled up."

A sterling example of the trust going both ways and part of the reason why Jacaranda would quit Trysting at summer's end. Better to end their dalliance than let Worth Kettering know he'd climbed into bed with a dissembling woman.

Because whatever lay between him and his brother, Jacaranda was certain a dissembling woman had been part of it.

"Was he mortified to seek your help?" She put an arm under his neck and stroked her hand through his hair—which soothed her.

"I was mortified. Jacaranda, I wanted to put my hand over his mouth and push his words back into silence. He's been struggling away up there in

Cumberland, selling off his beloved hunters, the art he enjoys so much, and God knows what else, and it's pathetic. Papa left him a cocked-up mess and not one clue how to go about fixing it. He refuses to raise the rents, and I have to applaud him for that, given the price of corn lately."

Jacaranda kept her hand moving slowly through his hair. "You suspected he'd traveled alone out of economy, and you were right. He probably doesn't entertain for the same reason."

"I wish I'd been wrong." Worth closed his eyes, his lashes glancing delicately against her palm. "We'll get him sorted out, eventually."

She kissed his forehead, nuzzling his hair to catch a whiff of his scent. "If anybody can straighten out a monetary situation, it's you, and that you're willing to try likely means more to his lordship than that you succeed."

"Why do you say that?"

"He misses his brother. Money grows behind every hedge compared to brothers."

She realized too late how much truth, how much homesickness her words held, but Worth kissed her breast, and all thoughts of cottages and brothers flew from her head.

"Jacaranda? You never answered my question: Did you miss me? For I assuredly missed you, dear heart."

\* \* \*

Worth needed to hear the words, which was silly, insecure and unbecoming, but he wanted at least some words from Jacaranda: *I missed you*. Every night when he climbed into her bed, she put up her token protest.

He accepted that and bantered and teased and cuddled his way past it.

Then he cast around for something of substance they could talk about. He could see her cottage clearly in his mind's eye, so thoroughly had he made her describe it. He could smell the sea, hear the sea birds, feel the piercing brightness of the summer sun blazing in the Dorset sky.

He'd told her as much as he could recall of Grampion.

Told her as much as he could recall of Moira, and even a few things about his long-dead mother.

Jacaranda listened, she asked a few questions, and she answered most questions he put to her. She sometimes even made small overtures, such as stroking his hair.

But Worth could not divine what was in her mind, and increasingly, he suspected his lady was keeping more of herself from him than she shared with him. The last time he'd had this same uneasy feeling, his intended had ended up married to his brother.

"You were hardly gone," she said against his forehead. "Two days. How could you miss me in such a short time?"

A besotted man missed his beloved when she ventured into the next room, that's how.

"I simply did." He shifted up over her. "I think of you far more than is dignified, and I can only hope you suffer a similar preoccupation regarding me."

He was naked, she was dressed in only her summer nightgown, so he let her feel the blunt length of his nascent arousal by settling his body loosely on hers.

"You are driving me beyond reason, Jacaranda Wyeth."

She might have been formulating some prim, off-putting reply, but he wasn't having any of her starch and vinegar. He pressed his lips to hers, determined that if she'd never missed him thus far, in future she'd have a reason to.

She was at first merely passive, just as she never exactly welcomed him into her bed. He was out of patience with her diffidence—had been out of patience for days. Now he was determined. Very, very determined.

So he grazed his lips over hers lightly, again and again, until she parted her mouth on a sigh, and then he slid his tongue over her bottom lip. She drew back against her pillows.

Jacaranda had tasted him before, but perhaps she grasped that he'd recalled his sense of purpose now, because she went still, waiting, until he dipped inside her mouth again. Then her top lip, then the soft folds between her lips and her teeth.

He drew back a quarter inch, enough to make a point. She lapped at his bottom lip and wrapped a hand around the back of his neck, urging him forward.

"No. You kiss me." His voice held a slight rasp, for he issued not a command but a plea.

Slowly, she raised her mouth to his, eyes open, watching him until she made contact. Then it was his hand anchored in her hair, her eyes closing on a soft, yearning sound.

He kissed her with his whole body, plundering the damp heat of her mouth while his weight gently pinned her to the mattress. He let her feel his cock, rampant now against the softness of her belly, held her hand in his above her head. He set up a rhythm with his hips, slow and insistent, a deliberate call to her body.

God bless the woman, she answered. Her tongue came questing to explore his mouth, and by the smallest degrees, she arched up into him and followed his rhythm.

"Too much," she whispered against his mouth.

Relief twined through Worth's arousal, for Jacaranda Wyeth was at least in the grip of a fierce attraction, and he could build on that.

"We're barely getting started."

"No." She brought her mouth back to his without elaborating. Nonetheless, he'd heard that one damnable syllable and was frustrated enough to take his mouth from hers.

"Not *no*. You may have your *no* if you're refusing me your body, but we will have our pleasure. Say *yes* to that much at least."

She didn't understand. He could see bewilderment in her eyes, so he let go of the hand he'd pinned to her pillow and settled his palm over her breast. Through the soft fabric of her nightgown, the fullness of her practically drove him to begging. Her nipple crested against his palm, and she inhaled sharply as he teased at her with his fingers.

"You will let me pleasure you, Jacaranda," he said, watching her face. "Or you'll tell me to leave this instant. Choose."

The sensible part of him, the part that watched him make a hash of what should have been a protracted seduction, that part understood that forcing any choice on this lady was bound to fail. Stupid—disastrous—any use of coercion. This was a woman who'd turned her back on family for the privilege of ordering about maids and footmen. She would not be forced in any regard.

The *man* in him, though, the man who'd gone without assurances for too long, the man who'd gone without *closeness* for far too long, that fellow kissed the hell out of her, surging into her mouth as he surged over her body.

Two passionate instants later, she hauled back on his hair, stoutly, then smoothed her hand over his head.

"Soon, I must return to that cottage, Worth. I've made promises to my family."

What was she going on about? They'd make a damned wedding journey to her cottage.

"And I must return to Grampion. I understand that, and we can discuss our travels at length, some other time. For now, it's your nightgown that must go somewhere else." He grasped the hem and lifted it, but something in her bearing gave him pause.

The infernal woman wanted to talk *right this minute*. He ascertained her intent by the way she shifted back against the gathered fabric of her nightgown, resisting but not exactly protesting.

"We will talk, Jacaranda, I promise you that, but *not now*."

She relented, raising her shoulders enough to let him draw her only garment over her head and toss it away.

The pleasure of her naked flesh against his had him sealing his body to hers, wrapping her close simply to indulge himself in the sensation of her skin next to his, belly to belly, chest to breast. They could visit family six times a year, but this—this embrace, nothing between them but honest desire and mutual besottedness—was *home*.

"God, yes," he breathed against her throat, though he wanted to give her promises and vows while her whiny family and their musty little cottage could go hang.

Then he rolled so she straddled him, and he fleetingly considered getting up to light branches of candles.

She crossed her arms over her breasts, and his momentum shifted.

He wouldn't make love to her in the next hour, not as intimately as he wanted to, but they were in new territory, naked, together, and she was trusting him—this far at least.

"You are beautiful," he said, meaning it as sincerely as he'd ever meant spoken words. "Please allow me to adore you."

"Adore?" Her single word bore a wealth of uncertainty, and she kept her arms crossed.

"Please." He levered up and kissed her jaw. "You've seen me, watched me lose every shred of dignity and control. Let me see you."

Slowly, holding his gaze, she drew her arms down to rest at her sides.

Never had desire, trust, and vulnerability been as dearly—and arousingly—clothed in nudity. Worth swallowed around the lump in his throat and prayed for...

All manner of blessings.

Fortitude, to proceed despite risk to something of greater value than a mere few hundred thousand pounds.

Worthiness, because Jacaranda's trust should be surrendered into only worthy hands.

Gratitude, because she'd chosen to place her trust into *his* hands.

"I would like to touch you, Jacaranda Wyeth. I'd like it exceedingly."

"I would like that, too."

He didn't use his hands, not at first. He curled up and inhaled the fragrance of her between her breasts.

"The scent is sweet, Jacaranda. Like your neck or your hands, but more secret." He ran his nose all over her chest, grazing her collarbones, the soft undersides of her breasts, and around her nipples.

"I want..." She sighed, tried again. "Will you *touch* me?"

"Soon."

He rested his hands on her shoulders as he lay back against the bed. Sturdy shoulders, unapologetically solid, and yet still feminine.

She regarded him solemnly, waiting, and all his frustration, all his missing her was worth the anticipation he saw in her expression. Gently, he settled his hands over her breasts.

"You're silky," he said. "Warm, smooth, delicate, lovely..." With each word, he drew the backs of his fingers over her breasts, her nipples, around the undersides, up the slopes. "I could come simply by touching your breasts,

Jacaranda."

God help him, he spoke the truth. He could come, compose sonnets, and sing hymns to her breasts, and to the heart that beat swiftly under his palm.

As much to shut himself up as to gratify them both, he closed his mouth over her nipple. She arched toward him, and his cock leapt as desire rippled out from her to him and back again, ricocheting through him, through her, resonating endlessly.

"Worth…" Her fingers winnowed through his hair, and she clung to him.

"Ride me." He got a hand low on her back and anchored himself while she moved over him.

He would not, *would not*, shift his hips to penetrate her heat. She hadn't given him that permission, wasn't expecting that intimacy, and no matter how much pleasure he brought her, he'd never regain her trust if he presumed to cross that line now.

He tipped her so she hung over him, her braid slipping down, tickling his shoulder and arm as he made love to her breasts. The hand he'd used to guide her over him slid around the full curve of her flank, a satiny warm pleasure he'd explore later and thoroughly.

By slow increments, he brought his hand lower, to draw the backs of his fingers over her curls. He sensed surprise and pleasure vibrating through her, and she didn't draw back.

Thank God Almighty, she didn't draw back.

He traced her folds with one thumb, pleased to find dampness and heat and more pleased that she went motionless, allowing it.

"Move, love," he whispered against her breasts, letting his hand go still, waiting for her this time. Then, a tentative motion with her hips, forward against his hand, back, but not far.

"Just like that. Again."

In the quiet darkness, she found a rhythm—conservative, because she didn't know her destination yet as well as she soon would, but Worth fell in with it, applying and releasing pressure at the apex of her folds.

"Worth…what…?"

"The matter wants only patience and determination. You excel at both." He watched her face in the moonlight, and kept up enough pressure that her arousal escalated toward completion. "I'll get you there. No risk for you, all reward."

She said nothing, no doubt listening with her body for how to find more and more pleasure.

Worth's arousal became insistent, but he focused on her, on caressing one breast while he took the other in his mouth, on plying her sex with as much gentle insistence as one half-sane man could muster.

He sensed when passion overtook her restraint. Her back arched, driving her against his hand and his mouth, and she leaned into him hard, her body begging for what words could not convey.

"That's it," he whispered. "All reward."

"*Worth...*"

She hissed his name on a rasp of pleasure, and he drove a finger into her heat, her sex gripping hard around him, and that—that was too much. He held on to her like a bankrupt clutches his last, shiny gold sovereign and let the pleasure reverberate through him even as she was overwhelmed by it as well.

The sounds of their harsh breathing mingled, then eased, and still Worth held on.

Jacaranda stroked his hair, clinging to him, too, as he relaxed back against the bed.

"Come here." He urged her down onto his chest, needing to hold her, needing to keep her close.

She went easily, despite his spent seed all over his belly, despite the aftershocks he sensed rippling through her.

What words could he give her now? What could he say, in thanks or reassurance? He was at sea still, for this was an aspect of intimate pleasure he'd not experienced before—the desire to linger and comfort and be comforted.

He kissed her temple, stroked her back, and prayed for the right words.

Any right words at all.

* * *

Jacaranda tried to get her mind to function, to form sentences, but her body was still too absorbed with marvelous sensations. Her skin buzzed with pleasure, her breasts hummed with it. Between her legs the fire of Worth's touch lingered, and inside, deep inside where a woman carried new life, bodily exultation had yet to entirely fade.

What to say?

"I missed you, too." The ridiculous words were out without Jacaranda having any idea where they'd come from. They were honest, but ye gods. *I missed you?* After *that?*

He came alert beneath her, and it was too late to call the words back. "I beg your pardon?"

"I said, I missed you, too."

"Good." His hand started moving on her back again. "That's good."

What did "good" mean? She searched for basic vocabulary.

"Hold me." Those words *were* right, and Worth's arms closing more securely around her were more right still.

"Better?"

She nodded against his chest and wondered what came next, but then the comfort of his embrace stole even curiosity from her grip. Worth knew what came next, and that was all she needed for the moment.

His lips moved at her temple. "Sleep, love. I've got you."

"You won't leave?"

"Not yet."

When she next opened her eyes, she was cast adrift over the great, lovely expanse of Worth Kettering. His hands caressed her back, his chest rose and fell beneath her.

"I should move." Straight back to Dorset, and soon.

"You shouldn't go far. We could do with a wash, though."

So one talked about that. Two did. "I'll see to it."

"You will not."

One argued about it, even. She wanted to smile—no, to *smirk*. She did not want to move back to Dorset.

"You sprawl here in feminine splendor while I see to it," Worth said, and he was smiling outright, his teeth gleaming in the darkness.

"I do not sprawl, Worth Kettering." She climbed off him, an ungainly production, and hit the mattress on her back. Her stomach was sticky, so she didn't draw the sheets up.

"You will acquire the knack of sprawling if I have anything to say to it." He bounced off the mattress, his tone as brisk as his movements. "Sprawling, lounging, reclining, what have you. A well-pleasured lady is entitled to certain privileges." He came back to the bed with a flannel in his hand, looking her over in the moonlight.

Jacaranda held out her hand. "I'll take that."

He sat at her hip, ignored her hand, and put the cool, damp cloth on her belly.

"You sprawl," he said, tidying her up. "Unless you'd like to perform this courtesy for me?"

"Good heavens." So many ways to be intimate, and she wasn't even truly his lover.

He rubbed at himself briskly. "Maybe next time. Now we sprawl together. I rather like this part."

"You didn't like the other?"

More wrong words. When would her wits come back to life?

Worth positioned himself over her, and that was nice, to be gathered beneath him again. Despite her words, Jacaranda felt safe and close to him.

"I adored the other," he said, close to her ear. "I adore you." He climbed off her when she didn't have the confidence to ask him not to. "Now we sprawl. There's science to it. First, you get comfortable."

"I am comfortable."

"You usually sleep on your right side, love."

She wanted to argue, but didn't because she felt rather in charity with him, and with the rest of creation. She scooted to her right side.

"Just so. Then I get comfortable." He spooned himself around her, his warmth comfortable and comforting. "Then I tell you how much I enjoyed spending this time with you, more than words can say." He kissed her nape. "You are truly magnificent, Jacaranda Wyeth. Beyond words, beyond anything in my experience. I am humbled."

He sounded humbled, too. Jacaranda was grateful for the darkness, because his words made her blush.

"Now go to sleep." He settled a hand around her breast, and even that brought with it emotions warm and dear. "Dream of me, for I shall surely dream of you."

She went to sleep and she did dream of him.

Also of her cottage in Dorset.

* * *

Worth lingered in Jacaranda's bed until almost dawn, passing the night in a pleasurable twilight. He'd wake up, cuddle her closer, stroke his hands over her curves and hollows, kiss her cheek, her hair, her neck, and subside back into dreamy drowsing. He knew for a fact he'd never spent as much of an entire night with a throbbing cockstand, or enjoyed himself so much without having intercourse.

Before the sun peeked over the horizon, he stole down the corridor, boots in hand, much on his mind.

Jacaranda probably suspected his latest marriage proposal hadn't been a joke about raspberry jam. She was deucedly perceptive about things like jam pots.

The words had come out, heartfelt and sincere. Jacaranda had been surprised and nonplussed, which did not bode well for him.

As the day wore on, he confirmed his suspicion that part of what ran the household was his housekeeper's perpetual motion. She came to rest in her little sitting room for tea, but she also held audiences in there.

Cook joined her for a cup and emerged peering at a handful of menus.

Mr. Reilly passed the time of day with dear Mrs. Wyeth and then braced Worth on whether the bridle paths in the home wood ought to be cleared to permit access to Hunter's holding if the bridge should fail.

Carl disappeared into that sitting room and emerged clutching a list to take to Mr. Simmons, the printing so large and bold Worth could make it out from across the corridor.

With the head maid, another list of orders was dispatched. Then the vicar called, paying Worth and Hess a few courtesies before rising to go in search of Mrs. Wyeth.

Jacaranda Wyeth was more than a housekeeper, and not simply in the sense she was the woman Worth wanted for his wedded wife. She had infiltrated his household, systematically asserted her common sense, and made a large, neglected estate into a profitable, smoothly running home.

She'd invaded and taken over.

"What has you frowning so?" Hess asked as he ambled into the library.

"My housekeeper. I've been duped, Hessian. I like it not."

"By her? In what sense? She doesn't seem the duping kind."

"I only think I own this property," Worth said, tossing himself into a wing chair. "I'm a guest here."

"You weren't a guest yesterday." Hess took the other chair in a more decorous fashion. "I was ready to expire with worry, and your housekeeper had reached the end of her tether, too."

"She was worried she'd fail." The words were unfair, also true. Something or someone had driven Jacaranda to impossibly high expectations of herself.

"She was worried Yolanda had done something irreparably foolish," Hess corrected him. "Worried the girl was hurt, lost, set upon by ruffians."

"Ruffians on Trysting land?"

"With sufficient quantities of drink and stupidity, ruffians can be found in almost any corner of the realm. The point is, Mrs. Wyeth was beside herself, as was I, and you—Mr. I'm Only A Guest—were the only one with a cool head. You might feel like a guest, but you do own the place."

"I pay the taxes. That's not the same thing."

Hess's lips quirked at this pouting. "You are decidedly grumpy, brother. To what do we attribute your foul mood?"

"Hess, I want to marry her."

Hess's smile became sweet rather than teasing—and God above, *that* smile would bring the ladies of Polite Society to his side at a dead, panting run.

"Then procure a ring, take a knee, and be about it. We're not getting any younger, in case you hadn't noticed, and neither of our nurseries sports an heir."

"Hang the nurseries." Worth abandoned his chair to study the outdated maps of the enormous atlas. "She won't have me."

"Have you asked?"

"More or less." Mostly less. "She scolded me for being so forward the first time. The second time we made a raspberry joke of it. She natters about her family and some cottage in Dorset."

"I have no idea what a raspberry joke is, Worth, but the lady fancies you."

Clearing the bridle path would also create a shortcut into town—and let a closer eye be kept on Thomas Hunter.

"Has Jacaranda told you she fancies me?"

Worth understood about money, and all the ways human nature and money fit together, but Hess... Hess had been married. For years. Hess had dallied. Hess had a child, and he was the only sympathetic ear Worth was likely to find.

"Your housekeeper is an attractive female. My notice has been drawn to her, but every time I behold the lady, she's busy beholding you. And Worth, she has this wistful gleam in her eyes when she does. I do not think she's contemplating dusting you, either, or adorning you with a lace runner."

A smile threatened at the image of Jacaranda Wyeth using a feather duster on Worth's naked parts. He flipped the page of the atlas to find an elevation of Trysting before the conservatory had been added.

"Women like to hear the words," Hess said. "I haven't any pretty words for them, hence I am a non-competitor in the courting stakes."

"So stay here in the south with us." Worth left off perusing familial ancient history to regard his brother. His only brother, his only adult family in the entire world. "Get some practice, or at least get your ashes hauled regularly. Most women I know, the married ones anyway, are long past the need for any words besides 'faster,' 'harder,' and 'aren't you ready to give it another go yet?'"

"You poor abused old thing. No wonder Mrs. Wyeth has her doubts. What do we know about Mr. Wyeth?"

"Who? Oh, Mr. Wyeth. Not a thing. I doubt there was one."

Though there had been somebody, or no way on God's earth would Worth be pursuing Jacaranda in the manner he was.

"Many housekeepers make diplomatic use of the married form of address," Hess said, rising and coming to stand beside Worth. "I told Yolanda I wouldn't drag her north against her will. I'm not sure where that leaves us, when Grampion is the only roof I can afford to put over her head. She assured me she hadn't been running away."

As changes of subject went, Hess's gambit lacked subtlety, but Worth had gone over Hess's finances. The lesser holdings were either let out or soon to be rented, that much was fact.

"What about spending the winter in Town? Your vote would be an asset to your party."

Hess drew a finger along the façade of an older, more stately Trysting. "Winter up north is long, cold and harsh, but it's also beautiful, peaceful, and I'm used to it."

"We're both in a contrary mood, though that parade of footmen across yonder terrace means we're once again to be picnicking. Perhaps I'll go north with you, where the picnic season is so much shorter."

Where housekeepers were less likely to drive a man to unrequited longings that had him up most of the night, in more ways than one.

# CHAPTER FIFTEEN

Jacaranda managed to avoid her employer—Worth was still that—for most of the day, and she told herself that for the best, also necessary, because she needed to compose herself.

Or appear to compose herself.

She'd forgotten today was the day for Vicar's call and had nearly forgotten between a morning note and an afternoon response, that she'd asked for a moment of Mr. Reilly's time. If Cook hadn't come bustling by, Jacaranda would have neglected a week's worth of menus as well.

This was all *his* fault.

Jacaranda would never grow accustomed to spending the night naked and entwined in a man's arms. The pleasure was heady, wonderful and, when that man was Worth Kettering, overwhelmingly sweet. The caring and tenderness he was capable of in the simplest, fleeting touch—

Jacaranda's insides fluttered with the memory of his caresses, a fluttering that had afflicted her all day. She crossed her legs at the knee and encountered a tingling in places a lady doesn't tingle. She brushed her hair and recalled the feel of his hands sweeping through the length of it repeatedly, like he couldn't get enough of the sensation. She wiggled her feet out of her slippers and recalled him grasping the arch of her foot and holding her *foot* in a secure, warm embrace of the hand.

Holding her foot, and she'd wanted to swoon with the pleasure of it.

Angels abide.

Into this muddle of memories and sensations came emotions, heralded by long, gusty sighs, staring spells, and other behaviors Jacaranda had previously seen only in her younger sister, Daisy.

First came a yearning so desperate it scared her, a yearning to be more intimate with Worth than she'd already been, a yearning to share with him the act Jacaranda had experienced only once, years ago.

But following on that honest admission came the realization that what Jacaranda wanted was the entire man, not simply copulation with him, and that—that small, profound distinction—put her on precarious footing.

Worth Kettering was heir to an earl, quite possibly rich as a nabob, and completely unaware of his housekeeper's true origins. When Jacaranda told him, he'd feel obligated to marry her in truth, when she knew the last person he'd affix himself to was a woman who'd lied to him. He had learned his lesson, just as Jacaranda had learned hers.

Then there was her family, all expecting her to return to their loving, if noisy, disorganized and perpetually impecunious arms.

"There you are."

Worth Kettering stood in the doorway to Jacaranda's sitting room, his riding attire showing him off to great advantage, his hair tousled, his faint smile tugging at places low in Jacaranda's belly.

Even a day later, words eluded her.

"And there you are," Jacaranda answered, busying herself with afternoon tea. "I've wondered if it's your gaze I felt on me of late."

"Only my gaze?" He ambled into the room and wandered its small perimeter, stopping to sniff her late roses.

"Need I remind you the door is open, Mr. Kettering?"

He wandered closer and leaned in as if to sniff her.

"The next time I bring you pleasure, I want you to call out for *Mr. Kettering* in that exact tone, for it arouses me." He straightened, his eyes dancing.

"You've come to torment me. I suppose a day of peace and quiet was too much to ask."

"Far too much."

He settled into her rocking chair, and Jacaranda had to admit she liked the look of him there. Relaxed, thoughtful, a gleam in his eyes.

"Tea?"

"Please." He rested his chin on his palm, his elbow on the rocker's arm. "What have you found to do with yourself today, Mrs. Wyeth?"

Her name had never sounded so wicked, reminding Jacaranda that she hadn't even told Worth her true name.

"A little of this and that. Having the family in residence makes the day busier, but more pleasant, too."

"More pleasant?" He accepted his tea from her hands, cradling her fingers in his as he did. Wretch.

"Meaningful, maybe?" She tried to ignore his nonsense, tried to find honest words. "One doesn't tidy up and dust and direct the maids and footmen simply for the sake of the house. A house is a building. One cares for the house on behalf of the people who dwell there."

"For me, you mean?"

"For you, some," she allowed, and he looked so hopeful she added cream and sugar to her admission. "Mostly for you, because you are the head of this household."

"I am." He took a sip of his tea. "I don't feel like it, but I am. I'm wondering, though, if I shouldn't offer to spend the winter in Cumberland with Hess and the girls."

"You haven't been home in a long time." This was what came of admitting that she must return to Dorset. Perhaps among sophisticated, worldly adults, such a mention was all that was needed.

Worth had brought her pleasure upon pleasure in the dark of night, and now he casually acquiesced in her insistence that their dealings remain only a summer dalliance.

"Avery should see the family seat," Jacaranda went on. "Yolanda would feel less banished if you accompanied them."

"I'd feel banished," he said, grumpiness creeping into his tone. "Would you come with us?"

Grey would have an apoplexy if she broke her word again, Step-Mama would hunt her down with a press-gang. "I could not, not with any sort of reputation. You know that."

His stare became broody, his eyes shuttered, and she sensed she'd hurt him.

"I might want to," she relented and spoke the truth. "But I could not. My family would not tolerate such a great distance between us."

She thought he would let her answer stand unchallenged, but after a beat of silence, he was still watching her.

"Why not come with us? You could be Lannie's companion, because Miss Snyder is going back to her little finishing school come Michaelmas. The girls would like your company."

His eyelids dropped to half-mast, implying something else entirely, and God help her, Jacaranda was tempted.

She thought of Grey, and Will and Daisy, and of the boys. Of her two nephews and her niece, Step-Mama's pleading and threatening and begging.

Of her cottage.

Of the falsehoods now thoroughly rooted between Jacaranda and the man she loved.

"A housekeeper is not a suitable candidate to be a young lady's companion."

"The hell she isn't." Worth pushed out of his rocking chair, the lazy innuendo replaced with tension. "I want you to think about something, Mrs. Wyeth." He shot a glance at the open door and lowered his voice. "We have not consummated our dealings in the intimate sense, and for the next two weeks, given the risk of conception, I would not impose on you even were you willing. It's August, soon it will be September, and for all the patience I've shown, you're no closer to a decision than you were a month ago. You're a nervous investor, Mrs. Wyeth. No risk, no reward, though. That has ever been true."

He kissed her cheek and took his leave, while Jacaranda held her cooling tea and tried to think of a reply to his observation.

She came up with nothing but a cold cup of tea.

* * *

Yolanda's privacy was disturbed when Worth found her reading on a tartan blanket in the hay mow over the stables, a fat black tom cat asleep in a sunbeam beside her. She came here for privacy, and to revel in the way the scents of hay and horses put her in mind of Mr. Hunter.

Thomas.

"Hello, you." Worth sat right beside her in a manner that still unnerved and pleased her, as if they were siblings of long-standing, not recent acquaintances trying to rub along in an awkward situation. "I do believe you've grown prettier since leaving that school."

Did Thomas think her pretty?

"Hullo, Worth."

"You reading a fatuous novel?"

"Sir Walter Scott."

"I've always enjoyed his work." Worth drew a wisp of hay from the packed pile beneath them and batted the fat black cat on the nose. The beast didn't stir from its position in exact alignment with the sunbeam slanting through the hay port door.

"Are you hiding from Mrs. Wyeth, or from Avery, or perhaps from Hess?" Yolanda asked, closing her book around a single finger because, like a brother one-quarter his age, Worth was apparently intent on pestering her.

"I'm hiding from my life. Have you and Hessian come to some peace with each other?"

Yolanda stroked a hand over the cat, who yawned and began to purr.

"Some. Hess thought I'd be happy visiting here in the south with schoolmates and doesn't see why I would rather have spent my holidays mostly traveling to and from Cumberland."

From *home*, something a brother who dwelled there year after year ought to have appreciated.

"You, of course, assured him he was completely in error?"

"I told him there's a difference between sparing me travel and abandoning me for two years straight. Hess doesn't seem to need anybody but his hounds and horses. He doesn't let himself need family."

At least Worth had Avery, and Avery had Worth. Lucky them.

"Hessian is a Kettering." Worth scratched the cat's shoulders, and the beast tried to bite him. "We're prone to managing on our own, no matter the size of the load. Did you tell him about that cut on your wrist?"

Drat all brothers for being such noticing fellows. Thomas had wondered at the scar, too, but had been gentleman enough to keep his questions to himself. "The injury is healed. What is there to tell?"

"Something, when you're ready. Hessian is the head of our family, but I'm your brother, too, Lannie. You could tell me if you didn't want to impose on Hess."

How delicately Worth could express himself, when he chose to. "There's little to tell."

"You ladies." Worth tormented the cat again by tickling its nose with the hay, but the tom was again intent on ignoring him. "Why can't I be more like this fellow? Happy to pounce on mice, and be on my way after the occasional trifling scuffle?"

Safer ground entirely, and good of Worth to offer it. "Mrs. Wyeth has given you your congé?"

Worth's expression was perplexed, while the cat made a half-hearted swat at the hay, which Worth failed to notice. "Sixteen isn't so very young, is it?"

Yolanda's finger remained between the pages of her book, which was fortunate; otherwise, she might have patted Worth's hand.

"Mrs. Wyeth cares for you. That might be why she's not falling into your arms."

"I fear one shouldn't discuss such matters with a younger sister."

She paged through her book, for Worth apparently wanted to discuss his situation with somebody. "Hess certainly wouldn't discuss it with me, just as he doesn't discuss Belinda Evers with me."

Whom Hessian seemed to regard with equal parts bewilderment and wariness.

Worth smacked her nose with his stalk of hay, entirely the brother, but also affectionate. "Explain your female reasoning to me. Why would Mrs. Wyeth reject my suit if she cares for me?"

"Your *suit?*"

"Yes, my suit, brat. I've asked her to marry me more than once."

Good for Mrs. Wyeth. Yolanda had the sense few women refused the Kettering brothers anything of value. "Are you such a bargain, Worth?"

"See how many swains flock to your side when word of the dowry I've set aside for you gets out. I'm not exactly shoddy goods, Lannie Kettering."

How she loved the nickname he'd given her. "You're a good bargain," she said, in part because of that nickname, "but a husband is a complicated proposition."

"A long-term investment." He stroked his face with the straw the way Yolanda often touched a quill pen to her cheek when puzzling over some Latin. "One gathers you ladies view the long-term investments warily."

Warily, and incessantly. Most of the girls at school had been obsessed with Debrett's for the information it held concerning possible husbands.

"You have to offer her something she doesn't already have, Worth. She has a roof over her head and meaningful work and people to care about."

The notion intrigued him, for he ceased fussing with his bit of hay. "I can offer her wealth, an honorable before our name, all the entrée in Town she wants. She could be Hess's hostess, clothed in silk and jewels, own all the cottages in England."

He could also give her babies, though Yolanda did not point that out to him.

"I'm not sure what cottages have to do with it."

"Neither am I, but it's important to her. More important than I am."

How well she knew that feeling. "Don't sulk. While I was stuck in a cottage with Mr. Hunter for most of an hour, he had to remove my boot and wrap my foot with his bare hands, and he didn't permit himself the smallest liberty."

What a delight that had been, to be treated so properly, so carefully.

Also a towering disappointment.

"He had better not take any liberties." Worth tossed the hay at the sleeping cat and missed. "Do you fancy this yeoman, Lannie?"

Thomas smelled a great deal better than any yeoman Yolanda had stood downwind of. He quoted poetry, and he loved his children.

"I'm sixteen. If I say I do fancy him, you'll laugh at me. If I say I don't, you'll accuse me of lying. Brothers are awful."

"You didn't laugh at me," Worth pointed out. "If this is the fellow you want, Lannie, then do the pretty in Town next Season, but know that you'll be welcome to spend your summers here at Trysting."

Yolanda's exact plan, though she'd been unsure how to manage the part about summers at Trysting. Worth's generosity was too convenient not to be a little suspect, though.

"You aren't saying he's beneath my notice when I'm the daughter of an earl, my brother is an earl, and I'm generously dowered, for which I do thank you."

"You're my sister. Of course you'll have a decent portion, and I will not lecture you about your station. You're the acknowledged illegitimate daughter of an earl, and if you haven't already sensed it, the tabbies of Polite Society will ensure the distinction is noted by all."

Yolanda turned an idle page, though Worth's blunt acknowledgement of reality was comforting in a way his generous dowry could not be.

"School was no different. If I'd been the illegitimate daughter of a mere baronet, it might have been worse. Coin does seem to open doors."

"You are not like any sixteen-year-old of my acquaintance, Lannie Kettering. Next you'll be reading the financial pages."

Yolanda put her book aside, because he'd given her the opening she needed.

"I saw a piece in the *Times* about the Drummond being late for its scheduled return and you being a major source of investors. Are you in trouble, Worth?"

* * *

"Had I not been quizzing Avery on her fairy tales"—Hess handed his brother two fingers of brandy—"we would have had no conversation at dinner to speak of. Are you and your housekeeper feuding?"

"We are." When had Hess become Worth's drinking companion? "My thanks."

"Is this feud over the menus, perhaps?" Hess took the second of the library's two largest, most comfortable chairs. "Or maybe she wants a raise in her pay?"

"She deserves a raise in her pay." Though Jacaranda, in her contrary fashion, would regard a pay raise as an insult. "I asked her about traveling north with us next month, serving as Lannie's companion for the winter months at Grampion."

"Miss Snyder isn't willing to serve any longer?"

The question was posed casually, but Worth had been watching the glances exchanged at dinner. "You find Miss Snyder attractive?"

"Her papa is heir to a barony." Stated even more casually.

Worth set his drink on the low table. One Kettering brother in perpetual rut was one too many. "Go back to Town, Hess. Avail yourself of what Mary freely offers and settle your nerves."

"I did."

"I beg your pardon?"

"I did avail myself of what Mary so delightfully offered, and my nerves are settled." Hess took a contemplative sip of his drink, and indeed, he did appear to be more relaxed than he had upon arriving from the north.

Rotter.

"Settle them again. The activity bears repeating in the right company."

"Up to a point," Hess allowed. "Then it is merely an activity, and as pleasant as it is, I found my nerves adequately settled by the one occasion."

"Pleasant." Life had been simpler before Hess had resumed being a brother—also lonelier. "If it's merely pleasant, then you're going about it wrong, brother mine."

"I was never afflicted with the passions affecting the rest of our family."

Hess retrieved Worth's drink and handed it to him. "Back to your Mrs. Wyeth. What is the problem?"

The question of the hour.

"I delivered her an ultimatum," Worth said, "or as good as, and that after telling her she could have between now and forever to make up her mind." Though every half-witted, spotty legal clerk knew a decently drafted contract specified an exact period of performance.

"What did your ultimatum regard?"

"What do you think it regarded?" Worth paced to the window—the sparkling-clean window, which he was tempted to put his fist through. "I offered her marriage, she politely laughed in my face. Why should she give up all this freedom, the endless adventure of warring with the dust and the mice and the gossiping menials when all I offer is a ring? So I offered something less weighty—my heart on a platter—and she dithered. She's still dithering and talking about going to visit her family."

"Well, there's your answer, isn't it?"

"Must you be so honest?"

Hess rose and put a hand on Worth's shoulder. "I cannot fathom women, never have, never will. You've more than the normal complement of sense, though, Worth, and a Kettering's portion of pride. Why do you persist when the reception is feeble?"

"Because it isn't feeble, damn it. She nigh devours me when we're private."

"And you devour her?"

No, *that* was the question of the hour.

"I haven't yet." Worth traced his finger down the lattice-work of the mullioned window. "It's a near-run thing, Hess."

"You're in unfamiliar waters?"

"Deep, shark-infested unfamiliar waters with cross-currents and undertows."

"Then it's time for a strategic return to dry land, old man. You're the only brother I have, and I refuse to stand by and watch you dragged out to sea ever again."

Worth stood, staring out the window, long after Hess had sought his bed. He considered getting drunk, something he hadn't done for a decade or so, but if he imbibed, he was more likely to talk himself into visiting Jacaranda's boudoir.

He went for a long swim, diving frequently to the coldest reaches of the pond, and eventually sheer fatigue took the edge off his mood. He arrived to his rooms tired, chilled, and no clearer in his mind than he'd been earlier. While part of him was certain Jacaranda would dither and prevaricate on his offer for the rest of her natural days, another part of him wondered if she was waiting for some sign from him, some subtle indication of worth he'd failed to give.

So he fell into a restless sleep and dreamed of the Drummond coming to grief on rocky shoals within sight of port.

* * *

"Why is my stable master waltzing about the garden with Miss Snyder?"

"Good morning, Mr. Kettering." Jacaranda rose from her place at the table to stand beside him at the window to the breakfast parlor. "Roberts and Miss Snyder do not appear to be waltzing."

Simply standing near Worth had Jacaranda's pulse leaping, had her leaning infinitesimally closer to catch his scent.

"Promenading, then. Are they enamored of one another?"

"If they are?" she asked, resuming her seat.

"Then good for them," he said, taking his own. "At least somebody on this benighted estate is finding some pleasurable company."

She took a sip of tea and scalded her tongue. He'd very nearly hurt her feelings, though she *wasn't* good company.

"My apologies." Worth reached for the teapot. "I'm on tenterhooks regarding an investment, and my nerves are unsettled."

"You usually take it with cream and sugar," Jacaranda said as Worth winced at the taste of his tea.

Worth spooned the sugar in generously. "Does anything on this property escape your notice, Mrs. Wyeth?"

Her wits, her common sense, her ability to be honest with the man she'd come to love.

"Much," she said, wondering—hoping?—he was in this foul mood because he'd not come to her bed last night.

She'd missed him, missed him badly, and tossed and turned for hours. She'd made the decision to return home to Dorset, but longed to consummate her dealings with Worth Kettering before she did.

A woman already sunk in falsehoods might as well steal some memories, too.

"I take leave to doubt you miss anything of significance, madam. Is that all you're eating?"

Toast and butter. Daisy's breakfast in the early weeks of her pregnancies. "My appetite is off."

His gaze narrowed. "Is it really? What a pity."

"You are not a mean man. What has got into you?"

"Do you recall telling me I could have your coin?"

Not an answer, and he was busy putting more omelet onto Jacaranda's plate. "I recall that, yes."

He stopped heaping eggs before her. "Why won't you marry me?"

"Oh, Worth." She stared at her plate, trying to form an answer as tears welled. "Not fair."

"What isn't fair," he said, his voice low, "is that you pleasure me like a siren in the night, find bliss in my arms, and then turn up diffident and prim at the breakfast table. Am I really such poor husband material, Jacaranda?"

She fell back on the truth.

She dabbed at her eyes with her serviette. "I honestly do feel an obligation to my family, but you and I also hardly know each other. I am not the ideal wife for an earl's heir. You would agree with me if you knew me better."

"The earl's heir? I'm not asking you to marry Grampion's unborn children," Worth said. "Trust me, Hess is getting up the nerve to find himself a countess. I know the look, and he's a smart lad. Winters are long in the north, and families tend to be large."

"Hush." Jacaranda rose. *I love you, I love you.* "One doesn't pick a husband like a new mount at Tatt's. You and I suit in one regard, I'm confident of that, but I sense others have suited you as well, and you know you're not my first."

He rose. "Dear heart, that can hardly matter to me when you won't even permit me to be your second."

His eyes held puzzlement, hurt, and not a little determination, so Jacaranda left the room at the fastest walk dignity would allow.

* * *

Worth pushed the remains of his breakfast away and went in search of his brother, resisting the urge to chase after his unwilling intended. Instinct suggested that if he pursued Jacaranda too tenaciously, she'd flee not simply to her sitting room, but clear back to that cottage in Dorset she seemed so fond of.

He could not fathom *why.* Some secret tormented her or some familial obligation. Perhaps she had a child in her brother's care in Dorset—

Walking by the library, Worth was surprised to hear an otherwise peaceful morning punctuated by Yolanda's voice, nearly raised at her older brother.

"You said you wouldn't drag me north against my will!"

Hess's voice came next, civil, but tense from the tone, the words indistinguishable.

Worth debated mentally, then pushed the door open. He loved them both, and they were clearly in difficulties.

"Greetings, siblings. A pleasant day for a disagreement, is it not?"

"We weren't disagreeing," Hess began, as Yolanda crossed her arms and declared, "Wonderfully so."

"What seems to be the trouble?" Though for once, no part of Worth relished a touchy negotiation, no part of him was eager to see if he could untangle the Gordian knot of Hess's sense of duty, Yolanda's injured pride, and his own desire to remain as close to Trysting as possible.

Yolanda's chin jutted in Hess's direction. "*He* says we need to think of repairing to Grampion. He wouldn't invite me home when I was desperately homesick, but we must hare off there now when you've perfectly lovely accommodations for us all here in the south."

"She wants to make sheep's eyes at that dratted farmer," Hess retorted. "If I leave her here, you'll need to post a watch on her."

Yolanda's eyes glittered ominously. "Unfair, Hessian. If I'd wanted to misbehave in that manner, I would have accepted all the invitations I received to join the school's gardener in his charming little shed, wouldn't I?"

"What?!" Both brothers spoke—bellowed, more like—at once. Worth recovered first.

"What invitations, Yolanda Kettering? And don't think to prevaricate with us now."

Her expression was chillingly blank for such a young lady. "His name was Arnold, and he was a nuisance, but he was Mrs. Peese's nephew, so my complaints weren't considered noteworthy."

"Of what exactly," Hess asked, "did you complain?"

Yolanda's gaze traveled from one brother to the other. She settled on the sofa, in the same manner the accused takes the dock. "Promise me you won't yell at me?" "We promise." In unison.

"You won't throw things?"

The brothers exchanged a look.

"We won't throw things of value at you," Worth said. "Stop fretting and tell us."

"He started with a few little touches, at first," Yolanda said, staring at her hands. "The other girls thought it was daring, because he's not...he's not spotty. Some of them said he was handsome in a common sort of way."

"Famous," Hess hissed. "You've been subjected to the attentions of a not-spotty gardener in the one place a girl should be free of such bother."

Worth sent his brother a quelling look. "Go on, Lannie. We're listening."

"He must have known he wouldn't get in trouble, because he started leaving me notes then, in personal places."

"Personal places, Lannie?" Hess asked.

"Under my pillow, among my clothes."

"With your unmentionables," Worth said. "He's a dead gardener, this spotless wonder."

"You mustn't," Yolanda wailed quietly. "All the girls knew, and to them, daring progressed to amusing."

"But not to you." Worth settled beside her. "To you it became frightening."

"He waited in my room one night and k-kissed me." Yolanda grimaced at the memory. "It was horrid. He was horrid, and he said things."

Hess took a cushioned chair, his fingers drumming on the arm. "*Things?*"

"Things he wanted to do to me. You didn't answer my letters, and Mrs.

Peese said I was imagining it all, but I wasn't."

"God in heaven." Worth brushed back a lock of Yolanda's hair. "Did he manage to do more than threaten you, kiss you, and scare you witless?"

"He had better not have," Hess said, back on his feet. "I'll see the place shut down, I will."

"You mustn't." Yolanda leaned into Worth. "When Mrs. Peese asked the other girls, they said they'd seen nothing, heard nothing, but they all knew he'd treated another student the same way the previous year. She was a by-blow, too."

"So, little lunatic that you are, you cut yourself," Worth guessed. "Beat them at their own game, brought me running, and got free of the scoundrel. Well done." He kissed her forehead and glared at Hess over her shoulder.

"Right," Hess said, "well damned done indeed. I'm surprised you didn't call the idiot out, or entice him into his lowly garden bower, then wallop him with a shovel where it counts."

Yolanda dropped her forehead to Worth's shoulder. "I thought about it, but nobody supported my version of events, and a violent lunatic is worse than a hysterical female. I didn't know if Worth would come fetch me or not."

"Worth came," Hess said.

"I will always come when you ask it. You're my sister."

"You didn't know that." Yolanda took Hess's proffered handkerchief. "You were so dark and stern and brisk. You never said I was your sister until recently."

"You're my sister." He hugged her, pushing the words past an abruptly tight throat. "Hess is my brother, you are my sister. Avery is our niece. We're a family."

"I will not drag you north," Hess said, clearing his throat. "I will, however, offer a medicinal tot all around."

Yolanda sat up. "Brandy? For me?"

"It's medicinal." Hess passed her a scant portion and Worth a more generous serving. "I really do want to see that school closed."

"But what will the girls think?"

"What will their families think, to know such a situation wasn't dealt with appropriately?" Hess countered. "Consider another girl, Lannie, younger than you, not as resourceful, not as brave. She won't think of a scheme to get herself sent down. She won't even protest."

"Like the girl last year," Yolanda said. "She didn't come back for Hilary term, and nobody said anything."

"Ketterings don't meekly allow such injustices, and they don't quietly tolerate another's dissembling," Worth said. "Either the gardener takes a post where he can't prey on girls or the school will be closed. Between Hess and me, we've the connections to see to it."

"We do," Hess said. "I'll give it a day, then draft a letter for you two to look over. It's the right course, Lannie."

"It is," she agreed, taking a shuddery breath. "This brandy does help with one's nerves."

Worth downed his at a swallow, more proud of his siblings than he could bear. "Having family helps, too."

"Here, here." Hess held up his glass, as did Yolanda. A knock on the door interrupted Yolanda's maiden attempt at a toast.

"A note for Mr. Kettering," Carl said. Worth took the folded and sealed missive, dreading any news that took him away from Trysting

"A pigeon up from Devon," he said, crumpling the paper into a ball.

"It's urgent?" Yolanda asked.

"Pigeons generally are. The timing is miserable."

"You fear for the Drummond?" Hess asked.

"I do." And, worse, he feared for his future as Jacaranda Wyeth's husband. "Somebody should have passed along some gossip by now, something from one of the Cape Town ships, or Lisbon. Some-damned-where between here and the Antipodes, somebody has to have seen the Drummond under way and headed home."

"Unless it came to grief again," Yolanda said. "Oh, Worth—"

"I'm for Town," Worth interrupted her. "Hess, I'd appreciate it if you'd hold the reins here. Lannie?"

"Worth?"

"You did the right thing. You defended yourself the best you knew how, and I am sorry as hell I haven't been a better brother to you."

"You needn't—" Yolanda began, but Hess interrupted.

"We need to, both of us, Lannie. I'm sorry, too. I should have paid attention, should have protected you. I am sorry. I won't let you down like that again."

He aimed a look at Worth as he said that last, a look that implied unspoken apology, and a full complement of Kettering determination. A fraction of Worth's anxiety eased.

"Does this mean you'll invite Mr. Hunter to dinner?" Yolanda asked.

"I'm leaving," Worth said. "Hess is the head of our family, he can deal with the difficult decisions."

Worth all but ran from the library, knowing Hess faced no decision at all. At this rate, Yolanda Kettering would soon be vying with Jacaranda Wyeth for honors as queen of the parish, if not the shire. The gardener had been lucky she hadn't taken a knife to his parts.

He put away for another time the self-flagellation resulting from the knowledge that Yolanda had resorted to self-harm to get herself rescued. What if the knife had slipped? What if the wound had become infected? What if Peese's letter had gone astray?

God's toothbrush.

And now, now of all times, Worth did not want to leave Trysting. He had a miserable, low-down hunch that Jacaranda was up to something, looking for another post, taking a permanent leave to see her family, somehow withdrawing from the field and refusing his several offers.

He couldn't let that happen. Could not.

# CHAPTER SIXTEEN

The timing was awful, as of course, timing must be when one's life was becoming a complete shambles.

"It's my step-mother," Jacaranda said, barely containing her tears. "She's leaving, and Mrs. Dankle is quitting in truth, and Daisy can't step in because she still has a child at the breast. They need me."

Mr. Simmons's expression was gratifyingly miserable. "Family is the worst. If my grandda hadn't shouted my dam down, I'd still be back in Rabbit Hollow, mooning after Miss Sophie Dale—except Sophie's dead these ten years and more. Grandda said I was tall enough and handsome enough for service."

Half a century ago, that might have been true. "More biscuits, Mr. Simmons?"

"Biscuits make my teeth ache." He took two anyway. "Why must your step-mother up and leave now?"

Yes, why, why, why? Jacaranda wanted to burn Step-Mama's letter, though the summons it brought was inevitable.

"She says she's lonely, and she refuses to grow old shouting at grown men to leave their muddy boots in the hall. Without her or Dankle, the house will soon be a ruin, my brothers' clothing a disgrace. Grey must spend part of the year in Town, and Will hasn't the temperament for exercising authority. Step-Mama says she's worn out, and they can all go to blazes. She says if I won't take them in hand, I'll regret it all my days, for they're my family."

Simmons took a nibble of biscuit, leaving a trail of crumbs on Jacaranda's carpet. "Can't argue with that. Not all ladies are like you, Mrs. Wyeth. Most of them are cursed with delicate nerves."

"Step-Mama's nerves are very delicate, from so many births, she says. Mr. Simmons, when you left Rabbit Hollow, did you think you'd never return?"

Simmons was not always nice, but he was old, and Jacaranda had no doubt he was capable of kindness.

"Rabbit Hollow is the English. In my grandda's day, we still used the Gaelic for it, even in Cumberland. I went back a time or two, and one of my sisters used to live in Hampshire before she died, but my family is here now, at Trysting."

And she'd be leaving that family, leaving Worth, to preserve her brothers' lives from chaos. She'd promised.

Jacaranda began to cry. Simmons passed her his uneaten biscuit, patted her shoulder, and left.

\* \* \*

Worth went in search of Jacaranda, taking the better part of an hour to track her to her own sitting room rather than resort to interrogating the maids and giving himself away.

"Wyeth, what the hell do you think you're doing?"

"W—Mr. Kettering, you startled me."

"That is a box, Jacaranda Wyeth." Worth closed the door quietly by sheer effort of will. *Mr. Kettering?* "You are putting your personal collection of books into a box suited to conveying the books over a distance."

"They are my books," she said, a volume of Wordsworth held to her chest. "I can do with them as I please."

"What is it you're doing?" He took the Wordsworth from her and opened it, then closed it with a snap. How dear to his heart, indeed.

"Packing." She snatched the book back. "To leave."

Her words weren't a surprise, but they still stung like a clean, sharp knife, sliding silently between his ribs, taking a palpable moment before the pain built toward blackness.

"Leaving *me?*"

"Leaving Trysting." She put the book in the bloody bedamned box, calm as you please. "And you."

"Why Jacaranda?" He kept his hands at his sides, opening and closing his fists. "Why now?"

"Why not now?" Another book, then another. "I've promised my family over and over that I'll return to Dorset, and I've broken my word repeatedly. Now my step-mother is abandoning her post, and I suspect she talked the housekeeper into quitting as well. You abhor dissembling of any kind, surely you can understand that my siblings expect me to keep my word eventually. I've been your housekeeper for five years. That's long enough to polish your silver, air your sheets, and beat your rugs, don't you think?"

Her attempt at a practical tone was a form of dissembling, and he did, absolutely, abhor it. "No, damn it, I do not *think*. You shall not leave me."

"Yes, I shall." Her tone was gentle, painfully so. "I've told you repeatedly I could not remain at my post indefinitely."

"I had hoped you'd take up a different post. As my wife." Though Jacaranda had told him often enough that *she* hoped to return to Dorset. Perhaps she had not only a child in Dorset, but a husband.

She tossed a volume of Sir Walter's *Waverley* into the box like so much old crockery. "I value you...your friendship, Worth, but marriage must have a firmer foundation."

"The hell it must." The temptation to dump out her bloody box was nigh overwhelming. "You can't leave this house without its general."

She stopped filling the box, a minor relief to his nerves. "I beg your pardon?"

"Do you already have your next post lined up?"

She nodded, having the grace to look chagrined.

"Was it something I said?" "It's time, Worth. You are traveling north. Sooner or later, our encounters would have come to the attention of your family, and I miss my siblings."

In all their dealings, she'd never once mentioned a family member by name other than the one brother—Blue or something—and now she *had* to be with family?

How was he to compete with family? He barely knew Yolanda, and yet he was willing to beat a gardener's lights out for her.

Worth had negotiated successfully with angry princes and irate, titled nabobs. He calmly fired his biggest cannon directly at her overactive sense of duty.

"Leave then if you must, but Trysting does not deserve to be abandoned this way." *And neither do I.* "Simmons's knees are acting up, Cook can't plan a menu to save herself, and Reilly will forget to repair Hunter's bridge if you turn tail on us now."

Her posture grew two inches taller. "What do you mean? I manage the maids only, and that other... Those matters are not within my purview."

She was a great believer in honesty, so he'd be honest.

"Right. You don't make a weekly list for Carl, printed large enough for Simmons to read and fuss over? You don't plan the menus, right down to Avery's breakfast porridge? You don't choose the wines to serve with dinner? You don't meet at least daily with Roberts to learn of the doings in the stable? You don't have the maids spying on the footmen, the footmen on the maids, and Reilly relying on you for his every move?"

She sat, a woman whose wind had dropped abruptly from her sails, though this was his Jacaranda, and not even guilt would becalm her for very long.

"I'm sorry. If I've overstepped, I'm sorry."

"You've overstepped," he said, desperation making him merciless. "You've charged past every limit ever put on a housekeeper's authority and made all and sundry dependent on your guidance. You owe me and this household the time I need to find a successor, Jacaranda Wyeth. I'll write you a bad character and run it in the *Times* if you bolt on me now."

"I wouldn't bolt," she said, sounding contrite—as if mere contrition would serve. "I'm preparing for the transition."

"Preparing to bolt." She was leaving him now, now when he had to get to London post-haste. "You ought to be ashamed."

"Oh, I am. I ought to be and I am."

His resolve nearly faltered at the sheer misery in her tone. "I want your promise you'll be here when I return."

Her head came up. "Where are you off to?"

"Bloody London. It's always damned Town and my damned clients, and I want your last damned groat, Jacaranda."

"You want my funds?"

"I want the authority to invest them as I please, your power of attorney, and a signed note of hand for the sum." At least he could prevent her having the coin to take ship or remove herself to the ends of the earth.

"You need it?" She sounded more curious than concerned, but all Worth knew was that she'd stopped packing and she wasn't leaving—yet.

"I need it." A lie, and the God's honest truth. "I'm leaving as soon as Goliath is saddled. Meet me in my room in fifteen minutes."

He left before he could start kissing her silly, or throwing things of value, or tossing more useless proposals at her. She was leaving him, leaving him, and when he ought to have locked the door and pleasured her senseless, he was getting on his damned horse and wearing his arse out over blighted, blasted, bedamned, benighted *business*.

Never again. He'd deal with whatever the mess of the moment was, report to his Regent, and get the hell out of the endless demands that comprised his business. Jones could deal with the opera dancers, Lewis could peddle the lace, the titled clients could go pester some other man to make them wealthy while they sat on their pampered, drunken backsides.

He silently ranted on as he retrieved the power of attorney and promissory note he'd drafted earlier on the strength of earlier discussions with his deserter of a housekeeper. He summoned Carl and Hess to witness the signatures, then ordered them from his sitting room.

"I would have told you," Jacaranda said, eyeing the closed door. "I wouldn't have disappeared like a thief in the night, but I'm worried about my family."

"Like a thief in the day then. Will you at least give us your direction?"

"We can talk about that later," she said, moving toward the door. He beat her there, holding it closed with a hand over her shoulder as she lifted the latch.

They stood like that for a moment, her back to his front, until Worth swept her hair from the side of her neck.

"You're stronger than I, Jacaranda, to turn your back on this." He pressed a kiss to the spot below her ear, the skin so warm and fragrant and tender he had to linger there, breathing her in. "Promise me you'll be here when I return."

She nodded as her breath caught.

"Jacaranda?"

"I'll s-stay."

"Oh, love." He turned her gently and took her into his arms while she pressed a teary cheek to his shoulder. "You won't tell me what these tears are for?"

"For us."

"Is there someone else? A Mr. Wyeth?" A mere husband was an obstacle he could surmount, for divorce was simply a matter of influence, exorbitant sums, and vast patience. The patience might be a challenge.

"No Mr. Wyeth, no one else."

A weight lifted from Worth's heart. "Then why?"

A silence measured the distance between his plea and her answer. "You could not respect me if I betrayed a trust placed in me by someone who loves me."

She'd got her female brain fixed on some emotional star he couldn't begin to sight—something to do with her long-lost, useless brothers, and he couldn't change her mind in the next five minutes. She at least hadn't tried to deny her feelings for him.

To hell with siblings who didn't understand that a woman was entitled to a family of her own—an encouraging thought. "You'll stay until I return?"

He had to hear the words again.

"Only until then."

"I won't have a replacement hired that soon." Pathetic, to suggest the household Jacaranda had run for five years wouldn't be able to soldier on a while without her. Twenty years from now, the footmen would still be quoting her.

"Mary can manage here for a bit. You should go."

"Promise me. I need to hear your promise, love."

"I promise...I promise I won't leave until you return, but Worth? Don't tarry in Town."

"Dear heart, I never have." He kissed her gently and lingeringly, when he wanted to put a wealth of fire and possession into their parting intimacies. If he gave into that impulse, he'd have her on the bed in the next room in about two heartbeats, and haste and desperation would not do.

Not for their first time, not for their last time, and certainly not for their only time.

* * *

"Where's the damned note?"

Worth fired the question at Benjamin, Earl of Hazelton, a sort of neighbor in Town, and a sort of business associate. Maybe even a sort of friend. More to the point, Hazelton kept a dovecote full of homing pigeons connected with all points of the realm. Nothing stopped the birds save truly ugly weather. Hazelton claimed his pigeons could cover up to thirty miles in an hour, which meant word of a ship's passing Land's End could reach Town in a day, rather than a week.

"Here's the damned note." Hazelton tossed a small, folded piece of paper to him. "Hello to you, too."

"Apologies for my attire," Worth said, for he was muddy, rumpled, and the hour was late.

"Read your note. Shall I ring for a tray?"

"Please." Worth read the few words on the page, and felt…nothing. The fate of the Drummond and all the risk connected to it made no difference.

"Bad news?"

"Nothing of any moment." Hazelton could be trusted, but Worth had no reason to burden him with confidences. As far as Worth knew, his lordship held no shares in the Drummond. The source of Hazelton's wealth was mysterious, and Worth had no interest in unraveling the mystery, though Hazelton's pretty countess likely had a hand in matters.

Jacaranda Wyeth had done this to him. Taken a fine solicitor and investment manager and turned him into a walking ghost.

"Kettering?" Hazelton stood not two feet away, holding out a tumbler of whiskey in Worth's direction.

"My thanks." Hazelton had connections that ensured he offered only the finest spirits. Worth suspected a certain marquess among Hazelton's associations, but had never pried. "When did the bird arrive?"

Hazelton poured himself a drink and held the glass under a nose more bold than aristocratic. "Noon. He left Devon yesterday midday."

"You've a slacker in your mews, then." Worth let a swallow of very fine old whiskey slide down his throat.

Hazelton shrugged. "Or there are storms on the coast. Do you want word sent anywhere in particular?"

"No. The truth of the matter will be readily apparent in due course. Where do you find your libation, Hazelton?"

Hazelton smiled faintly and took a delicate sip. "I took that in trade for services. If I tell you from whom, I'll violate a client confidence."

"Bloody clients." Worth threw himself into a well-upholstered chair as a patter of rain spanked the library windows.

"For many years, clients paid my way in this life." Hazelton took the sofa facing a crackling fire, and they drank in silence until a footman appeared with a laden tray.

"Your kitchen dotes on you," Worth said.

"My countess dotes on me, and I on her." Hazelton gestured to the tray. "You look peckish."

Worth ate, swilled more whiskey, and let Hazelton detain him until there was a break in the showers, then walked Goliath home through the remaining drizzle, the weather suiting his mood.

He'd make various arrangements tomorrow at the office, track down his regent, send a messenger to Hess, who would be on tenterhooks until he got word, and then…

Then he'd go home, for Trysting was home now, because of *her*. When he got there, he'd beg if he had to. He'd plead, he'd cry. Well, he wouldn't cry, perhaps, but he would feel like crying.

He already did feel like crying.

And when he dreamed that night, he dreamed the Drummond had sunk, her cargo tossed about on the waves for the scavengers to salvage.

* * *

"What is that damned dog doing in the house?" Grey snapped.

The beast looked anxious, until Will stroked a hand over her head. "You'll hurt George's feelings, and that's not wise when I bring a warning that trouble has come to call."

Grey marched off in the direction of the Dorning family wing, where Trouble was a permanent guest.

"Trouble cannot come to call. Nobody should call, for Mrs. Dankle has gone and done it this time."

Will fell in beside him, the dog trotting at his heels, tail waving merrily. "Dankle killed Francine? I'd say you should double her wages."

"I cannot afford to double her wages again, and I won't be paying her wages in any case. She's taken French leave, decamped for the charms of her drooling grandbabies. I don't think she's coming back either, Will."

"Dankle has to come back. She loves us."

The hound looked worried again—smart dog.

"No, she does not. Between my muddy boots, your hounds, Cam's mischief with the maids, and Ash's mechanical experiments, Dankle would probably prefer Bedlam to another month at Dorning House."

"At least she won't have to put up with Francine," Will said as they reached the double doors opening on the family wing. "That should be good for morale among the domestics."

An itching that had started up between Grey's shoulder blades weeks ago, nagged at him.

"What do you mean, we won't have to put up with Francine?"

Grey stayed where he was, because forewarned was forearmed, and he had every confidence Francine was behind Dankle's defection to the ranks of contented grannies.

For which, he would make his dear step-mama pay.

"Some baron fellow is pacing about the front parlor," Will said, "clearing his throat, and muttering about fetching his bride. I told the footman to bring him the very best brandy we've been able to hide from Cam, because any fellow who's meeting Franny at the altar is a friend of mine."

The dog remained obediently by Will's side, her tail still waving gently as if she shared her owner's sanguine outlook. Behind Will, a mirror with a crack across the bottom hung slightly askew, and a bouquet of roses had long since needed replacing.

"This is not good, Will. Without Dankle, Francine might have at least tried to hold the staff together until I could hire a replacement."

Though the baron was welcome to Francine, for she created a lot of work for the staff.

"This is not bad, either," Will said, streaking a finger through the dust on the mirror. "Francine is unhappy, and an unhappy female is the definition of trouble."

True enough. While an unhappy earl was the definition of one whose damned roses wouldn't cross.

Or something.

"Come with me," Grey said, resuming his progress. "We can ask Francine about this fiancé she neglected to let anybody know she'd attached."

When they reached her ladyship's suite of rooms, they were met by footmen hauling a series of trunks from the room.

"Those are my trunks," Will muttered.

"Think of your friend in the parlor," Grey replied, leading the way into a chaos of gowns, hats, and boxes strewn about the room. "Your ladyship, what's afoot?"

The dog sniffed at a stocking dangling from her ladyship's vanity, then padded over to Will's side, her tail no longer wagging.

"You might knock before entering a lady's chambers," Francine said. "What is that dog doing in my rooms?"

"She's sitting," Grey said, as a maid stacked three hat boxes in a tower and departed with the lot. "While you appear to be going somewhere."

For all Francine was unhappy, as Will had said, Grey was still uneasy to see her boxing up her every slipper and glove.

Particularly without a word of warning to the head of her household.

"I'm leaving for Bath," Francine said, closing the doors to an empty wardrobe. "Baron Hathaway has offered to share his coach with me."

"Will says the baron has offered to share a bit more than that with you," Grey observed, "and when were you planning to tell me yesterday was Dankle's last day?"

Francine turned, the wardrobe at her back. "When were you planning to get that sister of yours to come home, so my existence here was not an endless round of feuding housemaids, lazy footmen, and ridiculous economies?"

Francine truly was leaving, else she would not have been as obvious about her motivations. If her departure to Bath were merely temporary, then she'd resume fretting over Jacaranda's good name, or natter on about missing dear Jacaranda, or coo over family needing to be together.

"Do you hate Jacaranda?" Will asked, his tone for once sharp.

"No, I do not," Francine said, snatching up the dangling stocking and rolling it into a tight ball. "I'm in truth fond of the girl and have only her best interests in mind, but you lot seem content to turn Dorning House into the largest gentleman's club in England. Jacaranda can manage you, and she'll likely even be able to find wives for you. I wash my hands of you all. *She* is not plagued by delicate nerves—not yet."

Francine pitched the stocking into an open hat box with an accuracy many a cricket team would envy, and while she tried to hide it, Grey detected a gleam of triumph in her eyes.

"Francine, you may elope with your baron, and I will wish you all the very best. I hope for Daisy's sake and the sake of your grandchildren, we continue to remain cordial. Whatever you've done, whatever scheme you've concocted, you had best tell us now, or we'll inform the baron you've changed your mind."

The dog rose from her haunches, her alert gaze swinging from Grey to Francine.

"Hathaway will not believe you," Francine said. "As for my schemes, I've planned a little house party to keep you gentlemen entertained, a few dozen of Society's finest heiresses and prettiest debutantes selected from the best families. The list is in my escritoire, and while I'd really rather stay and allow you to bid me a proper thanks, I must instead make my farewell."

She swept out, the last of the maids following with another tower of hat boxes.

With a sense of foreboding, Grey approached the escritoire and opened the top drawer. On a piece of vellum—no foolscap for Francine—in the tidy hand that was likely recognized all over the realm, a list of names marched down one page and onto the next.

"How bad is it?" Will asked.

Grey took the delicate Louis Quinze chair before his knees could buckle.

"I wouldn't say it's bad, exactly," he replied, reading down the third page. "I'd say if we don't retrieve Jack immediately, we're facing a bloody damned disaster."

George strolled over to the vanity, sniffed the skirt, squatted, and peed on the carpet.

\* \* \*

Worth wasted another blighted rainy day chasing down Prinny and whispering the appropriate warnings into the royal ear. With His Royal Highness, a confidence might be kept, or passed along to titillate the inner circle at Carlton House. It made little difference now, in any case.

Worth had seen to his paperwork, made the last arrangements, given his stewards and clerks the appropriate stern but appreciative lectures, and once again put his tired arse in Goliath's well-worn saddle.

The shift in his finances would make no real difference. He'd never lived extravagantly, and man didn't arrive to a half million in worth without suffering both gains and losses. The fate of the Drummond should have mattered to him, but it didn't.

"So this is love," he informed his horse, when they'd stopped for a drink at one of the better posting inns between Town and Trysting. Worth swilled his ale while Goliath did his best to drain the water trough.

Mostly though, horse and rider were dawdling. Autumn lurked in the shade, in the mud that made the king's highway slow going, in the yellowing of the undergrowth along the road. In the north, the season would be well advanced.

"Come along, horse. Your fool master must meet his fate, lest the lady bolt before she's taken proper leave of me."

Goliath flicked an ear beginning to grow fuzzy with the approach of colder weather.

Though Worth didn't travel faster than a relaxed trot, still he made Trysting before tea time. He dreaded the news that Jacaranda had fled, dreaded seeing her, dreaded dinner with his family looking on.

Dreaded the rest of his life without Jacaranda to tease and love and grow old with.

As he bathed and changed, it occurred to him that before, when he'd left Grampion as a much younger man, he'd been this bewildered, hurt and confused.

But he'd been angry, too. He'd been gloriously, righteously angry with everyone he loved, and even with the woman he thought he loved. Somewhere inside, he was angry now at Jacaranda, but he recognized that the anger was driven by hurt and a kind of confused shame that she should reject him.

He was wealthy, relative to her, still.

He was an earl's heir.

He was not bad looking, if a bit too largish.

He loved her.

Maybe she didn't want love, he thought as he dragged a brush through his hair. He would have to ask her.

He went to the kitchen, learning that Jacaranda intended to take a tray in her room for dinner. The coward was in the library, cleaning the window next to his desk. The scent of vinegar seemed an appropriate counterpoint to her usual sweet fragrance.

"Mrs. Wyeth, greetings." He did not cross the room, did not wrap his arms around her.

"Mr. Kettering. I trust your journey was productive?" She didn't even turn to face him, but kept moving her rag vigorously over the already sparkling glass.

Where the hell were the maids, and why polish a spotless window?

"My journey was an exercise in wasted time, for the most part. You'll scrub through that glass do you persist much longer."

She stopped, her shoulders slumping.

"And you're taking a tray in your room tonight," Worth went on, "the better to avoid me?"

"Not to avoid you." She stepped down from her stool. "I'm trying to avoid further aggravation for both of us."

"By fleeing. I know all about fleeing, Jacaranda. I run off whenever my feelings are hurt, or my pride, or my dignity, but I could not run off this time. I could only run to you, do you understand?"

"Yes." She folded her rag as if it were pristine linen. "I understand about running, but you must think I'm running from you, when I'm running *to* something I never should have turned my back on. I've finally found the courage to put right some things I put wrong in the past, and you will not lecture or bully me into changing my mind at this late date."

After *five years*, this courage just happened to befall her when Worth offered marriage?

"Nobody can apparently change that block of stone you call your mind," he said, his ire gathering. "Not for love nor money will you consider another's viewpoint might have more merit than your own."

She pitched her rag at his chest but missed. "You haven't the first clue what you ask of me."

"So tell me," he said, his voice lowering as he advanced on her. "We're running out of time, Jacaranda, and I want to know what it is you find so much more compelling than a future with me."

Tears gathered in her eyes, but Worth could not afford to relent. His happiness hung in the balance, and he would have bet his entire remaining fortune that hers did, too.

"For the love of God, Jacaranda, please tell me what keeps us apart. If it's a dragon, I may not slay it, but I'll tame the damned beast until it eats from your hand."

"You'll hate me if I tell you why I must leave. I'd rather skip to the leaving part and have you merely wroth with me. I'm trying to find my courage, Worth. I don't want to leave you, but I fear I left the greater part of it in Dorset."

She believed that convoluted, inverted, inside-out female pronouncement, and yet, Worth also saw hesitation in her eyes, and longing, and—most encouraging of all—love. The dratted, dear woman had somehow determined that she had to leave *for him*.

"Jacaranda, I'm a solicitor. I solve problems for a living. I thrive on difficulties and averting scandal. I'm resourceful, persistent, and creative. I have means, and more important than all of that—" He loved her, though one shouldn't hurl those words at the object of his devotion.

A soft tap, and then the door banged open to reveal an entire crowd of big, dark, windblown young men and a mastiff who might have been a near relation to Goliath.

The tallest of the lot strode into the room, murder in his eyes.

"Whoever you are, get the hell away from my sister *now*."

# CHAPTER SEVENTEEN

"Grey?" Jacaranda's brows rose as the pitch of her voice went up. "Grey Dorning? What are you doing here now?"

Worth turned to face his unwanted guests, and he'd be damned if he'd leave Jacaranda's side. "Are you a housebreaker, Dorning, to intrude on a man in his own library?"

"When that man is bellowing at my sister," Dorning replied, "I will intrude at Carlton House itself. Stand away from my sister."

"Excuse me." Hess came sauntering through the crowd at the door. "Casriel? I wasn't aware you were acquainted with my brother."

"Grampion." Dorning bowed slightly, some of the tension going out of him. "I have no quarrel with you or your brother, but I've come to take Lady Jacaranda home. Her step-mother has created circumstances that make Lady Jacaranda's presence at Dorning House a matter of urgency."

"Step-Mama didn't ask you to come barging in here like Blucher at Waterloo," Jacaranda said. "All I've asked for is the indefinite hospitality of Dorning House when I leave here."

Saints be praised, Jacaranda was not pleased to see this interfering baboon. Better still, she'd been abandoning Worth to go home, not for the pleasure of another fellow's broom closets. Victory loomed within Worth's grasp, until one small word intruded on his budding sense of triumph—

Lady Jacaranda. *Lady* Jacaranda?

Worth's entire reality came to a snorting, rearing halt. His housekeeper was the daughter of an earl, at least, to have her own courtesy title.

He'd fished an earl's daughter out of his pond. Importuned her repeatedly for her favors, invited himself repeatedly *into her bed*—

"Worth, with your permission I will alert the kitchen that we're to have a considerable number of guests," Hess said. "Casriel here can make the introductions."

"I'll talk to Cook," Jacaranda cut in. "With your permission, Mr. Kettering?"

Worth could not read her expression. She was leaving him, but first she was seeing to his kitchen, and she was a lady—a *duplicitous* lady. He disliked that revelation, and yet, of course she was a lady. Her station had been evident in her generalship of his house, in her inherent dignity, her poise.

He nodded, not the master dismissing his housekeeper, but the intimate, allowing the woman he cared for a strategic and dignified retreat.

"I suppose that leaves me to handle the pretty," Hess said. "Grey Dorning, Earl of Casriel, may I make known to you Worth Kettering, my younger brother and heir. As to these other fine gentlemen, I'm sure Casriel will enlighten us."

One by one, Worth was introduced to the forest of young manhood that was Jacaranda's family. Grey Birch Dorning, the earl, followed by Willow—"call me Will"—Ash, Oak, Hawthorne, Valerian and a sapling by the name of Sycamore.

They were handsome devils, the lot of them, and big. They all sported the peculiar hue of lavender eyes that looked so lovely on their sister.

"Do we take it you're staying again at the local inn?" Hess asked as he distributed the brandy Worth poured.

"Again?" Worth asked.

"Casriel and I shared an enjoyable evening at my final stop on the way to your doorstep," Hess said. "We served on a committee together in the Lords, or wasted time in the same meetings."

"We didn't stop to arrange accommodations this time," Casriel said. "Step-Mama has planned a house party and invited half the dowered young ladies of the realm."

"Then she took off for Bath, and the housekeeper quit," young Sycamore said. "So we thundered up from Dorset because now Jack has to come home. It was fun."

He downed his brandy like a much older man. What else might this pack of sylvan giants think was fun?

"You are welcome to stay here tonight," Worth heard himself saying. "The weather is threatening misery, and I can vouch for the readiness of my household to comfortably accommodate you all."

"Jack wouldn't have it any other way," Will said. "I can recall how Dorning House was before she got a flea in her ear."

"Willow." The earl's tone was warning.

Will peered at his empty brandy glass, his expression forlorn. "Jack kept us in line, and she did it without shouting, much. We miss her, and she didn't come home to visit this summer, not even to see the baby. We worried."

Worry was something Worth could understand, albeit grudgingly.

"I think she's been happy here," he said, praying it was so. "I know she's kept the house running like a top. The whole estate, actually."

Casriel ran a hand through thick, dark hair.

"She does that," he said quietly, almost…sheepishly? "I've gone through three stewards since she left. My housekeeper threatened to retire at least a half-dozen times before actually quitting, and that's after I've doubled her wages, twice."

His admission was followed by a silence, then Will lumbered over to the decanter and helped himself to another drink.

"We can't keep maids either, and it's not what you think." Will passed the decanter to the next brother, and it circled the room until coming back to the sideboard, quite empty. "We don't pester them, or not much. Grey won't stand for it, but they don't stay. They run off with the footmen, or the tenants, or they simply run off."

"When Jack was around," the one named Ash said, "they stayed long enough to be friendly."

Grey frowned. "You weren't even at university then."

Ash shrugged. "I was out of short-coats. I'm a Dorning."

They went on like that, raising a slow, fraternal lament for the sister who'd kept them organized and out of trouble until Worth wanted to scream. These fellows needed their sister, and she would go with them and spend her days running their household, stepping and fetching for them, when they should have been stepping and fetching for her. They arranged themselves all over the room, on the chairs, the table, the sofa, the hearth, the floor, the largest band of orphans Worth had ever seen.

And a house party bore down on them, arranged by this fiend of an errant step-mother, toward whom Jacaranda no doubt felt buckets of loyalty and guilt.

"Don't you lot have another sister?" Worth asked. "I know Mrs.—Lady Jacaranda mentioned a sister."

"Daisy." Sycamore rolled his eyes. "She's married to Eric and having babies."

"Shouldn't Jacaranda be married and having babies?" Worth certainly thought so. Married to him, having his babies.

"She isn't the marrying kind," Grey said. "Her heart was broken once long ago, and she hasn't any interest in finding a husband. She told me that herself, though not the particulars. Why else do you think I'd tolerate this housekeeping nonsense from her?"

Worth searched the gaze of each brother, but it wasn't until he got to his own brother that he felt some relief. Though Hess's expression was bland, in his eyes Worth could see his thoughts: *What a driveling lot of pathetic fools, kidnapping their only sensible relation so she can rescue them from—horrors!—a house full of heiresses and debutantes.*

"I will confer with Lady Jacaranda to see which rooms we're putting you in," Worth said, "and then you'll be free to freshen up for dinner. We dine as a family, and you'll be introduced to our sister, Miss Yolanda Kettering, and our niece, Miss Avery, as well as Miss Snyder and Mrs. Hartwick."

He bowed and left the room before anybody could prevent him from conferring with his own housekeeper. Jacaranda *was* his housekeeper, and he'd trade on that for as long as he could.

Which might be for one more day, give or take a few hours.

He found her in her room, where she seemed to be spending increasing amounts of time. Her pretty gentian eyes were haunted, and all the ire Worth had felt toward her receded behind genuine concern.

"You weren't expecting the entire tribe, were you?" he asked, closing the door.

"I haven't seen them since last year. They seem to keep growing."

Worth took a seat beside her on the settee. She was hunched forward, so he could only see her face in profile.

"You must have been in a very great rage to leave so many helpless men behind you." His words were soft, so was his touch as he smoothed back her hair. "They miss you terribly."

"They miss having their every need met without them thinking about it," she said. "They're dear, and I do love them, and Grey especially tries, but Step-Mama knew I'd never leave the boys to deal with a house party. You see that, I hope. I can't allow them to flounder along before half the gossips of Polite Society, bankrupting Grey's coffers, preyed upon by heiresses, wrecking the house—"

"Who broke your heart, Jacaranda?"

She scooted as if to rise. Worth put a hand on her arm.

"You can tell me. I've wondered why you ran away from home, and that was before I knew you were an earl's daughter."

He said it for her, because apparently, she'd never intended to say it to him herself. Some purveyor of confidences, he.

"An impoverished earl." She settled back, and when Worth put an arm around her shoulders, she let him have her weight. "Papa had more kindness than sense, and more amateur botanical inclinations than money. I had a small portion left me by a grandmother, though."

"Go on," Worth said, stealing a whiff of her hair.

"My younger sister, Daisy, was sickly—my half-sister. Of all of us, she's the only one who isn't a giant."

"You're not a giant." Nor was she his housekeeper. The simple sight of those buffoons in the library, and she'd already on some level abandoned her post at Trysting. She'd get them organized for this house party, see that the staff acquitted themselves as if serving foreign royalty, and by then that cottage would have wrapped its ivy tentacles around her heart.

"Daisy's lungs were weak as a child," Jacaranda went on as if Worth hadn't spoken. "For several winters we feared we might lose her. Papa had the solicitors put my portion in Daisy's name, because Step-Mama convinced him no man would want a sickly wife."

Kind, botanical, and none too bright. No wonder Jacaranda felt she had to fend for her menfolk.

"Let me guess," Worth said. "Dear Daisy used her portion to snabble a swain, and she's been in the pink of health ever since, while you've been slaving away here in Surrey for a man who doesn't even bother to learn what his housekeeper looks like."

"You rather know what I look like."

"So now you leave me?"

She turned her face into his shoulder. "I'm not leaving you. Well, I am, a little, maybe. We were only dallying, Worth."

"We weren't *even* dallying."

She fell silent, and again, he wanted to kick something fragile and bellow obscenities, but he knew when to let a negotiating opponent stew, and this little tale was more complicated than Jacaranda had disclosed.

"I did dally, once," she said. "I do mean once. One time."

"Not a memorable occasion?" Whoever he was, Worth wanted to kill him, not for despoiling Jacaranda—she was free to dally where she chose, thank the Deity—but for disappointing her.

She tucked closer, as if to hide. "Eric was so sweet, not loud and ribald like my brothers, but mannerly and soft-spoken. When he kissed me, I felt pretty. He's handsome, Eric is, refined."

The bastard was shrewd, too. "He had the sense to pay you some attention."

If Jacaranda tucked herself any closer, Worth would give in to the temptation to haul her into his lap.

"His attentions befell me when no one was about—I thought he was exercising gentlemanly discretion. My brothers trusted him, because we've known the family forever. They trusted me because no man in his right mind would bother flirting with me."

"In God's name why not? You're gorgeous, brilliant, tireless—"

She kissed his cheek, a scolding, hushing kiss, and Worth had the uncomfortable suspicion his words wounded her.

"I didn't know any better," she said. "I thought Eric was courting me, and I was pleased to think it so."

"You would have married him?"

"At the time, I would have rejoiced to marry him. I was infatuated."

"How old were you?"

"Past twenty. I'd had my Seasons and was facing yet another year as the tallest, plainest, most awkward woman in every ballroom. Marriage to Eric would have spared me that. He hasn't a title, but his father is gentry and prosperous."

Gentry, prosperous, and conniving as hell. "This lovely, discreet gentleman married your sister."

She was a ball of hurting female against his side, and Worth kicked himself for not having the patience to prompt this story from her before. This part of her past mattered to her, so it should have mattered to him.

"I was increasingly willing to permit him liberties. I thought we were anticipating the vows."

*Oh, my love.* "What happened?"

"I let him...have me, and it was awkward and untidy, and he was so pleased with himself over it, I said nothing. He hadn't finished buttoning his falls before he was explaining to me that his father believed a married man should make his own way, so it was Daisy he'd have to marry—she had that nice little settlement, after all—but there was no reason he and I couldn't continue to enjoy each other's company."

"He got your portion, and your sister got him."

"She's welcome to him," Jacaranda said. "I've saved some money working for you, a fair bit for a housekeeper, and if I invest it well, I'll manage. And as for Eric..."

Worth had invested that money for her, lest she forget—a discussion for some other day. "He deserves the French pox, at least, for how he treated you. Do your brothers know?"

"Grey suspects." Jacaranda fell silent for a moment, still leaning on him. He wanted to store the moment up like a happy memory, except it wasn't happy. Not for her, not for him, but it was important. "When he wanted to demand answers and create a fuss, I argued him out of it. He made them have a long engagement, but my oldest nephew was born four months after the wedding."

"Eric is a randy bugger, isn't he?"

"He seems devoted to Daisy." Jacaranda was trying to convince herself, because how could she know this when she dwelled far from her family—unless her sister tortured her by correspondence? "Leaving was far easier than staying and watching them raise their children, but now it has been five years, and I still haven't put things right with my only sister."

"One can understand that a reckoning would be important to you. If it makes any difference, I am sorry." Particularly when wounded pride had also sent one fleeing his own home more than a decade ago.

"Sorry? For?"

"For what you went through. I'm not sure I would have importuned you if I'd known."

"You knew I was used goods; you did not know that I was also a lying baggage of used goods. I'm sorry for that. I could not find the right time to explain my situation to you, and I knew I was bound to return to Dorset soon anyway."

She still hadn't entirely explained her situation to him, though Worth had acquired a fine grasp of the havoc unfinished business between siblings could wreak.

"Hush, Jacaranda Dorning. You are not used goods any more than I am. We're adults, we've taken some knocks. Are you sure you don't want to remain here, though? You don't have to marry me. You don't even have to see me. I'll go north, I'll stay in Town, I'll buy a few more properties and keep myself from your sight."

What was he offering? Lies, certainly. He might try to stay away, but some pressing contrivance would see him on Trysting's doorstep within a month. He'd ride William the Pig if it meant he could share a roof with Jacaranda.

"You don't like it in Town," she said, smoothing her palm down his lapel.

"I realize that now, but I don't want you keeping house for that lot of handsome louts when they couldn't even see your heart was broken." Though he did want her to put things to rights with her sister. That was important, when one had only a single sister.

She looked away, and Worth felt his frustration with her rising again. What had he said? What had he missed? He understood that this house party nonsense required her presence in Dorset for a time, but why was it so important for her to *stay away* from him?

"Would you do me a very great favor, Mr. Kettering?"

"Anything, Mrs. Wyeth."

"Hold me."

And while she cried as if her heart were breaking all over again, he held her and knew for a certainty his was breaking, too.

* * *

"I've been meaning to tell you something." Hess settled in beside Worth on the library sofa.

"We have brandy left?" Worth marveled as Hess passed him a drink.

"Your cellar has been kept in good stock, probably thanks to old Simmons."

"Thanks to my housekeeper, who thinks she's abandoning me." Hess was turning him into a sot, that was the trouble.

"That is what I wanted to bring up. I haven't known exactly how."

Worth took a sip of good brandy, the everyday having fallen victim to the Dorset tribe of Visigoths.

"There's nothing to bring up. We got through dinner with the plague of locusts, now we'll go to bed. When I wake in the morning, the only woman I've loved will ride out of my life, because assigning beds at some house party is more important than being in my bed. End of fairy tale." He would muster the determination to fetch her back, of course—Ketterings were determined—but what if she didn't want to be fetched?

"Mrs. Wyeth is the only woman you've loved?"

The way Hess posed the question, so delicately, alerted Worth to the focus of the discussion.

"You loved another," Hess said. "Years ago, and yet I married her."

"Must we?"

"I was never quite sure why you hared off." Hess's voice was meditative. "Did she say something to you?"

"No words were necessary. She and I had arranged to meet in the stables, and I saw the two of you there. Your attentions to her were not those of a future brother-in-law."

"The stables."

"In the saddle room, embracing rather enthusiastically." Consuming each other, or so it had appeared at the time. "This is excellent brandy. My compliments to the host."

"Ah."

"What does that mean? 'Ah'? Maybe earls understand such profundities. I can't fathom them. Perhaps if you refresh my drink my comprehension will improve."

"Have you ever wondered why, of all the young ladies in the shire, I chose to single out your intended?"

Worth slugged back the rest of his drink. "We're brothers, we were occasionally rivals. She was pretty."

"She was neither the prettiest girl in the shire nor the wealthiest."

She'd apparently been the most determined—and lo, she'd ended up a Kettering. "She was wealthy enough. Pretty enough." Except sitting there with good brandy sloshing in his brain, Worth couldn't exactly recall the lady's looks. Blond, he was fairly certain of that.

Only that. He couldn't say what color her eyes had been or what the texture of her hair had been.

"I've suspected for some time that we were played for fools, Worth." Hess rose and brought the decanter to the low table before the sofa. The flames from the hearth gave the brandy a depth of color, like a magic potion.

"No more for me. Tomorrow will be difficult enough without a bad head."

Hess sat on the table—did earls sit on tables?—and poured himself another finger.

"You did not see me kissing Elise." Hess set the decanter aside. "You saw her kissing me."

"A distinction without a difference, as we solicitors say." He saluted with his now empty glass.

"Not so. She came to me, claiming your ardor was cooling, so prettily distressed, so young, and so uncertain. I told myself I was comforting her when she threw herself into my arms. She began to throw herself into my embrace frequently."

"You were young and lusty." Worth eyed the decanter with desperate longing. "We really do not need to revisit this."

"I was young, lusty and stupid, and so were you." Hess put his drink down. "She began to kiss me, all the while apologizing for forgetting herself. I was so very like her dear Worth, you know? And what was I supposed to do, peel her off of me and scold her soundly? I did, several times, but by then you'd drawn your own conclusions."

"Why not scold her again and send her on her way?" Worth asked, though the question was moot when Jacaranda was leaving with her fraternal forest in the morning. "Why did you have to marry her, Hessian?"

"She said you'd had carnal knowledge of her and begged me to grant her the clemency of marriage."

Silence, while Worth considered his empty glass and his empty life.

"Were life a stage play, her falsehood would have been hilariously clever," he said. "I might have once run a glancing hand over her corseted and clothed breast, Hess. Nothing more. I swear it."

"I concluded that even before the wedding night confirmed it."

"God's holy underlinen." Worth set his glass down rather than smash it and earn a scold from his departing housekeeper. "She simply wanted the title and saw a way to get it."

"I took several years to come to the same conclusion, and when she was ill, she apologized for as much."

"And you were married to her. I'm sorry, Hess. It never occurred to me you were the injured party."

"We were both injured parties."

Earls did not sit on tables, but brothers did. Brothers also put the past behind them. Entirely behind them.

"Elise wrote to me," Worth said. "I carefully opened the letter, read her plea to rescue her from your cold and indifferent company, sealed it back up with equal care, and returned it to her, to all appearances unopened."

"At least you got that much right."

"I know you never be cold and indifferent to your countess."

"I came to be." Hess ran his finger around the lip of his glass in a slow, perpetual circle. "She tolerated my advances with all the warmth of a martyr at the stake, and each time I wondered if she was thinking instead of you."

"I stopped thinking of her within a few months."

Another silence, equally considering, not as pained.

"Will you come north with us, Worth?"

"You want me underfoot when I was the reason you ended up leg-shackled to a brainless, grasping twit?" Who hadn't even presented Hess with a needed heir?

"I should have taken the brainless, grasping twit by the hand, dragged her to you, and accused her to her face of scheming behind your back, but I was young, full of my own consequence, and eager to impress Papa. Then you wouldn't have spent half your life as a stranger to the only home you've known. Of course, then Papa would not have got his hands on her settlement, which was likely why he was so happy to bless the union."

Worth considered that and admitted Hess had put his finger on a truth, and a relieving truth at that: They were *both* injured parties. Worth didn't have to be careful around his brother anymore, didn't have to suspect Hess's motives, didn't have to tiptoe around their past for the sake of the girls.

If Jacaranda remained at Trysting, she'd never reach this sort of understanding with her sister, much less with the tribe of louts who could not be bothered to keep mud out of their own home. The awkwardness would grow, until the rift affected the next generation, and even the next after that.

He could not reconcile with her family for her, and he did not want her to choose him simply because he preserved her from dealing with old hurts.

"I'll go north with you," Worth said. "I'm not saying I'll stay all winter, but I'll get you home, show Avery the family seat and do the pretty."

Hess shifted to sit beside his brother again. "Grampion is beautiful in winter."

"I remember. Truly beautiful."

And Grampion truly had been his home, once upon a time.

* * *

Jacaranda loved Worth Reverence Kettering. She'd been infatuated with Eric, though at the time she'd had no means of comparing an abiding tenderness for a man with the combustible combination of ignorance, insecurity, rebellion and loneliness that had propelled her into Eric's skinny arms.

She'd go home to Dorning House, to the rough and tumble of life with her brothers and the beauty of the Dorset coast. She had messes to tidy up there, and she had missed her home.

Though not for a moment had she ever missed it as much as she already missed Worth Kettering. That mess might well not admit of any tidying.

The house was silent and dark around her, and if she'd been able to sleep, she would have passed the night in dreams. She hadn't been able to sleep. Worth was one floor below her, and they wouldn't share a roof ever again.

She rose, belted a night robe around her waist, and left her rooms.

He was abed when she let herself into his suite, the click of the door latch sounding loudly behind her.

"You might as well lock it."

Worth's voice came from across his sitting room, and Jacaranda could just make out his shape in a rocker by the cold grate.

She locked the door and waited, feet growing cold in more ways than one.

He held out a hand. "I was about to go to you. You couldn't sleep either?"

She crossed the room, feeling awkward and desolate. No room for her in the rocker, giantess that she was.

He tugged her onto his lap and wrapped his arms around her.

"If you have come merely to talk, Jacaranda, I'll try to listen." His lips grazed her temple. "I'm somewhat the worse for drink, though, and I've spent a lot of nights behaving with you. I'm not sure I have another increment of saintliness in me, not when I know you're leaving me tomorrow."

His arms tightened around her, but she was holding him, too. Beneath her, he was becoming aroused, and what a relief that was. She curled in his lap, battling a longing for him that had simmered inside her since she'd leaned against him weeks ago in the kitchen, wet, angry and bruised.

"No saintliness," she said, stroking his hair. "Not for you, not for me. We deserve this night for ourselves."

He pressed his face to her throat, and Jacaranda wasn't sure, but she thought his shoulders hitched, almost as if he'd been weeping.

"Take me to bed, Worth, please."

He rose with her in his arms, as if she weighed nothing, and crossed to his bedroom. "You're sure, Jacaranda?"

"Of this much, yes." If he'd followed his question with another proposal, her answer would have been very different from her previous replies. A lifetime managing messes and counting somebody else's silver had abruptly lost its appeal.

Worth laid her on the bed and peeled off his dressing gown and pajama pants with gratifying haste. He sat at her hip, untying the bows of her chemise, one by one as they marched down the center of her body. Gently, he spread the sides of her clothing, leaving her exposed in the moonlight.

"Gorgeous," he said, "breathtaking, wonderful, lovely, sweet, adorable, beautiful, luscious." He leaned down and pressed his cheek over her heart. "We should talk, of course. You doubtless want to talk, until I'm nearly agreeing that you should go. I'd rather not be put through that, if you don't mind, though I understand that you must return to Dorset."

"No talk then." For he wasn't entirely wrong.

"I don't think I can go slowly, Jacaranda. Not the first time. I've wanted you too badly for too long."

"Not slow, then. Not for either of us." She held out her arms, and then he was over her, settling the magnificent length of his body snug up against her, the velvety heat of his arousal probing at her sex.

"You'll tell me if you're uncomfortable?"

Jacaranda wrapped her legs around him. "I'm uncomfortable now. Uncomfortable with wanting you, needing you. Stop fretting and dithering, Worth, and love me."

He laughed, a strained gesture toward humor, but he also got a hand under her backside and shifted the angle of her hips. Then he was there, right there at the entrance to her body, big, hot, and blunt, exactly what she craved, almost where she craved him.

She wiggled, she strained, she smacked his muscular backside, but he wouldn't move.

"Kiss me, Jacaranda." He kissed her on the cheek, the forehead, the jaw, and slowly she surrendered her will to his. Her body softened, she let herself kiss him back for long, quiet moments.

"Better," he murmured against her mouth. He ran his nose along her jaw and cradled the back of her head against his palm. Jacaranda had just formed the thought, *How much longer?* When his cock nudged gently at her sex.

"Worth, please…"

"Hold me." He tucked her leg up higher around his flank, then began to move his hips in the smallest increments of forward and retreat. He teased at her until she was mindless with yearning, her ankles locked low on his back, all but dragging him into her body.

"Such a managing little thing you are," he said.

"Now, Worth, please, God, now."

"Soon," he said, his voice a whisper rasped in her ear.

"But I need…"

He'd shifted over her, the first thick inch of him penetrating her heat, then withdrawing to penetrate again. She couldn't help it, didn't know how or why she'd want to stop herself, when her body clamped hard around him in sheer, blinding ecstasy.

"That's it," he whispered, surging into her deeply. "Let go for me."

And holy angels, did she let go. She let go of reason, dignity, past and future, her body and soul flying to pieces in the pleasure he gave her. She moaned against his throat, the delight shuddering through her and rebounding to leave her shaking and keening in his arms.

"Worth Reverence Kettering, hold me."

He was hilted inside her, unmoving, while he petted her hair and nibbled at her ear. Jacaranda's breathing slowed, and her world gradually righted itself.

"I like how you feel inside me."

"You are my every feeble imagining of earthly bliss made manifest ten times over," he said. "I knew you would be."

"And yet we've wasted our summer." She stroked his shoulders. Such broad shoulders, and they held up worlds of responsibility. She knew that now. "I will miss you, Worth."

"I'm here now." He shifted slightly, setting of shocks of pleasure inside her. "I'm loving you, exactly where I want to be. You can abandon me for the charms of Dorset, Jacaranda Wyeth, but this is not finished and you will not forget me."

He moved inside her again, raising himself up on his arms. He met her gaze in the shadowy darkness, and Jacaranda had to close her eyes. He was watching her as he moved in her, watching her again lose herself to him, to the pleasure he deluged her with. Worth as a lover was as relentless as Worth in every other facet of his life. Twice more he sent her over the edge, each climb shorter and steeper than the last.

When he finally followed her into pleasure, Jacaranda held him to her with every fiber of her strength. He was silent with his satisfaction. Silent for endless moments while passion racked the length and depth of him. When he subsided against her, Jacaranda was in tears beneath him.

"Did I hurt you?"

"Never." And he'd been right about something else: This was not finished.

His thumb brushed her cheek, and Jacaranda was reminded of how they'd met, in the dark, her head ringing, her sense of balance unreliable. She felt as battered now, except her heart was the organ in jeopardy.

When she woke up, it wasn't light yet, but the birdsong coming through the window suggested dawn approached.

"You aren't returning to your own room yet," Worth rumbled beneath her.

"Let me off of you," she said, trying to hoist a stiff leg across his body.

"I liked you where you were," Worth groused. But he let her shift to a place beside him, then spooned himself around her. "I liked it a lot."

"I liked it, too," Jacaranda said, an odd joy welling up from among all her sorrows. "I must thank you for this night, Worth."

"And I you. Will you write?"

"I don't think that's wise, do you?"

"I know you and Daisy must resolve what's between you, and then there's this Dorsetshire Bacchanal that your step-mother schemed to drop in your lap.

I still have your money, though, and I intend to get it back to you."

He'd keep hold of her heart, though. "You're good for the money." She kissed the hairy male forearm banding her collarbones. "When will you go north?"

"By Michaelmas. I haven't committed to stay the winter, but Avery should see the ancestral pile, and it's…it might be time I spent some time there. Hess and I had an interesting conversation last night."

"He's protective of you," Jacaranda said, treasuring the feel of Worth, big and warm, and dearly familiar cuddled around her.

"Hess and I have wasted years more or less as a result of not being protective of one another. It leaves one sad, but I understand about you needing to go home."

"You couldn't possibly."

"Yes, love, I could. We both left home in a towering pout and took on the management of the world. Well, the world's somewhat taken in hand, the pout has worn off, and family is still family."

"You make it sound so prosaic."

"Prosaic and profound, like what passes between a man and wife in bed. Babies, snoring, cuddling, cold feet. Mundane existence with little doses of heaven mixed in."

"Life." She nuzzled his arm this time.

"You are my glimpse of heaven, Jacaranda," he said, and she knew they were words of parting. "I will spend the rest of my life missing you if you insist on making this remove to tend your family permanent."

"Not yet." She rolled to her back. "Please don't start missing me yet."

He made love to her again, slowly, with a wealth of tenderness, his sorrow at their parting palpable in his every caress and sigh. Jacaranda didn't want their joining to end, yet the twining of the sorrow with the delight became an unbearable combination, until she was weeping in Worth's arms, even as she was consumed one last time by pleasure.

# CHAPTER EIGHTEEN

"So you're simply letting her leave?"

Grey Birch Dorning, Earl of Casriel, tossed the question at Worth as his lordship mounded omelet onto his plate at the sideboard. There probably wasn't an egg in the whole of Surrey that hadn't gone into the morning's meal, and at least three entire loaves of bread were toasted and buttered as well.

Jacaranda had kept the lot of them fed, clothed, housed, and more or less out of trouble since her girlhood.

"You'd best eat," Casriel went on. "Until Jacaranda comes down, the boys will think nothing of taking the food off your plate."

"Grampion was so busy pouring my best spirits down their thirsty little throats last night, I doubt they'll be up and about this early." Worth put a goodly pile of eggs on his plate for show. God knew he wasn't hungry.

"Sycamore—Cam—can out-eat any one of us," Casriel said, setting his plate at the place to Worth's right. "He'll be the tallest, though he's the youngest, and certain older brothers of his will regret some teasing they've done. You're avoiding my question."

"Regarding your sister," Worth said, passing the teapot over. The table boasted three this morning. "It's gunpowder. Hess and I prefer it."

"I didn't put the two together," Casriel said, pouring his tea. "I know Grampion in passing, and I knew Jacaranda's employer was some dithering little cipher in the City, Somebody Kettering. Never made the connection."

"I don't dither." Nor were his offices in the City. Worth pushed over the cream and sugar. The cream was in a milk pitcher today. Better than a quart of it awaiting the Dorset Horde. "Your sister is a lady in every sense. She should not have been allowed to go into service. Had I known her station, I would have returned her to you five years ago."

"I, for one, am glad you didn't," Casriel said around a mouthful of eggs. "I was having a grand time in Town, new to the title, years past university, and she sent me a letter warning me Daisy was being courted and telling me to get myself down to Dorset as head of the family, because Jacaranda was tired of cleaning up after me. She said if she had to spend a life in service, she at least wanted to be paid for it."

Worth poured himself more tea while he still could, wanting to toast the lady in absentia.

And yet, the earl sounded genuinely contrite. "Go on, Casriel. The barbarians will soon sack the sideboard and take the teapots prisoner, unless I'm mistaken."

"Jack saw what I did not. I had no authority as head of our family because I was little more than a boy myself and acting as stupidly as most others in my position. My step-mother has ever enjoyed delicate nerves, and my brothers were terrorizing their tutors, the maids, the local girls. Jacaranda contained them as best she could. While my brothers and I weren't looking, somebody stole a march on us and treated her ill."

"Do you know who the somebody is?"

Casriel set his fork down, just so, on his plate.

"That's a bit delicate. A family as big as ours is a balancing act. If I buy Ash a horse, must I buy one for all five of my other brothers? If Daisy got flute lessons, did I owe Valerian the cello he claimed he'd practice five hours a day as well? You can't always know what the just outcome is, and when you do, sometimes you wish you didn't."

"Not in this case," Worth said. "In this case, you let the man who abused one sister turn around and marry the other." He felt not the least sympathy for an earl whose brothers were decimating Worth's pantries and his stores of civility as they stole Jacaranda for their own. "Oh, and you let Jacaranda's portion be tucked in among the wedding presents."

Casriel's gentian eyes narrowed. "The trust was transferred by my own father, and that's Lady Jacaranda to you."

On Jacaranda, those eyes were beautiful. On Casriel, they were merely odd, to Worth anyway.

"Lady Jacaranda, my housekeeper. I at least gave her a generous wage for her hard work. You let her sister—or, more properly, her step-mother—steal from her."

"Daisy's lungs—"

"Were as hale as yours by the time this Eric weasel came sniffing around your sisters."

Casriel glanced at the door. "Look, Kettering. There I was, a grown boy, one sister begging me to let her go off into service, the other sister bound and determined to get her hands on this squire's son. I could not afford many more Seasons for Jack, and Daisy would spare me the whole Town do if I could get her married. Haven't you ever been young and stupid?"

Well, hell.

Worth had been young and stupid, and last night, he'd been not young but still stupid, because he'd taken no measures to protect Jacaranda from conceiving a child. He was still trying to untangle his motivations for that, and hers for allowing the risk.

"What will you do now?" Worth asked. "Let her molder away on the coast, cleaning up after those bull calves you call brothers?"

"I wish they were bull calves. Then my course would be clear-cut, so to speak."

"Good morning, all." Hess sauntered in, looking well rested and elegant, damn him.

"Hessian." Worth poured himself more tea. "Casriel encourages us aging bumblers to eat before the locusts descend from their bedrooms."

"Jack can put away her fair share, too," Casriel said, slathering jam on his toast.

"Lady Jacaranda to you," Worth retorted, balling up his serviette and rising. "She hates to be called Jack."

\* \* \*

Worth helped Jacaranda dress. His attentiveness broke her heart in a whole different way, but he topped that accomplishment by helping with the last of her packing, too.

Both of those heartbreaks were different from the heartbreak of making love with him.

Different from the pain of waking in his arms.

Different from the anticipation of him coming home from Town.

Different from sharing the single tea cup with him when her morning tray came up.

And it all hurt unbearably.

"Before you go downstairs," Worth said, drawing her down beside him on the settee, "we need to discuss something."

"Not my money." She could not bear to see him looking so solemn. "You may borrow it as long as you want. I'll have a roof over my head at Dorning and coal for the hearth. We manage. I'm not sure how Grey does it, but we do manage."

"Not providing his sisters any dowry probably helps." Worth's scathing tone was at variance with the gentle caress of his thumb over her knuckles.

"He has to see my brothers educated, Worth. Don't judge him."

Worth's smile was crooked and sad. "You love him. I'll keep my judgmental mouth shut on that score. My dear, last night—"

"Last night was lovely."

"Last night was beyond lovely," he countered, "but there could be a child, Jacaranda. I want you to promise me we'll marry if there is."

His words implied they would not marry *unless* a child came along. She had refused his proposals, after all.

"Think of the child, love." He brought her hand to his lips. "Think of the scandal to your family, when your brother ought to be finding himself a countess."

She studied their joined hands. "He ought, oughtn't he? Given the timing, I doubt there will be consequences."

"Is Wyeth any part of your name?"

"Jacaranda Wyeth Dorning. No missus, though. That was a misrepresentation." Another misrepresentation.

"A liberty," he said. "Promise me, Jacaranda Wyeth Dorning. I would not force you into marriage, but it is my right to provide for my child and the child's mother. My privilege."

She kissed his knuckles and nodded.

"Say the words, my love."

Oh, that hurt. Those little words—my love—said with such patience and tenderness while he looked at her as if she were precious.

"I promise, if we've conceived a child, I will tell you and you can make proper provision."

"Thank you, Jacaranda."

"I'm about to cry."

"You cried enough last night," he said, though his tone assured her his words were meant kindly, bracingly. "A pack of hyenas is scavenging every scrap of food from my larder, my housekeeper is leaving me, my brother wants me to winter in Cumberland, for God's sake, and you think you're entitled to cry?"

"Suppose not." She might well have the rest of her life to cry. "Will you see me off?"

"If that is what you want. I've a suggestion," Worth said, drawing her to her feet. "Why don't we send you and Casriel on your way? Your brothers can come after you when they rise."

"They might not be up and about for hours."

"Trust me," Worth said, stepping back and tucking a strand of her hair behind her ear. "They'll be no more than two hours behind you, and Casriel will want to take his time because he's escorting a lady. You'll have your knights at your side by noon."

"Anxious to get rid of me, Worth?" She paused by the door, wanting nothing more than to feel his arms around her one more time.

"Anxious to get the pain of parting behind you, yes."

"I'm glad you're capable of thinking," she said as he led her toward the stairs. "I'm not."

"You're exhausted. I can send you home in my coach if you like."

"No, thank you. The fresh air will do me good." Left to herself in a coach, she'd give way to tears all the way to Dorset. "Grey and I will spend the morning catching up."

By the time Worth had brought her to the breakfast room, Jacaranda's chin was up, her shoulders were back, and she'd resolved to get through the next hour with some dignity. Grey acceded easily to Worth's plan, and Worth excused himself to alert the stables to the arrangements.

When Jacaranda saw Worth next, the tea and toast she'd managed to down were sitting miserably in her stomach, and Grey was making a polite production out of conferring with Hess over by the gardens. She waited by the mounting block as Worth emerged from the stables.

He was so dear. She'd always liked his looks, liked how easy he was with his size and his strength. She liked his humor, his odd touches of modesty and fastidiousness, liked how he was a good brother and a devoted uncle.

He was conscientious with his clients, and with her he'd been so careful, so confoundedly caring it was easy to forget that Jacaranda's brothers needed her.

Then too, Step-Mama—among others—had some significant explaining to do.

"Let's stroll a little, shall we?" Worth appropriated her arm, wrapping his hand over hers. "Hess will keep Casriel busy as long as we need him to. Did you know Roberts and the maid named Muriel were spying for your brother?"

"I suspected. I would feel eyes on me from time to time."

"We've been discreet, Jacaranda. You're not to let that pack of jackanapes run roughshod over you because you think you've been naughty."

"I'm not?" She had been naughty, wonderfully naughty. A skein of happiness trickled through her sorrow. She'd been naughty, and this time, she was not remotely ashamed.

She was glad.

"But for the youngest couple, your brothers are grown men, off to university and back, and you are not their nursemaid."

"Are you lecturing me?"

"I am." He paused in their perambulation. "I want you to be happy, and that lot isn't intent on the same priority. I know, I was a jackanapes once myself, and we're a selfish bunch. Promise me this is what you want."

"I want this," she said, able to mean it in some sense, because five years at

Trysting had only made some problems worse, not better. "You'll make my good-byes to Yolanda and Avery, Miss Snyder and Mrs. Hartwick?"

"No. They've all got their noses pressed to the windows in the nursery wing, I've no doubt of it. Wave and they'll see you."

She waved and caught a flutter of movement from the third-floor windows.

"I'm about to kiss you good-bye, my love."

"I'm about to let you."

He kissed her when she desperately wanted him to talk her out of leaving. Not a naughty kiss either, which made it worse. His kiss was sweet, tender, almost chaste, and all too quickly over.

"Ready?" His gaze was steady and steadying.

"As I shall ever be." She took his arm and processed to the mounting block, feeling as if it might have been the gallows at the Old Bailey.

"We'll be off then," Casriel said. "Thanks for the hospitality, and if the boys give you any trouble, a bullwhip sometimes helps. They know which inns we use, and they'll come along because I'm the only one carrying enough blunt to stand their meals."

"Lady Jacaranda." The Earl of Grampion bowed over her hand. "It has been a pleasure and an inspiration."

She blinked, seeing kindness and understanding in the earl's eyes. Oh, dear…

"Come." Worth turned her by the arm. "Your steed awaits."

"My….Goliath? You're lending me Goliath?"

"He's taken to the country," Worth said. "If you find he doesn't suit, you can send him back with one of your brothers, but you and he are friends, and he's of a size to carry you. Then too, Casriel says that due to yet another unforgivable oversight on your family's part, you have no personal mount, and you deserve one."

"Just for a loan," she said, patting the beast's glossy black neck. "A short-term loan."

"For as long as you need him," Worth said, and he was looking at her with such focus, Jacaranda had to wonder at the significance of this extravagant gesture.

This lovable gesture. The loan of Goliath was generous and kind, easing their parting and leaving them one detail of business to connect them. She threw her arms around Worth, heedless of Grey clearing his throat on his mount. Worth caught her to him in a fierce embrace, then let her go and stepped back, her gloved hand in his.

"Safe journey home, Lady Jacaranda. Lord Casriel, you will send us word when you've seen the lady back to Dorset."

"Of course."

Worth held Goliath's reins while Jacaranda mounted. When her skirts were arranged, he petted the horse's shoulder.

"She's precious, old friend, so don't put a foot wrong." He looked up at Jacaranda, his eyes the same impossible blue as when she'd first met him, but so much more dear to her. "God-speed." He blew her a kiss, and then somehow, the horse was cantering down the driveway, taking her away from the only man she'd ever loved.

The only man she ever would love.

\* \* \*

"I am near tears," Hess said, standing beside Worth.

"Stubble it, Hessian." Worth turned toward the house. "That is my future wife, though before she admits that, she must face again the choice between her happiness and her family's dictates. Last time she confronted that reckoning, she chose neither. This time, I've every confidence she'll see she for herself that she can have both—and a fine husband into the bargain."

Worth was counting on it, maybe the way Hessian had been counting on him to ask for a reconciliation.

Which had taken more than a damned decade to bring about.

"She didn't even give me her direction," Worth added, because he and Hess *were* reconciled. "I am in no mood to be teased."

"She didn't need to give it to you," Hess said, holding up a piece of folded paper. "Casriel generously provided *his* direction to me, while her ladyship sipped tea and made not the least fuss."

Worth coasted to a stop, like a ship gliding home to the dock. "Hessian, I love you. I might not have always said as much, or been much of a brother, but I…what?"

Hess passed him the paper.

"I've done my part," he said. "With or without you, I must leave for Grampion in a few weeks. Now what will you do with that address?"

"Nothing, for now. Jacaranda isn't the only one with some reckoning to do."

Hess said nothing, but walked with him back to the house where six bleary-eyed young men were rousted, dressed, fed and put on their mounts in record time.

\* \* \*

"I wondered when you would come see me," Daisy said, hugging her sister.

"I saw you at dinner last week at Dorning House," Jacaranda replied, though the final dinner of the house party had been more like a mêlée. "I know the children keep you busy, and I didn't want to intrude."

"Come." Daisy took her hand and walked beside her through the tidy manor house. "Her Highness is asleep, and that's the best time to visit her. Before I can get the tea tray ready, she'll be up and fussing."

Daisy led Jacaranda up the stairs to the third floor and quietly pushed open a door left slightly ajar. Still holding her sister's hand, Daisy crossed the room, stopping beside a white bassinette.

"She's beautiful, Daze." The infant had her mother's perfect skin, a thistledown head of white-blond hair, a perfect Cupid's bow mouth, and the tiniest, sweetest little fingers.

"She's beautiful now," Daisy said. "Give it an hour, and she'll be a terror. She puts me in mind of my own mother when Mama's nerves are troubling her."

They drew back from the sleeping infant, though Jacaranda wanted to linger. She already knew she wasn't carrying Worth Kettering's child, and while that was a relief—it truly was—it was also the unkindest cut.

"You're wool-gathering again," Daisy said when they'd repaired to a sunny morning parlor.

"I'm sorry. She's a disconcertingly beautiful child."

"Eric loves the children, which is why I don't leave him."

"I beg your pardon? Daisy Fromm, you aren't thinking of leaving your husband? You've been married but five years."

Was this why Jacaranda had come home? To prevent her sister from abandoning a marriage Jacaranda had resented for years?

"I know what you're thinking." Daisy took one seat and gestured for her sister to take the other. "We have three children, so we must be compatible in the essentials."

"Daisy, your unwed sister is not the one to receive these confidences." Jacaranda took her seat, wondering where her dear little sister had gone, leaving this tired, somewhat resigned-looking young matron in her place.

"Grey pulled me aside at dinner and said you and I are overdue for an honest chat. I thought it might help if you knew Eric and I have already descended into tolerating each other."

*Angels abide.* "Of course it doesn't help. Why would it help? What would it help?"

"Jack…Jacaranda, all those years ago, Eric was about to offer for you. He confided in me when we found ourselves on the garden swing in a shockingly friendly moment, one I am ashamed to say I instigated in part because Mama suggested Eric was trying to choose between us. I told him you weren't inclined to marry. Otherwise, why would you have given me your portion?"

This revelation should have pierced Jacaranda to the quick. Instead, she stifled a curious inclination to *snicker*. "Oh, my poor Daisy."

"I am Eric's poor Daisy." She fiddled with the tea service, an everyday Jasperware sporting a chip on the spout of the cream pitcher. "I don't know how you can stand to look at me."

"You were seventeen," Jacaranda reminded her, "and Eric didn't truly love me or he wouldn't have been swayed by the money." She'd taken five years to admit that, to see that she'd had a narrow escape.

Daisy glanced around at the tidy comfort of their surroundings. "Enough to buy this place and keep up the three tenant farms fairly well."

"You're doing the managing, aren't you?" Unlike Jacaranda, Daisy wasn't comforted by ordering a domestic universe for others.

"Eric isn't a bad man," Daisy said, peering into the teapot. The scent of a delicate gunpowder provoked memories of Trysting. "Eric is simply in want of guidance."

"Do you suppose Francine is providing that exact guidance to her baron?" For Step-Mama's campaign at Bath had borne fruit, and Daisy had a new step-papa, may God help the man.

"She's beggaring him," Daisy said dryly, "or she will soon. Grey says the money he'll save not having to pay Mama's bills will exceed what he would have spent on three house parties. I'm sorry you were plucked from Surrey, but Jacaranda, Mama was driving us all to Bedlam."

"I've written her my best wishes and made a few suggestions for how she might curry favor with the baron's housekeeper. I don't believe she'll take my suggestions to heart."

They shared a sororal smile, then Daisy started giggling and Jacaranda was pouring tea, and five years of distance and hurt were eased aside in an afternoon.

As much as Jacaranda missed Worth, missed him bitterly moment by moment, she took some pleasure in knowing she'd at least put matters right with Daisy, who'd also been manipulated by Francine's marital schemes. Jacaranda had hired Grey a housekeeper who would not tolerate juvenile behavior from grown men, and she'd written what would likely be her last letter to her step-mother for some time.

Dorning House was again the family home, and yet, the longer Jacaranda missed Worth, the more she realized that home *for her* was no longer a dwelling, but rather a certain handsome, ruthless, dear and difficult solicitor.

\* \* \*

"You and Daisy must have found something to talk about," Grey said as Jacaranda rode Goliath into the Dorning stable yard.

"I had to wait for the baby to wake up to properly dote on her." Jacaranda let her brother help her dismount, a courtesy he wouldn't have known to offer five years ago.

"Did Fromm show his face?"

"He did. He's aged." Not matured, aged. Poor Daisy.

"He has responsibilities," Grey said carefully. He waited until a groom led Goliath away to speak further. "You didn't call him out?"

"He offered me no dishonor I didn't invite, Grey." Jacaranda looped her arm through his, sparing herself his searching gaze. "I see him now, and he's not an old man, but he's going soft in the middle, his hair's thinning, and he still has puny arms."

"Puny arms? What has that to do with anything?"

"I doubt he could manage Goliath in a snaffle." She gently guided her brother toward the house. "Eric has no bottom, so to speak, and he's lucky Daisy will have him."

"I see."

"Do you? How much do you know, Grey?"

"More than I want to. Enough to know the topic can be dropped now and forever."

"It can," Jacaranda said, and what a relief that was, not to have to dodge and cringe and tiptoe around the past with either her sister or her oldest and dearest brother. The past was the past, and the future… Jacaranda had decided to return Goliath to his owner in person.

Maybe Worth had known she would?

And yet, Grey looked worried. "Does this mean I can bring up your former employer?"

"If you must."

"Roberts will be returning to Surrey," Grey said as he held the front door to the house for her—another small, dear courtesy he hadn't shown her five years ago. "You could send along a note."

"A lady does not correspond with a single gentleman to whom she is not related, unless to offer condolences or other socially acceptable sentiments."

"Jacaranda, the poor blighter's in love with you," Grey said when they reached the family parlor. "For once in your life, have pity on the male of the species. Write to him."

She was well and truly done having pity on the males of the species.

"What I have to say to Worth Kettering can be said in person, Grey. I've made the mistake once before of thinking my sentiments were returned, and I was egregiously in error. Now I *know* my sentiments are shared with the object of my affections, and I owe the man an honest recitation. His affection for me was not in doubt when I left Trysting, I can only hope he still holds me in high regard."

Vaguely, she heard somebody clearing his throat behind her, but she went on even in front of some embarrassed footman, because Grey needed to let this drop once and for all.

"I have come home, I've seen you through the house party, I've sorted out matters with Daisy. I've put your house to rights, and even dispensed advice to Francine, but it's time I put my own house in order, Grey."

She'd known she loved Worth Kettering when she'd left Surrey. Now she knew that she needed him as well. She didn't need him as a large household needed organization and effort to run smoothly, she needed him as a woman needs to love and be loved.

"Er, Jacaranda?" Grey, who never dithered, was dithering.

"You must simply learn to muddle along without me," she went on, because this was something Grey should understand. "I have my own life to live, my own matters to tend to. I never told Worth Kettering I loved him. I didn't think I deserved to impose my feeling on him, didn't want to risk that he might not—what?"

Grey looked like he'd swallowed bad fish, but he managed to point over Jacaranda's left shoulder. She turned and saw Worth Kettering standing in the family parlor, his expression arrested while the butler beside him wrung his hands.

"Lady Jacaranda has a caller. Mr. Worth Kettering," the butler explained, his ears as red as the fall mums gracing the sideboard.

"*Worth?*" There he was, looking just as handsome and fit as ever, though not particularly happy.

"I'm sure you two have things to chat about." Grey sketched a bow and escaped right behind the retreating butler, leaving Jacaranda ready to melt into a puddle of mortification.

Joyful mortification, if such a thing were possible.

"Have you come for your horse?" she asked, taking two steps into the family parlor.

Worth walked right past her and pulled the door shut with a definitive bang. The next thing she knew, he was kissing her like they'd been parted for years, not mere weeks.

Though weeks could be eternities when a woman was in love.

"So give me the words," he growled. "Don't make me drag them from you, because I haven't come for the damned horse. I've come to retrieve my heart."

"Your h-heart?"

"Say the words, Jacaranda, and then, by God, it's my turn."

"I've missed you," she said, searching his face, for his mood was not that of a man glad to hear a lady's declaration. His mood was like nothing she'd observed in him before.

He dropped his hands from her arms. "I've brought you a bank draft."

"Thank you." Because he could have resorted to the mails or to a messenger. He hadn't, and Jacaranda's heart rejoiced simply to see him.

"Don't you want to know the amount of the draft?"

"You don't owe me interest, Worth, not for a few weeks' loan of such a paltry amount."

Still his expression gave away nothing.

"I wanted you to have your cottage, Lady Jacaranda. I can go home again to Grampion in part because of you, and I wanted you to be able to buy your cottage, though that's not all I want." He passed her an official-looking paper. Jacaranda couldn't spare it a glance.

"You mean Complaisance Cottage?"

"If it's ever for sale, you can afford it now."

She glanced at the document and saw a sum many times what she'd lent him. "Worth, there's a mistake. I know you are a conscientious solicitor, but this—"

"Thank the captain of the Drummond. My ship came in, so to speak."

"Yolanda told me about the Drummond. She was very worried for you." Jacaranda had worried for him, too, but not about his finances. Never that. "What did you do?"

"May we sit?"

Sitting meant he wasn't leaving, and Jacaranda would get her turn to speak. "Of course. Shall I ring for tea?"

"Hang the damned tea."

Hang the damned tea?

"Don't look at me like I've sprouted horns, a tail and cloven feet." He patted the place beside him. "Sit where my nose at least can plunder your charms."

That sounded more promising, more like her Mr. Kettering. "Worth, you aren't making sense."

"No, I suppose I'm not." He didn't say another word until she'd dutifully taken her place exactly where she wanted to be, right against his side. "Better," he said. "I invested your funds in shares in a ship thought lost at sea. The shares were available for a pittance, the cargo was very valuable, and here you are."

Here you are, a small fortune, simple as that. "But why?"

"Because when you take your morning tea at your cottage, tossing the crumbs to the sea birds, I wanted you to think of me and the pleasures we shared. I wanted to make you happy, though you've said things that lead me to hope I might see this cottage."

A pure, piercing joy curled up from Jacaranda's middle. She'd been determined to fight to regain his esteem, but Worth was so generous, so kind, and his actions spoke so very, wonderfully loudly.

"The cottage is leased. Grey has to lease it out when he can, but I'd love to show it to you."

Worth pushed her hair behind her ear. "Buy out the rest of the leasehold. You can afford it easily, my dear. Put a new steeple on the local church if it suits your whim. You're modestly wealthy, Jacaranda, and you can do as you please."

"I have a much better sense now of what will please me."

"About time you had a care for your own happiness," he said, glaring at her. "Which brings me to the next negotiating point."

"You look very stern, Worth, but I am grateful for the money."

"I care that"—he snapped his fingers before her nose—"for the money. You had ten shares, Jacaranda. I had two hundred, Prinny had two hundred, my brother had fifty, and the other forty were owned by other small investors."

"Two hundred?"

"I did not think it wise to earn more than my sovereign."

"Angels abide." Two hundred? She gave up trying to do the math.

"You are stalling, Lady Jacaranda." Worth still looked ferociously stern. "I overheard your charming diatribe to your brother and must disabuse you of an odd misperception."

She did not say a word lest the hope beating in her chest find some foolish admission with which to mortify her.

"In some matters, a lady is not allowed to go first. *I love you.* Does that put your house in order? I want you for my wife and for my lady—I'm to suffer a damned barony for this summer's folly. A knighthood simply won't do when Prinny's in a magnanimous mood. I want to wake up beside you every morning until I'm so old, I know you're there only because your fragrance assures me it's so. If I'd known you were willing, I would have brought a special license with me, for God's sake. I love you, I will always love you. Is that clear enough?"

"You're quite sure?" How she would love teasing him, and managing his households, and his babies, and his—

"I said…" He was winding up for a shouting match, and then he fell silent. He slid to his knee, and not in any romantically debonair posture. He laid his cheek against her thigh and circled her waist with his arms.

"I love you," he said, quietly but clearly. "I did not feel it fair to inflict my sentiments on you when all you wanted was a frolic or some comfort when far from home. Then, I did not feel it fair to inflict my sentiments on you when your family needed you so. After that, I did not think it fair to make you choose between my importuning and setting things to rights with your siblings. I finally get up my courage to come here and pluck you from your fairy cottage, and I find you telling your damned idiot brother—"

She stroked her fingers over his hair.

"You didn't let me have my turn, Worth. I'm slow at this business of setting things to rights. I must have a turn, too."

"I'm a solicitor. We're long-winded, and I'm not finished." He subsided against her knees. "I love you, you make my house a home, you brought my family together. I have my brother back, a sister…" He fell silent again, holding her as if his every dream and wish hung on her next utterance, though he had to know how she felt.

Jacaranda took a moment to let wonder and joy flood through her while she tried to organize words that would equal the ones he'd given her. She slid to her knees, too, holding on to him as if he was her every happy memory, including those yet unborn.

"I love you, Worth Reverence Kettering. I love the physical strength and competence of you, the way you sit that great black beast as if you were born on his back—and he misses you, too, by the way. I love your mind, it's as quick and brilliant as lightning, and I love your kindness to the opera dancers, and to me, and your family, and I love your generosity, for I know of no other who would share a fortune with both the Regent and the small investors, I love your body—"

He smothered the rest of her litany with his kisses, and right there on the floor behind the locked door to the Dorning family parlor, Lord and Lady Trysting conceived the first of their many lovely daughters.

They turned out to be great strapping beauties, with their father's head for money and their mother's ability to manage anything—and anybody—they took a fancy to.

And they all, all of them, with their cousins and uncles and eventually with some brave aunties as well, lived happily ever after.

THE END

Continue reading for an excerpt from *The Captive*, by Grace Burrowes (July 2014), first book in The Captive Hearts trilogy

"Your Grace, you have a caller."

Christian had been at his London town house for three days and nights, and still his entire household, from butler to boot boy, seemed helpless not to beam at him.

He'd been *tortured*, repeatedly, for months, and they were grinning like dolts. To see them happy, to feel the weight of the entire household smiling at him around every turn made him furious, and that—his unabating, irrational reaction—made him anxious.

Even Carlton House had sent an invitation, and Christian's court attire would hang on him like some ridiculous shroud.

The butler cleared his throat.

Right. A caller. "This late?"

"She says her business is urgent."

By the standards of London in springtime, nine in the evening was one of the more pleasant hours, but by no means did one receive calls at such an hour.

"Who is she?"

Meems crossed the study, a silver tray in his hand bearing a single card on cream vellum.

"I do not recall a Lady Greendale." Though a Greendale estate lay several hours ride from Severn. Lord Greendale was a pompous old curmudgeon forever going on in the Lords about proper respect and decent society. An embossed black band crossed one corner of the card, indicating the woman was a widow, perhaps still in mourning.

"I'm seeing no callers, Meems. You know that."

"Yes, quite, Your Grace, as you're recovering. Quite. She says she's family." Behind the smile Meems barely contained lurked a worse offense yet: hope. The old fellow *hoped* His Grace might admit somebody past the threshold of Mercia House besides a man of business or running footman.

Christian ran his fingertip over the crisp edge of the card. Gillian, Countess of Greendale, begged the favor of a call. Some elderly cousin of his departed parents, perhaps. His memory was not to be relied upon in any case.

Duty came in strange doses. Like the need to sign dozens of papers simply so the coin earned by the duchy could be used to pay the expenses incurred by the duchy. Learning to sign his name with his right hand had been a frustrating exercise in duty. Christian had limited himself to balling up papers and tossing them into the grate rather than pitching the ink pot.

"Show her into the family parlor."

"There will be no need for that." A small blond woman brushed past Meems and marched up to Christian's desk. "Good evening, Your Grace. Gillian, Lady Greendale."

She bobbed a miniscule curtsy suggesting a miniscule grasp of the deference due his rank, much less of Meems's responsibility for announcing guests. "We have family business to discuss."

No, Christian silently amended, she had *no* grasp whatsoever, and based on her widow's weeds, no husband to correct the lack.

And yet, this lady was in mourning, and around her mouth were brackets of fatigue. She was not in any sense smiling, and looked as if she might have forgotten how.

A welcome divergence from the servants' expressions.

"Meems, a tray, and please close the door as you leave."

Christian rose from his desk, intent on shifting to stand near the fire, but the lady twitched a jacket from her shoulders and handed it to him. Her garment was a gorgeous black silk business, embroidered with aubergine thread along its hems. The feel of the material was sumptuous in Christian's hands, soft, sleek, luxurious, and warm from her body heat. He wanted to hold it—simply to hold it—and to bring it to his nose, for it bore the soft floral scent of not a woman, but a *lady*.

The reminders he suffered of his recent deprivations increased rather than decreased with time.

"Now, then," she said, sweeping the room with her gaze.

He was curious enough at her presumption that he folded her jacket, draped it over a chair, and let a silence build for several slow ticks of the mantel clock.

"Now, then," he said, more quietly than she, "if you'd care to have a seat, Lady Greendale?"

She had to be a May-December confection gobbled up in Lord Greendale's dotage. The woman wasn't thirty years old, and she had a curvy little figure that caught a man's eye. Or it would catch a man's eye, had he not been more preoccupied with how he'd deal with tea-tray inanities when he couldn't stomach tea.

She took a seat on the sofa facing the fire, which was fortunate, because it allowed Christian his desired proximity to the heat. He propped an elbow on the mantel and wished, once again, that he'd tarried at Severn.

"My lady, you have me at a loss. You claim a family connection, and yet memory doesn't reveal it to me."

"That's certainly to the point." By the firelight, her hair looked like antique gold, not merely blond. Her tidy bun held coppery highlights, and her eyebrows looked even more reddish. Still, her appearance did not tickle a memory, and he preferred willowy blonds in any case.

Had preferred them.

"I thought we'd chitchat until the help is done eavesdropping, Your Grace. Perhaps exchange condolences. You have mine, by the way. Very sincerely."

Her piquant features softened with her words, her sympathy clear in her blue eyes, though it took Christian a moment to puzzle out for what.

Ah. The loss of his wife and son. That.

She pattered on, like shallow water rippling over smooth stones, sparing him the need to make any reply. Christian eventually figured out that this torrent of speech was a sign of nerves.

Had Girard blathered like this, philosophizing, sermonizing, and threatening as a function of nerves? Christian rejected the very notion rather than attribute to his tormenter even a single human quality.

"Helene was my cousin," the lady said, recapturing Christian's attention, because nobody had referred to the late duchess by name in his presence. "The family was planning to offer you me, but then Greendale started sniffing around me, and Helene was by far the prettier, so she went for a duchess while I am merely a countess. Shouldn't the tea be here by now?"

Now he did remember, the way the first few lines of a poem will reveal the entire stanza. He'd met this Lady Greendale. She had a prosaic, solidly English name he could not recall—perhaps she'd just told him what it was, perhaps he'd seen it somewhere—but she'd been an attendant at his wedding, his and Helene's. Greendale's gaze had followed his young wife with a kind of porcine possessiveness, and the wife had scurried about like a whipped dog.

Christian had pitied her at the time. He didn't pity her now.

But then, he didn't feel much of anything when his day was going well.

"Here's the thing—" She was mercifully interrupted by the arrival of the tea tray. Except it wasn't simply a tray, as Christian had ordered. The trolley bore a silver tea service, a plate of cakes, a plate of finger sandwiches, and a bowl of oranges, because his smiling, hopeful, attentive staff was determined to put flesh on him.

His digestion was determined to make it a slow process.

"Shall I pour?" She had her gloves off and was rearranging the tray before Christian could respond. "One wonders what ladies do in countries not obsessed with their tea. Do they make such a ritual out of coffee? You take yours plain, I believe. Helene told me that."

What odd conversations women must have, comparing how their husbands took tea. "I no longer drink tea. I drink...nursery tea."

A man whose every bodily function had been observed for months should not be embarrassed to admit such a thing, and Christian wasn't. He was, rather, humiliated and enraged out of all proportion to the moment.

"Hence the hot water," she said, peering at the silver pot that held same. "Do you intend to loom over me up there, or will you come down here beside me for some tea?"

He did not want to move a single inch.

She chattered, and her hands fluttered over the tea service like mating songbirds, making visual noise to go with her blathering. She cut up his peace, such as it was, and he already knew she would put demands on him he didn't care to meet.

And yet, she hadn't smiled, hadn't pretended grown dukes drank nursery tea every night. Whatever else was true about the lady, she had an honesty about her Christian approved of.

He sat on the sofa, several feet away from her.

She made no remark on his choice of seat.

"I suppose you've heard about that dreadful business involving Greendale. Had Mr. Stoneleigh not thought to produce the bottle of belladonna drops for the magistrate—the full, unopened bottle, still in its seal—you might have been spared my presence permanently. I can't help but think old Greendale did it apurpose, gave me the drops just to put poison in my hands. Easterbrook probably sent them from the Continent all unsuspecting. Greendale wanted me buried with him, like some old pharaoh's wife. Your tea."

She'd made him a cup of hot water, sugar, and cream—nursery tea, served to small children to spare them tea's stimulant effects.

"I'll fix you a plate too, shall I?" A sandwich, then two, as well as two cakes were piled onto a plate by her busy, noisy hands.

"An orange will do."

She looked at the full plate as if surprised to find all that food there, shrugged, and set it aside. "I'll peel it for you, then. A lady has fingernails suited for the purpose."

She set about stripping the peel from the hapless orange as effectively as she was stripping Christian's nerves, though in truth, she wasn't gawking, she wasn't simpering, she wasn't smiling. The lady had business to transact, and she'd dispatch it as efficiently as she dispatched the peel from the orange.

Those busy hands were graceful. Christian wanted to watch them work, wanted to watch them be feminine, competent, and pretty, because this too— the simple pleasure of a lady's hands—had been denied him.

He took a sip of his nursery tea, finding it hot, sweet, soothing, and somehow unsatisfying. "Perhaps you'd be good enough to state the reason for your call, Lady Greendale?"

"We're not to chat over tea, even? One forgets you've spent the last few years among soldiers, Your Grace, but then the officers on leave are usually such gallant fellows." She focused on the orange, which was half-naked on the plate in her lap. "This is just perfectly ripe, and the scent is divine."

The scent was...good. Not a scent with any negative associations, not overpowering, not French.

"You are welcome to share it with me," he said, sipping his little-boy tea and envying her the speed with which she'd denuded the orange of its peel.

Peeling an orange was a two-handed undertaking, something he'd had occasion to recall in the past three days. This constant bumping up against his limitations wearied him, as Girard's philosophizing never had. Yes, he was free from Girard's torture, but everywhere, he was greeted with loss, duress, and decisions.

"Your orange?" She held out three quarters of a peeled orange to him, no smile, no faintly bemused expression to suggest he'd been woolgathering— again.

"You know, it really wasn't very well done of you, Your Grace." She popped a section of orange into her mouth and chewed busily before going on. "When one has been traveling, one ought to go home first, don't you think? But you came straight up to Town, and your staff at Severn was concerned for you."

Concerned for him. Of what use had this concern been when Girard's thugs were mutilating his hand? Though to be fair, Girard had been outraged to find his pet prisoner disfigured, and ah, what a pleasure to see Girard dealing with insubordination.

Though indignation and outrage were also human traits, and thus should have been beyond Girard's ken.

"You're not eating your orange, Your Grace. It's very good." She held up a section in her hand, her busy, graceful little lady's hand. He leaned forward and nipped the orange section from her fingers with his teeth.

She sat back, for once quiet. She was attractive when she was quiet, her features classic, though her nose missed perfection by a shade of boldness, and her eyebrows were a touch on the dramatic side. A man would notice this woman before he'd notice a merely pretty woman, and—absent torture by the French—he would recall her when the pretty ones had slipped from his memory.

"Now then, madam. We've eaten, we've sipped our tea. The weather is delightful. What is your business?"

"It isn't my business, really," she said, regarding not him, not the food, but the fire kept burning in the grate at all hours. "It's your business, if you can call it business."

Something about the way she clasped her hands together in her lap gave her away. She was no more comfortable calling as darkness fell than he was receiving her. She'd barely tasted her orange, and all of her blather had been nerves.

Lady Greendale was afraid of him.

Order your copy now: *The Captive*
Book Two in the Captive Hearts trilogy: *The Traitor*
Book Three in the Captive Heart trilogy: *The Laird*

# ABOUT THE AUTHOR

*New York Times* and *USA Today* bestselling author Grace Burrowes hit the bestseller lists with her debut, *The Heir*, followed by *The Soldier, Lady Maggie's Secret Scandal*, and *Lady Eve's Indiscretion*. *The Heir* was a *Publishers Weekly* Best Book of 2010, *The Soldier* was a *Publishers Weekly* Best Spring Romance of 2011, *Lady Sophie's Christmas Wish* won Best Historical Romance of the Year from RT Reviewers' Choice Awards, *Lady Louisa's Christmas Knight* was a *Library Journal* Best Book of 2012, and *The Bridegroom Wore Plaid*, the first in her trilogy of Scotland-set Victorian romances, was a *Publishers Weekly* Best Book of 2012. All of her historical romances have received extensive praise, including several starred reviews from *Publishers Weekly* and *Booklist*. *Darius*, the first in her groundbreaking Regency series The Lonely Lords, was named one of iBookstore's Best Romances of 2013.

Grace is a practicing family law attorney and lives in rural Maryland. She loves to hear from her readers and can be reached through her website at graceburrowes.com.

Made in the USA
Middletown, DE
03 January 2023

21134631R00156

wind mag

# No. 86

ISSN 0361-2481

Leaves: 11.01

What if bombs
just floated
whispered
lightly,
softly,
down?


—Richard
Arnold

wind magazine
po box 24548
lexington, ky
40524

editor
chris green

fiction editor
arwen donahue

poetry editor
rebecca howell

contributing editors
whitney baker
julie brooks barbour
jenny hobson
christine luft
eric shields

interning editor
robert lowell clark, jr.

cover art by
mark butler

**wind magazine** is a tri-annual magazine, published in Lexington, Kentucky. Subscriptions are $15 ($21 foreign/$18 institutional) for one year or three issues.**wind's** goal is to publish a wide scope of literary work from diverse communities. We operate on the metaphor of neighborly conversation between writers about the differing worlds they live in. Unsolicited and simultaneous submissions are accepted year round. For submission guidelines, write or visit our web site at wind.wind.org. Send all subscriptions or submissions to **wind magazine**/PO box 24548/Lexington, KY 40524. Advertising space is available; guidelines and prices available upon request.

# Poetry

# Fiction

# Reviews

## Community Spotlight
### Bloomington Free Verse Poets

## **wind magazine** short fiction award

## Artist Portfolio

## The **wind magazine** Community Letter

# Contributors' Notes

# Direction

North is where the sea spreads its gray blanket.
I refuse to add another sea poem
to the world's too long list, but
there you have it, sea divided
from sky by Hingham's blurred line.
A lighthouse winks red,
smaller than a needle's eye.
An occasional seagull bobs,
contained as any small boat.

A crabapple tree pins down the South corner.
In May its branch-hands toss bridal confetti,
crumbs for starlings and mockingbirds.
Do brides marry in May because azaleas
match their bridesmaids' dresses?
Or is it simply habit and lack of imagination?
It could be the weather, dependable yet crisp
so that the bride won't smother in that satin number.
She may smother anyway, or freeze;
that's not related to the sun's position,
but to what the trees shed onto her path.

To the East sits a Homes and Garden's staple
complete with slick white paint and phallic pier.
Well-manicured, the suburban postcard that no one really takes,
but takes seriously. It's chockfull
of enough greenery and sneezery
to declare a personal Manifest Destiny.
Clipped and snipped and neat as fingernails,
a fine green stretch of pool table with no balls
or players.

West sits the German Spy House,
a phrase that sent imaginations spinning
fifty years ago. The spy is long extricated:
hung, banished (no one's heard the tale's end.)
His myth inhabits the house's husk,
already overcrowded with resident ghosts:
divorcees, tabby cats, Republicans,
parakeets, alcoholics, teachers,
artists, bouquets of bright children,
manics and mechanics, none of whom I know.
The German Spy House and mine
will remain respectful neighbors, slightly
turned away from one another, decades after my own path
ends, strewn with God-knows-what
and crabapple blossoms.

*Dave Bonta*

## Congruence

*at the Cafe Gourmet Ltd.*

James Brown counts out

the beat on

the cafe stereo

loud enough

to be heard on

the street

corner by

the man with half

a face

    hunching

over to tip

his cigarette into

the glowing

cave of

his palms

      & the

bearded woman

rocking back

and forth on

her bare

feet to smooth a

route to slumber for

the wide-

eyed infant

on her hip:

      this

arrangement only

lasts for one

full measure

before the man

moves on,

      perhaps

to keep

his smoke away

from the baby

whose

occasional fervent

cries start coming

faster &

the Godfather

of Soul goes

on chanting

*get up*

*get up.*

*Kim Bridgford*

## Listening to the Wind

Some days I cannot see enough:
The prayerful heads of children newly clean
From bathing for their God; the women who
Brush their loosened hair for half
An hour. A tulip unfurls its blood-red fan
In Easter green. It must be that,
In the moment, there's a shadow there,
Translucent, with the brimming rim of it

Beneath the surface; and when it breaks
It makes me think of all the longing I've
Known, the way each touch holds its own death.
But in the frieze when the body locks
With another, there's time that dances on the grave;
And in a child's birth; and in the sound
Of voices round a table talking late
Into the night, until the wine is drained.

I remember once, when sitting on
A hill, seeing a town spread out beneath,
And all the lights trembled, then flickered off,
And I felt the loneliness of one
Who knows a thing or two about the grief
Of man. There was not a scrap of light
To hold, and so I listened to the wind,
Its silvery breath, till long past midnight.

When I was young, I thought my days
Would realize their beauty like a leaf
Turned back upon itself, that early green
Distilled, by time, to alchemize
The almost-gone. Now it's the leitmotif
I know, the pleasure of refrain:
Lying down with others in the earth
Beneath the lasting tremors of the rain.

6

# Magnolias

September and Percy Sledge sang, *When a man loves
a woman,* from the 45 vinyl into the refrigerated
      classroom flanked by standing tables
          and string mops. It was
      my first teaching job and the creatures
had hopeful names —Suzy Rodriguez, Anthony Beasley.

Fay Fish, the cleanest, licked her finger and fanned
pages of a Sears catalogue, the washing machines
      and brassieres making breeze in her
          cornrow braids. Liz, the cretin,
      her ass high, wore pink stretch pants, pulled
hair, swept the floor for more, shrieked, eating the strands.

Beautiful Smith Sisters dying of a syndrome
more exotic than a Karma Sutra,
      shoving crayons in mouth-like eyes.
          Andrew Dickey, the doctor's son,
      blinking, brown lice in his eyebrows.
At first I feared these students who could not speak.

They were the stupid of the dumb. They had fermented
in old mothers' wombs, things the sonogram missed.
      I was afraid of their hands that became
          the temperature of what they touched
      like black skins of polar bears under the optic white,
long fingers flapping as I staggered them to the bathroom.

When the afternoons stopped, in that space of breaking
and settling down, Joanne Little, the teacher's aide,
      part Blackfoot, stroked their faces, called the stinking
          Rosa Ruiz *babe.* I held up Steven's head,
      his enormous forehead and ox-shaped cranium.
I was lulled by the bubble of spit forming on his lip.

He hummed, his head pressed my hand, wanting to drop.
I fought back yawns. "Hold your head up, Steven."
         The pits of his blue eyes stared into mine.
                  "Hold your head up, Steven," I repeated, as if
         hoping to take back the years he'd spent examining his lap.
His sleep came into me. My head dipped and bobbed.

I woke on the floor, the observation mirror studying me
— metallic sheen of reflector sunglasses.
         I had been humbled. Rubbing arms, I taught them
                  to finger paint, their hands naturals, swirling the violent
         reds and blacks, streaking butcher paper
with sunspots of orange and green.

Expecting nothing from each other,
we began to fall in love.  The way the heat was –
         sweating roper's jeans – I didn't want to wash the smell
                  of them off, even after the school day vanished
         into the magnolias, leaves fried from the cholera
fire of the sun, and I had laid with a man.

This was Houston. The tiny corpses
of stars shining over eight lanes of interstate.

## Dog Dreams

The rest of the household
is still downstairs, hanging on
to the end of the movie.  But this,
for the evening, is enough:
straightened sheets that smell
of last night's sleeping;
a whiff of wood smoke rising;
then cold air through a window,
which a dog's nose takes
for all the world's news.
They say
night air brings good dreams.
Again she sighs, and settles
straight dog-spine
against my own that aches
from work; her simple
breathing.

*Chris Kingsley*

## Dinner at Home with the Muses

I was having dinner one evening
with Thalia, the muse of comedy,
and her family. She seemed pleased
to see me but very tired somehow,
as though a deep exhaustion
smoldered  within her, emanating
a sadness that could fill a room.

She told me she has paid the price
of humor, which is sorrow,
which is a scorched heart that
shelters the spark of inspiration
that lights the wet branches of the soul.
I fell in love with her immediately and
struggled to keep my tears from
welling into my uneaten salad.

"Pass the wine, please, young man,"
interrupted her father, Jupiter.
I felt ashamed. Thalia and I might
as well have been alone for all
of the attention I paid to the rest
of the family who were sitting
around the table rather solemnly.
Evidently, Jupiter had been harking
back to a golden age of poetry,
a time when four of Thalia's sisters
were busy holding down full-time jobs.
Now they were gone, and there were
only a few sisters left, sadly muted,
as the TV glowed  in the background,
crackling with applause and laughter.

"They'll be back," Jupiter said of his
daughters Calliope, Euterpe, Erato,
and Polyhymnia, the muses of epic,
lyric, love and sacred poetry respectively.
"But in the meantime, Thalia has taken
up the slack. She has more work than
she can handle-the phone never stops
ringing, not to mention the barrage
of  messengers, emails and faxes."
He was trying to comfort his wife,
Mnemosyne, but without much success.
"It's an age of entertainment, dear,"
he said . "We've been through these
ups and downs before and we
always get through them, don't we?
Besides, comedy and poetry are very
close and the pendulum will swing again.
I've always thought that a good poem is
like a good joke except that nobody laughs,"
at which point Thalia pushed her plate
away and ran from the table crying.
"What?  I mean that in the best way,"
he said, taking a forkful of green beans,
looking around, weak and befuddled,
catching only the eye of his daughter,
Melpomene, the muse of tragedy,
who preened and giggled and squeezed
his hand hard.

## Guardian Blimp

It was the obsolescence of its technology,
the propensity to crash and burn,
that sealed our bond, that finally
made me a believer.

Sure, it was easy
to avoid it. To run
into tunnels, to take fast cars
or trains and then laugh at it
from a distance. Even a simple
body fake could send it careening
in the wrong direction for hours.

But what was the point?
Eventually it would find me,
sometimes week later, its benevolent,
moony visage bobbing over the horizon
once again, powered only
by intentions as pure
as hydrogen.

What good are angels
who glide snag-less through this world?
How could they protect me?
What do they know?

If you don't believe me, come
and walk with me one day
through a wide-open field,
and I'll show you.

"Will you save me?" I'll yell,
keeping my hands behind
my back (it's important that
no strings be attached).

If you stick around, you'll see,
a nod, a small, but not
imperceptible,

"yes."

## Near the Tornado

I broke a glass when the siren shrieked.
Some streets from here a window burst in knives,
so that a woman lay bleeding and died.

We hustled the girls in to crouch by the tub.
Gusts barked and slapped the doors. The baby cried
as my wife cooed and bounced her on a knee,

her own face pale above the bobbing head.
The big-eyed sister needed words from me,
but comfort stuck in my throat and failed.

The radio sputtered. A loose board clacked,
then solid wind punched the town, a fist
knuckled with sticks and roofing tin —

but not here. Our storm has whined and slacked
to everyday weather. Elsewhere, red lights twist
above a sheet seeping black stain.

The dry yard has sprouted streams and twigs.
Our laughing daughters' swimming pool
rocks a doll face-down in too much rain.

# Thinking of the Soul in the National Forest near High Knob

Where honeysuckle smell brims air like fever in the body,
surreal in its force, calling mid-August weather
as witness to the fiery orange blooms,
each a tiny opening into someone's image of hell,
cup of sweetness above the vine-tangle, threatening
to spill into the abandoned logging road's borders,
which shine with butterflies, thickening
in gem-weed, loosestrife, toadflax—

if we were entirely of this world,
this dear jostled meshing wild under the sun,
life with its leg in a trap and gnawing at the ankle, if we
were not part sky and the ceaseless gnashing of comparison,
no one would think "elixir of honeysuckle,"
honeysuckle abstract, essence and form
to which the aroma is not a palest shade, no one
would want to swallow that concept of sun-fired liquor,

dreading its touch at the lips like a first slug of death,
a sweetness past endurance, past corrosion.

# The Cathedral at Cologne, February 2001

It took 800 years to complete. Vaulting
into the sky, stretched thin between earth
and heaven. Centuries of labor, sacrifice,
commitment. I am talking about the human
heart, the time required to build a lasting
edifice of love. I am talking about intimacy.
I am talking about how we are all scored with pain.
Some of those wounds are vertical,
deep cuts leading us upward,
but it is the horizontal brokenness we don't see
that sanctifies our faith in one another.

I stood watching my husband, that militant Jew,
light a candle and chant the shehechiyanu,
thanking G-d for this moment. He bent
over his pocket to count the marks
into the offertory. He whispered a plea
he thought I didn't hear:
"Protect our children, Adonai, and let this marriage
survive." He prayed in this city of pogroms.
He prayed in the cathedral
that lacks a rose window
for fear of distracting the eye
from its celestial ascent
as if crosshatching
wasn't God's handwriting.

And I turned away with tears
knowing that faith itself is sometimes inadequate
forgiveness belated
and redemption a spire lost in clouds.
If heaven hears us, it is when we merge our differences
and geometry
like all broken vows
expires.

## The Future As An Act Of The Scissor

Dialing prospects, he purrs
with the voice of a flower farmer.
He gets to her number. She is watching
a greasy neighbor who rubs his car,
as if stroking the national woman,
beyond roses she pruned.

The flower lover lets the cold-caller's hint
wash the grease from her seeing.
She agrees to witness his samples, glides
from her window. Her dress rises
like a red rose lifting the lawn.

She sits on foam rubber
that bulges through the cracked plastic
of the salesman's rust and rattle on wheels.
He turns toward her with the shaved half
of his jaw. Half his hair is a tangle
of weeds and half is shaved.

Memory of shears weights
her hand. The future is a pruning,
she tells herself. If she can cut a flower
so that it grows, she can listen.

## Eve at the Bat

Now she is in Mudville.
She's given up slinging apples
and moved on to hickory.

Adam's busy working the earth,
his farmer's hat's pulled down,
God knows he won't look up.

She leaves him out in the field.
She's tired of endlessly disputing
how one piece of fruit caused such commotion.

She only wanted to know—
something— for once —besides
the babbling brooks and omnipresent sun.

Adam had been occupied anyway —
naming the animals, conversing with cherubim,
ceaselessly tending those borders.

He hardly saw her, until she offered
the apple she had bitten to the core.
Then, in the time it takes a snake

to strike, he saw red, and green,
and wanted them; a fly whistled
past his ear, he swatted, and missed.

Now he's doomed to the outfield,
and it's Eve who hits cleanup, turns double plays,
and always, always, knows the score.

# The Hundredth Sheep

> What man of you, having a hundred sheep,
> if he lose one of them, doth not leave the
> ninety nine in the wilderness, and go after
> that which is lost, until he find it?
> Luke 15:4

The hundredth sheep is not lost
but wanders in all the loveliest places:
the flame's blue core, the lilt
of dusk upon the hill, the shore
of the downy lake in the moonlight.
The ninety-nine are at peace
in dumb-sleep, their wanderlust
abandoned or never known,
their woolly heads crowded
in the comfort of bounded spaces.
I'll take the hundredth sheep,
who slipped the fence
and trembled alone in the wind,
a shepherd unto himself, a searcher
who sought to be found
without being missed,
who waited to be warmed
by the sun rising
in her own majestic loneliness.

## The Return of Beauty

While love has waited, patient and kind,
beauty has returned. Here, in the
grim sparkle of December,
I have made my own Byzantium.
Where there has been bronze,
I have made gold.
Where one blue tile might have done,
I have made twenty thousand.

My friend, I would sail with you
to this place defensible and lovely
beyond all centuries. While
faith and hope would abide
and basilicas and mosques shine upon us,
we would learn that love, tousled and warm,
love awakened by your cheek against my neck
— that love— is the greatest love of all.

And so you, one morning,
or twenty thousand mornings,
might arise here, your arms around me,
and teach me to speak in tongues,
while I would teach you the codes
of antiquity, and we would abide
in the city where beauty abides:
*our city, built of kiln, crossroads and love.*

# 2001 *Wind* Short Fiction Award

Elizabeth Winthrop is the recipient of *Wind*'s 2001 Short Fiction Award for her story "Boys."

 When asked to share a little about herself, Elizabeth wrote, "I was born and raised in New York City, and I graduated in June from Harvard College. I have loved to write creatively for as long as I can remember, and as an English major, I had the opportunity to write a creative thesis. This consisted of seven interconnected short stories, of which 'Boys' is the first. Currently, I am living in Gloucester, Massachusetts, and I plan to spend this year doing as much writing as I possibly can, just to see what comes of it all."

*Wind* is honored to be Ms. Winthrop's first publication.

*Elizabeth Winthrop*

## Boys

Saturdays, we circled the city like aimless dogs; we stopped to eat and piss and we soiled the stoops we rested on.

Stan was our hot dog man: seventy-first and Amsterdam, we hovered around his cart with our dogs and coke and breathed the salty, sultry steam that rushed from the cart's belly each time Stan opened the lid to reach in for a customer.

We pissed where we were when we had to: in the park's cool tunnels, against cars parked on side-streets, into the first-story window boxes of brownstones, through the reservoir's chain-link fencing.

We never could call a stoop our own for more than a couple weeks. Ladies would stumble over us lounging on their stone steps and yell at us to "disperse! disperse!" Some would pick their way around us with their skirts partly raised as if they were walking through mud, and at the bottom of the steps they would turn and ask us to leave, to take our bodies and butts and garbage and never return. Sometimes when we arrived at our afternoon stoop we found it fenced off or mounted with a sign: "DO NOT SIT ON STOOP," or "BEWARE OF DOG."

"Dog my ass," Max said. "I've been coming to this stoop for weeks and never seen any dog."

"Fucking wimps," Alex said. "They couldn't just tell us to get off to our face? They had to make some sign?" He scoffed; we all scoffed. We were proud to think that we intimidated, that we, sunk into the stone steps or draped over the banisters with our stale cigarettes and soda, could scare. Hands in our pockets, we would stand at the bottom of the cordoned stoop and look up at it one last time, at the bubble-gum clumps collecting dirt, the cigarette butts, the sticky trails of spilled coke; we grinned, then pressed on.

It was December when we settled on the eighty-third street stoop. I lived on a street like it five blocks north; both were sloping streets lined with iron-guarded trees and low brownstones whose stoops rolled outward like pouting lower lips.

A man and a pregnant woman lived in the brownstone, and as much as we spat and swore and stamped cigarettes into their steps, they didn't ask us to leave. Saturday afternoons we arrived, as usual, after lunch, with dried ketchup crusting in the corners of our mouths or sauerkraut strands caught between our teeth. We had always been there for the amount of time it took to smoke two cigarettes each when we heard first the banging of the inner iron-barred door as it swung shut, heavy on its hinges, and then whine of the outer door as the man opened it with the weight of his whole body. The woman would walk through the door as the man leaned with his back against it and then she'd wait for him at the top of the steps as he worked the door shut and locked it. Then the man would turn, offer his arm to the woman, and they'd walk together down the steps without acknowledging us.

It was infuriating, really. The first Saturday we spent on the stoop, after the couple had stepped over us without glance or comment, the four of us stared down the street after them, their red and brown-coated backs flickering as they walked in the shadows of bare and brittle trees. At the end of the block, they rounded the corner onto Amsterdam, and we were silent.

The next Saturday, we brought our hot dogs to the stoop with us, wrapped for us by Stan and packed in a brown paper bag with containers of extra ketchup, sauerkraut, pickles, and mustard. Denny sat on the round stone post at the banister's bottom with the condiment containers open and lodged between his legs. He decorated each of our hot dogs, one at a time, and handed them out.

"Alright Max," he said. "What'll it be?"

"I'll have it all," Max said, "red stuff, kraut, pickles, you name it."

Denny reached into the bag, unwrapped a dog from its cellophane, and started smearing the extras on. He looked up. "Mustard?"

Max nodded. "I'll have it all. Mustard included."

Denny handed the hot dog down to me, and I handed it to Max.

"Next?" Denny said. "Alex?"

"The works," Alex said.

Denny reached into the bag.

Then, "hold the kraut, pickles, and mustard," Alex said.

Denny paused, and looked up. "So you want ketchup. Ketchup only."

Alex reddened. "I want what I said."

Max chewed and nodded his head violently. "The works, man," he said. "Alex wants the fucking works. Hold the kraut, hold the pickles, hold the mustard." He turned his entire body to look at Alex. "You want him to hold the bun, too? Or maybe the dog, too? You could just, like, drink ketchup?"

Alex rolled his eyes. "Fuck off," he muttered.

"Here, man," Denny said, handing Alex his hot dog. "Billy?"

"Ketchup and kraut," I said. Denny handed me mine, then started in on his own, plain.

We ate quickly.

Stan had already dropped a stack of napkins into the paper bag, but we had each stuffed handfuls more into our pockets. After we had eaten, Denny hopped down from the banister post and handed each of us a condiment container.

"For you," he said, handing me the mustard, "and you," handing Max the sauerkraut, "and you," handing Alex the ketchup. "And I," he said, straightening up, "get the pickles."

Max tipped on his ass as he reached into his pocket for a napkin. Soaking it in kraut juice, he shook his head. "You know," he said, pinching the soggy napkin from the sauerkraut and holding it in the air before him, "they had it coming." Then he slammed the napkin down; it splattered kraut and plastered itself to the steps.

Alex flung a ketchup-soaked napkin against the steps. "I agree," he said. "One-hundred percent."

By the time we heard the inner door thud shut and the outer door's knob beginning to rattle, the stoop was strewn with soaked napkins and us, trembling inside but postured leisurely at Max's last minute insistence; "Don't even look up, man! Lie back!" he had hissed at the noise of the doors. Each of us sat leaning back with his elbows propped on the step behind him, feet stretched outward and ankles crossed.

The woman, as usual, walked through the outer door and waited on the top step. When the door had been shut and locked, she joined arms with the man and they walked down the stairs again without a glance or remark. They didn't alter their course; they walked directly down the middle of the staircase, stepping on splattered ketchup and crushing pickles with their heels.

The napkin incident took place the second Saturday in December; on the third, we graveled the couple's stairs with the cigarette butts we'd been collecting all week; the fourth Saturday we stuck chewed gum to the knob of the outer door.

But the man and the woman followed their routine as if we didn't exist: inner door, outer door, link arms, stroll to Amsterdam. They added hats and gloves and scarves to their uniform brown and red jackets; the woman's stomach swelled; the cold air fogged their breath; the street turned dull with winter. We sat on their stoop and craned our necks to stare up as they stepped over us, smiling at each other or glaring at each other or pointing at things down the street.

All December the sky seemed to sag under an enormous, snowy, silent weight; it wasn't until January that the sky's skin thinned to the point of surrender and let loose a rush of snow that fell and fell and hushed the city for weeks.

We got to eighty-third street the first Saturday in January just after lunch, as usual. Someone had shoveled a narrow path up the middle of the stoop, which had been otherwise smoothed flat with snow; there wasn't room to sit except if we sat one behind the next on the cleared strip of stairs, which we did when we tired of sledding the uncleared part of the stoop on our asses.

"All right, where the fuck are they?" Max panted as he slid his final slide from the stoop's top into the snowbank below. He lay there with his arms outstretched and his chin shiny with spit.

No one answered him. He dragged his mitten underneath his nose and held his hand up in front of him. Then, "hehe," he said, "frozen boogars."

"Here's a cab slowing down," Denny said, and Max scrambled to take his place at the bottom of the stoop. "That doesn't mean it's them, dumbass." Denny swatted at the back of Max's head.

"Ah, but it is them!" Max said as the cab stopped.

It wasn't them, though; it was the man alone. We watched through the cab's windows as he leaned forward and paid the driver, then waited as the driver flipped through smaller bills for change. The man's profile was dark against the bleached background out the far window; it wasn't until he swung the cab door open and climbed out that we could actually see his face.

He stood tall in the bulky brown of his coat and looked for what seemed a long time at the waist-high bank of snow between his home and the street where he stood, droop-necked enough so that his head seemed to hang lower than the rise of his back; the shape of him was bird-like, vulture-like, but unlike a vulture's, his posture seemed one of defeat. His eyes were wide as if at the overwhelming prospect of circumnavigating the snow that made his homecoming impossible.

The cab shuddered into motion and drove slowly away after the driver had re-pocketed his cash, but the exhaust from its tailpipe hung still thick in the cold as if it had frozen there; it didn't curl or lift at all, it seemed, until the man finally raised a foot to climb the snow, holding onto the narrow trunk of a curbside tree for balance, or maybe to keep himself from sinking into the pile entirely.

We watched as he made it down the sidewalk side of the snowbank; he stood before us at the bottom of the stoop and breathed out noisily as he rubbed his bare hands together. I felt my heart begin to beat more heavily in anticipation of what the man would do next. The four of us were sitting on the stoop's cleared path; there was no other way up, there was no way the man could just walk around us, there was no way we could go unacknowledged.

In a way, I wanted him to raise his voice. "Get out of the way, you little fucks!" I wanted him to shout, "Get the FUCK out of my way!" It would have felt good, then, to sit sullen and unmoving, to refuse to budge; it would have been honorable and brave. It would have given me the satisfaction that I got from following the women who kicked us off their stoops down the street and dropping bits of chewed gum in their hair.

"Excuse me, boys."

We didn't move.

"Excuse me," he said again, and still we didn't move.

The man exhaled a long, whistling breath and shut his eyes. He took a step sideways to the banister post, and, holding on, placed one foot on the sheer face of slippery hard-packed snow. He heaved himself up and placed his other foot on the slope in front of the first; he edged his hands up the banister to brace himself for the next step.

It took him several minutes to get to the flat platform of his doorway. He held onto the banister at all times; first he would slide his hands upward, then he would move his feet slowly forward. He left his body behind, at first; he hung awkwardly with his ass sticking out from beneath his flapping brown coattails and his back hunched weirdly as he paused to get his breath. Then he would haul his weight upward and rest it over his feet, and he'd pause again before sliding his hands forward up the banister, before beginning the cycle again. A couple of times his feet slipped as he brought his weight to rest on them and he had to throw the bulk of himself onto the banister; he looked, then, with his feet useless behind him and his head vanished over the banister rail, like a seasick passenger. He would blindly kick himself a toe-hold in the snow, ease his weight from the banister back onto his feet, and resume his climbing.

When he had finally made it up the staircase, when we had heard, without turning round to see, the doors clang shut behind us, we dared to swivel our heads and look at each other with gaping, astonished expressions. The silence of the past ten minutes—we had not spoken at all during the man's climb—was thick and begging to be broken; I felt as if I would burst unless I uttered some sort of human noise, and out of desperation, for a lack of words, I snorted into a hysterical laughter that cleared the way for a rush of jabbering from the others.

"Did you fucking *see* that!!?" Alex pounded his fists on his knees and nodded and shook his head violently.

"We win, we win, we win," Max was chanting, "we win, we win, we win. . . ."

Denny sat grinning.

And I kept laughing; I laughed until my stomach muscles cramped and doubled me over and my ribs, in the crunch, pinched the flesh of my insides and the tears on my face froze in the January cold.

The next Saturday, the stoop had been shoveled bare.

We sat. We smoked our cigarettes and watched our spit freeze on the concrete; our asses felt flat with cold against the cold stone slabs of the stairs.

"I'm cold," I said after it seemed like we'd been there long enough without anything happening that it seemed safe to assume that nothing would happen at all.

"I'm cold," Denny said.

"Yeah, let's go," Max said, and we left.

It was the same the next week, and the next; we didn't see the couple anymore going for their Saturday afternoon walks or pulling up in cabs, and soon it was too cold, too snowy to be outside, and we stopped coming.

The snow was still falling almost daily in February.

School was cancelled on Valentine's Day because of it; my mother sent me to the grocery store on eighty-first street to buy firewood, less because we needed it and more because I needed something to do.

Amsterdam was lined with mounds of buried cars; the few cars actually out driving drove slowly, skidding and swerving their ways down an avenue spread with a thick layer of snow unyielding to the salt the city-men shook over it day after day; it would not thaw.

The walkers went slowly, too; over icy, shoveled spots, we dragged our feet with each step so as never to lose contact with the ground; our feet caught in the unshoveled stretches of snow, and often our heels nearly lifted out from their boots.

It was barely past four o'clock, but already the dusk light was rolling in, dimming vision already dulled by a curtain of steadily falling snow; still, though, I was certain I saw the eighty-third street couple just a quarter of a block ahead of me; I recognized the red and brown of their coats. I hurried to catch up. I wanted to see them again, I wanted to be able to report to Alex and Denny and Max that I had seen them.

I only caught up to them directly in front of the eighty-first street store; they were going in there, too. They paused in the store's vestibule, where stamped-off snow had melted into slushy pools that ran beneath the red quarter-machines with their bubble gum and plastic jewelry, and it was only in that vaguely yellow light that I saw, over the woman's shoulder, the blue peak of a bundle she held against her chest. The automatic door whined closed, leaving me outside, and I stood and watched the couple through the door's streaked and foggy glass.

The woman stood with her back to me, and the man stepped around so that he was facing her, and, very gently, began fiddling with the strings attached to the bundle. That peak of blue that faced me over her shoulder looked weirdly like a cat's ass, smooth until the center hole where the material bunched and wrinkled tight. But then, as the man pulled strings and untied knots, the material loosened and the hole widened and a baby's hooded face emerged.

The left side of its face had collapsed in on itself; where an eye should have been was a hollow socket and the skin to coat a missing jaw sagged without its underskin bone, dragging down with it the lips of a drooling mouth. The baby's single eye was expressionless, and it seemed, through the blurred glass of the automatic door with the fog collected at its edges, through scarrings of peelings of old skateboard and cigarette stickers stuck to the glass, through streaks of icy drops rolled slantwise with the wind, to be looking directly at me.

I never actually went into the store; at home, I walked through the kitchen and my mother said, "what, they were out of wood?" and I grunted and went upstairs to my fourth floor room.

I sat by my window; I looked into the lit windows of the brownstones across the street, at bookshelves and desk lamps and bathroom sinks, or at the still gauze of a curtain. I looked at the way the tree branches sagged at least a foot under their snowy burden, and I watched the snow keep falling, the flakes glinting as they passed beneath the streetlamp in front of my house.

I looked down at my own stoop; the path I had cleared was being snowed over, and I would have to shovel again in the morning. School would be cancelled; I would go down with a rusting shovel and clear a foot-wide trail for my mother and father to climb and descend. I was too lazy to clear the whole stoop, just as the eighty-third street man had been to lazy, at first, to clear his. I could still see him climbing the uncleared part of his stoop; I could see him hanging back from his arms, exhausted, or rapidly shuffling his slippery feet to gain his balance, or hurling his torso fully onto the banister so he wouldn't fall.

I bit the insides of my lips to keep from smiling, but the more I tried not to think about the man, the harder it became not to laugh. Laughter forced itself out through my nose, and it hurt, so I let my mouth hang open and I laughed out loud until I was so breathless that my laughter made no noise.

I rubbed my eyes as I calmed and pressed my forehead against the window, my breath catching in my chest with each exhalation in the way that it does when you've been crying hard. I could hear the street's stillness broken by the hum and whine of a city plow making its way down our street; I saw the toss of its yellow light, faint at first and then brighter as the engine's groaning grew louder. Then, with noise and light increasing, I saw the thing itself; it was a lurching, slow, and yellow truck with a spinning, tired, yellow light that flashed the street and snow a sickly color, and mounted to its nose was a giant, rusting plow that scraped down to the ice and heaved snow in heaping scoops to the side of the road. It barged in on the stillness of the street's unbroken layer of snow and left in its wake chain-tire tracks and broken clumps of snow that rolled blackly down the road-side mounds of cars and snowdrift which, that afternoon, had been smoothed and whitened in the fresh falling.

I had expected, when the plow left, that the street would seem violated, or interrupted; I expected the upturned snow to quiver and flash still with the hum and light of the departed plow. But when the plow had gone, stillness settled on the street again as if it had never been broken. Fresh snow would cover up the stirred up dirt and icy balls of snow, and, in the morning, the plow would have to plow again.

# Coca-Cola

Of course Mr. Dog's Friend always had Coca-Cola, even in the dry season, when he kept it buried in wet sand, in a pot filled with water. Surely, with his knowledge of all things American, he'd never admit he had any suspicions about it at first. But then he's only a *jaisi* Brahman, he's not *upadhyay* like our own family, so maybe it's true the rumors didn't bother him like they bothered my mother.

When I was growing up there were two teashops within a five-minute walk. One was my mother's, under a lean-to tacked onto our house. We had a good location, at the heart of Simalpur, by the stone platform where people rest before choosing one of the unmarked trails that scratch their way toward a dozen villages and, in one case, all the way to India.

Mr. Dog's Friend had a good location too. His shop leaned into the schoolyard like an eager suitor, and just as disreputable. In the right breeze, he could scrub the smell of chalk right off the blackboard with the oily sizzle of his potato *pakaudi* or the crispy-sticky *jalebi* with their promise of syrup squirting on your tongue like an underground river. If only you had the money. Which mostly you didn't.

But the Sirs had credit, and most other adults, too. Credit is how any business runs in our village. Aama kept the list of debtors in her head, since she was born some time around 1945, long before there was such a thing as a school. She'd squint at my books with the usual comment of people her age, "Those black letters might as well be buffaloes," but if I offered to teach her she'd shrug indulgently, as if I had promised to teach her to fly, and say, "What's the use, to an old lady?"

In retrospect, she must have been barely thirty when she started to say that. She's never been certain about her birth date. It wasn't important to calculate it precisely, the way she did the mathematics of the teashop, at least after the year when the amounts payable got all jumbled in her head with the amounts receivable and she charged less for the glucose biscuits than she had paid. But after that rough start, Aama kept her mental records with the precision that most of our neighbors devoted to gossip.

Probably the matter of record-keeping worked the same way for Mr. Dog's Friend, who was even older. His face was all ridges and sucked-in shadows and yellow teeth at the angle of falling timber. People said he must have killed a cat long ago, because when he poured tea half of it spilled on the table, and a shaking hand is the divine punishment for cat killers.

But his nickname had nothing to do with cats. It was because of the American. I only recall the American as a long-ago blur of rice-water skin, but I was no more than four when he left. He didn't talk right, that I remember. Or maybe those are memories I got later, because Mr. Dog's Friend hung his photo in his shop and made people laugh about the way the guy said *"namaste"* when he heard a jackal howl, as if the jackal was his friend or something. People tried to call him sahib because he had dollars, and because he paid people to do things like cook for him, but he'd always respond in his flat nasal accent, *"Malai dog bhannos."*

Or that's what it sounded like. Call me "Dog." Simalpur compromised by turning him into Mr. Dog. He used to eat a watery stew of boiled pumpkin over his rice, the kind of thing we feed our buffaloes. But everyone was happy. Mr. Dog was happy because he thought he got good Nepali cooking, and his cook, who of course was Mr. Dog's Friend, was happy because he saved a lot of rupees to open a teashop later, right by the school. Guaranteed profits.

Especially with the stories he'd pour out with the milk tea. They swirled lazily in the steel cups. Waited to jump from the lips that touched the scalding rims. Curled up with the vapor that rose on wings of steam and vanished, carrying the hours into an invisible place that tasted of sugar and homegrown ginger and, yes, tasted of hot metal too.

The Sirs would go to his teashop for tiffin, and also during class for a break, telling us sternly, "Chant loudly so we can hear you." Then even the kids like Rag and Whitey who never went to school, the ones on their way to the forest, could hear the waves of our chanting —

> c-o-w COW, cow *mané GAI!*
> c-a-t CAT, cat *mané bi-ra-LO!*
> d-o-g DOG, dog *mané ku-KUR!*

— and the Sirs were satisfied we weren't being lazy. But if they just wanted water or *pan parag* they'd pull one of the boys out of class, so we got to know Mr. Dog's Friend well, and he taught us a lot. Like the old-time songs:

*Caw caw the blackbird crowed*
*Seeing black pubic hair*
*The dick got scared.*

You can hide in a tree and sing it when girls pass, although it's best to make sure they're from another village or they might recognize your voice and you'll get in trouble. Especially me. The son of a priest. Because that's how it was in our family: my mother ran the teashop, but my father was a priest, everyone called him *pandit-ji*, and our neighbors liked to sit under our thatched canopy and talk philosophy with him.

Of course, most of the time they just talked about crops, the weather, who was matchmaking, who was quarreling over land, who was quarreling over loose cows and goats, who was a greedy sonofabitch who not only cheated them out of their land but also let his cows steal their corn. The usual gossip.

It was mostly the same at the teashop of Mr. Dog's Friend, but not always. And that's one of the reasons he had his following. He was one of those old people who always reminded me of what's said about monkeys. If you lie really still in the forest, a monkey might come up and groom you for lice, nicely, as if you're its friend. But if it starts on the tickling you're done for. Because a monkey can kill you by tickling.

That's what Mr. Dog's Friend is like with his jokes. He's not the only old person like that, either. It's as if some people, when they get old, figure they've come to the point where fate has power over everything but their laughter. It's stolen their teeth, bent their spine, played a practical joke on their skin and eyes, so they might as well play a few jokes back.

That's why it can be risky to be around a *budha*—an old guy, pronounced with a quick *dh* sound, not like a *buddha* with a thick *ddh,* a wise or enlightened one. But also not a *bhuddhu.* Not a fool.

A *bhuddhu* would be someone like Whitey, a doughy, string-armed boy my age who spent a surprising amount of time tapping on a drum made of dried banana stalks. One day he brags to Mr. Dog's Friend, "Look at what my father got me." He shows off a new topi cap.

The old man looks it over. Striped Dhaka cloth, the real thing, made up in Tansen where all the good Dhaka cloth comes from.

But he just coughs, "That cheap thing? I'll tell you what to do
if you want a good topi. Some time when your mother is boiling milk,
when the fire is really blazing under the pot, put that pathetic cap in
the hearth. Burn it right up. Your father will get the message. He'll
get you a real good one, straight off."

Whitey did it. Like I said, he was a *bhuddhu*. From then on
Simalpur knew him as the kid who burned his cap to get a new one,
and wherever he went, it was as if Mr. Dog's Friend was fluttering
around him on flashes of laughter, calling out, "Watch out kid. Even
God is afraid of a fool."

It was a kind of comic mantra for him. And in a way, it's what
he got paid for. People came to his teashop to hear his jokes, because
he didn't have the other kind of mantra, the sacred kind. The thing
is, Mr. Dog's Friend may be Brahman like us, but he could never be a
*pandit-ji*. He could never be paid for the sacredness of his words, like
my father, whose mantras have actual monetary value. Somewhere in
the past an ancestor of Mr. Dog's Friend had married a non-Brahman
or a widow, so the family line had become *jaisi*, a little impure, and
his words aren't believed to have the same power as the words of
pure *upadhyay* Brahmans like us.

Of course, for practical purposes my parents are just farmers
like everyone else. But the way it is in Simalpur there's always a
need for extra rupees, so Aama has her teashop and Bua is a priest.
Once when I was an infant, he fasted and chanted until his words
ended a drought. This gave him a reputation locally, so later even the
American used to come to our teashop and ask Bua to teach him.

Mr. Dog's Friend, later, when he opened his own teashop up
the road, would do an imitation of the scene: The American is trying
to say in his imperfect grammar and jangly accent, "*Malai kasari
dhyan dine sikaunos*," Teach me how to meditate. But what actually
comes out is, "*kasari dhan dine sikaunos*," Teach me how to give
away money.

And Bua praying, "*hari om bhagwan*," praise God, and the
American repeating, "*hariyo bhagwan*." O great Green God.

At our home, the life of the teashop began only an hour or two
after the life of the house itself. Bua began his days with words;
Aama, with action. It was always Aama who awoke first, up before
dawn to re-plaster the floor with a brothy mix of clay and fresh dung.
Sometimes the battery radio would still be playing because Bua had
fallen asleep with it by his ear even though Aama said that was just
burning money. He listened to Radio Nepal, to the BBC news in

Nepali, sometimes to the Voice of America. It would ratchet through the muffled darkness like some sort of nasal music, only a few words comprehensible: Russia, Iran, Yasser Arafat.

As Aama sloshes the dung over the floor, her slap-slap-slap and the hollow shrill of roosters rousing the household, Bua switches off the radio. Into the tingling air comes the grunting of buffaloes, the distant sound of hawking and spitting. Morning crawls in under the quilt.

The floor doesn't know much difference between itself and the earth outside, so when I step out of bed in the hot season the tamped dirt is dry and pleasantly cool, but in the monsoon it's clammy and exhales mildew. As for winter, the floor gets so icy it'll suck the warmth right out through the soles, so you learn to let your courage get out of bed before your feet.

All around Simalpur, our neighbors stand in the gathering light, clearing their throats onto the dirt, breathing the season into their lungs. Chickens scramble to pluck up ribbons of phlegm like worms. The air grabs the village by the shoulder and shakes. It has a sharpness that scrubs the night off your body even before the pump creaks and releases a gush of water with a mineral taste to set teeth on edge.

Bua bows to the earth, says a brief prayer, and only then does he step onto the floor to begin his day. Meanwhile Aama squats by the stove barefoot, not out of poverty but out of habit, blowing through a bamboo pipe to stoke the fire for the sweet milk tea that warms us from the inside out. First she'll make tea for our family, then she'll start making it for the village.

At the edge of the world a flush of color escapes, as if there, too, embers are being blown into life. Wide open fields pinken in the dawn, delicately at first, until a band of orange and rose explodes out of the horizon into the vast turquoise of the lowland sky. And then it evaporates. Bleaches into morning. Pearlizes.

A cool dew still sparkles like eyewash on the banana leaves and elephant grass and wild bamboo when everyone goes to the forest. Often the men of high caste — not only Bua but Mr. Dog's Friend, the school teachers, old Ekraj Adhikari who was a rich landholder before his three wives and 22 children, dozens and dozens of farmers — return from their strolls with their sacred threads still looped around their left ears. That's how you keep it pure and holy when you pee or squat.

On the homeward path Bua will snap a neem twig to brush his teeth and recite his mantras and after that you'd better not disturb him. For hours and hours, as Aama chats with our neighbors, sprinkling gossip and jokes into the milk tea with the sugar and ginger, Bua would be cross-legged by the shrine with prayers rolling out of his mouth in husky waves, strings and strings of long phrases like "*brahmannasyamukhamasiddha.*" They were long like that and always in Sanskrit and sometimes he'd say, "Listen, son. That means, whatever comes from a Brahman's mouth must be pure and true."

And if Aama heard him she'd turn to me and warn, "So don't go eating foods that are taboo. They'll pollute your mouth."

Aama doesn't meditate, it's a man thing. But she knows her duty and when the Coca-Cola first arrives you wouldn't catch her trying it. Not so Mr. Dog's Friend. Two cases rattle up to his shop in a gaily painted bicycle rickshaw loaded also with Gluco biscuits, bottled ink, pan parag, Amla hair oil, cigarettes of Finest Virginia Tobacco to be sold by the stick.

Naturally, because he's no bumpkin, he's been the cook of a man with dollars, Mr. Dog's Friend has often enjoyed Coca-Cola himself. He says it's from America. He learned this from the original Mr. Dog, who often used to send him to a whole other district to purchase foreign things. But Aama doesn't care what they drink in some cow-eating country. If you ask her that stuff is the color of beer.

She's not the only one to notice this. The rumor goes around among the more observant Brahmans that Coca-Cola contains liquor. And Aama knows her duty. She won't stock any of it. She knows the stories, particularly the one relevant to the matter at hand, the story of the gods and the demons. Bua is a *pandit-ji* so he knows it in Sanskrit but Aama knows it in her own way, and the way she tells it goes something like this:

Once the gods wanted to churn the ocean to bring up the nectar of immortality and they convinced the demons to help, using a mountain as a churning stick and a monstrous snake as a cord. They gave its head to the demons and it spit venom like the cobras that sneak up to chicken sheds and just like that—*pffffffft*—th e chickens are dead. You've got to be careful about snakes or you might end up like Tika Tiwari who was nursing her baby under a mango tree at night and reached up to slap a mosquito, but it was no mosquito, it was a cobra. Old Shaman-Brother tried to save her by sucking and blowing and shaking his rattle, but it did no good.

"She should have gone to a hospital," the teachers would say. They divided their loyalties between the teashop of Mr. Dog's Friend (which was closest to the school) and our own teashop (where they'd talk philosophy with Bua and debate the meaning of words in Sanskrit).

But Aama would say, "What to do? It was her dying time." Tika had been a few years ahead of me in school, but she'd gotten married in class eight, like my sister.

Anyway, the snake that was churning the ocean spit poison, but what to do, everyone has to die sometime, so lots of demons died but the others weren't bothered, they kept at it and said, "We want whatever comes up first." Which turned out to be liquor. They drank it all, had a wild party, and when the nectar came out of the sea they were too drunk to notice and after all that work they lost out on immortality.

"All because of foolishness and greed," Bua would say. "Never touch liquor, it will disrupt your meditation."

So Aama doesn't touch the Coca-Cola. And she won't sell it. Nor will she sell those instant noodles in the bright cellophane wrappers, because maybe at the factory they added some cow meat or eggs, pork or chicken or something else taboo. Everyone knows this is the Kali Yuga, the era of wickedness that started 5,000 years ago and will only go downhill for the next 400,000 years until the god Vishnu comes to set things right. So in the meantime no one can tell what a factory owner might put into the noodles.

In time it becomes clear that, in spite of Mr. Dog's Friend's entreaties, people don't care about the Coca-Cola, not because liquor is a suspected ingredient (which would only bother the more observant Brahmans) but because most of Simalpur has decided it's mainly colored water.

This makes Aama even more certain of her business savvy and convinced that her teashop will win more customers than Mr. Dog's Friend, in spite of his location by the school. She takes to saying, "Who's going to throw money into water?" Liquor or not, Coca-Cola is a city thing, like shoes for children. And if it's an American drink, then the Americans aren't only cow-eaters, they also must be hucksters or fools, because colored water is a thing only a huckster would sell and fool would buy.

But Mr. Dog's Friend gets a cheery red-and-white sign to advertise it, and he hangs it over his only table, next to a calendar picture of Laxmi, goddess of wealth, glued with cowdung to the pallid wall of wattle and daub. She has bee-stung lips, black eyes, fair skin like a Hindi film star. Or like Mr. Dog, whose photo hangs by a storage shelf, one meaty arm draped around the much-smaller shoulder of Mr. Dog's Friend, who looks like a shadow in comparison.

The Coke itself is stacked prominently, and not very usefully if you ask Aama, like the watch the old man got as a parting present from his old boss. It sits slackly around his thin, taut wrist, a flash of dull silver among rubbed gray hairs. Above the watch his arm is veined coarsely, the way dried creepers curl around hardwood. He never takes the watch off. I realized one day that it was broken.

The hot season arrives. Crawls up from the south, spitting dust and flies. Settles into Simalpur with a heavy, head-hollowing dullness. The fields are sullen and cracked. Dung dries on the trail shortly after it lands, and soon it's road dust. The Coca-Cola is still unsold. The crisp sign in English is grayed by the sand that blows everywhere, and the liquid it advertises is like boiled water.

But Mr. Dog's Friend digs a hole in the earth, packs it with wet sand, and inserts some water-filled clay pots in which to cool the bottles that are waiting for somebody (a Kathmandu cousin, a man on his annual visit from a job in India, another aid worker) who has some money to throw into water.

Time passes, unmarked on the broken watch. The Coca-Cola waits in its shell of clay pots, in a darkness spun of sand. Waiting, like a caterpillar in its chrysalis.

My cousin Dilli isn't looking for Coca-Cola when he comes to the teashop, where the old shopkeeper is resting on his rope charpoy for lack of business. Dilli just wants the regular kind of water. If he'd been less thirsty he'd have waited until he got to Aama's teashop, out of loyalty, but as it is he thought there could be no harm in asking for water, although of course he doesn't plan to buy anything.

The main thing to know about Dilli is he had just moved to Simalpur from our family's old village of Alubari, which is quite a different place. Simalpur is in the lowlands, and not even an hour from a road. But Alubari is high in the mountains, and to reach a road takes a day of walking. So his family had come to Simalpur for a better, more sophisticated life. Everyone knows our village is about to be developed. Hadn't Mr. Dog himself come for just that reason, so many years before?

It wasn't long after Dilli arrived that Mr. Dog's Friend wanted to know all about him. "That boy you were with the other day," he had said, "He's your cousin, isn't he? I heard someone say he's *pandit-ji*'s brother's son."

"Actually, he's Aama's brother's son," I said. "From the hills." I was at the teashop to fetch one of the Sirs some *pan parag* and a cup of water, and I was in no hurry to go back to the class, so I told a few stories. "You know what he said when he saw a motorcycle? He said, 'How does it eat its grass? Where does it poop from?' He's such a *pakhé.*"

The old man laughed, "Oh really? Well, that's how it is with some people. Real bumpkins. Don't know a thing, not a thing."

As I walked back to the classroom with the *pan parag* and water, I felt disloyal. The story was true, but it had actually happened when Dilli was five or six, the first time he visited. I liked Dilli. The only thing wrong about him was he didn't know the ways of the lowlands.

One day Dilli walks up to the teashop. He'd been sent on some errand to another village. By the time he's heading back, the hot *loo* wind is baking the moisture off anyone foolish or unlucky enough to be on the road. The light has a pale, dustblown quality. The only sound at the teashop is the flies, who drone sluggishly as they trace a vague, purposeless circuit along the benches, the plank table, on the rim of a saucepan of coagulating milk tea.

When Dilli asks for a glass of water the old man is awake, though lying down. He looks up from his string cot and sees a long narrow face, eyes swollen with a chronic touch of conjunctivitis, sun-boiled ears winging out beneath a squashed-down topi cap.

"Of course, son," the old man says. "But to my mind, in this weather, wouldn't Coca-Cola taste better?"

He leans down, extracts a bottle from its underground chamber. It's the deep brown of unfiltered honey. Trickles of water lick its curves, tracing the contours, each droplet a flicker of changeable light.

Dilli shrugs. "I don't have a single rupee with me."

"That's all right. Maybe you can trade some oranges for a bottle."

"We don't have any. In the hills they grow everywhere. So many oranges, tangerines. Really sweet. But I haven't seen any here at all."

"Well, seeing as you're *pandit-ji*'s nephew, you may be new here but it's like you're family. So I'll let you in on a secret. There's an orange grove just across the river, by a little stick hut, and I just saw the owner, oh, it wasn't 10 minutes ago. He's going to market. He'll be gone all day, I'm sure of it. You know, my business isn't very good right now, but if I could just get some oranges to sell I'm sure it would be worth a lot to me. I've got all this Coca-Cola, you know, and it's pretty valuable, but I could make a deal."

He pours Dilli some tepid water. "Used to be you couldn't get Coca-Cola around here. It's American, you know. In America you can just turn on a tap and get it. First time I ever had it, I was with my American friend. Ever tried it?"

Dilli hadn't. On the plank table, in its curved bottle, the jeweled syrup gleams like liquefied shade.

Probably he'd have agreed to the deal no matter what he was offered in return, anyone would have, especially if they didn't know Mr. Dog's Friend. All of us kids would steal fruit whenever we had the chance. But the bait is irresistible.

Dilli borrows a sack and runs off and soon in the forest he finds a rough hut, woven of sticks, and sure enough there's a fruit grove. But they don't look like the orange trees he knows, and he feels foolish. Doesn't he know oranges when he sees them?

He stops for a minute, thinking. He decides the lowlands must have a different kind of orange. He pulls himself up from a low-hanging bough and starts filling the sack.

He's got a good collection when there's a parched voice from below, crackling like twigs. "What thief is that in my tree?" Coming from the hut is a gaunt figure with a tangled mat of dreadlocks and bare nipples. "You sisterfucker, you little thief, I'll fuck you in the ass." There's the flash of an ax.

Dilli tumbles down and makes a rabbity dash for the dried river, darts through underbrush boiling with brambles, skids down eroded bluffs. He runs without stopping, as if the curses are a swarm of bees, and the man chases him, "You sisterfucker thief, stealing my fruit," dreadlocks flopping like a shawl of snakes, arm pumping as if the ax is an oar. It actually seems to make him run faster.

Dilli is so scared he doesn't even think to drop the fruit, he's in a cloud of dust and he's sweating so much it's clinging to him like wet flour, he thinks he can hear the old man's bony legs and they're just like scissors, *snip snip,* he darts around the trees and once he trips but still he doesn't drop that fruit. Finally he reaches the fallow fields at the edge of the village and then the curses grow fainter, as if the bees don't want to go far from the hive, in case someone else steals the honey. Dilli's eyes are watering but in the distance he can make out a stick figure on a bluff, slicing an arc in the air with his ax.

When he reaches the teashop his body is so shiny with sweat it has turned almost blue, except around his eyes, which are swollen in the dust. Damp pink eyes in a damp blue-black face. He is breathing heavily and squints down through the miserable hot slits of his eyes and somehow, as if it's been glued to his hands by all the sweat, the sack of fruit is still there.

The shopkeeper tips his chin back, smiles a broad cave smile that exposes a black canine. "Hot day, isn't it?"

"There was a crazy *sadhu*. With an ax."

"Ehh, really? Well, I'm sure it was worth it. You got a lot, I see. Smart boy. How are they? Sweet? Have one yourself, go ahead, go ahead."

Dilli takes a bite. Then he springs back, as if stung. The lower half of his face shrivels, the upper part is nearly in tears. The old man doubles over with laughter. Soon Mr. Dog's Friend is calling all the villagers to tell them about the new boy in town — the nephew of *pandit-ji*, Aama's brother's son — who is such a bumpkin he nearly got chopped in two by Banchariya for a sack of lemons.

And for a week that's all Simalpur hears, and everyone adds their own stories about Banchariya who's no *sadhu* but only a *sawadhu*, a self-server.

"Renunciation, ha," someone says. "All he renounces are his clothes. He claims to be a hermit but haven't you seen him going to the house of that widow?"

The story is told so often, and people get so many chances to try to top it, that even the Nepali Sir defects from his after-school philosophy sessions at our teashop. He orders cup after cup and teases, with a hint of local pride, "It's true that even God is afraid of a fool. But our elder brother here"— no one called him Mr. Dog's Friend to his face —" our brother here, God is doubly afraid of him."

"Why is that?"

"Because he is a creator of fools."

That week, our family just has to surrender. Aama's tea and Bua's philosophy have no way to compete with Mr. Dog's Friend and his comic mantra. Everyone goes over to bask in the talk, to fan themselves among the stories. In the butterfly wings of a cooling laughter. They buy a lot of tea and even a few bottles of Coca-Cola, so in the end the trick on our family turns out to be better for business than stolen fruit. Better even than American water, buried in the earth until it's suitable for Simalpur.

# Limbs

I sat on my porch in late August, learning how to tell time from the shifting moon. I stared at the moon until a single pecan broke from its bloom and collided with the tin above my head. A single pecan broke from its bloom and brought me back.

It brought me back to earlier that morning, when I had used my chainsaw to cut up several pecan limbs while my grandfather watched me from a stump. I cut and stacked and cleaned all the tree limbs torn loose from the South Georgia thunderstorm that had rattled our windows and pounded our roofs all night the night before. Most of the shade we'd ever known was lying on the ground. My grandfather's face was cast in shadow from his straw hat, but the sweat leaked from him in gallons, even as he sat unmoving on the stump.

Every few minutes he spoke of his last surviving brother who had died in a hospital the day before. They did all they could do for him, I guess, he said, and I agreed, pulling the rope to the chainsaw one two three times before it screamed.

"They did all they could do, I guess," he said again, as soon as the saw was off. Then he pointed to my hands and cocked his head and asked if the gloves I wore were his. He'd lost his gloves, he said, and he couldn't think of where they could've gone. I told him no, they weren't his gloves, and for the moment he seemed satisfied.

His brother was the person I'd been named after, the man who, with my grandfather, assumed the role of my absent father. Together, they taught me everything they thought a man should know: bats and balls, hammers and nails, knives and guns; engines and plows, levels and saws; rivers and woods. Don't complain and don't explain. Study how the rooster plants its talons in a hen's back when mating. Watch how he'll peck her until he pierces the skin and pulls her intestines out. Drop dead chickens into scalding water for easy plucking. Chicken shit is too strong a fertilizer for tomatoes. The tide is highest on a new moon and a northeast wind. Train the ear to know when to allow more air and less gas or more gas and less air into the carburetor. Don't drink before five p.m. Hold the fists so the knuckles on the first two fingers do the work. Shooting has to do with breathing, and successful fighting has to do with cruelty and the will to go down swinging.

"Are those my gloves?" my grandfather asked again, and again, I told him no.

I separated the wood we would use in our fireplace from the rotten wood I'd throw away. I cut the good wood into fifteen-inch pieces, and threw the remainder in the truck.

I was twenty-one years old, and didn't have a job. The family paid me a hundred dollars a month to take care of my grandfather and his place—prepare his meals, feed his chickens, cut his grass, tend his garden, wash his soiled clothes, bathe him, and keep him company during televised baseball games. The nights got lonely sometimes after he went to bed, but I didn't mind it much. I never imagined moving to a city, or pursuing what people fondly refer to as a career.

I stacked the good wood and listened to my grandfather retell the story of how he and his brother had once pulled their drowned brother from the river, body blue and bloated, a stiff arm raised above his head as if he'd had time to orchestrate his final gesture into a wave. I stopped what I was doing. My grandfather was sobbing. His whole body was shaking. But he wouldn't look at me. He lifted his head, stared into the top of a tree, and began a composed lecture about how pecan limbs absorb more moisture than the limbs of other trees and grow too heavy to hold on.

I took a load of limbs to the riverside brush pile, where, in another week, I'd burn it, waiting for the green to fall away so it'd be dry enough to torch. Then I'd sit and watch it for as long as it took to finish burning.

When I returned, my grandfather was shuffling toward a small twig as if the earth was the deck of a boat being rocked by waves. He wore shoes held on by velcro straps because he'd forgotten how to tie his shoes. He reached the twig and began to bend, but I reached it first and snatched it away.

"They've done all they could do, I guess," he said again, and I agreed. He labored to straighten his back and then brushed his hands on his dark brown trousers.

I'd seen Uncle Ervin in the hospital two nights before, after twenty-three straight days of my mother asking where was I, and was it going to be like this when she was old and dying and needed so badly some small sign from her only son.

And so I went, and saw him dying. The poisons had risen in waves and he no longer recognized the wife who had woken up beside him for sixty years. His hands were tied to the bed to keep him from pulling out the tubes in his nose which instinct told him did not belong. He babbled incoherently and his wife whispered for him to speak more clearly please. He seemed to see something that frightened him. Though I couldn't see it, it frightened me too.

In the midst of his babbling, he said, "oh boy oh boy oh boy oh boy oh boy oh boy."

His wife had sent his only suit to the cleaners and asked me to pick it up for her. I took it to her house, hoping she wouldn't be there, but she'd come home for a couple of hours to write his obituary. I hung the suit in a closet, and she chastised herself for her failed faith in miracles.

She'd written his obituary on the back of a telephone bill, fearing she'd forget something if it were left to do afterward, when the order of dates and places would fade into the blackest portion of her already darkening memory. She wanted me to stay, offering tea and cake, but I made some excuse and left.

I told my grandfather that our work was done, that I'd take a shower, and fix some hot dogs we could eat in front of the ballgame.

"Seven-thirty sharp," he said.

I said I knew.

But I went for the first of countless beers and left him sleeping in his recliner. Left him without supper. Left him without his bath. Left him sleeping in soiled underwear. I settled on the porch with a cooler full of beer, feeling the day's work settle stiffly into my bones. I drank the beer and watched the remaining pockets of clear sky turn to black.

I took the phone so it wouldn't wake him, and when it rang, it was my mother, asking where were we, that the family had gathered at my aunt's house for the sake of solace, and that we should come and eat of all the food that had been brought as gifts. But I was filthy and already too much into the beer, and couldn't possibly stomach the idea of sitting in that musty living room with all the dour faces who would speak of how the doctors had done everything that they could do.

I stayed on the porch, drank beer, and watched the moon float above the river.

After an hour, I called Mary, a woman I thought I could love —a nurse —to see if she would come over as she did some nights after my grandfather went to bed. I wanted to put my ear to her chest and hear her heart and I wanted to put my lips on her mouth and taste her breath. But when I called she said she was sick and couldn't possibly get out of bed. She'd watched someone die on her shift the night before, she said, and this always had a way of depressing her immovably into bed. She didn't give any details. I didn't ask for any. I didn't give any of my own. We were silent for awhile. I didn't want to hang up, but I didn't know what to say. We were silent for awhile longer. We were silent until she couldn't handle it anymore, and then she hung up.

I stayed on the porch, drank beer and watched the silent moon slide past the river. I thought ahead to the funeral, when I would carry a corner of the casket and stand beside it at the graveside, facing my family. I would find my mother's face, and she'd be looking toward the woods at a row of old oaks that held Spanish moss like a thousand grey handkerchiefs from history. A preacher would keep us too long beneath the August sun, explaining how the angels had carried my uncle through the valley of the shadow. My mother would flap a fan in her father's face to keep him cool, though his mouth would crack open and the sweat would fall in buckets from his head.

I stared at the white light of the waning moon and tried to remember what day it was. I tried to think of what I'd need to do the next day to prepare myself for the funeral, but I couldn't locate the day of the week, and so I couldn't think at all. I felt like a child on the days when I wandered too deeply into the woods, got lost and had to scream for my uncle or my grandfather to come and rescue me.

I stared at the moon until a single pecan broke from its bloom and crashed on the tin above my head. A single pecan broke from its bloom and brought me back.

I remembered then that I needed to buy a suit. I'd wear the suit to the funeral and then I'd have it cleaned. They'd give it back to me wrapped in plastic and I'd keep it in a closet and forget about it, though I'd brush against it every time I reached for something else.

# Death of a Salesian

"Define, boys, if you will, the following. . . Or, can we," (Fr Lafayette pauses at the board) "can we at least, gentlemen, in this opening sentence of Milton's great epic, Heron, Donnelly, can we at the very least indicate, to begin with, now, the main verb?"

Our heads go down. Five years along and few of us can dare to meet Fr Lafayette's stern, blue-eyed gaze. Expectantly, he stares down into our souls, like God will.

"Farrell, boy, you?"

His voice has that rough Northern Irish boom, like an IRA bomb going off in your class. Soon, we all hope, Tom Christensen, the cleverest boy in the school, if not the world, will engage him in a discussion of some point only himself, Lafayette and Milton could appreciate, and the rest of us can switch off for twenty minutes. Which is as it should be, I think, on a morning like this one.

Fr Lafayette is not a nice man, it says on the wall of the Sixth Form boys toilet, and below that, in thick black ink, it also says, *Fr John walks on water.* Irony of ironies. All is irony.

Lafayette looks at me now. "Stevie?"

"Is it 'sing', Father? Line six, Father. *Sing, Heavenly Muse...*"

A pause (staring) while he checks the righteousness of my answer, and, for once, is satisfied. "Yes, Stevie, 'sing'. . . *Of Man's first disobedience and the fruit of that forbidden tree, Sing, Heavenly Muse . . .*"

Slowly he walks along the front of the class, his long black cassock almost touching the floor. Fr John was a nice man, now drowned, we believe, on a school trip up a mountain. When the bell rings for the end of class this morning, it'll be time for his service in the school hall. All the elderly Salesians we don't usually see will be there, wheeled out from the Priests' House for the occasion, like at Fr Drum's funeral back in our first year. Latin chanting and *paso doble*, in scarlet and gold. Fun for all.

Eccentric Fr John (or 'Mad' Fr John, as we called him) was our form-master, then, in our first year. Tall, ungainly, pigeon-toed; with his upper class accent and manners, he seemed as though from

another world than ours, a world of bicycle clips and Radio 4, spe-
lunking in Wales, cross-country rambles and, as ever, God. That
morning, he gave us the first of his annual Before-this-year-is-out-
one-of-you-boys-will-be-dead sermons: blood and fire. Though each
year we never paid him much attention, he was always right. Patrick
Fitzpatrick, Christensen's older brother, and Jonah.

Fr Lafayette's face is set like a gravestone. "*What in me is
dark illumine, what is low raise and support...*" His hands clench into
fists as big as any docker's fists, his boots promise violence. Of all the
Salesian brothers, Lafayette is by far the most fierce. Neither Lynch
nor 'Pig' Dooley, the champion truffle hunter of all France, come
close, even when in a pad. Lafayette's discipline knows no quarter,
shows no mercy. An eye for an eye. "*That, to the height of this great
argument I may assert Eternal Providence . . .*" He pauses once more
by the window, a huge silhouette against the grey sky outside. Then
comes the voice, brassy and loud: "Can we not agree, then, gentlemen
. . ."

I notice Christensen sit back in his chair, arms folded,
waiting, ready. A pity about Christensen. Last year his brother died
from leukaemia; Christensen himself was suspended from school for
two months for what he did to his mock RE exam script. Now, his
long, thin fingers quiver nervously; an explosion of red welts mark
and scar his face. He sends a cold, ironic look in my direction, then
turns away. We haven't really been friends, I suppose, since the
Third Form, when I beat him in English. These days he calls me
usually either 'Suffering-Jesus' or, even worse, 'Matter-Not', a play
on my name.

". . . De facto, Mr Cahil! De facto and not de jure!"

Fr Lafayette thunders his point, whatever it is, then falls
silent. His eyes scan the classroom for dissent. At last, satisfied that
we all agree, he moves on. Or begins to. Like a perfectly timed foul
tackle at football, Christensen's voice drags him to a halt.

"Well, I'm not sure I do agree, Father, or not, about what you
say, but I think, if anything, it's probably the most Protestant of
poems, isn't it?"

Fr Lafayette's grave expression blackens further. He takes a
step back. "Yes, Thomas?"

And so, they're off— even on a day like today there's no
putting aside the inquisition, their eye for an eye.

It's funny how I can't remember the title of Fr John's
Christmas play. The Boys of Shark Island, or something like that.

I'll have to ask Christensen later. What I can remember, though, are the rehearsals on all those dark nights after school—how strange it felt backstage, for instance, or Fr John, up a ladder, painting palm trees on the scenery; and Jonah in costume, with his red fox-brush of hair showing up even redder under the stage lights.

These memories have stuck in my head like the lines of some poem I've never actually understood until now. I think the three of us—that is, Jonah, Christensen and myself—only got involved in the first place because we were the three shortest boys in the first form, and because Jonah complained too loudly one day in Fr John's Tutor Group that he was bored, a bad move. Fr John showed little patience with any complaints of boredom, especially from boys in his own form. I can see him now as though he were suddenly close-by, peering down at us, his thick-set eyebrows arched quizzically over those black-rimmed glasses:

"How can you possibly claim to be bored, Jones, at your age? O, there's nothing to do? Well, open your eyes, boy, there's everything still to do! Start a club! Read a book! Go abseiling with Fr Lynch! Remember, Jones, only boring people allow themselves the luxury of boredom. Join the school play!"

And so his litany ran on, until the three of us agreed reluctantly to stay behind after school and help with the play—Jonah's fault, we felt. Little did we think that we would actually enjoy it, and none of us more so than Jonah!

The night of our big performance, I remember it now: just before Christmas, in front of all the boys' parents. I preferred to be backstage but Jonah was in his element in the spotlight, performing—or, as it was usually called in class, showing off. I remember how before the start a surprising amount of general noise rose up from the darkened hall, like at midnight mass in the cathedral on Christmas eve; then came the laughter as the play sprang to life around us (laughter connected to what we were doing on stage—strange sensation!), and when it was all over we had what felt like waves of wild applause from the audience, curtain calls, whistles from the older boys which were probably ironic, as ours would be now. Jonah was buzzing, even though his part had only been a small one really. Fr John, his wonders to perform.

Now as I look back at it all, I see Fr John was quite right about Jonah; I suppose in the end it was just boredom, nothing more, nothing less. He didn't get involved in anything again—Jonah, I mean, at school; and neither have I much since the play, if I'm honest about it. All of us scholarship boys, Jonah, Christensen, myself even. And the rest, what's happened to us all?

It's like last year when we had all that trouble with *Top Of The Form*, or whatever it is, the radio show. The man from the BBC had primed us all before the start, about when to clap or cheer, and we'd all gone along with that. Up on stage were Burke (Head Boy), Flynn, Donnelly, I think, and someone else, Baker; 'Pig' Dooley was fussing around distractedly behind them like he does, looking as if he'd lost something he didn't want anyone else to find. Then, as the theme music faded out, the man from the BBC counted us all in for our first big live cheer and, as one, the entire Fifth Form —I think of it now as a response to the situation that we all just seemed to understand at the same time —stayed completely silent in our seats, nothing. Dooley's face passed through several flustered hues of crimson as he floundered about, stage-left and then stage-right, in almost a fit of disbelief. Over the radio link we could hear our opponents at the other end of the country, cheering for all the world as though they meant it, like schoolboys. And it went on like that, no clapping, no cheering, just the tinny noise of the opposition (a Protestant school, no less) coming over the loudspeakers like so much interference after every round. I remember looking around at the others and thinking this was something really great, a brilliant rebellion, and then at the same time worrying like mad about whether we'd gone too far this time, about all the probable consequences.

At an early point in all of this Dooley had exited stage-left, florid-faced, as good as if pursued by a bear. And shortly afterwards, about halfway through the quiz (which we lost), Lafayette came into the hall and glared down at us all from the stage, his fierce blue eyes blazing silent anger.

Then, long before the end —a sidedoor swinging, and he was gone.
A victory, then.
But today, it makes me ashamed just to think of it.

I don't know what it is, this rift between us and them. Maybe it's us; perhaps we just can't hear them anymore . . .

I think it's like that parable we did in RE class lately, the one about the stony ground: we're like that. What they tell us doesn't take root.

Take Jonah, for instance. Right from the start, I don't think any of it ever really went in. I remember that role-play we did in class once for Fr John, about finding a purse with £20 inside. This was back in the Third Form, I'm almost sure. We had to argue the case between us either for handing it in, or for saying nothing and keeping it ourselves. Fr John — or so it seemed to me at the time —was watching us curiously throughout it all, peeling his apple with his pocket-knife, like he did at some point in class every day. Out of the corner of my eye I could see his short white socks dangling over the foot of the desk, distractingly. Jonah, for his part, began playing it up for the benefit of his new cronies, the tough boys from the Secondary Modern School. I'd started off with something like we should really hand the purse in to the driver or at the depot (we'd found it on a bus, apparently), or failing that, then, at a police station, because that would be the right thing to do —but he just didn't want to know: Why should we give it back? Didn't I realise that the driver or a copper— or anyone, even —would just pocket it themselves? What was the matter with me? Did I know nothing?  — His face had that sly, conniving look it often had when he thought he was getting one over on you. This was the start of the era when Jonah's parents took up their increasingly frequent visits to Fr Lafayette's office, to discuss young Michael's worrying behaviour. "Well," I said to him in counter-argument, "we could give it to a charity. Just because we can't give it back doesn't mean that we should keep it . . ." Or something like this. But it was no good. You might as well argue with the wind or next-door's cat. At every turn Jonah twisted, leapt, settled where he wanted, indifferent. He wasn't even listening, really.

Perhaps for them, it's like that with all of us, all of the time. I don't know . . .

Whatever I said that day was just lost on the breeze . . .

Afterwards, I remember, I took quite a bit of stick from almost everyone in class for acting the Holy-Joe —but especially from Jonah. He said I practically was one of St Joe's, the way I'd gone on. The ironic thing is, that, at the time, I'd actually agreed with him about what to do with the purse —in practice, that is. I agreed with Fr John in principle, if with Jonah in practice. I'm sure I know what really would have happened if Jonah and me had actually found a purse together on the back of a bus.

I could still see what the right thing to do would be, though; Jonah couldn't, which is probably why we ated it out in class like that in the first place.

That's how I see it all now anyway, looking back at it like this . . .

I think it was from about then, or shortly afterwards, that Jonah began to give me a wide berth, and I did the same with him. He got himself mixed up in some stuff that didn't interest me, fighting after four o'clock with the Senate House School boys, for instance, and I deliberately didn't want to know. If the truth be known, I suppose I hadn't forgiven him for what had happened next that afternoon in Fr John's RE class —something and nothing, really, in the end. Or at least, ironically, it felt like something to me, if nothing to Jonah and everyone else.

A few half-cheers went up in the class for Jonah at one point, Heron, Flynn, and some others, the new boys. ("You give your half to a flaming charity, then, if you want to! I'll keep mine!") Without any warning, Fr John had risen up up from the desk and crossed the room, depositing the peeled rind complete into the waste-basket. He stopped beside us, coring that apple of his, still with a detached air. Even now, I've a particulary strong memory of this process: the halving and paring, then quartering; though I suppose I had witnessed it on many occasions. But Jonah went on (and on!) regardless, playing-up, twisting my argument around to suit himself: "Isn't that right, Father? Why should she get to keep it? A single mother! It'd be her Wages of Sin, wouldn't it? Isn't that right, then, Father!"

Fr John paused, looked down at Jonah. He'd finished what he was doing, both with the apple and us. His expression was pointed, cutting, sharp, like the knife he was folding away coolly into his black jacket pocket. Then, he said, with a reproach in his voice that was worse to me than any threat of violence from Lafayette, something very like the following:

"You might be many things these days, Jones... A twister, a liar, or perhaps, worse..no? — But I know — Are you listening, boy?—I do know, Jones, that you aren't anywhere near as selfish or hard-hearted as you like to think yourself these days. Now, one day, Michael, if it's not too late, you may let yourself realise this."

"If you say so, Father. Do I get the £20 now?"

Another —much bigger this time —cheer again in class. In the face of such outright defiance Fr John stiffened, took a step or two back towards his desk, and without any hesitation from almost any of us, it quickly became one of those moments when the general din of the classroom suddenly rises to a deafening cacophony — out of control, louder and louder.

Who'd be a priest today, that's what I ask myself. Let alone a Salesian Brother having to teach the likes of us lot! I once asked Fr John this question, why he became a priest. This was only recently, in the Lower Sixth common room after one of the more mature sort of RE seminars we tend to have today, or did. We were sat over by the ping-pong table; everybody else in the group had filtered away. Fr John was packing up his tape-deck (for playing Radio 4's 'Thought For The Day', taped at some ungodly hour that morning), and assorted papers — the famous old battered 1941 briefcase was open. He stopped completely, was probably surprised by the question coming totally out of the blue like that. I waited for what seemed like an age while he contemplated his answer; his head bowed thoughtfully, seriously, like in prayer. I'd expected him to say something about vocation. God had called him one day and he knew he'd have to give up everything and answer the call, the sort of thing we'd hear at least once a year in assembly from one of the St Joe's Brothers on the lookout for recruits. Instead, to my surprise, he said quite straightforwardly that it occurred to him somebody had to do it. That's all. He carried on packing up his things, then. I was puzzled at the time but I suppose I can see the sense of it, now. Somebody does have to do it. When you think of it like that, it does make some sense, maybe . . .

I suppose I have to make up my mind next what to do about this retreat Fr John asked me to go on next month over at St Joe's, or rather, that he asked me to lead, with boys from all years of the school going over there with me. Talk about from out of the blue! I was more than a little gobsmacked when he asked me, and flattered! I asked him why he didn't pick Baker, the goody-goody Deputy-Head Boy everybody likes, even Lafayette. This would be more in his line. "The world would be a very boring place if everyone was like Baker," he said, which I took as a backhanded compliment. I was still honest with him, though, and said I'd have to think about it. To be truthful, despite the good feeling I got from being picked out, I didn't really fancy it. Retreat. Sounds too much like going backwards for my liking. I didn't fancy getting involved.

To think this all just happened a week ago, and now everything's so different. Or I suppose I'm just seeing things differently now than how I used to see them . . .

Christensen and Lafayette: both still going for it, as if the bad feeling between them were something neither one could do without, the leather strop on which they sharpen their wits. You can understand why Christensen hates them all so much, perhaps. When his elder brother John came down with leukaemia, the Brothers here virtually turned it into a sideshow for Christ, which can't have been nice to witness every morning at assembly when it's your sick brother they're going on about. *"We visited Christensen in hospital again last night, and his continuing cheerfulness, strength and good faith in the face of this terrible illness should be a lesson to all you boys fortunate enough to be in perfect health here today..."* The usual sort of stuff. Except Tom Christensen tells us it was hardly like that at all; his brother was just sick, especially towards the end. That funeral turned out a no holds barred affair, as well. Full battle dress, choirboys from St Joe's, the entire school in attendance, just like we'll probably get this morning. The works.

I remember Christensen's brother as a very quiet, scholarly boy, two years older than we were. Like Tom, he was fantastically intelligent; he'd already passed the Oxbridge entrance exam. Then fate, cruel as any nun, took him off. Ironic.

You have to wonder about it all. I suppose they made a big fuss about John Christensen because he was such a model student, an example for us all. Someone like Jonah, on the other hand —who in a sense the school fails, even if it's mostly his own fault, I'm not denying that—someone like Jonah gets put in the ground without so much as a prayer for the dead in morning assembly. Just an oblique warning from Lafayette, about those boys straying from the paths of righteousness, was all that was said. Lafayette, the clanging cymbal as ever, sounding brass.

I guess I still find it hard to accept that it was Jonah who was driving the car that himself and the other three boys were killed in, like some of them in school said he was. I suppose I don't want to accept it; I just don't see how they would know one way or the other.

What not many people here do know is that Fr John came to the funeral— Jonah's, I mean. The service was performed at St Jude's by the parish priest, Fr O'Reilly, not by anyone from school. In fact, virtually no one else from school was there, apart from me and one or two others, and I only went partly because I knew his Mum and Dad. I still see them now and then, at the shops or on the bus to town. You think of things like what if I hadn't stopped being Jonah's friend like I did, or had made more of an effort, but then you remember how he was in school those last two years, in trouble or sagging off with his new tough pals, his face like a clenched fist in yours when you did see him.

Fr John turned up at the graveside, a tall figure in black, pigeon-toed, head bowed. Perhaps he had slipped into the service, at the back, and I hadn't seen him. A horrid, grey day it was, and when we all turned away from the grave it began to drizzle windily in every direction. I walked back slowly, deliberately behind all the others so I wouldn't have to talk to anyone. Fr John walked up ahead with Jonah's Mum, who was crying and talking to him, and his Dad, who had his face set off somewhere in the rain and wind. I could see Fr John saying 'Yes' over and over in a serious way to Jonah's Mum, breaking his long stride to keep pace with her, his head down and towards her, a sympathetic ear while she mourned her dead son.

He's right; somebody does have to do it.

\*     \*     \*

"Yes, very well, Thomas; if you will, I think we'll just have to agree to disagree on this point, as usual, now shan't we? Now, then, gentlemen .." Christensen must have had Lafayette over a barrel yet again, and the old devil's about to be saved by the bell, as usual. "For next time, gentlemen, I want you to prepare, Mr Heron, Mr Gill, this includes you, too, lines 156-270: 'So Satan spake; and him Beelzebub thus answered.' You will know .." I missed it all, for what it was worth. Any second now the bell will go, and we'll all troop off to the school chapel for another funeral extravaganza —or rather, memorial service—this one having no body as such to inter. I fold my book away. You wonder if all this isn't a bit too soon; I mean, it's only been a week since he went missing, though on Snowdonia in that sort of weather . . . Still, you never know: he might turn up yet, coring his apple or producing 'Thoughts for the Day' from his battered old briefcase.

I say something to this effect to Christensen on our way out the door. He fixes me with his standard cold ironic look:

"Don't be stupid, Matter-Not," he says to me. "The daft old bugger's well dead."

*Faruk Ulay*

# The Somnambulist Caught Naked

(Translated by Meryem D. Grant and Nat Gertler)

The sudden summer shower snarls traffic. She folds her arms on the steering wheel, leaning her head on them. A couple of drivers leave their cars in the middle of the street and run to the newsstand on the corner. The rain punishes them by coming down faster. Once it's obvious that the traffic will be locked for a long time, she stops the engine, turns off the radio, and listens to the sound of the rain.

The sun that occasionally breaks through the rapidly-rolling clouds plays light games on the hood of the car. It makes miniature rainbows and then dismantles them. She changes the focus of her eyes by squinting. To play her game, she focuses on the windshield, on the roof of the car in front of her, or on the place where her hood ornament is attached. When she concentrates completely on the drops that fall on the center of the hood, she notices one that moves more slowly than the others. The drop casually falls and, just before hitting the hood, rises back up. When she sees some other raindrops behave the same way, she realizes she is drifting into sleep. A comforting warmth soothes her consciousness. Her gaze dims and she yawns while watching the summer rain falling up. Her eyelids grow heavier but don't close; she sleeps with her eyes open.

She discovered that she had been leading a sleeping life during a weekend that she had reserved for relaxation, when she found an envelope in her apartment. Since her teenage years she had hesitated to even look in the mirror while undressed, so she was utterly surprised to open the envelope and find a nude image of herself. When she read the note that explained where the picture was taken, she rushed to the open window and found her neighbor smiling at her from the window opposite.

"I sent both the picture and the negative. I meant no harm. I just wanted you to be careful," called out the man.

She could hear what the man said, but her responses came out as whispers. According to the man, she was murmuring in her sleep.

"I was afraid something might befall you, but didn't know how to tell you that you're a somnambulist, a sleepwalker."

Although she could not speak, she could command her neck muscles enough to gesture in a way that asked, "How?"

"Some of us spend almost all the day like this, while others escape consciousness for merely a handful of minutes. I suspect you belong to the former group."

She didn't want to believe this man and stared at the picture that embarrassed her. The whiteness of her bikini line emphasized her nakedness.

The man asked, "Have you ever witnessed plummeting objects change their mind and return to their source instead of falling down?"

She nodded.

"Then look around you more carefully. It's a sign you're drifting into sleep. When you see a falling item defy gravity, you are in a somnambulistic state. However, the falling objects do fall; only those who sleepwalk fail to see them. So you can deduce that you have left the waking state and entered the sleeping state. If you don't believe me, watch this," he said, releasing a towel from his hand. Instead of being pulled downward, the towel started upward, passed between them and disappeared into the sky.

Meanwhile, the bar of soap the man threw at her hit her square in the chest and woke her up. When she looked down, she saw the towel on the grass.

"So it is. Sleepwalking is not a bad thing, as long as you are aware of it. You'll grow accustomed to it over time," he said.

"But it is awful. Things fall down and I am convinced that they are not actually falling, and when I awaken, I will see that all I had to believe while sleeping truly happened."

"Don't make too big a thing of it. You will only believe that things are not falling. This indicates that you're asleep at the time. If you want my opinion, it's quite poetic actually."

"But nothing will ever be the same again."

"Why not? Nothing has changed in your life except you're now aware that you're a sleepwalker. And think of how many people would love to be in your shoes, having the chance to see the rain rise, right?"

She never saw the man again after this little conversation.

Now in the middle of traffic, snarled by the sudden and unmerciful summer rain, she is in the car, in a twilight state between awake and asleep. She's looking at the raindrops whirling around and sees that the windshield is now dry and the mini-rainbows have all dissipated. She also notices that the car is already collecting dust, and sees a yellow leaf fly up out of nowhere, turning green instead of landing in the space between cars. Is she still sleeping? She has to wake up to find the answer. When she does, she'll see that it's already autumn. And she will remember the man who reminded her of her sleepwalking as he rises up between their buildings. As the rain lets up, the traffic clears. She turns the key and runs into the truck next to her while trying to avoid a leaf that is stuck to the asphalt.

# Featured Literary Community

## *Bloomington Free Verse Poets*

Top Row, from Left to Right: C. E. Greer, Karol Hovis, John
Sherman, Rebecca Beck, Marie Deer, Jenny Kander
Bottom: Thomas Tokarski, Antonia Matthew, Roger Pfingston

## *Rebecca Beck*

4|2

### Delivery

You tend my torn nail —
contemplate the depth of its break,
decide which pair of scissors
would work best.
Gently you cut, halting at my grimace.

This could have been our child
you were delivering,
gently working back folds of skin
to reveal dark hair crowning,
cupping your hand under my hips,
charting evidence of pain
in my eyes.

This could have been a proposal,
you, contemplating the odds of my response,
taking my hand,
the one with the broken nail
a trace of cool sweat forming on your brow.

*Rebecca Beck*

## This Boston Cabby

hailed from Haiti.
Luscious African-Caribbean
drawl resonated the car.
Chunky braids
wrapped her head
in their own island turban.
Her lack of verb agreements
strutted through her singy tone;
I wanted to leave the cab
talking her lingo.

We talked colds and flu,
health care seeming to be only for the rich.
Her ninety-four year-old grandma
raised her on the island,
a woman with plants
and no need for hospitals,
and we agreed this was best.
People from the States
visited the woman
wanting to learn her secrets,
how to stay continent at 90
with clear sinuses
and a honey-clean memory.

So much swing in her voice,
my cabby had survived
a migration
from an ankle-iron government,
the relief in her voice —
so happy to drive a cab,
to boldly singspeak
her way through this city.

## As if I Were the Mother,

my mother holds her thumb
to me for comfort.
A jagged cave erodes
the middle of her nail —
more unwelcome reminders
of her decline —
her wounds that don't heal,
the erasing of skin on her leg,
bulbous swellings on her wrist.

Snarled parts of her unresolved past
mark their presence
as festering tattoos.
Here on her surface
they reside —

as far from her depths
as they can escape.

# My Mother Falls Out of Love

On the screen, the 8mm film sputters and
jumps to 1959. My mother is lean
with light brown curls and capri pants.
She's so young, she hasn't lost the way
kids attempt to stifle signs of youth
in their wide open eyes,
yet, she's already raked-over
from loving my father.

 It's in her face, as the camera eyes her
in the prow of the fishing boat.
Her hands shade the sun,
but really deflect the photographer, my father.
He works to catch her smiling into him;
she only looks over his shoulder.

To him, she's a marble statue
wrapped in bright plastic.
In transit to a new city,
she shimmers in sunlight
as a yellow crane deposits her
on a red steamer.

He wishes this statue were ice instead of stone.
Through the lens, he wants her sunhat and canvas shoes
to melt, her skin to glisten with heat,
and the glass blue in her eyes
to look deep into the camera
and put it all behind.

## Upstage in the Kitchen

*We're caught in a trap,*
*can't get out...*
As if on signal,
Lana and I took up the melody
lip synching to Elvis,
bumping hips, snapping wrists in rhythm,
arms stretched
angular
tangoing each other
across the kitchen.

We were the Pointer Sisters
on stage
backlit, lustrous
red nails accenting every gesture
swaying in the kitchen
knowing, with mother-daughter chemistry
when to flip our heads in unison,
when to kick-up a skillful twirl.

We were famous
in our kitchen
in the immaculate way
we read each other's impulses,
in the way our moving abandoned anger,
and opened our eyes
to floodlights.

As a member of Bloomington Free Verse Poets, I feel a deep sense of appreciation for this diverse group of writers who indulge me with their careful attention, who share the gifts of their insights with me, and who gently, and with humor, propel me forward as a writer. Even when we're tired and edgy, we're still ready to give our best to each other, and that's a gift to treasure.

# Mad Playground

We are the anger family.
I was taught, and I'm teaching you.
We are on the mad seesaw.

We drop our things where we stand.
Strike now, notice damage later.
We are the anger family. Here the last straw.

Smart, so smart. Brilliant screaming raw.
We understand all the wrong things.
We are on the mad seesaw.

Twenty minutes between this
and your dark bed, scared, and you bait me. We learn
to shout in the anger family, choke on the last straw.

I yank you to the anger playground. We claw
and swarm the fury monkey bars. We are booby skaters
on a collision course with the mad seesaw.

Swift, we are kings of the castle indignant behind our safe draw.
Who will depose us, hammer the alligators?
We are the crowned anger family. Ha! The final straw.
We are the dynasty on the mad seesaw.

## Leaving Kinshasa

Under the highrise we sit on our suitcases, green
off the Zurich train. My bell-bottoms, new for the trip,

are suddenly wrong. The concierge says
our place isn't ready. Mommy counts

our seventeen pieces of luggage again while Daddy
negotiates fast. I sit. I sit in the wind on the concrete apron

of my brand-new Strasbourg highrise, and consider
my bell-bottoms. I wished for them in the crook

of the frangipane tree, but in this Alsatian September
they are too floppy and too thin. Dizzy from looking up,

I don't know which twelfth-story
windowsill is going to be mine. I have no idea

we'll keep our butter up there, outside on the ledge, in a few
months when the tiny French fridge is full. Fresh

from my barefoot days, I don't know
I will dream up there, over and over,

of arriving at French school in fuzzy slippers. Each
on a suitcase, we sit and my bellbottoms are too bright.

# Wife School

## BEGINNERS

How to be one.
How to be a good one.
How to be one till one of you dies.

How to drive if he doesn't; how not to if he does.

Why your husband is the least of your troubles.

Why Mrs. God didn't change her name.
How Mrs. Holsopple kept the baby in a sunflooded crib on the living room floor in the converted apartment that had been my third-grade classroom.
What Mrs. Ellington said when she couldn't keep quiet about hot flashes, about pierced ears being of the devil, about how unbelievably fat I was, home from my freshman year in college.

## ADVANCED

How to be decorative.
How to be useful and decorative at the same time.
How to become like a limb to him, so that if you are ever separated he will feel the constant phantom tingling of you.

How to know Greek if expected and not know Greek when it wouldn't be right.

Why wife school is no place for you.

Why not to be Mrs. Alvy, breaking my high-school heart six ways, loving her husband, teaching me love songs, swooning in sashes over chocolate kahluas, ducking good-byes, and not staying married, disappearing, after all that.

Whether to bother.

# Belated Note to a Landlady

Forgive me, Frau Erhard. You must have died, but I'm juicy and
    breathing and pink
and if you're still decked out in your teeth, sitting up nights with
    the TV lights,

waiting for me to come door-slamming home, I'll eat your garden
    mud clogs.
I never wrote you in twenty years, Frau Rosel Erhard Im
    Buschgewann, whatever

that means, Im Buschgewann, but you can't have died. A hundred
    years old
and still parading me to the neighbors, the butcher, *hands off the*
    *prize*

*big American girl*, the grin, your steering elbow. You must have
    died,
your grandchildren grandparents, but who then is chopping the
    wood for the bath,

who will you let touch your fifties kitchen? I'll eat your TV and
    your beer
and your teeth and your short white fence and your apron flowers

if you're not sitting there, watching my phantom fingers go
like crazy, nights in your living room letters out, typing
    SAVE ME,

you praising my work lust. You just won't teach me what you
    know:
*hands off the ax! away from the stove!* Frau Erhard, Frau Erhard,

I'm sorry you're dead, if you're dead, but if you're bright alive
I'll eat the underpants off the line, your wool ones that keep you warm,
    and mine.

# Just Bring Me Things

In the icebox of myself I come to know everything.
I shake you comers off. You are below everything.

The families adopting me are the wrong ones.
My people are swimming somewhere. Their breaths blow
     everything.

I  am in a hurry to grow up so that I can grow old.
In myself is my whole world. I am embryo everything.

I know I have people somewhere, just like me. We come late
     to things.
We are slow kissers, slow drivers, slow listeners, slow everything.

I have nothing to say. I stand here and preach only because
I like my voice better than yours. You don't know everything.

I examine myself to know my people, they are somewhere.
I cannot hear them, but I must learn to echo everything.

Don't, don't teach me, I am learning myself. I am Marie.
I will trumpet my answers when I know, I will crow everything.

Marie Deer is a textbook editor by day and a fan of aquafitness, fat theory
and word games. New in Bloomington, she's tremendously grateful to the
Free Verse Poets for their careful poets' readings of what she writes and
for the pleasure and stimulation it gives her to read and think about the
poems they bring to the group.

*C. E. Greer*

# Equus

When afternoon begins
dissolving, I lead Spud
and Snook to pasture,
each on a line, with me between,
both roiling energy
to burst at the gate and pound
up the field, flanks hard
and eyes high, daring
any challenge to their fleet
dominion of that open world.

But there is a moment
before the gate
where our way narrows
between rank cedars and dogwood
by the lane, when their nimble
urgency not to be last
through that tapering speeds them,
and I must keep my feet
safe from theirs, my elbows high,

so as they surge
the crowding will lift and carry me,

so three rib cages crush and drive
in one flow, three backs weld
to rock as one, and I become
part of the deep charge
against all fettering,
of shoulders churning
like boulders in a flood

to deliver us
hoof-drumming ancient plains
with sun and new stems
waving belly high,
so we can keep with distance
this heart safe
from what would creep
against our swifting
over the rolling globe —

all in a few strides
before the cedars are behind,
Spud and Snook ballet wider,
and, feet on the ground now
at the gate, I loosen their leads
so we stream apart

to know again the separate sky
and close clothing of breeze,
to feel again so sharp the greeny
beckoning of grass.

## Bonpas Creek

Long rain the last day of May,
and we camped at a muddy pond

where one old bullfrog boomed
all night, under the blurry moon:

*be glad with me
that everlasting earth*

*is so good a home
for all our bones.*

## Blood Test

Lucid autumn afternoon,
and a father with two sons
wove through back forest ways.
One boy made the coveted sighting
at an aspen-scattered edge of airy
clearing. Softly sculpted heads
came up, moved through dappled light
and shade, but did not swing away
as the father held his trance
across all afternoon, brought
quick powers to a bead
in the empty, practical moment,

then made the whole woods shake
and leap alive with smooth,
frenetic bounds in echo waves
that left behind one buck
struggling in so much silence,
so many brittle twigs.

The other son exploded
a footrace with excitement
to where it thrashed,
but dropped in the grass
at his shouted name,
burning with the quick shame
of having so thoughtlessly run
too soon in front of the gun —
preventing a second shot and
revealing his unreadiness
for that day's deep fraternity.

It fixed in him a vision of the buck
laboring, spine broken, until the rifle
was put at its heart, and it lay still —
glossy wild gray trimmed sharp white
in settled leaves as they knelt around
and a knife came out, to begin
with cutting at the testicles.

*C. E. Greer*

## Wild Plums

The bushes grow halfway up
the sage and short grass bank
where we pulled over one hot day
and got out to stand by the pickup
with the long curve of the river
running below,

stand and pick the pink-orange fruit
hanging so thick on the bush we'd seen
it from the road and my father told me
to stop —some of it still sour and some
with a delicate sweetness having changed
the sour. We ate our fill, then made a pile
on the seat between us for mother,
who couldn't leave the house anymore.

He said in sixty years up and down
that road he'd never stopped, though
the bushes always bore a heavy crop.
Now I see them every year alone, but
haven't stopped since that last day
he and I drove out of the canyon
then across the open valley home
held in level sun of August afternoon.

The Free Verse group is one of those times in life when things just click. You find yourself with some other people really hitting a lick. Nobody knows why, and nobody thinks to analyze why. It happened one day with my high school track team. We always had good sports teams but never won anything big until a certain hot day in late May. I threw the shot and ran in the mile relay, and everybody else did the same things they usually did, and it just felt good. And at the end of the day we had won the championship. We were very happy, but not that surprised because it fit the way the whole day had felt. That's how it is with Free Verse Poets.

## Regeneration

My wife and I rose in a plane
over Indiana fields, soared
above Colorado peaks

remembering the quick decade
when both children blossomed
in hardwooded Wabash ribs
of the continent, before
each left to follow an earth-
encircling dream.

Now both were back
from Pacific sojourns —
Kenai, Shinjuku, Moresby;
Balboa, Wanneroo,
and both newly wed
to make us a fresh six
first-mixing at that strand

where sea lions lolled on coast rocks
sprung up sheer from the frothing sea,
clear streams descended through redwoods
to wend heathery bluffs,
embrace the ebbing sea.

As they compared new plans
for Sonoma and Seoul,
I could hear my mother's old refrains:

*Four brothers came from Scotland*
*to the hills of Tennessee.*

*As a girl Great grandmother left*
*Montrose, and sailed to Grand Manan*
*Island, off the coast of Maine.*

Then twilight stilled the Mendocino shore,
crimson sky-patch and seabird calls all gone,
and, breathing eucalyptus, we walked together
out the lupine dunes
to open, darkling beach

where land was one dim line,
tide all the power,
and stars came high and random —
soft, quick, new.

## Sierra Madre Lumina

Camp is quiet, the full moon
screened by solid cloud,

and a distant lake sheening late
prints the only odd-lobed spot
on darkness wide enough

to blank a boundless
valley-wrinkled world,
while close

by a tent peg
new Queen Anne's lace looms
the sure and delicate template

it must keep
through all this yawning,
ragged mountain night.

## Poem for Julie

Remembering
>    1984. Our bodies above the river, voices
>    a shimmer beneath god-toss of July stars.
What we loved
>    was there, on the sandbar, the brown water
>    rushing against us, under our talk
About fire.
>    About thunder. Sparks
>    from our fingertips, words
>    whispered among plague-weed and stone angels.
And everything
>    that year came true! the shadows
>    beneath the bed *did* grab our ankles, and somewhere,
>    back in the woods, a cottage was built cookie by sweet.
We danced
>    down the banks; we had not learned to be
>    afraid. Our hands wove spells above the silver sand,
>    we would cast our futures like runes
>    and we would be fearless, we would!
Around
>    our feet, the river rose and broke,
>    murmuring the names of those
>    we would someday lose; rising and breaking
>    and not once
>    did we hear our own names among them.

Karol Hovis

## Finding Out

My son, six this week, is enthralled
with menstruation, the very idea of painless
blood a novelty that he doesn't quite believe.
Through the closed bathroom door,
he questions me in his unembarrassed shout:
Does this happen to his daddy? his grandma?
what about girl dogs?
His fine forehead has been creased
with concern since he found out,
his voice apologetic when he asks
if I am really, *really* all right.

Days later, he still hasn't grasped the inconstancy
of periods. As I step from the shower
he barges in, proudly bearing gifts:
tampons ferreted from the hallway closet,
cupped like treasures in the earnest cradle of his hands.


## What My Father Tells His Fishing Buddies These Days

What can he say, now that I am no longer "the teacher"?
Now that I am some sort of inexplicable hippie chick daughter
and he must say instead, "Well, she makes soap.
Some damn thing. I don't know," while here
in the Indiana heat, the dogs sleep in piles around the unkept yard
and I keep having babies with that foreigner I married.
My father can't know how gladly I walked away, left
behind the first husband in his spotless cool house;
school desks groups around the sterile classroom,
the constant hands of the wall clock. He would not believe
the peace of this new life—the black enameled pots lifted
from the shelf, the oils and lye stirred by hand,
stirred until that elemental change comes forth, a shift
in consistency so subtle at first that it is more emotion
than proof, and I lay down the molds and pour.

## Poem for a Fourteen Year Old Son

That evening, you found your parakeet dead
in the corner of his cage, and the force of your grief
drove you against me, clutching and mute.
I held you and said the motherwords that are natural
after fourteen years, and hid that small secret
gladness —the joy I couldn't help at this unexpected chance,
perhaps the last time you would come to me for comfort.
A month from now, a year, you would begin to hide
your bruises and sorrows. You would say *it's fine*
when your gerbil died, and lock yourself in your bedroom
when your girlfriend moved away, and I
would begin the unending process of letting go.
There in your bright bedroom I cried with you,
grieving my own losses, safekeeping each moment
and offering hush-quiet thanks to poor Crackers
silent behind his thin chrome bars, huddled
beautiful and calm in his yellows and greens.

## Love Poem

I am waiting for you to be able
to tell me the rest, although I imagine
that I already know. How it must have been
that hot Georgia afternoon, when your uncle
took you for a walk after supper —he asked you
about seventh grade and if you liked to fish, and waited
until you had passed the first row of trees before he laid
one heavy hand on your shoulder. Too shy to shrug
it away, you watched your cheap blue sneakers
nudging through the dusty gravel, moving one
past the other as sweat and the first cotton of fear
began to warm your head. Two more rows into the orchard,
the peaches almost-ripe in the low branches,
he stopped and pulled you to him, and the world
you know narrowed down to that small section of ground,
his voice mumbling about things *just between us;*
his hands hot and trembling on yours, and your stomach
sick with realization and dread.

My love, I am watching that child, helpless
in the lane scented with fruit. I was once held down,
shoulders pressed into the rough ground, by a man
raging and strong beyond my young comprehension.
What happened there was a bloody war, and I grieved
in that place for years, weeping and fighting my ghosts,
and finally came home scarred and changed, but whole.
My love, I am waiting for your call, and then
I am gathering my bandages, I am flexing my strong
hands and back, and I am coming in after you.

# What It's Like

You pick yourself up from the sharp ground, push
your hair from your face, shake away the shards of darkness
that still falter behind your eyes. You realize
you are still alive, you have survived; already
you are beginning a list of people you will never tell. He
is gone now, but he will still be there, just beyond corners,
breathing from the dark living room,
hovering just above you as you sleep.
His rough hands will wake you in nightmares,
and always, this man will be a part of your body,
inscribed on your cells in profane cipher.
Some day, still damp from the shower, you will gaze
into the fogged mirror and wonder
that others can't see what you see —the bitemarks,
the black scar over your heart, that void
left by something taken. You envision
your soul, small coin of your being
spilled onto a stranger's nightchest with the random change
from his day, saved for laundry
or a six pack. All of this you are realizing
as you pull your clothes back into place, and this
is the beginning of what it's like.

Working with the Free Verse Poets has enhanced and change my life in
ways more profound than poetry itself. I have found, with their guidance
and support, that I am able to write loudly, painfully, and truthfully.
Their willingness to hear has inspired me, time and again, to speak.

*Jenny Kander*

## Lens

Surely she was lovely before age and illness
penned lines, hollows, into their own gaunt tale.
Supported by her husband, at the doctor's office
she sinks stiffly into a chair.

Whistling softly, lifting gloved fingers up
before her face, she capers them back and forth,

pauses to ask  *aren't they pretty?*

                    *You'll scare*
*the people half to death, Mother,*  the old man smiles,
one hand on her arm. *Do you need anything Papaw?*
she answers. *Are you alright?*
                    *I'm just fine,* he says,
and again, for her dancing fingers, she's whistling.

One chickadee, perky in his skullcap, hops
onto the feeder near the window.
                    *See the little bird, Mother?*
*Will you just look at that?*  Her tune fluting
from pursed lips, she glances outside, returns
to frolicking her fingers, stops long enough

to ask  *aren't they pretty?*

# The Aunts

Old Violet, gasping she'd never
regretted kissing a series of squash-faced,
snorting pekinese, died from asthma
while dusting her bobbled lampshades.
A lump-knuckled parental finger
had been shaken in warning when,
as a child, she'd been caught
nuzzling dogs, and so, for the ensuing
seventy years, kissing and snuggling
she'd expected to wheeze her
way out of this life.

Aunty Win, the oldest sister,
whose body resembled a small
hatbox, insisted her lack of any
waist was due, not to her nightly
sherries and then wine, but
to bath oil unavoidably absorbed
while she sat in her steaming green tub,

while Fran, deaf as the dead, thought
she'd heard that a clove of garlic
pushed half-way into one ear
prevented hearing loss, but never could
remember which ear it was,

and dear Evangeline, voluptuous,
imaginative, who had always been
uncomfortable at the zoo, sported
leopard skin bras to the very end.

Ada, by far the youngest, skinny, brash
and wild, dyed her hair red and shocked
her sisters early on by buying four multi-
coloured urns for their ashes
and using them, *until the old bags'*
*time came*, for tea bags, and reefers.

## Hysterectomy II

Three tiny keyholes barely
more than slits,
secret entrances left, right,
and just below the unseeing
eye of the navel.

In each, the key
a knife springing the locks,
riving ovaries, and from the centre,
my womb,

severing them to ensure
their rivered passage downward,
to be drawn forth like
my child but
leaving me dispossessed.

## Horse Collage

Penciled creases, fine runnels
as the neck swings, head arcs ...

Palm muscle's curve, power,
outlines of thrust, veering and return,
speed's contours defining the vein-
patterned pelt.

Shape space between sounds: bridle
rattle, turf-crop and slow munch,
the percussive canter, leap's
sudden silence.

A creased bougainvillea calyx,
crisp coral tinge, contrasts

thud's umber resonance
in dark and hay-strewn stable,
a whinny's descending spiral,
iron's looped density: horseshoes
along thrust of splintering beam:

Trace mane's texture
and high tail's sweep, nostril-soft
flare, the sloping limber
hush of shoulder, flank; a swift
drop to fetlock, the done of hoof.

# Ars Poetica VI

Pale lingual membranes
within slide-smooth shells

      tide-swept

granules assail flesh    shifting
shifting    yet unable to shrug  away
frustration of edges

Time streams
through privacy

      layer by sheened layer

nacreous sheaths transform
kernels    harvested    assembled

each nub    each strand

      articulate

About eight years ago a number of us gathered to form the Bloomington Free
Verse Poets' group, meeting every three weeks to read our poems to one
another, critique and be critiqued in an atmosphere of friendship, support
and gentle honesty. Three years later a couple of us formed a second Free
Verse group, with some new members, also meeting three-weekly, on a
different Tuesday —the highlight evenings of my weeks!

It is almost impossible to say how much I owe these groups. The debt is
fourfold: for growth as a poet, owing to the quality of what each member has
to offer; for the sense of community we share; for the privilege of friendship
with such special men and women, and for the opportunity we've created to
offer poetry into the larger Bloomington community through readings and
yearly (well-attended) performances.

*Antonia Matthew*

## Juice

While my grandmother,
pink rose in hand,
chats to a neighbor
I've set down the basket
of cut flowers
and escaped.

Deep in the blackberry patch,
at the end of the long garden
— legs  scratched,
    stained blouse untucked,
    fingers purple —
I lick the sweet juice
from off my lips . . .

"You'd try the patience of Job!"
  —my grandmother's voice behind me.

Then, "Beatrice!"
  —to  my mother who sits in the shade
sipping tea from a delicate cup —

"Your daughter has gone wild."

# Solar Eclipse on Christmas Day, 2000

Only a squirrel is around,
stuffing her mouth with snowy seeds
fallen from the bird feeder,
as I stand outside,
— no hat or gloves, how foolish —
my back to the sun
holding up two pieces of card,
one with a pin prick.
On the other I can see
the bite of darkness
formed by the moon sliding
across the face of the sun.

The snow throws out reflected light.
There's none of the dimness
I remember in1994
after returning from a visit
with my mother, knowing
she had Alzheimer's.
Then the air at noon
took on a dusky thickness
and birds were silent.

Now at this rather unremarkable
happening, there are no neighbors,
cats or birds joining me;
and my children on the West Coast
probably slept through it.

The squirrel keeps eating.
I stand here long enough
to see the shape change,
the crescent of light enlarge,

then I go back in,
light a candle for my mother
dying on this day, five years ago
and for my stepfather,
mourned this past September.

It's the first time in thirty five years
I have not called England on Christmas Day.

## Postwar child:
Woolacombe Beach, Devonshire, 1946

The old photo,
turning brown
reminds me:

> Pushing and shoving each other
> the boys chant, "I'm the King
> of the Castle. Get down you
> Dirty Rascal."
> But I'm too busy to play,
> packing handfuls of sand
> into holes the incoming tide
> eats in our castle, then running down
> with the retreating foam to push up
> a sand wall against the waves'
> next surge.

Didn't I know I was losing?
Soon parents would call us back
as the high tide swept towards
our picnic place, strengthening
the undertow —warning notices
posted along the dunes —that made
even wading dangerous, and disturbed
lumps of oil, from tankers
sunk during the war.  In the photo
I can't see any oil stains on my feet
or hands, but by the end of each day
I was always sticky.

Who waded out and took this picture?
My mother would have been too busy
talking, flirting even, I realize now.

I'm the only girl out here
in the sharp wind off the sea,
spray from the waves thrown
in my face, like rain
that threatens in the grey sky.

The other girls must have been
back at the picnic spot, still eating
their tea or making little shapes
in the sand with buckets and spades.

My bare legs are smeared with sand,
my bare toes dig in, I can feel streaks
drying on my face where I've tried
to brush the hair out of my eyes.

Seaweed is carried in on each wave;
we pound the dark tangle
into the sides of our castle. The pods
make squelching sounds as they split.
When the big waves break, gulls flap up
screaming. We shout at each other, "Here."
"No, here, stupid!" "Oh, look out."
and the boys start throwing
wet sand at each other.

I'm left alone on top,
— the sea washing around my ankles —
sinking as the castle falls apart,

and that's the moment,

my face serious, still holding
a handful of sand,
the wind blowing my hair ribbon
loose

the picture was taken.

Someone else's father,
hearing my mother's increasingly strident
"Antonia, come <u>here</u>!" waded out,
snapped me and when a wave pulled back
took my hand and ran up the beach with me.

Then, I'd have picked up my towel,
put on my shoes and socks, helped my mother
shake crumbs off our blanket,
trying not to listen as she scolded me loudly
embarrassing the others,
and, upset, trailed behind
as everyone walked to the hotel, chatting.

At the top of the dunes
—I   can see myself now—I stopped
and looked back.
The sea had covered it all.

Since the 1970's Adrienne Rich has been a major influence on my writing because of the courage and clarity of her writing, the way she lives her life, and how she deals with a chronic health condition. The life-long influence on my writing has been the experience of growing up in England during the Second World War. That gave me an expectation of loss and disaster. But it also gave me a knowledge of the strength of women and the power of women's community. A recent influence on my writing is the experience of growing old and the increasing frailty of my body. I find the support and expertise of this writing group, invaluable. The careful reading that the members give to a piece, the positive comments and suggestions that they make, and the on -going nature of the group, all helps me to keep writing!

*Roger Pfingston*

5|2

## For the Birds

Stepping outside, ten degrees
in a backyard gone crunchy
with old snow, he carries a failure
of popcorn balls stacked
like geodes in a metal pan.

"Not a one worth eating,"
his wife said. "Never again!"

As he rolls them, lopsided, light
in the wind onto the picnic table,
he wonders about the sticky threat,
the cheap trick of such treats,
fearing a ruin of guts and beaks,
the imagined carnage still strewn
over the lawn come spring.

No

# The Best Looking Man at the Funeral

It was the wife of the deceased who said
I was the best looking man at the funeral.
And I did look rather spiffy in my blue
blazer, light blue shirt, dark blue tie
and pants of a complementary hue,
a proper ensemble sliding to a dark closure
of black wingtips with a slightly cleated,
selfishly comfortable sole, though nothing
disrespectful or inappropriate.

I blushed at her words, more so when
she followed up with *When's your next movie?*
as if I were some sort of Sean Connery
or Kenny Rogers, with whom, I'm told,
I share certain features. Speechless,
her husband lying just beyond the crowd
of mourners moving slowly past the casket,
I stepped back and merged with the other suits,
my face blood hot, burning still with mortal pleasure.

No

## In the Living Room After Dinner

Sitting next to each other,
my mother smiling and holding
his hand, my dad tells about
his four widow women
in the neighborhood,
their needs and worries,
the funny, sad stories they become,
these women who call on him
to fix things:  replace a broken pane,
mend a torn screen, re-caulk
the tub or sink. And even though
a stroke has left him legally blind
(my mother his octogenarian chauffeur,
to his chagrin), he still can read up close
and at a slant, see well enough to please
these women in their widowhood.

## I Want

"The word I love best in Lorca is 'quiero'...."
                    -Robert Bly

From summer on I want the mammoth sunflowers,
those Russian beauties, to flourish year round.
I want them free of birds though bees may cling,
nine in all encircling the pampas grass,
their faces married to the sun, that ocean of blood,

while autumn offers plenitude imbued with all
the hues of death. Let winter carp, coughing
sleet and snow till spring, the clever one, sings
renewal with a sensuous lisp of rain, a treachery
of pastels and twisting winds as still the tall ones

tower, yellow tongues licking the sour light.

## Paper Work

Unused to the requirement of death
he rises from his desk,
retreats to the backyard
with a rake and a book of matches.
Under a darkening sky he claws
smoldering clumps of leaves,
letting them breathe and burn.

He tries to imagine his wife
beside him still,
lighter than a bird's breath —the finch
that nested on the windowsill last spring.

When the first drops fall
he curses the rain and flings
the rake against the maple, obscured
by smoke, then turns toward the house
resigned to paper work.

## Lush or Dry
Indiana '98

Such a warm winter...
El Niño's doing. They
said it would lessen spring,
kill off unsuspecting buds,
the early ones like lovers
who can't help themselves,
the wet opening suddenly shot
with late frost, and yet
the world is lush again,
more so perhaps: at the end
of the driveway, one tulip,
cup so ablaze with red
and yellow, a drink from it
would risk rapture.
And this morning, along
the highway, flaming out
of a rock wall, a bright loner
of a redbud below the steep
ground above, rich with sheep
and trees and tall mottled
grasses measured by a line
of barbed wire, one man's
rusty grip on the world as he
sees it, no matter lush or dry.

During the '70s and '80s I was a founding member of the Bloomington Poetry Workshop that met on a monthly basis and included such fine poets as Alice Friman, Roger Mitchell, Richard Pflum, and Bonnie Maurer. Eventually the workshop moved to Indianapolis and dissolved. I missed the camaraderie and the invaulable critiquing, but I thought that maybe I really didn't need the workshop atmosphere anymore at my "advanced stage". Wrong. I realized just how wrong when invited to be a part of The Bloomington Free Verse Poets. It's been a couple of years, and I don't think I've ever left one of our sessions without coming away with something significant to think about or reconsider. Equally important, of course, is the friendship, not to mention the delectable goodies served up at each meeting.

6 4\4

# Well

well I say to fill up a silence
between something too hastily said
and something needing a careful reply
giving me the time to think
while a chorus of other wells
joins mine as elbow rubbers
around the stove and table
nod their heads and think
upon whatever it is

well I say and the word drawn out
lets me acknowledge that I am listening
though it doesn't say I agree

I grew up listening to my mother say well
to bolder folk including me
well she'd say and sort of smile or frown
and look into her coffee cup
and not commit to anything
and it would anger me most
because I knew I had a future
of coffee cups to look forward to

as the kitchen fills up with my maternal people
saying their wells
rocking back and forth on crepe soled shoes
picking their teeth
even before the meal is ready
making jokes about each other
and funny neighbors
who think them likewise strange
discussing the crops
and the president
and unhappy with both
no matter when the season

and one then two then three wells are heard
and a head seen nodded
and an elbow rubbed

then the hand goes back
to beating the batter
or wiping the cabinet
before the dishes are set down

## Samson

if I were samson
I would give myself a buzz
tell delilah to (screw herself)
and live out a life
free of macho constraints
relaxing
reading
making myself
a veritable
pillar of wisdom

*John Sherman*

# On Contemplating the Afikpo Onye Ocha Mask

images of white men
things falling apart
no one any longer at ease

cultural murderers
destroying shrines
trying to wrest souls
from the horrors of
other gods

is this me
do I look like this
more important:
do I act like this
making changes
where changes should not be
bearing blue jeans and
bubble gum
as surely as others brought
bibles and guns

try I tell myself
try to be an observer
sit at the edge of the crowd
as unobtrusive as your pigment
will allow

don't make judgments
laugh when they do
clap when they clap
move in their rhythm
sway in the same direction
at the same time

speak little

listen a lot

## Maria Benitez

I knew I would come home
to write about maria benitez
I knew I might dance
with the keys
as she so fiercely swirled
in front of us

I had sat there
afraid to move
when she twisted
and turned her skirts
bared her teeth
thrust up her head
and stamped so hard
upon that wooden floor

staccato beats
cantor wails
swishing of satin against satin
is something I wanted
to capture
but could not

my wife read that first poem about maria
and said:
*a dispassionate poem about a passionate subject*
and I had to agree
it got wadded and tossed
and I fretted that I could not
get down in this medium
the sensual madness
of maria benitez

I wanted to dance against her:
make my feet echo hers
throw my arms in the air
as hers were coming down
gaze without touching her face
and almost press my body against her own

I wanted to dance my words against her image:
the high cheekboned face so hard and suppressed
the body tight within the sheen
her feet hitting again and again
the boards of my soul

John Sherman's third book of poetry, *Marjorie Main: Rural Documentary Poetry* (Mesa Verde Press, 1999), provides rich details of his experiences growing up an Indiana farm in the 1940s and 1950s. He has also published short fiction and is the author of pictorial history books on Santa Fe and Taos, New Mexico. John, who lives in Indianapolis, joined the Bloomington Free Verse Poets in 2001. "The group provides me with the opportunity to share in an honest, beneficial exchange of criticism. I am discovering my own work anew."

*Thomas Tokarski*

## November Flowers

In early morning
I rise to be present
in the quiet.

On a low table,
the last mums of the year
splay
from a rough, clay pot.

Stillness,
the gentlest of mirrors,
defines me.

I search the single row
of mauve petals
circling a softly yellow center.
My callused finger
touches translucence
and I feel nothing.
Leaning closer,
I absorb
the faintly sweet smell
of wildness.

After many days
the blossoms curl.
I keep them
while they darken and shrivel
to a ragged maze.

As the days of lightness diminish,
the woods gone skeletal,
so these last flowers
mark the dusty mauve
of withdrawal,
the coming years
of rueful
patience.

165 1

## Memory

In the arctic an animal dies.  Seeds,
blown by the wind,
catch in the bones
of the skull and chest.
As the animal comes apart it becomes
a small garden plot on the tundra —
flowers for the animal whose death
favored them.
Sustained
over many years,
they remember.

(Adapted from: *The Private Lives of Plants*,
by David Attenborough)

# Beyond the Storm

Summer night, distant storm.
Far-off lightning flashes
in your anxious eyes.

Through muted thunder's rumors
we are quiet, knowing
there will be no release of rain.

The storm will not crackle,
and hiss around us, the wind
will not force us
to seek shelter.

We will remain here
locked in complications
until even the anger is gone.

## Wisteria
(To the editor)

This poem is not about Wisteria.
I just used the word to get your attention —what
an ethereal word —Wisteria —
a spirit's whisper.

Such a sultry flower,
sweet to smell, in dense,
purple racemes among
the humid green
of warm summer mornings.

But this poem is not about that!

This poem is about death,
and child abuse, sadness and darkness,
people violating each other
in all their various ways.

It's about bringing Wisteria
to graves because
Wisteria
is just a flower —
the adornment
but not the subject.
Poems  should only be
about people,
their lives in distress.

Or so you said.

Wisteria, Wisteria.
If you insist on sadness
you will find the tear.

# Bloodroot

White
worthless thing.
It cannot give the homeless
homes, or feed the hungry child.
Fragile, transient form
of mere delicate stuff.
Petals folded like suppliant fingers
pass through the soil
and splay in the sun
to rays of light that serve
their own need,
reassuring, without meaning to be.
Not a rare thing
it cannot stop the dozer's treads.
Closer still I see the petals tremble
in the slightest breeze
like an outstretched hand —offered
blindly, across the border
on nonhuman urgency —
an apparition, waiting
to be taken by the needful hands
of the human mind
to form
a flower.

## Unfired

Sandra gave me a small clay pot.
Made with her hands,
it fits easily into the palm of my hand.
Unfired, polished with a stone
to the smoothness of a glaze,
its tan surface is lined
as the braided sediments of earth,
or the imagined weave
of a distant planet.
Inside the vessel I keep
her other gift to me —
the found wing of a butterfly.

The first artists to draw on cave walls were probably in a writer's group. I can imagine them deciding which animals to portray: "How about my antelope, Org?" "Cool man, but the tail's a little long. How do you like my bison?" "Well, you know, I feel clubbed by the form so the deeper meaning escapes me." That's how it all started.

For a writer the most important thing is to find a compatible group, one that respects diversity. In our group we help each other but expect to have the flaws in our work pointed out. Leave your ego at the door, but not your self assurance or individual perceptions. Positive criticism is almost always more helpful, but negative criticism can be enlightening. I like to know when my artistic zipper is wide open.

Being on a regular meeting schedule keeps me writing when it would be easy to put it off. So I'm more productive. It is also easier for a group to schedule a public reading and have a reasonable number of people in the audience. We have found it increases interest if we incorporate other artists in our performances —musicians and dancers. It's more work, but also more fun.

*Bloomington Free Verse Poets*

# WIND REVIEWS

Susan Donnelly. *Transit*. Iris Press, 2001. 82 pp. $12.00 (paper). ISBN
0-916078-53-1. The Iris Publishing Group, 1345 Oak Ridge
Turnpike, PMB # 328, Oak Ridge, TN 37830. www.irisbooks.com

Susan Donnelly's *Transit* exposes the reader to varied themes and
rhythms, but movement of one form or another pervades the work, as the
title suggests. Poems like "Chanson on the Red Line," "Transit," and "Tide"
provide concrete metaphors of motion, but all of these generally well-crafted
poems represent journeys of discovery.

"Chanson on the Red Line" opens the collection, preparing the
reader for Donnelly's unique vision with the invocation "The heart opens / in
such unlikely places" before describing a subway platform scene alive with
the sudden song of a street artist, and the "peopled solitude" so prevalent in
our urban landscapes. The speaker relates that she "wore a black and white
cloak / of impossibilities / that smoked like dry ice," an appropriate image for
the possibilities of the poems in this collection. Donnelly's voice remains cool
and reflective throughout, but she consistently provides metaphorical smoke
for her reader with startling images and moments of intense empathy with
the characters in the poems.

A keen eye for the unusual juxtaposition of natural and urban
images informs many of the poems. In "Saturday Morning, East Harlem,"
the speaker notes:

> Spring explodes
> like firecrackers under the wheels
> of a Trailways bus. A woman hurries
> from a Check Cashing store. Tulips
> in cans outside the *groceria*. No patch
> of earth's too small or grudging
> for the troweling will that coaxes lettuces
> from broken glass.

One gathers the impression from this poem that, like those miniscule patches
of earth, no image is too small or grudging for Donnelly to construct a poem
out of. Other poems display these surprising connections as well.
"Honeysuckle" conveys the speaker's reaction at the unexpected discovery of
the plant in a city:

> To come across it suddenly
> between one footstep and the next
>
> at 8 a.m. on a quiet street
> is to enter,
> by surprise as always,
>
> the ravishment of flesh,
>
> but you want more . . .

Like the speaker —who buries her "face / in bed-tousled blossoms" to take in the scent —one cannot help wanting to experience these poems more deeply.

Perhaps the most personal poems within the book deal with inner journeys, such as "To R.D.," in which a mother observes that "daughters become friends just as they leave" and sees a "suggestion / of winter trees, leavetakings, distances" in the window behind her image in the charcoal portrait drawn by her daughter, R.D. "Nocturnal" portrays another of these inner conflicts, comparing "letting in sadness / when you think / you've overcome it" to a visit "to the night building / at the London Zoo." The short lines of this poem mimic the interminable movement of the slow loris, as it decides:

> to reach one
> arm to the next branch, its
> whole body following
> like mud down a hill.

The speaker concludes with a wish for the reduction of sadness to imperceptibility, like the motion of the loris, so that one will mind it no more than "the stars with their / year-long stories" and feel it no more than "the rotations of earth."

The philosophy that this collection seems to carry across to the reader may be best described in "Pictures from the Floating World." The poet claims that "everything suggests something else, / if you know how to see it." Later in the poem, she paints her own picture of a Japanese print by Harunobu:

> Those girls, stringing
> a cat's cradle, wild geese in the distance,
> suggest a lute plucked in early spring,
> at the edge of a river, by the young
> prostitutes of Edo, in their off-hours.

She concludes that "the viewer would have known / the song they sing just by these hints / and walked away, humming." Just as the prints she describes convey more than one level of sensory information by way of a striking visual image, her own poems succeed through the power of suggestive images, according a level of satisfaction to her reader comparable to that experienced by the humming viewer she depicts.

Reviewed by Robert Callen

Stephen Dunn and Lawrence Raab. *Winter at the Caspian Sea.* 18 pp.
$15.00 (paper). ISBN: 1-891508-24-5 Palanquin Press, 2001
Palanquin Press, Department of English, University of South
Carolina Aiken, Aiken, S.C. 29801

*Winter at the Caspian Sea,* a short collection of poems by Stephen
Dunn and Lawrence Raab, is a lovely little book. At first glance, I was struck
by beauty of the stark cover, crisp as the seaside winter day that the title
suggests, and by the minimal precision of the layout. But this visually
stunning design is only a hint of the marvelous collection of poems inside. As
unpredictable as the sea itself, these poems froth with a lyrical play of image
and emotion.

As a true example of poetic play, Dunn and Raab composed the
poems during several summer vacations at the New Jersey shore, in a game
that only lovers of language would play. In this game, each poet quickly
writes a few lines and folds the page to reveal only the last line to which the
other responds. While there are some structural regularities pre-established
and the revision process did require some correction for clarity, these poems
emerge as a poetic frolic, with each lilting line inspiring greater expansion
from the other. The result is intentionally infectious as the introduction
explains, "We wanted in writing them to have as much fun as we could with
words-with what Wallace Stevens calls 'the gaiety of language' and we hope
some of those pleasures may be available" (vii). This sense of play reveals
itself again and again throughout this marvelous collection. For example, in
the work "When Enough Is Enough" the poets muse,

He had forgotten why he ever took anything seriously,

so what else was there to do but dance the tarantella
until dawn, make love shamelessly, do some wrong thing right
before he set out on that long road? (20-23)

In other works, like "Winter at the Caspian Sea," the poet's sense of humor
emerges in lines that tease,

I added that once in Madagascar I pulled back
The veil and kissed her on her forbidden lips.
How about saying hello? She suggested. (6-8)

In addition to the playfulness, there is an intensity present in the poems,
especially evident in the haunting images and soaring metaphors that are the
greatest strengths of this book. Publisher Phebe Davidson aptly described
these works as a "virtuoso of whimsy with an undercurrent of purposeful
engagement with the world." The verbal wordplay has a breathless power
that drives towards connection-connection with the world and with others.
The paired poems at the center of the book, "After the Long Party" and
"Silence" are examples of the drive to connect as they explore the
relationships between language, silence, and power.

'The saddest silence," you said, 'tries to conceal itself.'
[ . . . . .]
'Yes,' I said, 'I know what you mean.'
Were you smiling to yourself?
Were you shaking your head? (10,17-19)

In another memorable example, "The Bluest Day," Dunn and Raab explore
the ache caused by words not spoken as the poetic persona concludes,

Anyone in his right mind, he concluded, would stop
worrying about significance, would decide
to love those women instead of listening
to what he would never hear them saying,
and perhaps someone wiser would know, as he did not,

how far to take their beautiful, unfinished sentences. (21-26)

In conclusion, this book, the most recent release from Palanquin Press, a
micro-press that produces only twelve to fifteen chapbooks each year, is easy
to love. In fact, this book makes it clear that we should expect great things
from this South Carolina based press. Dunn and Raab, already well-
established poets, have turned the inherent weakness of this experimental
format, the surprising, even startling nature of improvisation into their
greatest strength. They have allowed themselves the freedom of play and
encourage their readers to join in the game. This book is about the discovery
and surprise of language, a game worth playing.

Review by Emily Biggs

---

## Matters of Identity

Leatha Kendrick. *Heartcake.* Sow's Ear Press, 2000. 65pp. $14.00 (paper).
ISBN: 1-885912-24-2. The Sow's Ear Press, 19535 Pleasant View
Drive Abingdon, VA 24211-6827

Life is a constant attempt to identify oneself apart from and among
others. Leatha Kendrick's collection of poems, *Heartcake*, is a reflection of
this. Her poems reveal the complexity of a task that seems so simple when
brought to a few words but which, in fact, is the one thing we spend our
entire lives doing. Yet, as Kendrick's poems suggest, we can easily lose that
sense of self while trying to find it. The collection is divided into three
sections, each representing a different theme: section one—id entity through
the body; section two —identity through family; and section three —claiming
one's own identity.
One spectacular moment in Kendrick's book happens within the first
section. Kendrick focuses on a very "primitive" theme here: the remembrance
of the body. (I call it primitive because it's not the mind that remembers a

touch, a jolt, or a slap.) In "Learning to Read," the speaker remembers the hardness of floor that "meet(s) her bones" while she recognizes letters in the Sunday paper; she remembers playing "horsey" on her father's leg, his "foot cocked." This becomes a poem not of actually learning to read a paper or book, but of learning to read things around us through our five senses: "a sentence/ strung across the air, a spell/ without letters, only for my ear —/ a secret song." "Touching the Cat" is similar to this conversation through the body, learning to talk with each other without words. Just as the cat responds to a human hand, ("her whole body rises rhythmically to fill/ the cupped emptiness of my hand"), so do husband and wife, mother and child communicate with each other. There is certainly a life without words. As section one progresses, we find ourselves in the beginnings of self-discovery: a teenager waits for her body to take shape and is finally granted her wish; then, she discovers sex.

Though Kendrick's poems are not narrative in form, they do tell stories and it is these stories that remind us of the importance of memory. How else could we map the structure of the selves we have become? It is in the second and third sections of the book that the mind takes over the body, but not completely: the body reappears to remind us of what we sometimes lose, even in death. In "Never Nowhere Without the No," the identity of the family has become habit, "moves perfected/ with practice of our motionless safety." The speaker's mother is dying. Her children have always relied on her authority to guide them, to tell them who they are. Later, after the mother's death, in "The Shape of His Need," a daughter tries to console her father, pretending she is her mother: "I replicate her potato soup,/ cook her roast, my rice pudding,/ losing all will to save myself." The daughter becomes lost in supplying her father with the solace and comfort he needs after this death. "Now/ can't you see how better/ I am than she was." The speaker is not interested in her own identity, but challenging the identity of her mother. She loses her own identity within this oneupmanship.

To want to be given a resolution on how to find our own identities from these poems would be selfish. Kendrick does not give advice. She only offers her own stories in exact measure, which is all a poet can do. It is the readers that have to find the truth, and Kendrick does offer bits of truth for us to savor, such as in "Beauty's Bitter Smell":

> What do I want from this world
> but a speaking part, a mark, a spot —
> a tongue lifted from the buried
> bud, loud as the narcissus'
> bloom and stink.

Near the end of Kendrick's book, we begin to see a potential blossoming of true identity, but she never gives the reader a full view. This is not a shortcoming but rather a strong point of the collection. Through the poems, we watch an individual struggle with her own identity and herein lies the hard truth: that we must each struggle, alone, and it isn't easy.

What eases the sadness of this truth is Kendrick's beautiful imagery and language, and the care she has taken to bring her poems to such exactness. This is a book to come back to again and again.

Review by Julie Brooks Barbour

---

Kat Meads. *Not Waving.* Livingston Press, 2001. 214 pp. $12.95 (paper), $28.00 (cloth). ISBN: 0-942979-83-4 (paper), 0-942979-84-2 (hardbound). Livingston Press, Station 22, The University of West Alabama, Livingston, AL 35470

Kat Meads's first collection of short stories, *Not Waving,* is a joy to read. The epigraph from Stevie Smith's *Collected Poems* beautifully tips the reader off to Meads's style; the epigraph states:
> Nobody heard him, the dead man,
> But still he lay moaning:
> I was much further out than you thought
> And not waving but drowning.

Just as the drowning man explains that while observers thought he was waving in glee in reality he was drowning, Meads' writing forces us to recognize that what we think we see does not even scratch the surface. Her stories explore the lives of the everyday, the mundane, making us realize that the lives of her characters are anything but mundane.

Meads provides few superfluous details in her stories, but rather than being a deficiency, this is an asset of a skilled writer. As a poet, she chooses the words that give her reader the clearest picture of life. In "Gene and Nikki, Nikki and Gene," we learn very few details about Gene's family, any character's physical appearance, or any character's innermost thoughts; however, when we finish the story, we feel as if we have known Gene and Nikki forever. This is more than a "poor boy meets rich girl" story; it is a story about loyalty, friendship, and roots. Meads unquestionably extracts a great deal of plot from her characters' seemingly lackluster lives.

The same is true of her other stories. In "Husbands Found Dead," we encounter a group of widows who gather weekly to socialize. While we first think that they have formed a support group, we soon realize that they are anything but supportive; they are a group obsessed. When their newest member runs out of the meeting, we cheer her on; as we loathe the group of widows, we simultaneously identify with them because we have all felt the pain of letting go. In "How Olive Plans to Die," we see a woman who regularly visits her neighbor to plan her suicide. Then again, is dying really what she has in mind, or does she simply want the attention? Again, Meads makes us recognize that what we think we see is far from reality; the seemingly ordinary rarely is.

Although this is the first collection of short fiction from Meads, anyone who values first-class fiction will be delighted with *Not Waving.*

Reviewed by Robin Gray

# the
# wind magazine
# community

## a letter from us to you

In my life as a writer, poems come to me, not me to them. It is my disposition to most times find this unfortunate and to sometimes find myself jealous of writers who can approach their work deliberately. I don't want you to misunderstand. I am not a writer who simply waits for inspiration; I just find myself with a writing schedule that must look more from the outside like a Buddhist's practice of meditation than a writer's work session.

I thought that I had come around that corner recently. Sometime last year I began to hear poems consistently and I thought that I had earned some right to their consistent arrival, as if I had learned a lesson the universe was now rewarding me for. I'm sure I don't have to tell you; things just don't work that way. These days I am drafting my first book, and while doing so I have experienced that same sense of heightened awareness I used to have when writing single poems. I don't know how to describe it, except to tell you that it is the same feeling I would always get when I would play in the store for too long while my mother was shopping —that feeling of sudden fear that your way home has left without you.

Recently, I was trying to explain these feelings to a fiction writer with whom I am close. She is a woman whose work and life have mothered me over the past few years. A few months prior to this conversation, she had given me a memorable reading of the first draft of my book —so detailed and attentive you would have thought it was her own work she was critiquing. Unfortunately, for all my strife, I couldn't do anything with the reading —despite weeks and weeks of work, I couldn't seem to make good on the changes she so clearly saw needed to be made. During this conversation, while I was explaining this to her, she simply told me to forget about it. "I really think you should be writing new poems right now, anyway," she said.

I did. I went right to work on new poems and found my ear full of them, and found pleasure in writing again. To top it off, from here it seems as though I am also accomplishing the goals set for the book. I guess I just needed to look at things in a new way, find the back door in, so to speak. Sometimes, I think we all need a new way to look at the things in our lives—to give things a chance to change and become more than out former expectations would have otherwise allowed them to be.

Likewise (as you've probably already noticed) we've taken this issue as a chance to reconsider wind magazine's appearance. No reason, really, except that we wanted a new way to see the magazine and a new way for the magazine to see itself. We hope you like it. Drop a line, if you have a chance, and tell us what you think.

—Rebecca Howell

# Contributors Notes

**Hom Raj Acharya's** first poems were written on slates and scratched into the walls of his childhood home in a Nepali village, which is remembered as "Simalpur" in "Coca Cola." He has since published a novel, a collection of poetry and numerous essays in Nepali. His poems have also been published in English in *Strategic Confusion, Isis Rising: The Goddess in the New Aeon*, and upcoming in *Salt Hill*. He is president of the Academy of Nepali Poets and Writers, a nonprofit organization dedicated to promoting a reading culture in Nepal.

**Sally Acharya** is an American journalist who has won national awards for news and feature reporting. While living in Nepal, she wrote for a travel magazine and collaborated with her husband on a bilingual book for rural children, which she also illustrated. Hom Raj and Sally currently live in Washington, DC.

A native of Alabama, a former naval officer, now a teacher and explorer on Vancouver Island, B.C., **Richard Arnold** is saddened by the environmental impact of war —which is often ignored. His poetic and prose writings have appeared in numerous venues in the U.S. and Canada, including *Snowy Egret, Tower, Barbaric Yawp*, and *Cotyledon*.

**Rebecca Beck** writes poetry as a way to celebrate those 'minor' experiences in life that can pass us by when we're not awake to them. Rebecca has been a member of Bloomington Free Verse Poets since 1992. Her poems have appeared in *Earth's Daughters*, and *Poems That Thump in the Dark*.

**Rachel Bloom** is a teacher, poet, and traveler. Her last trip was to Russia, but her favorite city to explores is her own, Boston. She has an MA from the University of Massachusetts and has had poems in myriad little magazines such as *Bluster, Mind in Motion, Insomnia & Poetry, The Boston Poet, Abbey, Free Focus, Kimera, Meanie, Nomad's Choir, 96 Inc., Bellowing Ark, Slugfest, Thin Air, Mobius,* and *Lucid Stone*.

**Dave Bonta** lives in the Appalachian mountains of central Pennsylvania. His poems have appeared in such diverse places as *Bird Watcher's Digest, The Sun, Art Times, Studies in Contemporary Satire, West Branch*, and *Pivot*. So far he has completed two unpublished manuscripts of poetry —companion volumes entitled *Spoil* and *Capturing the Hive*—a nd is hard at work on a third. He is also proud of his efforts to promote the cause of poetry and local poets in the State College area over the last 20 years.

**Kim Bridgford** directs the writing program at Fairfield University. Her poetry has appeared, or is forthcoming, in *North American Review, The Christian Science Monitor*, and *The Iowa Review*, her fiction in *Redbook, The Georgia Review*, and *Witness*. She received a 1999-2000 NEA fellowship.

**Matthew Cashion** grew up in Brunswick, Georgia, and now teaches English at Mitchell Community College, in Statesville, NC.

**Marie Deer** is a professional editor. She's working on her first volume of poems.

**Stephanie Dickinson** was raised in rural Iowa and now lives in the Bowery. Her poetry and fiction appear in *Mudfish, Cream City Review, Chelsea, Fourteen Hills, Washington Square, Iron Horse Review,* among others. She recently finished her first novel entitled *Shot.* Linear Arts brought out her poetry collection, *Corn Goddess (1997).*

**Malcolm Dixon's** fiction has been published in the *Newport Review, Gentle Reader, Streamlines* and *Monopoly.* In 1997 he was runner-up in the prestigious Stand Magazine Short Story Competition and in 2000 was short-listed for the Three Rivers Fiction Prize. Originally from Liverpool, he lived in London until quite recently, and now lives in the medieval city of Canterbury, England.

**Taylor Graham** is a volunteer search-and-rescue dog handler. Her poems have appeared in *The Chattahoochee Review, The Iowa Review, Poetry International, Yankee* and elsewhere. Her latest collection, *An Hour in the Cougar's Grace,* received a Pipistrelle Best of the Small Press Award.

A former teacher, **Karol Hovis** now spends her days caring for her four children, making soap and candles, working as a free lance proofreader, writing poetry, and watching the seasons change outside her Indiana home.

**Elizabeth Izzo** is a Chicago native who has been away from city residence for 15 years. She is self-taught in the visual arts although she did study some printmaking and photography at Indiana University. Her visual artwork is steeped in saturated colors and shaped with intuitive form. She has one daughter and lives outside Bloomington Indiana with her fiancé.

**Jenny Kander** emigrated from S. Africa to the U.S. 10 years ago; she loves mangos, windy days, silence and feather pillows, and records poetry programs, *The Linen of Words* (daily), *The Linen of Distances* and *The Poets Weave* (weekly) for two local radio stations.

**Chris Kingsley** has recently completed a poetry manuscript, *America's Most Beautiful Highway,* and is currently writing a novel based on the journals of his dog, Milo. He lives in New Hamburg, NY, with his wife and children.

**Antonia Matthew** was born in England and has lived in the United States since 1965.

Originally from Southwest Virginia, **James Owens** lives in Northport, Alabama, where he is putting the finishing touches on an MFA in Creative

Writing from the University of Alabama. He is also the editor of *The Sow's Ear Poetry Review*, and his poems have been published in numerous online and print journals, including recent work in *Now & Then* and the *Adirondack Review*, and have been accepted for upcoming issues of *Switched-On Gutenberg* and *3rd Muse*.

Four years ago, at 57, **Roger Pfingston** retired after teaching English and photography for 31 years at the secondary level. He now devotes his time to writing poems and making photographs. A chapbook, *Singing to the Garden*, is forthcoming from Parallel Press at the University of Wisconsin—Madison.

**John Sherman** loves to write. His next book, *War Stories: A Memoir of Nigeria and Biafra* (Mesa Verde Press), will appear in 2002. John is also working on a book-length satire of American history, a short-story collection, and an opera libretto. And, in his spare time, he continues to write poetry.

**Traci L. Slatton** is a writer and healer who lives in New York City with her two daughters and a Westie, all three of whom are highly opinionated creatures. She received her BA in English from Yale University and her MFA in Creative Writing from Columbia University. In 1996 Traci graduated from the renowned Barbara Brennan School of Healing, a four-year training in healing arts and sciences. Currently she is writing novels and screenplays, seeing clients, raising her children, and engaging the god-in-all-things in discussion both earnest and humorous.

**Mark Taksa** has poems appearing in *Laurel Review*, *Slant*, *Pacific Review*, *Permafrost*, and *Lullwater Review*. Chapbooks: *Choice At The Blossom Cafe* (March Street Press), *Cradlesong* (Pudding House), and *Truant Bather* (Berkeley Poets Workshop & Press).

**Thomas Tokarski** lives and writes in a rural area near Bloomington, Indiana. He has published poems in *Bathtub Gin*, *Indiannual 5*, and *Snowy Egret*. In 1993 he won first prize for poetry in a writing contest sponsored by the Ohio Valley Writers Guild. Recently, one of his poems was selected to ride a public transit bus in the "Words On Wheels" project in Bloomington. "My poems are condensed from a profound interest in, and respect for, this complex, beautiful, fragile planet and all the strange creatures that inhabit it, including us. It is the only home we will ever have."

**Faruk Ulay** was born in Istanbul, Turkey and now lives in Pasadena, CA. He is the author of two collections of stories, a novel, a book of experimental texts, and other works; a new collection of his stories will be published early next year. He is currently at work on his second novel. Ulay's short stories and nonfiction appear regularly in various Turkish literary and cultural journals. In the US, his stories can be found in *Private Arts*, *eye-rhyme*, *The Cafe Irreal*, *The Blue Moon Review*, *The Raven Chronicles*, and *Locus Novus*.

**Susan Wheatley** is an estate planning and probate lawyer in Cincinnati. She is married to an artist and has two children.